Clare Shaw trained and worked as a speech and language therapist before discovering that she preferred writing to talking. So she became a freelance writer, contributing to parents' magazines and writing five books offering advice to parents, including *Prepare Your Child for School* and *Help Your Child Be Confident*. Clare then produced two daughters so that she could put her own advice into practice. This proved impossible, so she returned to speech therapy and started to talk to people again. But the call of the word processor was loud, and *The Mother and Daughter Diaries* is the result.

Behind every woman writer is a man bringing her cups of tea, and John boils her kettle at their home in Essex, with help from their two daughters, Emma and Jessica.

Further information can be found at www.mirabooks.co.uk/clareshaw or www.clareshaw.com.

THE MOTHER AND DAUGHTER DIARIES

CLARE SHAW

MIRA®

First published in Great Britain 2008 by Harlequin Mills & Boon Limited, Eton House, 18-24 Paradise Road, Richmond, Surrey TW9 1SR

THE MOTHER AND DAUGHTER DIARIES © Clare Shaw 2008

ISBN: 978 0 7783 0201 8

58-0308

Printed in Great Britain by Clays Ltd, St Ives plc

Acknowledgements

My thanks to the families of Essex and Suffolk, who shared their stories of daughters and food with me. Thanks to agent extraordinaire, Judith Murdoch, and to Catherine Burke and everyone at MIRA for their hard work and enthusiasm. Also to Robyn Karney for her precision editing. Special thanks to John, Emma and Jessica for their endless support and encouragement. And to Mike Harwood for kickstarting me into this strange world of fiction.

To Abigail

ONE

SOMETIMES I look back and try and work out when I first started to worry about Jo, as if that's when it all started to go wrong. But that's a bit like asking yourself when you first fell in love or when you first grew up. These things tend to creep up on you slowly and one day you just notice them, notice something that has always been hovering there, waiting to be recognised. Perhaps I've always been worried about Jo—after all, I'm a mother and anxiety is on the job description. It all starts before your child is born, worrying in case he—or in my case she—comes out with three heads or twenty fingers. Then you worry about the contents of her nappies, whether she'll make friends at playgroup, whether that marble she shoved up her nose will cause permanent damage and whether the teacher will know that you helped her to colour in her picture. But this is all just gentle preparation for the teenage years when suddenly the world seems to be flooded with alcohol, drugs and piercings in places you never knew could be pierced.

The worry may have always been there, but was there a day when it struck me that there was something I really did need to worry about? Something more than the usual adolescent anxieties? I can't remember, but I'm always drawn back to the day of my niece's wedding. Perhaps, underneath my camouflage of denial and pretence, I knew then.

At times I blame myself that Jo hit those difficult teenage years just as I was learning to play out my new role as a single mother, still raw and bleeding from the pain and confusion of divorce. Yet if only Jo had accepted the separation as easily as her younger sister had, then maybe we could all have held hands and taken the journey together, as a family, as one. Now I understand that we each had our own journey to take and that sometimes our paths would run parallel, sometimes converge and sometimes divert onto very different courses. And when Jo's path led her off into what I believed was completely the wrong direction, I tried to pull her back onto mine. And yet that direction was wrong too. For her.

So perhaps the story really started with me. With me being plucked out of my comfortable existence, relabelled and thrown back into something unknown, frightening even. And as I struggled to make sense of my new life, I soon realised that my old life had been fraught with difficulty as well: that I had been hiding behind a veneer of perfect wife and mother, hoping that if I pretended long enough it would all come true. But it hadn't really been a life after all.

As a sixteen-year-old teenager teetering from childhood to the brink of womanhood, Jo had every reason to be finding herself, breaking away to discover who she was and where she was going. But what on earth was I doing, in my forties, suddenly questioning what I, Lizzie Trounce, was all about? For somewhere along the way I had left myself behind and had carried on living with no real identity, just a few useful labels so that people would understand what I did—mother, sand-wich maker, wife (now ex-wife), friend, neighbour, occa-sional beer drinker, part-time film buff.

I remember working at the sandwich bar alongside Trish the day before the wedding. Even then, I was trying to change direction, perhaps even hoping to find myself by looking somewhere different. But you can only change direction when you know exactly where you are in the first place and, un-knowingly, I was lost.

'The first rush is over—time for our own sustenance,' Trish said, pouring out a couple of coffees.

'You know, this place would be better if we had room for more tables and chairs. It would make it more of a café than just a takeaway sandwich bar.'

'There's five stools.' Trish nodded towards the long bar with the stools for any customers who might want to eat or drink on the premises. 'And they're usually empty.'

'That's because they're not comfortable and the room is so narrow you have to drink while being pushed and shoved by the queue. The chances of getting an umbrella in the ear and being slapped around the bottom with a briefcase are ex-tremely high. If only we had bigger premises.'

'Yeah, great. So we have to serve tables as well. Twice the work for the same money,' Trish pointed out. She was only ten years older than me but was content to float easily towards retirement.

'But if we owned the café…'

Suddenly I saw myself as a businesswoman with a chain of restaurants to oversee, bank managers grovelling at my feet, power suit, shoes clicking authoritatively across the restau-rant floor.

'If only I'd done that business course Roger suggested,' I sighed.

Trish laughed. 'I really can't see you on a business course. It's not exactly you, is it?'

But what exactly was me? I'd been bright at school with three good A levels to my name, but then I took a gap year, before gap years even existed, and that turned into a gap five years as I happily drifted from job to job, travelling the world in between, until I met Roger. The next thing I knew, I'd given up my flat with the giant sunflowers in the window box and was trimming the privet hedge in a neat, four-bedroomed cube in a convenient location on the edge of town, with favourable commuter services into London. Desirable, quiet, sought after, practical. And dull.

'Perhaps you're right,' I acknowledged, After all, how could I possibly run a business when I was struggling to make sense of the electricity bill, the car insurance, tax credit and all the things Roger had dealt with until six months earlier when everything, just everything, had been turned upside down and given a shake I could measure on the Richter scale. Of course, I thought, Roger's new partner Alice could probably quote her National Insurance number at will, juggle bank accounts around like oranges and get a tax rebate on…well, whatever people got tax rebates for. I still cringe when I think of the first time I met her and described myself as a sandwich designer and beverage entrepreneur. And I'm still trying to convince myself that her stiff smile was one of admiration.

As Trish and I started to prepare a fresh supply of sandwiches for the lunch trade, I realised that my job was the one constant, unchanging, predictable event in my shaken-up life and I needed to keep it exactly as it was. So I set about losing myself in the routine of the day and shoved everything else to the back of my mind.

I got home from work that day feeling exhausted. Exhausted by responsibility, regret, bitterness and the intense love I had for the children I thought I'd let down. It was as if I had been pulling everything together so hard that my limbs were aching and my resolve slowly breaking down. My neighbour waved at me, and then stared at my overgrown lawn and the triffid-like borders of nettles and determined weeds. I waved back and shrugged my shoulders. It had hardly been an accusation from her and it wasn't much of an explanation from me, but I sensed we understood each other. I would deal with the front garden when I could, but as yet I had no idea when that would be.

When I got to the front door, I turned round to look at the small wilderness behind me. There was something rather pleasing about the wild garden which somehow distracted from the predictable box of a house which stood symmetrically between two identical boxes. I liked it, and decided to put a bird table and sundial somewhere among the long grasses. It seemed rebellious and slightly daring, and I went into the house feeling a little better about myself.

I put the Chinese takeaway I had collected on the way home on the table and called the girls. Eliza danced in and gave me a hug.

'Chinese—great,' she enthused, and started pulling the lids off the cartons.

The dishwasher was packed full and I had forgotten to switch it on before work. I rummaged around in the cupboard and found some paper plates left over from Eliza's birthday tea some months earlier.

'Great, like a party,' Eliza said, and as I waited for Jo to make an appearance, I reminded myself never to compare the two of them.

'Shout up for Jo, would you, darling?' I asked Eliza.

Eliza and I were halfway through our meal by the time Jo drooped in, wearing pyjama trousers and a baggy jumper which looked like an old one of Roger's. She hung her head like a soft toy with no stuffing.

'Not another bloody takeaway,' she muttered. 'I'll get something later.'

'I'm sorry, it's just…' But Jo was gone, leaving behind a large helping of guilt for me to digest with my dinner.

'I can't wait for the wedding tomorrow,' Eliza said, helping herself to more spare ribs.

'Yes, it should be fun,' I tried to enthuse, but my voice sounded like a nervous children's TV presenter.

My niece was getting married the next day and it would be our first big occasion as an incomplete family. Part of me was looking forward to it, part of me dreaded it. I knew I would be dying to announce to everyone that the breakdown of my marriage had not been my fault, that Roger had gone off with a younger woman as part of his mid-life crisis. I wanted to be able to laugh about it, to show the world that I was carefree, happy and in control. But was I? And had it in some way been my fault?

As Eliza ran out urgently to phone one of her friends, I looked around the kitchen. Roger had planned to decorate the whole house the previous year and had scheduled it into his diary as he scheduled everything in—meetings, DIY projects, liaison time with the girls, sex probably. Yet it had never happened, presumably because of his well-scheduled plans to leave me, so the house was beginning to look a little frayed: nothing extreme, just the odd scuff mark here and there, the occasional patch of peeling paint or faded curtain. But there was something more, something that had changed the feel of the entire kitchen, and I realised that it was my piles of, well, stuff. With Roger, there had been a place for everything. Anything that could be filed was filed, anything that could be put on a shelf was put on one and extra shelves had been continuously added to accommodate any item inadvertently left lying about.

Now I indulged myself in allowing things to be left lying about, and I specialised in piling up books and photos, magazines and CDs, letters and odd pieces of clothing. Every room in the house was littered with piles of miscellaneous objects so that the lounge carpet looked like a lake with stepping stones across the middle and my bedroom an entry for the Turner prize. Yet it was not chaotic, I knew where everything was and the piles were somehow neatly piled. And I had every intention of sorting them into something else—well-ordered piles maybe.

The truth was I missed Roger, not as a partner but as someone who had sorted out the bills, put things away and knew where the stopcock was. Now I had to do everything and there never seemed to be the time. I wasted so many hours just sitting in the cluttered kitchen wondering where it had all gone wrong, how I had ended up in this characterless house doing an unchallenging job, a divorce statistic with a stroppy teenager who could tear my self-worth apart just by walking into the kitchen and looking around at what it had become.

Still, I loved Jo more than anything and went upstairs to talk to her about the wedding the next day.

'Hi, Jo, are you looking forward to tomorrow?'

'Suppose.'

'Looks like the weather's going to be good.'

'Yeah.'

'It's a bit of a long trek so we'll have to set off about eight. Is that OK?'

'Yeah.'

'Sorry about the takeaway. We'll have a roast on Sunday, shall we? Like old times.'

'Except it won't be like old times, will it?'

'No, of course. Still, you like a roast. What about now? Shall I make you an omelette?'

'I'm all right.'

'Right, well, I'd better go and iron my dress for tomorrow. I don't want to look like a wrung-out dishcloth.'

I laughed, I winked, I smiled, I patted Jo maternally.

I decided to go out into the garden and talk to the plants, reassure them that I cared and would soon be pulling out all those intrusive weeds which were strangling them and blocking the light. But perhaps I should have been saying the same things to Jo.

I listened at the lounge door but heard Eliza still chatting excitedly on the phone, underlining key words as she spoke.

'It's going to be <u>wicked</u>. You should see what I'm <u>wearing</u>. I'm on the stage practically all the time. And right at the <u>front</u>.'

Back in the kitchen, I thought about Jo again, although, looking back, I never stopped thinking about Jo. It was continuous. She had her own place in the worry zone of my brain, and I knew with intuitive certainty that there was something wrong, very wrong, with her. Of course she didn't tell me everything, she was a teenager and was still adjusting to her parents' separation, that was normal. But it was more than that. There was something I couldn't quite put my finger on. Out in the world she was often so different, speaking out eloquently, standing tall and proud and looking at her life ahead with some optimism. Was it this house that was stifling her, gagging her so that only a few words could be spluttered out of her mouth at one time? Or was it me?

I stared out of the window at the overgrown garden. It had begun to rain heavily so I put off my idea of going out and chatting to my neglected plants. I wondered if it would be all right to just shout out a few words of encouragement through the window, and immediately wondered what Roger would think. What he would think of my piles of stuff scattered across the floor like lilies; what he would make of me shouting out of the window at the plants… Would he despair of me phoning up the emergency gas line because I couldn't work the timer on the central-heating system? I could taste his disapproval as if he were there in the room with me, and yet I knew that if only I let it, that very thought could set me free because I no longer needed anyone's approval, except my own. But that was the most difficult approval to get.

I opened the window.

'Hi, plants, how are you doing?' I almost whispered—I wasn't quite ready for this.

'Hello, plants and trees.' A loud voice from behind me shouted over my shoulder. It was Eliza. We fell about like drunk chimpanzees and then I realised that the rain was slanting in and I shut the window. There was never any need to explain with Eliza.

'Just getting a yoghurt,' she said, and skipped out of the kitchen again.

My mind turned back to Jo as I tried to remember her pre-adolescent years. It had all been so different then. She had spent so many hours with Roger, talking about exams and how to invest her pocket money and planning her future. Now she was changed, and by more than adolescence. I knew then that I had to talk to someone about her, about me even, before we drowned in the sea of silence we found ourselves in. I picked up the phone and pressed out a number.

'Hi, Trish. Just called to say thanks for doing my shift to-morrow. Gina should be there about nine.'

'That's great. You have a wonderful day, Lizzie. Enjoy the wedding.'

'We certainly will. It'll seem funny without…on my own.'

'You won't be on your own. You'll have the girls with you.'

'Of course I will. They're really looking forward to it.'

'I bet they are.'

'Trish?'

'Yes?'

'I'll bring you back a piece of cake.'

So, I'd got it all off my chest, then. For someone who found it so easy to talk, the words crashing out of my mouth like coins from a slot machine, I found it very difficult to actually say anything. Later I learnt that there are other powerful ways to communicate, but back then, on the eve of my niece's wedding, I did at least manage to laugh at myself. You have to laugh, otherwise you end up crying, I thought. It was only after Lily came into our lives that I realised you sometimes have to cry as well. It took an enigmatic, mysterious stranger to teach me that, a stranger called Lily Finnegan.

TWO

BEFORE I started to write it all down, I wrote 'Lily Finnegan' at the top of the page. Then I found out Mum had done the same thing. Like this is all about Lily or something. Well, maybe it is. I'm not writing my life story—nothing like that. How can I? I'm still a teenager and everything stretches out before me. But I had to write about this slice of my life because Lily told me to. And because it changed things. For ever.

Did I have a happy childhood? Kind of. My parents divorced. Shit time but a lot of kids go through it. It was easier for my sister, Eliza. She thinks she's in a play or a film. That's why she's happier than me.

I was happy being me once. It was when I stopped being me that it went wrong. I couldn't put a date on it—'I got screwed up on 20th April 2001'—nothing like that. I just remember that I had to perform, so I started to pretend. And I guess the performance gradually took over from reality. I knew how to make other people happy—you just pretend to be who they want you to be. Act your knickers off. Smile on top, cry underneath. I can see all that now, but there was no set plan at the time. It just happened. I totally lost control of me.

One of my biggest performances was at my cousin

Victoria's wedding when I played the part of the perfect daughter. Oscar-winning stuff, but my mask slipped off. I went out of character. I let the real me show through, and raw emotions frighten people. I wasn't the only one playing a part. I had a talented supporting cast. Mum was acting out the role of the perfect mother of a jolly happy Sunday roast family. Me? I was eager to please, but at that time I didn't understand why.

When I got up that day and saw the dress hanging there, it looked boring and ordinary. It was suitable—for the weather, for the occasion, for someone who was frightened of standing out in the crowd yet who wanted to. The part of me that wanted to stand out felt a sort of regret. I draped the dress onto me and looked in the mirror. It looked better than it had in the shop. There would be boys at the wedding and I looked good. I had lost some weight for the event and the dress hung off me as if it were on a coat hanger. Perfect. Victoria would be the one in the wedding dress. I knew I would be envious. She was the one with the boyfriend, soon to be husband, but I was slim and very nearly elegant. And he might go off her.

Sixteen and no boyfriend. Sad or what?

Eliza came in.

'Where's your dress?' I asked.

'Oh, I'm wearing this,' she explained casually, fiddling with the make-up on my table.

I was stunned. It hadn't occurred to me that you could do that. Ignore the dress put out by your mother.

Eliza started to sing.

'Get out, Eliza, there's no singing in here.'

Eliza made me feel like a blob.

'Hello, I'm Jo, Lizzie's eldest daughter,' I practised.

Mum came in and sighed. She was relieved to see the version of the daughter she wanted.

'Do I look fat in this?' I asked.

She laughed. People don't always pick up their cues in this pantomime we call life. I told Mum I was excited about the wedding. I told Eliza it would be fun. Sometimes saying it can even make it happen and I think I *was* excited, but my feelings were damp that day. Ever since getting my GCSE results, it felt as if the only emotion that dared speak its mind was anger.

I remember sitting upright in the car when we drove up to the school on results day.

'You'll be fine,' Mum had said. It was expected. By the school, by Mum, by me. Expectation had its own pressure. Failure would be a steep fall, and I was nervous when I glanced at the piece of paper in my sweaty palm. Eight A* grades, four A grades. Best results in the school. Nearly perfect. I felt relief and pride and ecstatic joy. For about four minutes, before a feeling of disappointment and then indifference misted up my mind and dampened the positive stuff. I felt like screaming out, 'So what!' I phoned up friends and relatives, hoping their pleasure and excitement would transfer to me. Like catching chickenpox. But I was immune. A blob.

Still, I think I really did feel excited about the wedding. Underneath. Perhaps I had just forgotten how to let my emotions show, like a Coke bottle with the cap stuck on. Even shaking it up wouldn't help get the fizz out.

Mum sorted out the seating arrangements in the car. She organised who could choose the radio stations. She controlled the steering-wheel and the conversation. We sang and laughed and it sounded like happiness. Or something... We had to drive all the way to the end of Norfolk, miles and miles and miles. The end of the world.

Mum drove in trainers. She had gone on and on about her new shoes. Mostly she goes on and on about my exams, on and on about Eliza's talents, on and on about the food she sells at work and on and on about how you have to laugh. No option—you *have* to laugh. These are permanent ramblings, they never change and she recycles them on a daily basis, like the repeats on TV—you know what's coming but there's nothing else to tune in to. Then there are the new episodes. Like the shoes.

When we arrived, Eliza leant over the back of the seat and retrieved the shoes. Giggling, we hid them behind our backs and waited for Mum to open the boot and think she'd forgotten them.

We often played jokes on Mum. And on Dad. Mum and I often played jokes on Eliza. But nobody ever played a joke on me. People were too careful with me. As if I had a 'Handle with Care' sticker across my soul. Was I really that fragile, even then?

The church was beautiful, with flowers and everyone dressed up and the choir and the organ. It was so traditional and sort of old-fashioned. And everyone was looking warmly at Victoria, pleased she was so happy. I wanted to be pleased for her, but jealousy is in my blood. I could feel it then, pumping around my arteries, and nothing could stop the flow. Jealousy is hot. It makes blood simmer, gently at first, then violently. You cannot see, hear, feel, taste or touch anything. Not in your own skin. Not if you want to be in someone else's skin. Feel what they're feeling, see what they're seeing.

'Very young, but in the circumstances…'

I could sense my mother's thoughts, smug judgements as she perched between the daughters she thought she knew well. I thought about my life, I thought about love, I thought about meaning. Big thoughts. Scary thoughts. And then we laughed at a fat woman's hat.

Outside Mum pushed me into talking to old ladies. I must impress them, make my mum look good—by proxy. I hated it. Didn't they see my unease? Sense my reluctance? But maternal eyes were on me and I wanted to please. Why? I wanted to please *and* I wanted to rebel. The definition of unhappiness: wanting two opposite actions at the same time. Can't choose. Can't decide. Makes you feel like shit. I talked pleasantly. Kind of.

'How's your budgie doing?' I asked sarcastically. I'd guessed correctly that the lavendered aunt kept a budgie. She was the sort. Liked garibaldi biscuits, crocheted cardigans, watched *Countdown*, supported animal charities, never said 'vagina' out loud.

We went to Uncle George's house for the reception. Mum made the same joke to everyone about what a nice tent it was. Eliza escaped into her own world, I was stuck in this one. I was still on display. Here we have Lizzie's fabulous daughter. How clever. How bright. How charming. How tall. What big hips. I stuck to the script—exams, hockey, university, violin lessons, youth hostelling. Don't mention Dad—Mum's unspoken law.

'I haven't decided yet but I'm thinking about medicine or maybe pharmacy… Yes, Eliza was brilliant in *Annie*… She's got another show coming up… Maybe Cambridge. The school think I've got a chance… Not much time for boyfriends. I did have one but I've been really busy… That's right, Eliza's my sister. Yes, very talented… Duke of Edinburgh, yes—I'm doing my silver… Yes, Eliza is quite a character.'

Yes, I hate Eliza sometimes. Yes, I get fed up talking about her. Yes, I wish my whole existence wasn't chained to exams. Yes, I do want to scream out loud. Yes, I do need to punch someone full on in the face. You and you and you. But mainly me. Don't worry, I won't. Mum can rely on me.

I was introduced to Stephen and Ben. Ben was just about to start sixth form like me. Stephen was younger.

'They could do with some decent music in here later,' suggested Ben. 'Screamhead are local to these parts. They should have booked them.'

'That would be totally awesome,' I replied.

'You like them?'

'Yeah, I've got their CD—*All Quiet*.' Well, I was thinking of getting it.

'A girl of good taste as well as good looks.'

I looked in his eyes for a flicker of sarcasm, but he meant it. My diet had paid off. Nearly an hour with the hair straighteners had been worth it.

'See you later, Jo, I've got to do the relative thing, yawn, yawn.'

'Tell me about it, puke, puke.'

I found Eliza behind the marquee with another little girl.

'Hey, I like your routine, that's wicked.'

I loved my sister—at that moment.

I wandered around the garden. I was happy to be with my own thoughts, now that my thoughts were good ones. Amazing gardens. Uncle George and Auntie Sue are rich. I could be rich if I wanted. But I could end up poor. I didn't want to think about the future. I didn't want the future to happen. I was sixteen. That's old enough. Listening to Screamhead is better than having a mortgage. The now that I know is better than the then that I don't.

I saw Ben again on his mobile. He waved. I went over.

'My girlfriend checking up on me,' he said with a grin.

Victoria and her new husband were coming towards us. We watched them gliding along the lawn. It took a long time. We waited. Then we talked about weddings. Eventually I excused myself. I said I had to find my mother. As if. I walked around the outside of the marquee. The canvas rippled in the breeze and looked vulnerable. Surely torrential rain could get through the thin material. Surely a raging storm could blow it clean away. But storms and torrential rain rarely happen. Life is full of showers and brief interludes of sunny spells. Or so it seemed.

I slid into the marquee. A big cluster of guests was gathered at one end as if the ground had been tipped up and everyone had fallen together. A solitary figure stood staring at the food. My mother.

She loved food. All her plans were about food. Her plans for the day always included mealtimes, her plans for the future involved a restaurant. When I was little, there was always a picnic. A trip to the beach plus picnic. An outing to the zoo plus picnic. A tedious journey to a forgotten relative—plus a break for a picnic. Before we left, the kitchen would smell of picnics. A mixture of mayonnaise, coffee and plastic. The basket was like Little Red Riding Hood's. Food bulging out like buttocks under a red and white checked cloth. Gross.

There was an excitement about a picnic—my mother would whisk off the tablecloth with a flick of her wrist, like a magician—but there was no surprise. It was always the same. Soggy egg sandwiches. Lemonade. A flask of coffee. Ginger cake. Bruised apples.

'Eat up, eat up,' my mother would trill, like the repetitive cry of a seagull.

And there she was, smiling at the wedding food. Then she turned around and smiled at me. I think she smiled—there was some distance between us. I heard Ben's voice behind me, talking about football. Boys always talk about football at a wedding. My father tells a story about a wedding he went to on cup final day. All the men in front of the telly, missing the speeches.

Suddenly I knew that I didn't want to eat the food. I felt sick. I needed some air.

Uncle George was on the bench. I sat down next to him.

'Enjoying yourself?'

'I'm feeling a bit sick.'

'The car journey?'

'Probably.'

'Seen Victoria?'

'Yeah. She looks great.'

'Yes.'

'You proud?'

'Yes. After everything.'

'Yes.'

'It's hard growing up.'

'Yes.'

'These days.'

'Yes.'

'You don't do drugs, do you, Jo?'

'No, nothing like that.'

'I'm proud of you, Jo. Are you happy?'

'Sometimes.'

'That's all you can expect. Sometimes. Don't expect too much, that's the secret Jo. Don't expect too much of people.'

'I won't.'

But I did.

Women are meant to be better communicators, good with words, intuitive with the non-verbal stuff. But I prefer male speak. My mother uses too many words. So does Auntie Sue. Words to analyse, predict, accuse. Most of all, selfish words: look what this does to me, after everything I've done, what will people think about me? Me, me, me. You make me look good, you make me look bad.

If I'm sick, it's me who's sick. No one else need throw up on my behalf.

As my mother waved and called 'Coo-ee,' my stomach churned. My chest heaved. My throat went into spasm. I headed for the house. Walls make me feel safer than the open air. Or canvas.

Later, I was sitting in the marquee feeling a little better. My mother skipped over, full of sympathy. Sympathy for herself because her daughter couldn't perform any more—she had pulled a sickie.

She said, 'You must be a doctor when you grow up and you must eat this bread. Then I will tell you what else you must do.' Or words to that effect.

Anger hides round corners. If you listen carefully, you'll hear it rumbling, swishing. Like lava surfacing. You feel your body tightening as it grips your muscles and tendons and seeps into your nervous system, and you become hot, steamy, rigid. You can't keep it trapped inside, it will make its escape.

I pushed the plate away with too much force. I spoke with too much aggression. Then I sat back and let my mother turn my anger into guilt.

'Sorry, I was only trying to help, I forgot you weren't feeling well. I thought you'd want to meet that medical student. It's your life, but I'm here to support you, and it's just that you need to gather all the information you can. Talk to people, ask questions, and something will come up and you'll think, Yes, that's for me. But there's no hurry, just keep all your options open.'

'I just feel like…I don't know.'

'Go on.'

'I feel pushed. Kind of.'

'Well, it's you pushing yourself most of the time. No one else is pushing you in any way. You're completely wrong about this, you have nothing to be angry about. I simply don't want you to have any regrets, that's all. Regret can niggle you for the rest of your life.'

'Sorry.'

'That's all right. No harm done. Here you are, you can have my bread.'

'Can I go and play outside?' asked Eliza. She had scoffed down her food like eating's an Olympic event or something.

'I don't suppose children have to stay for the speeches, Eliza. Off you go then. Jo and I will be here if you need us.'

Ben walked past and winked at me. I smiled. Then I saw him wink at the girl in the pink chiffon dress.

The wedding party was sitting in a line like they were waiting for a bus or something. Victoria and her husband kept looking at each other. Uncle George and Auntie Sue kept looking at each other. The in-laws kept looking at each other.

People seem to come in pairs, like book ends. Or shoes. One by one, the men in the line stood up to speak. The audience joined in with romantic sighs, laughter, applause. I saw myself sitting up there in a white dress. My mum and dad beside me. Eliza one of a pair of identical bridesmaids. Everyone in pairs. Perfect.

I miss being a complete family. Two parents. Two children. Two gerbils. I like everything neat and tidy. Life arranged to perfection.

The speeches were over and Mum was chatting to some random man. Middle-aged men in suits all smell the same. She picked a piece of fluff off his shoulder. She smoothed down her skirt. She pushed a piece of hair behind her ear. She said it was a nice tent. She said the mother-in-law's hat looked like a pancake. She threw back her head and laughed. He laughed too. She said, 'You have to laugh.'

I stood up and went over.

'Ah, my daughter, Jo. This is Gordon.'

'I don't feel well.'

'Do you want to go and lie down in the house? Uncle George won't mind.'

'I really, really don't feel well.'

'Oh, dear, let me think…'

'I want to go home.'

The challenge. Who comes first?

'I'll catch you later.' Gordon slunk off quietly.

We got into the car in a cloud of apologies. Apology and regret equals blame. We stopped at the end of the village.

'Jo, if you're feeling sick, perhaps you'd better swap with Eliza and sit in the front. It was your turn to sit in the front anyway.'

'It's all right. I'm feeling much better.'

'But it was your turn.'

'Get a life.'

There are different types of silences. There's the easy, comfortable silence you share with friends. I can sit with my best friend, Scarlet. We can sit in silence like soaking in a warm bath. Then there's solitary silence, but your own thoughts make it a noisy, frantic silence. The silence in the car was thick and heavy. Like wet concrete waiting to set into something solid. Eliza eased into the silence with soft humming. I thought my mother would slice through it with laughter. Or a shrug-of-the-shoulders remark. Instead, she made us sit in it. She turned on the radio. Radio Two. She hummed along. But too high-pitched.

When did I first feel I'd let my parents down?

I remember when I was six years old. It was our school sports day. I was entered in the sack race and the obstacle race. Lucy Button was better than me. On the day, I stayed at home. I told my mother I hated school. I never wanted to go again. Mum and Dad argued. Dad had taken the day off work. Mum liked to talk to the other mums. I was off reading schemes. I could read what I wanted and Mum liked to tell everyone.

After that, I practised running in a sack all year. I practised crawling under tarpaulins. I practised throwing a bean bag into a hoop. The next year I won both my races but Mum was in hospital, having Eliza. Dad was with her. When I got home, I had to go to the hospital. I saw that Eliza was ugly. I didn't want her to live in our house. She had my mother's name and I didn't. I asked why. I said what about me?

I think Dad was on my side. I don't know, but there was shouting, right there in the hospital. I had caused a rift be-

tween my parents. So? They'd missed me winning my races.
Life needed to be balanced like that. Neat and tidy. Ordered
and fair.

When we got home from the wedding, I went straight to bed.
I was still feeling shitty. That night I dreamt I was running
along a winding path towards a big house. I knew I had to run
through the house and get to the other side. I didn't know why,
I just knew it had to be done. I ran along corridors but kept
coming across dead ends. Then I realised I had to go down
some stone steps into a dark cellar. That way I would be able
to run through the cellar, climb up some steps at the other end
and get through the house. But I lost my way in the dark. Then
I woke up and my stomach felt full. I felt like I had been
stuffed with cotton wool like a teddy bear. My throat was dry.
My forehead was hot. In the morning, Mum left warm toast
and a mug of steaming tea on my bedside table. She told me
to rest.

There were two weeks left before term started. Sixth form
waited ahead like a mountain. Daunting, imposing, frightening. Somehow the wedding had changed things. Another
mountain was in view. The future was too steep to climb.

I would make a list. A list limited the time ahead you had
to think about. I would make a list of what I needed to do in
the remaining two weeks. I got out my pad and pen and stared
at the blank page. I didn't like blank pages. They looked uncertain, open, ambiguous. I started to write, to cure the page
of its emptiness, to cure the future of its uncertainty.

- *Read through AS curriculums.*
- *File away GCSE work.*

- *Tidy desk drawers.*
- *Keep dream diary.*
- *Buy Screamhead's new album.*
- *Mend puncture on bike.*
- *Collect photographs.*
- *Get a new boyfriend.*
- *Lose a stone.*
- *Phone Scarlet.*

I decided to start at the end and work backwards. Maybe life should be like that. Start off as a crinkly with all that experience. Then feel yourself getting younger and fitter. Life would get better, not worse.

'Hi, Scarlet. Do you want to come over or shall we meet in town or something?'

Mum came into my room.

'Only two weeks left of the holiday. It's flown past, hasn't it? Eliza's round at Katie's for the day. I thought you and I would hit the shops.'

'I'm going out.'

'Oh. Right. Where are you off to?'

'Just out.'

'Are you meeting Scarlet?'

'Probably.'

'Well, maybe we could meet up afterwards. I've got a few things to do in town. What do you say?'

But I said nothing. I don't know why. The wedding seemed to have changed everything. Maybe that's why I keep thinking back to that day. Even now. It was the start of something. Or the end of something. It was an unhappy day, I know that. It's just been so hard to recall the feelings, the essence, of the day. All I really remember is the sequence of events, like it was a film or something.

I met Scarlet at Tramps coffee-bar. I had a black coffee. Scarlet had a latte. She spooned three sugars into it, automatically, and stirred it round and round and round. Her arm jangled with the rows of bracelets. The dolphin tattoo on her shoulder bobbed up and down. She put her elbow on the table and propped her head up with her hand. She carried on stirring.

Tramps had an uneven wooden floor and thick pine tables which wobbled when you leant on them. The hiss and splutter of the coffee-machines, the droning chatter of its young customers, the revs and buzz of the traffic outside drowned out our silence. The place smelt of froth and coffee beans and sweat and cinnamon.

'Life is full of shit,' sighed Scarlet eventually.

'Something wrong?'

'My parents are splitting up—no big surprise—and Blaise has dumped me and I think I've picked the wrong subjects for AS levels. It's all happening at once and I feel like shite. I am so-o-o-o stressed.'

Scarlet started to cry. Large solitary tears like a tap dripping slowly. She cried easily, unashamedly, as if it was normal.

'Look at me.' She laughed, and brushed her tears away with the back of her hand.

'Do you want to talk about it?' I asked, and put my hand on her shoulder. Then we hugged. Scarlet was the only person I touched, except perhaps Mum. Mum doesn't know how to hug me any more. Except sometimes when she forgets I'm grown up. Am I grown up? Anyway, she hugs me like I'm three or something. Like she wants to kiss it better and put a plaster on it. Scarlet's my best friend and her secrets are my secrets. And my secrets… Well, you have to know what they are yourself first. We hugged in the café so I could share some of my strength. If only I'd had any.

'Not much to say really,' she said.

But there was. Scarlet told me her dad was moving thirty miles away and that she had known it was coming but it was still a shock when it happened. That she'd racked her brains to see if there was anything she could have done. That Blaise was a bastard and she hated him. That she thought sciences would be too hard and would make her so-o-o stressed but she might stick with biology. That she felt uncertain and confused and muddled and shitty.

And all the time she cried and sniffed. She blew her nose on her napkin. She didn't hide her face or go to the toilets. She seemed locked into that space, that time, that moment. The bustle of coffee-bar life ground on, but Scarlet seemed totally unaffected by everything around us.

Eventually she shrugged it off.

'How was the wedding?' she asked. 'Any fit guys?'

'Mostly mingers. But there was one cute guy, Ben.'

'Tell me more.'

I leant over the table like there was someone listening or something.

'He's a Screamhead freak. We had so-o-o much in common. It was like we'd known each other years. I reckon he works out some. Muscles all over.'

I was whispering. Confiding in Scarlet. Confiding a lie, half a lie anyway.

'All over?' said Scarlet, and spluttered out a laugh so that the froth on her coffee went up her nose and made her cough.

We giggled and I nearly felt happy. I had made Scarlet laugh and that would make her feel better. Perhaps it would make me feel better. By osmosis or something.

'Are you seeing him again?'

'Might do. Bit of a distance.'

'Still, you had a good time.'

Did I? Did I have a good time? I wasn't well, there was something sad about it all, but otherwise...

'So we've both got divorced oldies now,' I said. I was sure I could help Scarlet out. That would make sense. I could tell her what it was like and then she'd understand and feel OK about it. Maybe.

I looked at Scarlet. How did she manage to cry without getting blotches? Her skin was perfect. Pale under her spiky blonde hair. She looked like a pretty pixie. Petite, small slightly turned-up nose, sparkling green eyes. I preferred long hair, but the style suited her. She made me feel clumsy. She said she wished she was tall. But she meant tall and elegant. Not tall and awkward. I liked my shoulder-length hair. I liked my brown eyes. I only got the occasional spot. But my body was all wrong. It was like a puzzle of different body parts all put together wrongly so that somebody else had some of my pieces. I had haphazard bulges here and there. In the wrong places.

We finished our drinks and Scarlet came to the music shop with me and to collect my photographs from Boots. While we were there, we fiddled around with the make-up samples. We sprayed perfume on our wrists and we weighed ourselves.

I got home with my photos and my CD and a number on a piece of paper. I looked at my list. I ticked off 'Phone Scarlet', 'Collect photographs', and 'Buy Screamhead's new album'. I got a pad out and wrote 'DREAMS' on the cover. I looked at the first blank page. I wrote about my dream of trying to run through the cellar. I wrote a number next to 'Lose a stone'.

This was the first time I'd felt happy for months. Was it happiness? I'm not sure now. Can you have happiness without contentment? But I was organised. I was crossing items off a list. I was on a roll. And something felt right.

I rushed out to the bike shed and wrenched the wheel off my bike.

'Coo-ee,' shouted Mum. 'I'm making myself a sandwich for lunch—do you want one?'

'I ate in town.'

You would think Mum would want something different to eat on a Sunday, her day off from the sandwich shop.

I stayed in the shed while Mum ate her sandwich. Soon, I was glueing the small fabric square onto the inner tube. I left it to dry. I wondered what it would be like to live in the shed. It would be like having your own flat. Cool. I spent the next hour slowly and methodically filing away my work from my GCSE courses and another two tidying out my desk drawers. I threw away a bin bag of paper. More than could have fitted into the drawers. Or so it seemed.

I got out the curriculum papers for my AS level subjects and started to read.

'Can I have mine in my room?' I asked Mum at suppertime. I didn't want to lose the momentum. Spaghetti Bolognese—better than a takeaway.

I carried on reading.

Three more items to tick off on my list.

I crossed off 'Lose a stone' and wrote 'Eat less' in its place.

I crossed off 'Get a new boyfriend' and wrote 'Prepare for a new boyfriend'. It was all in the wording, the semantics. Aims must be achievable, measurable, exact. Each day must have a new list. Each list must have ten items. I was in control.

My sister thinks she's so bloody perfect. So does my mum. Perfect. Someone ought to tell them.

THREE

I was kneading the dough on the wooden kitchen table, my rose-print apron wrapped around my hand-made gingham dress, when I had a maternal impulse to pat my two daughters on their plaited heads as they looked up at me with awe and gratitude…

Well, if you have no hope of being a perfect mother, you might as well imagine it.

'We've run out of milk again,' Jo whinged, crashing the fridge door shut. I abandoned my Walton fantasy to deal with the latest domestic crisis. 'There's plenty in there if you'd only looked properly,' I shouted in my best bad-mother screech.

'I have skimmed milk now, I told you.'

'You never…' But Jo was out of the door, slamming it behind her as if I were on a train about to leave the station. If only.

I checked the fridge and there was plenty of ordinary milk there. Not much else, though. I thought about going up to Jo's room to apologise for shouting but I sensed that might be the wrong tactic. I always felt so apologetic, apologetic for being inadequate, I suppose. But whenever I tried to say sorry or explain myself, Jo looked at me with an adolescent contempt as if admitting my shortcomings was in itself a shortcoming. I have always approached parenting as if trying to work a new washing machine without the instructions—by trial and error. What on earth does anyone else do? Yet part of me suspected that other mothers had received the instruction booklet with their children, while mine had been missing. Still, back to the Waltons…

Imagining is good strategy. It's so easy to imagine fresh ironed sheets on the bed, an Aga in the kitchen and a nanny in the back bedroom—a perfect lifestyle maybe. But imagining yourself as perfect comes a little bit harder, although it can be done with practice. And back then I was well practised. When the girls were little, I used to walk around with a picnic basket in one hand, a copy of *Parenting* magazine in the other, smiling confidently should Eliza or Jo fling herself onto the floor at Tesco in a temper tantrum. As if I knew exactly how to handle the situation. As if I were in complete control. Still, I muddled through those early years well enough, a permanent splodge of jam on my blouse like a bullet wound, play dough under my finger nails. I always seemed to be wiping one of the girls down with a licked handkerchief while forgetting even to clean my own teeth some days. I can't think why Roger left me and quickly moved in with the highly successful, designer-clothed, play-dough-free Alice.

Now I have a teenager, things are very different. I adore Jo, yet sometimes she is barely recognisable as the little girl I once knew. Sometimes she is barely recognisable as a human being, but I still adore her. If I'm honest, I would like to press my remote control and fast-forward her past the teenage years and straight into a mother and daughter bonding session in the spa pool, bypassing hormones completely. I desperately tried to hang on to my ideal vision of the future: shopping together without arguing; eating a meal together without an uncomfortable silence; talking together without…well, just talking together. Properly. I thought all it would take was for Jo to change, I didn't realise I had to change too. Not then, not before Lily Finnegan.

When we went to Victoria's wedding, I found myself chatting to a fellow parent-of-a-teenager, whom I'd spotted across the marquee—she had that tired, bewildered, confused expression we all share.

'What are teenagers actually for?' I asked her, as we stood looking at her daughter, who was sprawled on the ground in her pink frock and Doc Marten boots, with a Walkman plugged into her ears.

'To make us feel permanently inadequate,' she suggested.

'To make sure we never dare see ourselves as anything more than a taxi driver.'

'Or cash dispenser.'

As we tried to laugh about it all, I discreetly scanned the marquee to ensure Jo had not slouched off to sit in the car because it was all 'so sad'. In fact, Jo was in rather a good mood, chatting to all the relatives and smiling from time to time. Not a stray hormone in sight. I almost relaxed.

It was a happy day, as weddings so often are, and when Jo didn't feel well, I didn't give it another thought. The unwritten rule of teenage behaviour is to make a drama out of the mundane and Jo was no exception. One slight spot or blemish put her straight into quarantine in her own bedroom. One little tiff with her friend Scarlet had her announcing that nobody liked her, she might as well commit suicide, and when she did nobody would come to her funeral. So a slight period pain at the wedding meant leaving early with a view to hospitalisation later.

Should I have insisted she lie down in George's spare bed-room so that Eliza and I could carry on enjoying our day out? Did I do more harm than good by giving in to Jo's foibles? I have no idea, I simply made my decision knowing that it was probably the wrong one. As always.

There are no manuals on how to parent teenagers. It is assumed that once you get them sleeping through the night, using the potty and counting to ten, you can sit back and relax. Surely a parents' magazine for those of us with teenagers would be snapped off the shelves. We would be able to read articles like 'A Valium-free Method for Dealing with Your Child's Mood Swings' or 'Just Giving You the Benefit of My Experience'—and other phrases never to say to your teenager. All I could do was carry on with the washing-machine approach to parenting.

When we got home from the wedding, I made a positive decision not to ask Jo accusing questions about her apparent stomach problems.

'Are you better? You seem to have made a speedy recovery,' I said, the message from my brain not quite reaching my lips.

I must check the hinges on Jo's bedroom door, I thought, they may have worked loose by now.

The wedding had exhausted me. You never completely relax when you are out with growing children in an environment containing alcohol and collapsible tables. And I had sole responsibility for anything that might have gone wrong. The burden of being a parent on my own suddenly seemed to weigh heavily on me, for I had nobody to shift the responsibility onto, no one else to take the blame, no one else to share my doubts with. I sensed that the stress of lone parenting was beginning to take its toll on me.

The next day, I decided it was time her father got a taste

of what I had to deal with, and time I had a desperately needed break. So I dialled Roger's number, praying out loud as I held the receiver to my ear, 'Please don't let Alice answer, please don't let Alice answer...'

I hadn't heard the click on the line.

'I'm afraid it is Alice,' came the well-enunciated tones of my ex-husband's partner.

I put the phone down quickly and stared at it. It rang.

'Answer it, then,' sang Eliza as she danced past me and into the kitchen.

'Hello.'

'That's Lizzie, isn't it?'

'Well...yes.'

'It's Alice. I do believe you've just telephoned us.'

'No, it wasn't me. I've just this minute got in—the girls and I were out shopping.'

'That's funny...I pressed 1471 and your number came up as the previous caller. So I made the obvious deduction.' Ever the lawyer.

'Oh, it was Jo probably.'

'I thought she was out shopping with you.'

'She ran on ahead.'

'So does she want to speak to her father, then?'

'Yes. No. She did but she changed her mind. I'll speak to Roger, though, seeing as you've phoned.'

Roger and I have an amicable relationship.

When we split up, we gave each other leaving presents and vowed to remain best friends. I was so delighted when he met his young, attractive partner so soon after our separation that I sent Alice a bouquet of flowers...

Well, it could happen—in certain parts of America, perhaps. In reality, my main aim with Roger was to let him know how miserable he had made me.

'Hi, Roger, sorry I took so long to get back to you—the girls and I have been out shopping and having a wonderful, wonderful time. Together.'

'You phoned me.'

'Did I? Oh, yes. Sorry, I've had so many calls to make today—work, the hairdressers, Gordon, of course—just someone I met at Victoria's wedding. Now, what was it I needed to talk to you about?'

'Jo and Eliza, presumably.'

'Oh, yes, would you like Jo to stay for a few days next week?'

'Yes, that suits me fine. Eliza?'

'Rehearsals. But she could spend a couple of hours with you when I bring them over. If it's Sunday. Then I could bring her back again.'

'Fine. Look, you might as well stay to lunch. There's no need to go all the way home and come back again.'

'Fine. The only thing is, I would prefer it if your new partner wasn't there. Well, Jo would prefer it, I don't mind. After all, we're both meeting new people. All the time. Practically on a daily basis.'

'Alice lives here. Anyway, the girls have met her twice now and they all got on fine.'

'It's just something Jo said. About being just with you.'

'Alice did offer to go to her mother's but I think—'

'That's settled, then. About twelve-thirty.'

'Fine. Alice should be out of the house by then.'

'Will you be able to bring Jo back on the following Saturday?'

'Yes, I should think so.'

'About five o'clock would be good.'

'I'd rather make it in the evening. About eight maybe.'

'Six o'clock would be more convenient.'

'Between six and seven, then.'

'Fine.'

'Can I speak to them now?'

'They're busy. You could phone back later.'

'About six?'

'Seven.'

'Fine. It's been a pleasure doing business with you.'

'Bye, Roger.'

Roger had prepared a cold meat salad for us.

'You didn't tell me you were a vegetarian now, Jo,' he said.

'I thought Mum had told you.'

I had a choice of answers, starting with the fact that I didn't know myself, or 'it must have slipped my mind', or 'how come you ate my spaghetti Bolognese, then?' (which was provocative). I decided to remain completely silent and resist saying something meaningless.

'Well, there's vegetarian and there's vegetarian, isn't there?' I laughed.

Jo pushed her salad around on her plate as if she were designing a collage. She cut it up into smaller and smaller pieces, rearranged it, poked her fork into tomato and cucumber and hard-boiled egg and pulled it out again. Her mind was in orbit, it seemed, circling the world and searching for significance. When Jo thought, she thought deeply, penetrating her own soul, searching, probing, reasoning, analysing. She was a lot like I was at that age. Teenage angst, they call it. Eventually you learn to live on the surface, it's safer.

'Did you sign up for that additional course for next term?' asked Roger.

'Yes,' muttered Jo, glancing at me.

'What additional course?' I almost whispered, hoarsely. I cleared my throat.

'She's doing an additional course in IT,' explained Roger. He had clearly already done his additional course—in smugness.

After lunch, Roger sent the girls upstairs so that he and I could spend some quality time together. Maybe.

'What's happened to Jo?' he asked.

'What do you mean?'

'She looks like a hat stand, and she hasn't eaten any lunch.'

'For God's sake, Roger, she's a teenager—that's what they do.'

'Only Alice thought…'

'What the hell does Alice know about having children? She probably thinks ovaries, uterus and fertility are a firm of solicitors.'

'She's my daughter, too.'

It is always tempting at such times to launch into the 'I'm the one bringing them up and you're the one who walked out' speech, but I decided against it. Instead, I said nothing.

'Haven't you got anything to say on the subject?' Roger asked, eventually.

'Not really. I mean, I'm the one bringing them up and you, for whatever reason, decided to leave me to it.'

'Lizzie, let's not go over all that again.'

'No, you're right. Look, all her friends are the same, it's nothing to worry about, but if you like I'll talk to her when she gets back. Don't make a thing of it.'

'Fair enough. Does she eat at all?'

'Of course she does. She had spaghetti Bolognese only yesterday.'

'I thought she was a vegetarian.'

'Only a part-time one.'

On the way home, I wanted to think about what Roger had just said, make sense of what he seemed to be implying, but I pushed the thought from my mind as if thinking about it would give it some truth. I screeched to a halt at traffic lights I hadn't even noticed and banged hard on the steering-wheel, angry with myself for being so distracted, distracted by mere possibilities for nothing had actually happened. I started to sing, and right on cue Eliza joined in. There was a quiver in my voice, a quiver of fear, but I wasn't even sure what I was frightened of. I slapped my thigh like a pantomime character, grinned and sang louder until everything seemed all right again.

We got home at two-thirty and Eliza had to rush to get ready for her first rehearsal. There was a buzz and excitement about her which rubbed off on me like chalk dust. We sang songs from *Chicago* all the way to the rehearsal rooms with the car windows open, oblivious to the reactions of passersby. This was what being a good mother was all about and I mentally awarded myself a gold star. I drove back home still feeling exhilarated by Eliza's buoyant mood, as well as by a sense of freedom as if I had finally deposited my luggage with an airline and could wander around quite unencumbered. What Jo did or did not do for the next six days was not my problem. Or so I wanted to believe.

With both girls occupied elsewhere, I had the house to myself and three hours to do exactly what I wanted. So I

chose a particular CD which normally caused groans of com-
plaint, stripped off all my clothes and danced around in the
lounge to the thump and grind of Queen. As an afterthought,
I quickly closed the curtains then turned the heating up and
let myself go.

When I had exhausted myself, I simply wandered aim-
lessly around the house, looking at the photos on the wall and
fingering ornaments as if I were a tourist looking around a
stately home.

I found myself in the chaos of Eliza's room, clothes strewn
across the floor like the last day of the January sales, half-fin-
ished homework scattered across her desk, an old banana skin
on the window-sill. Then I wandered into Jo's room with its
tidy, ordered rows of books and files. An island in our chaotic
household. Lists and reminders were drawing-pinned to her
notice-board with symmetrical neatness and dated in the right-
hand corners. The bin had been emptied, clothes folded away,
and her dressing-gown hung where it should be, on the back
of her door. The walls had been painted magnolia when we
had bought the house but the paintwork had become chipped
and scuffed in places with the passing of time. Jo deserved
some fresh gloss, some new colour and brightness as a fitting
background to her tidiness.

I decided to go to the DIY store. Jo would have a surprise
waiting for her when she returned from her father's and I
would show her what a supportive, caring mother I really was.

Once at the store, I found myself staring helplessly at row
upon row of paint tins, stacked like a child's cylindrical building blocks, reaching to the ceiling. A small shelf, angled like
a lectern, sliced through the endless continuity of tins. On this
shelf lay books and leaflets containing square upon square,

each labelled with a reference number and name. It was like a colour-coded plan of a cemetery.

The spectrum of colours to choose from was overwhelming, not helped by my difficulty in visualising these tiny squares as complete walls in Jo's bedroom. It was like being given a daisy and expecting to know what Kew gardens looked like. I stared at the colour charts as if in a hypnotic trance until one square seemed to merge into the next so that all I saw was a swirl of pinks, purples and greens, like melted flavours of ice cream slowly mixing to one murky hue.

'Too many choices,' muttered a bewildered-looking man next to me.

'Like life really,' I answered philosophically. 'Easier when the decisions are made for you.'

'It's the names that put me off—Cornish Cream, Avocado Mousse, Blueberry Pie. It's more like a cookery book.'

'Or a holiday brochure. Look—Blue Lagoon, Californian Sunset, Icelandic River. They're not even accurate, I'd call that one Polluted Canal and that one Gangrenous Wound. Oh, look, here's Fungal Foot Infection.'

The man laughed and reached for two large tins.

'Well, I'm too set in my ways,' he sighed. 'It's Boring Old Fart for me, or Magnolia as it's known in the trade.'

Jo was not set in her ways, I decided. Surely there was a rebellious side to her that would respond to a black ceiling and purple walls, or clashing colours of orange or mauve. But I knew Jo was practical and sensible for one so young and would immediately see that such dark colours wouldn't reflect any natural light and would certainly not be conducive to studying. She would want something different, novel and young, but light, subtle and individual. I tried to recall the tone of her carpet and the shades of her bedroom furniture, but everything I visualised seemed greyer than it should be. I kept returning to the squares of green, one of Jo's favourite colours. There was a shade called Mint which almost tasted of those squares of mint chocolate. This, I felt sure, would be Jo's choice.

I put the tins into my trolley and headed for the checkout. Then I heard a familiar voice. I looked up and saw Alice in a grey trouser suit and chiffon scarf helping an elderly lady who was waving a stick and hobbling up the aisle.

'Come on, Mother,' she was saying, 'Let's get some nice new paint and then I can make a start on your bathroom. I SAID, "LET'S GET SOME NICE NEW PAINT, MOTHER." Oh, never mind.'

I swivelled my trolley round quickly to escape in another direction. If only the front wheel hadn't caught the edge of the paint tin at the bottom of the pyramid, I might have made it.

'Lizzie... Oh, dear. We can't just leave these here. I'll go and get someone.'

I couldn't really leave her deaf, disabled mother unattended so I just stood there awkwardly.

'Who are you?' she barked.

'LIZZIE, ROGER'S WIFE. Ex, I mean.'

'There's no need to shout. I'm not deaf. My daughter's staying for a few days. Pain in the arse. Wants to paint my bathroom. I bet she makes me have it done in pink.'

'You can choose what colour you want. It's your bathroom.'

'With Alice in charge? You're joking. Help me along to the paint area, then we can choose.'

With that, she sprinted down the aisle, holding her stick out in front of her, and was stretching up towards the tins of black and purple paint before I caught up with her.

'Take me to the checkout,' she said, linking her arm in mine.

Alice eventually caught up with us after her mother had bought the purple and black paint.

'Mother, my goodness. I see you've already purchased your paint. Marvellous.'

Alice's mother winked at me.

'Thank you, Lizzie,' Alice said. 'I had a feeling you and I would end up very good friends.'

I stopped myself from wincing and made a dash for the car before Alice noticed her mother's choice of paint and blamed me. With the paint in the boot, I just made it to the rehearsal rooms in time to pick up Eliza, congratulating myself on co-ordinating my afternoon so successfully. But as we approached the driveway, Eliza asked, 'What's for supper, Mum?'

…So I prepared her a farmhouse stew full of goodness and vitamins, went out into the yard to milk the cow and prepared to invite the neighbours round for a game of charades…

Actually, I'd somehow forgotten about the small matter of eating, and Eliza deserved a treat, I told myself. So we phoned for a takeaway pizza, slumped onto the settee and glued ourselves to her favourite film, *Chicago*. It should have been boring by this, our twentieth viewing, but I never tired of taking sideways glances to watch Eliza watch her two heroines.

If I looked right into Eliza's eyes, I could almost see her mind turning herself into Catherine Zeta Jones or Renee Zellweger. This time her focus was on Zeta Jones and Eliza was there in the film, tapping out every dance step in her mind, reaching for every note, feeling every emotion. Melted cheese and tomato dripped down her chin as she fed herself by touch, her eyes fixed firmly on the oblong screen in front of her. My vision as a perfect mother did not include slobbing in front of the telly with a pizza. Still, I told myself, it was a special occasion. Was that what it was? A special occasion because we did not have the adolescent tension of Jo in the air? I felt I had failed in some way but I quickly replaced that thought with a vision of Eliza and me singing a duet in a Hollywood musical. In Eliza's world, everyone would create a song and dance about everything.

Monday morning came and I had to put Jo's room on hold while I went to work.

I put on my black executive suit, threw some extremely important papers into my executive briefcase and made a quick phone call to ensure my executive car was on its way to pick me up and take me to the city where I would be handling investments of millions of pounds.

I arrived at the sandwich bar and put my vision on hold for later—I did still have that idea of running my own café. I rushed in, late as usual, washed my hands and got stuck into scraping butter across bread and spooning in the fillings for workers picking up their lunch sandwiches on the way in. Trish busied herself by dispensing caffeine to a hundred lethargic businessmen and we kept up this frantic pace for nearly an hour.

It was only later, when Trish went out in the delivery van, that I could no longer ignore my screaming thoughts about what Roger had said. Of course I had noticed that Jo was looking a bit thinner and of course I had been a bit worried. But Jo losing weight? That didn't fit. She had always been active and healthy, not one of those children who pick up every little cough and cold going round, always with a runny nose and alarmingly pale skin. In fact, I had rarely been to the doctor with Jo, for she had never suffered from anything more than the usual childhood ailments, which she always shook off very quickly, and she had barely missed a day of school. As I chopped up tomatoes and cucumbers, the word 'cancer' floated into my mind uninvited, but I soon pushed it out again. I clung to more logical explanations and somehow managed to keep my anxiety in check.

I reminded myself that Jo was pretty good for a teenager. She had largely conformed, and had kept her mood swings firmly locked in her bedroom, never opting for the throwing-crockery-at-your-mother option. I had had many a long chat with Scarlet's mother, who had torn clumps of her own hair out in the frustration of trying to control her daughter.

'If I tell Scarlet to be home by half past eleven, she'll turn up at a quarter to twelve just to prove a point. If I ask her to clear the coffee-cups out of her bedroom, she'll bring down just the one and then take up a new cup of coffee and a plate.'

Not much to complain about but I had noticed that Scarlet's mother had started to chew her fingernails lately. Scarlet had a belly piercing, one dolphin tattoo on her shoulder and another on her arm which nobody has dared ask the meaning of, and she had brought home at least three inarticulate, nicotine-stained boyfriends. A tame rebellion compared with many, but more than Jo had succumbed to. Jo didn't seem to have this drive to battle with authority, she had other priorities. It was much later that I realised she was rebelling in her own way, and I would gladly have swapped what happened next with any number of body piercings.

'I'm not sure I want this,' muttered one of my regular customers.

I looked at his sandwich. It did look rather thin and lank. He lifted up the top layer of bread to reveal a very thick spreading of butter but no filling whatsoever. He then lifted up the lid of his coffee-cup where, like a magician, he slowly revealed the whereabouts of the missing filling, which was floating on the coffee like seaweed in the ocean.

'Sorry, Reg, I was miles away.'

'Last week you were imagining yourself serving food in a beach bar on Mars. Where were you today?'

'I was solving the mystery of adolescence, but I think serving coffee on Mars is more realistic.'

That night it was fish and chips in front of a quiz, justified by my plan to make a start on the decorating. After supper, I creaked up the stairs to Jo's room, looked around, and decided I could muster up enough energy to shift the furniture to the centre of the room, pull back the carpet and get all my decorating gear ready.

I stood for a while and stared at the room. Beginning anything was always hard and I imagined Michelangelo must have felt the same as he stood inside the Sistine Chapel. Before I allowed my imagination to let me plan something rather too ambitious for Jo's ceiling, I went back to the kitchen and found a couple of cardboard boxes. I carted them upstairs and filled them up with books and ornaments.

Once I had begun the task, my earlier enthusiasm returned and I began to enjoy myself as I stripped the bed and lifted the notice-board off the wall. There was something very satisfying about this sort of job. It reminded me of taking down Christmas decorations, hoovering up the pine needles and starting a fresh new year with the old one wiped clean away along with its stale habits, overdone arguments, regrets and remorse.

I began to hum and whistle like a jovial morning milkman as I went about the business of dismantling Jo's room. It was as if I was taking her life apart to spring clean it, give it a lick of paint and then put it back together again—as if I was certain that that was what was needed.

It didn't take long to pack the loose items away and I set about the task of hauling the bed and chest into the middle of the room. I slid the top drawer out and found it neatly lined with underwear. At the back were two chocolate bars which Jo must have forgotten about.

The second drawer jammed and I had to rattle and shake it to pull it right out. It was full of black and grey tops and a couple of pairs of shorts which looked like Eliza's cast-offs. At the back of this drawer were two sandwiches which were as hard and dry as cardboard, the edges bending up like brittle autumn leaves. I took one out and held it in my palm studying it, trying to work out why it was there. Like frantic moths, answers flew into my mind but could not settle.

I placed the stale food on the window-sill and tugged out the remaining drawers, pulling jumpers and tops aside frantically, desperately, like a hungry dog trying to dig up a buried bone. Nothing.

Smiling at my own stupidity, I dropped the stale food into the bin liner and grabbed the radio from the hallway. I switched it on and allowed the rhythmic thump of some old rock music to smother any remaining illogical fears.

Almost cheerily, I pushed the bed away from the wall and picked up Jo's school bag which had been lying underneath. As I moved it, some books and a lunch box slapped down onto the floor. The lunch box was unexpectedly heavy and I peered through the plastic lid at its contents. There was no mistaking it. I peeled off the top to reveal the spaghetti bolognese I had served up days earlier. I stood still and stared at it for what seemed like hours. Then my brain jolted into action again and I tried to apply some logic.

Of course Jo had already unexpectedly declared herself a vegetarian so why hadn't she told me instead of stuffing the meat into a plastic box and hiding it under her bed? I supposed she must have thought I would be disapproving or critical. Would I have been? Possibly. I had always cracked jokes about vegetarians being wind-powered and likened tofu to small pieces of mattress. I cringed when I thought of all those stupid remarks I had made about deep-fried Brussels sprouts and plastic sandals. Perhaps the answer was to become a vegetarian myself and declare the house a meat-free zone, but then I thought about bacon. I could almost smell it. Still, surely I just had to reassure Jo that she didn't have to eat meat, and she simply had to reassure me that she would get her nutrition in other ways.

Yet I knew that such easy communication had broken down between us. Something told me that this wasn't going to be at all straightforward. If Eliza hadn't bounced into the room at that moment, I do believe I would have slumped down onto the bed and cried.

'What's wrong, Mum?'

'Nothing sweetie, it's just… Jo's become a…'

'Lesbian?'

'No.'

'Drug pusher?'

'No.'

'Prostitute?'

'Of course not. Jo's become a vegetarian.'

'Oh, is that all? How boring, everyone's a vegetarian.'

'Actually, Eliza, I don't think she's eating properly.'

'No one eats properly, Mum.'

'But Jo's so thin.'

'Then make sure she eats more.'

It didn't seem right to be confiding in a ten-year-old. Yet sometimes it takes a young soul to see everything in its simplest terms.

'How an earth can I get her to eat?'

'Use your imagination.'

Yes, I was good at that. Wasn't I?

FOUR

I WANTED to go to Dad's in August. Not because it 'made a pleasant change' as Mum said, but because he always left me alone to get on with it. To get on with what? Thinking, working it all out, making lists. He never went in for talking much. Talking can interfere with thinking. He'd moved to the country. It was only just under an hour's drive from us, but as you got nearer it got greener. Fields full of cows. That sort of thing. Decent cottage, I suppose. Bit small. In a kind of village full of commuters and ladies making jam and divorced fathers. There was a town nearby—market town, they call it. Never seen a market there, though. You could walk into town in twenty minutes. The bus was quicker, but always full of ladies with baskets, wearing brown macs and staring.

Mum and Eliza stayed for lunch. That was when I found out I couldn't eat in front of Mum. Eating is a bodily function and like all bodily functions it should be done in private. When Dad lived at home they would shout at each other. They would say what they thought. Everything would be on the surface, on view, like portraits in a gallery. Now they sit and smile and clip their words so they do not fly off in the wrong direction. It is the gaps between the sentences you have to listen out for. I preferred the arguing, the obvious tension.

Tension makes the air thick and difficult to breathe in. It makes voices high-pitched and annoying. It was like sitting in glue that lunchtime. Mum and Dad were trying to do and say the right thing. I knew how hard that was. I wanted to tell them not to bother, that it wasn't worth the effort. But effort made them feel noble and righteous, or something.

When Mum and Eliza left, the air cleared like the morning fog lifting and the sun coming through. We cleared the plates and talked of this and that. I asked about Alice.

'It's a pity Alice isn't here this week,' I said.

'She had to go and look after her mother.'

I wanted to ask whose idea it had been. I hesitated.

'Did Mum make her go?'

'Of course not, it's just how it worked out.'

I wished I hadn't asked. I invited the lie and then was disappointed when it came. Let down. Kind of.

'I'm playing darts tonight. Come along if you want, but I told Keith and Bev next door you might babysit—thought you could do with the money—but it's up to you, your choice.'

'Yeah, I'll babysit.'

The next morning I woke up and my period had started. It was about ten days early, dragged forward by a vicious moon. I hadn't come prepared. I padded my knickers out with toilet roll and went downstairs.

'No breakfast for me yet, I'm just going to the shop.'

The best thing about Dad—you didn't always have to explain yourself.

'I'll come too. We need some more milk.'

'I'll get the milk.'

'OK.'

The next best thing about Dad was he didn't feel the need to shadow me. And he was practical.

'Great. That gives me some more time. We're playing in a tournament at Brampton. Got to rush.' Dad coached an under-sixteens football team.

The worst thing about Dad? He never changed his arrangements because of me. Maybe that was good, I could never work it out.

I walked to the village shop two streets away. My body was slow and heavy. Every step was an effort, like I'd already walked ten miles or something. I folded my arms across my aching breasts. As if I could stop them getting bigger. I felt messy and grubby and infected. I had a disease that I didn't want and the only cure was to travel backwards in time.

I opened the shop door to let an old lady out. Then I backed in. I resented spending my babysitting money on tampons and paracetamol. I didn't look at the girl when I paid for them. I envied Eliza her pre-menstrual childhood.

When I was ten I would run everywhere. There was an urgency about life, as if time was running out. I ran to see friends, I ran up the stairs, I ran races with myself in the garden. Now, as if I wanted time to stand still, I swung my legs slowly back up to Dad's. I hauled myself up the path to the front door and heaved along the corridor to fall heavily onto the bed.

'Do you want to come to the football?'

'No, I'll get the bus into town.'

'OK, see you later.'

I had enough money to buy a new top. There was a free-dom about shopping in a strange town. Nobody knew me which meant I could be who I liked. I wanted to be myself but I'd forgotten how. Instead I would be a model, an actress, someone with style, money, good taste. I would buy a top to suit the new me. Buy a top she would buy. Something classy and sophisticated, and very very different. Something Eliza would envy and Mum would be unsure of.

I went to the usual shops and saw all the usual clothes. Then I saw a local shop called Hidden Scream and it sounded like a good omen. The interior was lit dimly and smelt of burning musk. I saw a rack of red tops. Crimson, rose, scarlet, blood. I picked out a crimson velvety bodice with a laced neckline and loose, Tudor sleeves. It was theatrical, bohemian, historical, vampish. I paid more than I'd meant to which made me feel daring.

I was thirsty but not daring enough to sit in a coffee-bar on my own. I bought a bottle of diet Coke and found a park near the bus station. A mother and two daughters were feeding the ducks. The eldest girl was about eight or nine. She was pleasing her mother by pulling off fistfuls of bread from a stale loaf and throwing them to the waddling birds.

'That one hasn't had any,' the mother was pointing out.

The girl threw the bread farther and looked at her mother to see if she'd done well.

'Well done, Georgie. Now try that one over there.'

It was as if the mother was conducting an orchestra. The eldest child was the lead violin and was playing to please. She in turn was encouraging her sister. The eagerness of the girl made me feel sad. No, not sad. More like numb.

My stomach felt heavy, pressing down as if it was trying to escape. A dull ache had spread across my front and down into my legs. I didn't want to stand up. I imagined sitting on this park bench into the night. Dew would form on my clothes, my bones would slowly turn rigid. Would anyone mind? Who would blame who? I opened my carrier bag and took out the new top. It wouldn't go with anything I had in my cupboard.

I can't remember going back to Dad's on the bus. It was as if I was in a trance, not wanting to think. Not wanting to feel. All I knew was the continuous ache.

The next day I felt better. The first day of my period was always the worst. I had some black coffee and a bowl of cereal. Dad had to go to work. He'd had one day off for the football tournament but couldn't take any more time. He was sorry, but he could drop me in town. We could go out for a meal in the evening. And to the cinema. I decided to stay at his house and read.

After he'd shut the front door, I felt free. I wandered around the house. I had a shower. I read a bit. I found some DVDs and slotted one in. The film and the space and the solitude made me feel vaguely happy.

The phone rang.

'Just phoning to say how much I'm missing you. It's not the same without you.'

Scarlet. So obviously Scarlet. Her words.

'I miss you too,' I said. 'What's happening?'

'Usual stuff. What about you? What's it like being at your dad's?'

I looked around the empty hallway. I listened to the silence.

'Cool,' I said. 'Once you get used to it. It's better. I've forgotten what it was like when they were together now.'

'I love you, Jo. You always make me feel better. Hey, guess what?'

'What?'

'Cathy's dumped Alfie.'

'No! Why?'

'Fran heard him telling Rob that he liked blondes the best, that he'd go for a blonde any time. Blonde with blue eyes and big tits, he said.'

'She could dye her hair.'

'Yeah, yeah, and get coloured contacts and a boob job. No, she's well out of it. No decent girl would change herself for a guy. Can you imagine a guy getting a penis extension just to please you, I mean, come *on*…'

I laughed. I wished I was like Scarlet.

'I wish I was funny like you,' I said.

'You are, you are. You just don't realise it. Got to go—text me, yeah?'

'Yeah.'

The hall was silent again. I thought about Scarlet. Missing me, loving me, thinking I'm funny. Funny in a good way. She should have been my sister. That would have worked better. I went and sat in the lounge and did nothing. And didn't think much. That was good, not thinking much.

Then Mum phoned.

It was as if she was there, in my space. Intruding. The silence had been invaded by voices. My freedom was slashed by her interrogation.

'Are you having a good time?', 'Is it raining where you are?', 'Did Scarlet get hold of you? I gave her the number.'

I kept my answers short. I wanted my time back again. Anything lost could never be retrieved. The questions were time-wasters, pointless, conversational, lightweight fillers that didn't mean anything. The next question had more weight.

'Has your tummy settled down now?'

'Yeah.'

I waited. It was a short, split-second of a wait that felt longer.

'Only the funniest thing happened. Well, it was going to be a surprise but you know how useless I am at surprises. I mean, remember your surprise party last year—mind you, I blame Scarlet for that—anyway, that's all under the bridge. Now, what was I saying?'

Yeah, what had she been saying? So many words, so little content. I knew what was coming. Like the punchline of an old schoolboy joke.

'I'm decorating your room as a surprise. There, I've told you.'

But she hadn't told me yet. I hung on for the punchline.

'The silly thing is…well, I found some food under your bed and in your drawer. I wasn't looking, I was decorating and, well…you know. I don't know if it's to do with this vegetarian thing or if it's your tummy. Still, well, you know…I had to laugh, seeing all those sandwiches you'd obviously forgotten about, then I thought, Oh, dear, perhaps you're not well. Only I could make a doctor's appointment if you want. I only mentioned it because I was phoning anyway.'

Why ask questions if you're going to supply your own answers? Why ask questions if you know the answer but will accept a different one? I remember Eliza's questions when she was about three. 'Why?' was enough to keep the conversation going. Any answer would do.

'I knew you were worried about my stomach,' I explained. 'I didn't want you to worry any more. I'm fine now.'

'I knew there was a simple explanation. Eliza's fine, by the way—her rehearsals are going well.'

'Great.'

'What are you up to today, then?'

If you have a dry, gristly piece of meat, cover it with pastry or sauce or aromatic herbs. Disguise the feel of it, the flavour, the quality. Maybe nobody will notice. But I always do.

I needed to make a list. No, two lists. A list for the day and a list for the week.

List One (Tuesday):

- *Wash hair.*
- *Buy magazine.*
- *Text Scarlet.*
- *Cook tea for Dad.*
- *Shave legs.*
- *Sew button on shirt.*
- *Try on new top.*
- *Read through chemistry curriculum.*
- *Find scales and weigh myself.*
- *Do fifty sit-ups.*

List Two (Weds—Sat):

- *Weigh self every day.*
- *Send postcard to Scarlet.*
- *Go to library and look at university prospectuses/ career books.*
- *Run every day.*
- *Measure waist.*
- *Start a novel.*
- *Bake a cake.*
- *Get money off Dad.*

- *Get hair cut.*
- *Make a plan for a better life.*

The day was my own again. I had reclaimed my space. I started at the end of my list. After fifty sit-ups I lay back on the lounge floor. It didn't seem enough. I did another fifty.

I went to the bathroom but there were no scales. I went into Dad's bedroom and opened the cupboard. Suits and shirts, dresses and skirts hung there like a row of headless people waiting in a bus queue. I glanced over at the bed. The bed where Dad and Alice slept. And didn't sleep. The middle-aged having sex is a thought to be pushed aside. Especially if a parent is involved. I was a sixteen-year-old virgin. I didn't want to save myself for love, I wanted it over and done with. Like an exam. But I was frightened of failing. I swotted up on it by talking to Scarlet. I studied magazines. I thought I would need to do it before I was eighteen—if I was to keep on schedule. But eighteen would roll around too quickly. The spin of the earth had speeded up, surely it had speeded up.

The scales were lying at the bottom of the cupboard, like a slab of concrete. They looked heavy and cumbersome but they were deceptively light. I weighed myself. I had lost another three pounds. Was it good enough? Was anything ever good enough? Were my results good enough? Probably. Would my next set of results be good enough? Good enough for who? Was I a good enough daughter, a good enough friend, a good enough sister, a good enough citizen? And who decides?

It's your own thoughts that try you, judge and condemn you. I wanted thoughts out of my head. I wanted to put my hand in and pull out what I didn't want. Give my mind a wash and a rinse. Being on my own made my thoughts my only company. I phoned Scarlet. No reply. I went to the shop for a magazine. I decided to smile at people on the way. I would pass a comment to the girl in the shop. I would discard the real me and be a friendly shopper. Everybody loves a friendly shopper.

I made the week pass slowly. I was a Time Lord. Or maybe that should be Lady. I worked out that when I got back home, there would be two days before term started. That was fixed. Not even a Time Lord could change it.

Mum looked nervous. I went upstairs and Mum, Dad and Eliza followed me. Like bodyguards. The room was green and everything was back in its place. It was like I'd been burgled or something. Worse than that—molested, violated. The space around me had been raped. It could never be the same. I had to be in that space and it was no longer mine.

'Do you like it?'

Did I? I didn't really know. The colour was OK. It didn't really matter.

'It's great. Thanks, Mum.'

I could hear the relief. We all knew it could have gone the other way. We all had a cup of tea. Everyone was happy. I sat in the lounge to read.

I felt sick again that night. Mum said she would phone the doctor. Just to be on the safe side.

The next day I wanted the house to myself, like it was at Dad's. But it was Sunday and Mum and Eliza were there. They take up a lot of space.

I phoned Scarlet. She was bored.

'I've got no money but we could go and sit in the park.'

So we did. We sat on the grass. The sun shone down on us. We talked. We laughed. We just sat. Doing nothing. Being us.

'What's it like, going to your dad's?' Scarlet asked again.

'It's cool.'

'I'm going to my dad's new place next weekend.'

'It'll be fine, honestly it'll be fine.'

'It'll seem odd, though, him in a different place. At the moment, it's just like he's away on business, but living somewhere else… I can't imagine it. I don't think he can even cook. And what will we talk about? We can't really talk about Mum, but I want to tell him about her, how she's crying and everything. Do you think he still cares? I don't want him to be bitchy about Mum. Can men be bitchy? Anyway, it all seems so shitty, you know—awkward.'

'You get used to it. Don't worry.'

Scarlet looked into me, pleading with me, wanting more than I could give.

'Sorry, I'm being a shit friend,' I pointed out. 'It's just I don't know what to say, everyone's different.'

'You're right, Jo. If you told me about how it is with your dad, I'd expect the same, but it won't be the same, will it? I think what you're saying is that I've got to work it out for myself. I suppose it just gets easier.'

'It does.'

'I just didn't expect to feel this churned up. Did you feel churned up?'

She asked like it was in the past, like I was over it. At the time, I cried. I think I might have cried a lot. Then I learnt not to.

'I guess I did. It's only natural.'

'Of course it is. Thanks, Jo.'

The park was spotted with small groups of people. Families

mostly and some groups of kids and teenagers. Anonymous faces. People I wouldn't recognise again in a line-up.

Everyone was smiling but they couldn't all be happy. Statistically impossible. I glanced at Scarlet. Her lips were turned up and her eyes were narrowed as she squinted towards the sun. Sad but smiling, it seemed. I held a mirror to myself. I put my hand towards my face. I was smiling too. In spite of everything. It was the hot August sun. It creased up people's faces into grimaces with laughter lines. Very deceptive.

'The bigger the arse, the more likely the chance of them wearing shorts,' I declared, nodding my head towards an obese woman, ice cream smeared across her chins. It was cruel, but it made Scarlet laugh. That was kind, making her laugh.

'If I looked like that, I wouldn't leave the house.' Scarlet could out-cruel me.

I scanned the horizon for more fat people. There were plenty to choose from. Disgusting white flesh oozing over tight clothes. Like lard in the gravy tray. I pointed to a fat husband and wife.

'How do they actually do it?' I asked Scarlet. 'They couldn't get near enough to each other.'

Scarlet rolled over with laughter. Her arms and legs splayed out like she was having a fit. Hysterical. Out of control. She really let herself go. I laughed too but swallowed some of it back again.

'Earthquake alert,' I whispered as a flabby woman jogged past. Thump, thump, wheeze.

Shared cruelty made us a team. It glued us together.

'That's more like it.' Scarlet sat up and smoothed her clothes down. She was looking at two guys with their tops off, kicking a football about. Showing off. Brown skin sweating in the heat. Aware of Scarlet's gaze. And mine. I turned away, looking for more people to laugh at. Scarlet nudged me; drew me back again.

'I'm boiling,' I moaned. 'Let's go and find some shade.'

We bought a couple of Cokes from the van and went and sat under the trees near the bandstand. It was sweltering. I thought about death.

'What are you thinking about?' asked Scarlet lazily.

'School tomorrow.'

School tomorrow, exams at the end of the year, more exams, a job, house, mortgage, life insurance, marriage maybe, children, middle age, menopause, stair lifts, death. Death is at the end of every list. Whatever route you take, whatever path you choose, they all end in the same place. Nowhere.

I remember when I was four years old. I lay on my bed. I couldn't sleep. I called for my mother.

'What if I die in the night?' I asked.

'You won't.' She smiled. 'You'll still be here in the morning.'

'Where do you go when you die?'

'To heaven. Everybody goes to heaven.'

Life was easy then. Somebody had all the answers. Total trust. Then one day you wake up and it hits you. Your parents know nothing. They make it up. They know about as much as you do. So you search for a guru.

Mrs Simms—my first teacher, Miss Castle next door, Mr Bradshaw, Katie's mum, Mrs Moore. They all promised such knowledge. Facts and figures, meaningless information. But they knew no more than I did, really. When I eventually met my real guru, I learnt that a guru didn't need to know more than I did. I just needed to be shown what I already knew deep inside. Lily Finnegan: my guru. On that day in the park, my guru was already getting her stuff together, preparing for the journey. Perhaps I was, too.

'Are you all right?' Scarlet asked.

'Do you think I'm depressed, Scarlet?'

'I don't know. Do you feel depressed?'

'I don't know. I don't think so.'

'Well, then.'

'I don't want to go to school tomorrow.'

'Neither do I.'

So I was normal, then. That was a relief. But my mind flipped over. I wanted to be normal, fit in, blend into the background. I also wanted to be special, unusual, better than the rest. There it was again. Wanting two opposite things at the same time equals unhappiness. I kicked my thoughts out and looked at the sun.

We sat in an easy silence, thinking, watching, being. The park buzzed with the children chattering. Now and then a shout rang out as an anonymous name was shrieked. I heard my own name and looked up startled. A young girl ran to her mother. A different Joanna.

Flies flitted round where we sat and I swatted them away from my face. The grass felt dry and brittle. I scuffed up the grainy dirt with my heels. Time must have been ticking by but it was going slowly. My thoughts were running ahead, bouncing from one thing to the next, but Scarlet was still thinking about school. Thoughts, for Scarlet, needed airing. Hung up against the skyline for all to see.

'The reason we don't want to go to school is that we don't have to. That's what I think, anyway. Till now it was the law, see. Now we have a choice. Perfectly legal to leave school, get a job. Leave home if you want. Get married at Gretna

Green. We're going back to school because we want to, and because our parents want us to, I suppose. But there's bound to be a bit of us that says, shit, I might leave. I reckon it was easier last year when we had to go. No choice, so there was nothing to think about really. Out of our control. Well, that's what I think anyway.'

I looked at Scarlet and smiled. I didn't know what to say.

'Do I talk too much?' she asked, seriously.

'Yeah, way too much.' I laughed, and I pushed her over on the grass and tickled her. Like we were ten or something.

The spots and splashes of yellow and white circled Scarlet's head like a spring aura. Daisies. I looked across the grassy area in front of us. They had been there all along. I hadn't seen what was in front of my eyes. I remembered pic-nics in a daisied field by a stream. Always by a stream. Dad, Mum, Eliza, Me. A complete daisy chain.

'Daisies!' I announced to Scarlet. Still ten.

I touched the tiny flowers carefully, picking the ones with the thicker stalks. They felt padded, pliable. Slowly, with my finger nail, I made a tiny slit in the centre of the first stalk. I took an-other daisy and threaded its stalk through the slit. I focused and took great care. I didn't want to waste a daisy by ripping at the slit. I picked them so that the stalks were long. I chose ones with the larger flowers, like egg yolks and feathers. I took my time.

'Hey!' said Scarlet. She started to thread daisy stalks too. At first she was careless. She threw discarded daisies over her shoul-der but then it got her gripped. It was hypnotic like you were in a trance or something. You made a daisy chain, you cleared your mind. How long is a daisy chain? It doesn't matter.

I held mine up and it hung there so delicately. Fragile. Vulnerable. It needed careful handling. I added more and more daisies. Slowly. It grew into a necklace, or something like it. I completed the circle. I finished the chain. Immediately I started another. Shorter this time. Total absorption. Partial amnesia.

Soon Scarlet was lifting her chain over my head. I bobbed down to let it pass over and sit on my shoulders. I put mine onto her head. A crown of flowers. She laughed. The chain broke. A fly got into the corner of my eye. I wiped away the salt water with the back of my hand.

Duty caught up with us. Scarlet felt she ought to go and support her mother. I felt I ought to go home too. Get my stuff ready for the next day.

One day my mother will greet me with a question: about my day or if I feel OK or ask me my news. Any greeting which did not contain the word 'sandwich' would do.

'We've eaten, you'll have to make yourself a sandwich,' was the greeting waiting for me when I got back from the park.

She was tense, uptight, edgy. And it was contagious.

'I feel a bit sick.' (My greetings were no better.)

'You'll have to go to the doctor.'

'I think I'll go and lie down.'

'You ought to get your bag ready for tomorrow. It's bound to be a rush in the morning.'

The snap of the elastic band.

'Lucky I've got you to tell me what to do—have to, ought to, should, that's all I ever hear.'

I wasn't looking for an argument, just an outlet. I didn't want a reply, I didn't want any interaction, so I turned away quickly and stomped upstairs. I slammed my bedroom door shut. Obligatory for a teenager and I was playing myself as a teenager. I lay on my bed. I stared at the green walls. I had wanted blue. I hated my mother. I loved my mother. I couldn't do both, surely I couldn't do both. I was torn between two emotions like they were both grabbing an arm each and ripping me down the middle. So I cried. I cried in blood for being ripped apart by my feelings. By my mother. By my bloody mother. I thought I would run at my pristinely decorated wall and splatter myself across it. Let my guts drip down onto the floor. Then she'd be sorry. If I were in pieces. If I were dead. I opened my mouth to scream but it didn't come out properly. It was stifled, half-hearted, too quiet. I couldn't do anger properly. I was a failure at being a failure. She didn't understand. I wanted her to understand. About school. About me. About eating. And not eating. But my bloody mother didn't understand. I sobbed. I sobbed with my head down on my arm, stifling the sound. When it was done, I felt better. But bad, too, like I'd done something wrong. And I did love my mother. Underneath all the pain.

I reached for my pad and pen. I needed a new list.

- *Don't forget to take Scarlet's book in tomorrow.*
- *Don't eat too much.*
- *Don't wear my new top to school.*
- *Don't put myself down for school lunches.*
- *Don't gossip about Scarlet's parents.*
- *Don't have a lift with Mum in the morning.*
- *Don't get chocolate out of the machine.*
- *Don't forget to sign up for aerobics or something.*
- *Don't let the work blob me out.*
- *Don't talk to Andy tomorrow.*

I stared at the last item. Why had I written that? Andy and I had gone out for three months. I'd only had one boyfriend before that. Piers. Lasted for four days. What was good about pulling Andy? Telling my friends, starting sentences with 'my boyfriend', borrowing his jumper, writing about it in my diary, being seen in the coffee-bar, being seen in the cinema, being seen in the precinct, being seen in the high street.

Kissing was OK. Holding hands was good. Him telling me I had great breasts was good. And bad. Him wanting sex with me was bad. And good. I dumped him so I didn't have to say no. The next day he pulled Melissa. A known slapper. Some-one who says yes a lot. Now I talked about my ex-boyfriend— my two ex-boyfriends. Some street cred in that.

There was something churning round in my stomach. It wasn't my period. That heavy, pushing ache you get was gone. This was more like a cement mixer, turning over and over. When I lay down, I got the taste of stale bread in my mouth. When I sat up, I tasted my own sick. Then my mouth suddenly filled up with saliva and I spat down the sink. I felt hot and then cold. I felt weak and dizzy. I was ill, there was no doubt. And I needed to take something. Pills, medicine—something to get this stuff out of my stomach, this stuff that was churning around.

Suddenly I felt drowsy. I could still feel the sun on my face. I had a dull ache at the back of my head, and closed my eyes. I remembered to lie on my right side. Best for dreaming. I willed myself to remember my dream. Daytime sleeping was the best. I could sleep right through till morning—but I had an alarm clock, my mother. My mother would wake me up and tell me to pack my school bag. And eat a sandwich.

As it happened I dreamt the same dream I had dreamt be-fore. The one where I'm trying to get through a house and out the other side. This time I arrive at the house on a bicycle and tie it up to a post like it's a dog or something. There's someone there to help me. The person is telling me which way to go but I don't want to listen. I tell the person to take my bicycle and go back home. Now I can go down into the cellar on my own. Then I realise that I have no bicycle and I know that I have to get another. I feel frustrated that I don't know where I'm going to get one from. Just as I think I've worked it out, I hear my name. I open my eyes and see Mum.

'Looks like you've got sunstroke,' she said.

Was she sympathetic? Accusing? Then she laughed. 'Your face is like a raspberry!'

Did she really have to laugh?

'It's all right,' she reassured me. 'It isn't really burnt. Only a little bit red. Do you feel all right?'

'Sick. Dizzy. Tired.' I was monosyllabic with sleep.

'Too much sun,' declared Mum. 'I'll get you some water.'

I wanted to ask for orange juice but she was gone.

Time took a leap. In a matter of seconds she was back with a jug of iced water. And a sandwich.

'I won't be well enough for school tomorrow,' I declared.

'Yes, you will. Then we'll go to the doctor, just for a check-up. A three-thousand-mile service,' she said with a laugh.

Mum put her hand on my hot forehead. For a moment she looked at me so kindly, like she was an angel or something. She poured out a glass of water and placed it in my hand. Then she turned briskly and walked out of the door to the sound of Eliza's call. Like a matron going off duty. End of shift.

I looked at the sandwich. I would weigh myself first, I thought. And afterwards, perhaps.

Green paint, sandwiches, school, doctors, a new dress for a wedding, an appointment on the calendar, Dad's girlfriend, spaghetti Bolognese, shopping. I had got myself another list. But it wasn't complete.

I remember knowing the French word for town hall but in my exam I couldn't reach it. Knowing something and not knowing something. It happens more than you think. Some people call it denial.

Mum came back in. She sat down on the side of my bed. She looked down at me serenely, rearranged my pillow gently. Like a proper mother.

'We'll sort it out,' she said.

But I felt like I had stepped onto the bottom of a long escalator. I was being carried along whether I liked it or not. It was almost impossible to turn round and run back down again. Almost.

FIVE

SOMEWHERE inside I knew the truth about what was wrong with Jo but I also knew it was impossible because it was what happened to other families. Families where the mother eats suppers consisting of a slimming drink and chips, families where the mother tries to push her acne-ridden, lanky daughter into modelling, families where the mother makes comments about the neighbour: 'She'd look better in something loose'; 'Oh, no, not the leggings'; 'At least she's got nice hair'.

I wasn't as bad as that, surely. But had I made my daughter lick the platter clean? Had she seen me reminisce about how I looked when I could fit into my size ten wedding dress? Was I, in fact, only one Ryvita away from the Hollywood-diet, celebrity-worshipping mother? Perhaps, in fact, it was all my fault…

The guilt that was sucking the sense out of me was magnified by the commercials on television. Cleaning fluids, gravy, the right medicine administered with loving care all shine the light on what it is to be the perfect mother. I didn't look like the advert mother and my house didn't look like the advert house. I was struggling to get Jo to the doctor, let alone tuck her up in bed and caringly spoon some wonder medicine into her, as seen on TV.

It was about that time, just before I eventually persuaded Jo to see the doctor, that I picked up the newspaper and read about the teenager who had literally cleaned herself to death. The girl was called Lisa and it seemed such a pretty, happy name, yet she scrubbed her hands with every cleaning fluid she could find in her mother's over-stocked cupboard. Still not satisfied, she would apparently bathe in bleach and wash her hair in a thick gluey substance normally used for unblocking sinks. She frequently ended up in Casualty on account of all the toxic fumes she was inhaling and the burnt areas on her skin. Her mother knew about it, but apparently did nothing.

Eventually Lisa swallowed some of the cleaning fluids, large quantities of the stuff, in fact, in an attempt to clean out her insides. Her mother, it transpired, was a stickler for cleanliness in the home and 'a friend' informed the paper that she would slap Lisa for coming home from school with the merest speck of school gravy on her blouse. 'What sort of mother…?' I found myself saying, but quickly suppressed the question in case I discovered that the answer was, 'A mother like you.'

For some reason, I cut out the article so I could read it again and again. Perhaps it comforted me in some strange way to find a mother worse than I could ever be, one who would have guilt stamped on her soul for the rest of her life. But it unsettled me, too, for I knew deep down that Jo had a problem and I knew that if I ignored it I would be like Lisa's mother, the one I was judging and condemning so easily. The story brought tears to my eyes and one day I sobbed over it as if I were reading an obituary of a loved one. I felt I knew Lisa and wished I could have done something to prevent her tragic story, and all the time Jo's tragic story seemed to be unfolding before my eyes. I knew my daughter needed help, more help than I could give her, and yet I had a responsibility. I was the one who needed to take control but was failing to do so.

In the end, I managed to get Jo to the doctor. I didn't know if it was the right thing to do but there seemed to be no other options. I had not yet taken Eliza's advice and used my imagination. That would come later. That would come with Lily Finnegan's strange approach.

'I don't need to go to the doctor's, I'm not ill,' Jo said when I suggested it.

'But your stomach…'

'I'm better. I'm OK.'

'You haven't been going to school, you've been—'

'I know, I know. Please, Mum, don't pressurise me. I'll be all right, I promise.'

Her eyes pleaded with me, she looked so sad, even desperate, and I couldn't reach her. I wanted to hug her, to tell her I loved her, that I missed the old Jo, that everything would be all right. But it was as if she had put a barbed-wire fence around herself to keep people out. To keep me out. Still, I tried to get through. I was not going to give up on my own daughter as, it seemed, Lisa's mother had.

'You *are* under pressure, I know,' I said as gently as I could manage. Yet my voice was shaking, unsteady, as if I were at an important interview. A test to see if I was a fit mother. 'School is full of pressure these days, I do understand. And the divorce, I realise you took it—'

'I'm over it, OK?'

'I know, but these things… Anyway, maybe a counsellor or a therapist or something…'

So Jo came to the doctor as the easier option, the more acceptable one, to both of us.

In my best hat and coat and clutching Jo's medical card and inoculation record, I helped my poorly daughter out of the car and into the doctor's surgery where I queued patiently to speak to the bright young receptionist who…

'You're late,' said the not so bright young receptionist.

'Sorry, couldn't start the car and then I've been queuing here so I wasn't as late as… Sorry, it's for my daughter, Joanna Trounce. Jo…? Jo?'

I went back to the car to get Jo.

'You didn't say it was for an actual appointment.'

'What did you think we were doing here? Having a pint and a game of darts?'

We sat among the coughs and heavy breathing of the waiting room, flicking through old magazines repetitively, rhythmically, as if searching for information.

'There are a lot of bugs around at the moment,' I told Jo and myself. 'The problem is when you feel unwell, you worry about it and that worry makes you worry even more. It's so easy to let these things get out of hand. I'm sure Dr Robinson will sort it all out.'

After my good-mother speech, I was carried along by a strong sense that everything would be all right in the morning, that a muddle would be unmuddled, that we would look back and laugh at it all. But the words 'eating disorder', 'anorexia', 'bulimia' repeated themselves over and over in my mind like a mantra wanting to push all other thoughts away.

It was with some relief that we were called into the surgery. I felt we had begun what we had come for and it would all be over soon, like taking your driving test. As we sat down, I decided not to take over but to allow Jo to describe her symptoms.

'Joanna is having difficulty eating, not difficulty as such, I mean her mouth works well enough! Yes, well, I mean she eats and then feels sick. She has some intermittent diarrhoea and her stomach hurts again, usually after eating. Of course, it's put her off eating, as you'd expect. She hasn't eaten anything the rest of the family haven't had so we don't think it's... Sorry, I'll let Jo tell you all about it.'

'I think that's a good idea, Mrs. Trounce. Perhaps you would like to wait outside. Is that all right with you, Joanna?'

I looked at Jo as if she were at school, choosing who she wanted to be her partner.

'That's fine,' she said eventually.

'I don't usually wait outside,' I objected. 'I mean, she is my daughter.'

'Mum...'

So I left the room like someone who has just failed a job interview and been eliminated for saying the wrong thing, only to sit in the waiting room and wonder what was being said about me. At least, I thought, the day couldn't get any worse. It could.

'Hello, Lizzie, I'm glad I ran into you.'

There stood the wonderful Alice, not looking the slightest bit ill. Still, it's hard to look sick in an Armani suit. I wondered what to say about Jo and thought about hinting at head lice, but Alice had other things on her mind.

'Have you been painting Jo's room?' she asked.

'Yes, it was a surprise.'

'Only I think we've ended up with your paint. Of course

Mother's got very muddled about it. I think you must have our tins of pink.'

'No, I've got the right paint, thanks. Maybe your mother wanted a black and purple bathroom.'

'How did you know she had black and purple paint?'

'Just a guess.'

'Are you here with Jo?' Alice asked—rather nosily, I thought.

For one second, I wanted to tell her the truth, to take the forced smile off my face and explain how bad everything was.

'It's that time of year,' I said instead, the smile remaining rigidly in place.

Just then the door to Dr Robinson's surgery opened and out came Jo.

'Hi, Alice,' Jo muttered.

'Hello, Jo, it's good to see you.'

I bundled Jo out of the surgery as quickly as I could before Alice asked any of her awkward questions. I thought I was protecting my daughter but perhaps I was trying to protect myself. I didn't stop to think seriously as to why Alice was visiting the doctor, my mind was too full of Jo.

'All right?' I asked as we got into the car. But what exactly was I asking?

'Yeah.'

'Do you need to make another appointment?'

'Yeah.'

'Let's do it now, then.'

'No. I meant not another appointment.'

'What do you mean? Do you or do you not need another appointment?'

Maybe it's all right to use a sharp, brittle, bad-mother's

voice if you say sorry afterwards. Sorry is the magic word your own mother told you about. It turns you into Saint Mary.

'Sorry,' I muttered. 'It's just…'

'I know.'

We looked at each other. For just a moment there seemed to be some joint understanding, some mutual emotion between us as if we were in it together, like musicians playing the same tune. But anxiety separates us from others. Laughter is a joint, shared display of emotion. You do anxiety on your own, even if it is in parallel.

We were silent on the way home and then I insisted on conversation, a sharing of information, my right to know. I stood firm. Jo tried to push me away, exclude me, fly solo, but I persuaded her I was there for her. This was not intrusion, this was loving care, wasn't it? They should extend those nanny-knows-best programmes to include stuff like this.

When in doubt, put the kettle on. Jo drank her coffee black. I sloshed some milk into mine and dunked a digestive into the hot liquid. We needed our drinks to focus on, to keep our hands busy, avert our eyes, give us something to do, a reason for sitting across from one another at the kitchen table. This was a chat over coffee, not an interrogation. Pauses were necessary to sip our drinks, not as a withholding of information or feelings.

'I've been referred to the eating disorders clinic.'

I felt the hot coffee drip down the back of my throat and warm my oesophagus. I could almost sense it arriving in my stomach. Its warmth was in welcome contrast to the cold, stark message from Jo. Yet still my fingernails clung onto a cliff edge that was not really there.

That's good. At least we know what's wrong now. I feel so much happier and calmer now I know. I could walk on air, skip through daisies, holding your hand as I guide you though this difficult time…

But those words were erased by fear and anger before they reached my lips.

'How does that bloody doctor know anything? Is he going to carry out any tests? Is he an expert on eating disorders or does he spend all day looking at gout, verrucas and snot? I think we should try another doctor.'

'I knew this would happen,' Jo snapped.

'Knew what would happen?'

'You'd go all hysterical.'

'I'm not hysterical.'

'I've seen the bloody doctor, I'm going to the bloody clinic. What more do you want? Sorry I'm not the perfect daughter.'

That sounded ridiculous to me. Why would I want a perfect daughter? I just wanted Jo, Jo as she was, with all her ups and downs, faults and blemishes, the whole package. But the eating disorder was wrong, it just didn't fit, it wasn't part of Jo. It was like one of those modern conservatories tacked onto the front of a beautiful, old, beamed Tudor house. Like a down-and-out with a bottle of meths and a Gucci handbag. I tried to change my anger into gentle understanding.

'All I'm doing is giving you some support. Perhaps I should have just let you walk to the doctor's.'

Oops, I had played my joker—the guilt card.

Guilt goes with motherhood. Guilt because we dare to go out to work, guilt because we failed to buy Barbie's health spa, jacuzzi and leg-waxing centre three Christmases ago, guilt because we sometimes buy pre-packed, e-numbered, shove-in-the-microwave suppers. And every now and then we try to disperse all that guilt in another direction.

Jo raged upstairs, stamping her feet on every step and leaving me sitting there like a damp firework. I knew I wasn't handling this very well but I felt out of control. Something was happening that I couldn't keep tabs on, it was running away with me, spinning out of my hands. I felt frustrated, inadequate, out of my depth. I just sat there, staring into my coffee-mug, weighed down by thoughts and emotions. I don't know how long I remained in that position, but when Jo appeared in the kitchen doorway I realised that my hands were numb from holding the weight of my head in them for so long.

'Mum, there really isn't anything to worry about,' began Jo. 'They're going to run some tests but the doctor was right and so were you—I'd just become frightened to eat, that's all. I suppose it's a sort of eating disorder and I have lost weight but not that much. The thing is, I've been to the doctor as a precaution but I can sort this out myself. I probably don't need the clinic at all. I might go just for a bit of one-off advice. I won't be like the others there.'

Suddenly the sun shone through the yellow curtains in our kitchen and we all danced together in the sunbeams, like fairies on a midsummer's evening.

When Jo was little, I used to read her stories about magical places. I also used to sit her in front of the television while I topped up on caffeine and magazine gossip. I used to take her to the park and push her on the swings for as long as she wanted, but then I would wheel her pushchair around the clothes shops until she was stiff with boredom. I was, in many ways, a near-perfect mother but on a part-time basis. Now I simply tried too hard to be that story-reading, swing-pushing mother.

'I think you should take things slowly,' I told Jo. 'So you sit there and I'll do one round of toast and just a teensy-weensy bit of scrambled egg.'

'Don't do this, Mum. Just leave it, will you?' Jo spoke calmly but her voice was rasping, as if she had just inhaled thick, smoky fumes. She turned around sharply and made for the stairs again.

All you really need to be an effective teenager is a flight of stairs and a door. A door can shake the house and all the people in it if it's slammed in the right way. It can create a barrier between a teenager and the rest of the world. It can enable desperate parents to tap on it hopefully, only to be rejected by the silence on the other side. It can allow a parent to invade a teenager's privacy if she dare face the consequences.

Stairs can be stomped up, marched up, slammed up, escaped up. They can be whispered up, creaked up, slouched up, sidled up and they can be the scene of a dramatic entrance. Or exit. Teenagers spend a lot of time going up and down stairs at various speeds. It fits in with the rise and fall of their emotionally charged hormones.

I waited for a while at the bottom of the stairs.

'What's wrong?' It was Eliza at the top.

'Nothing. Jo's tired, that's all.'

'You were shouting.'

I went to tuck Eliza in, where she slept surrounded by cuddly teddies and rabbits.

'It's all right,' I reassured her.

'I'm tired and I haven't done my homework yet.'

'Come on, I'll give you a hand. And if I can't do it, we'll say the dog ate it.'

'We haven't got a dog.'

'Then we'll go next door and borrow theirs.'

Eliza giggled and I hugged her. Then I tousled her hair playfully and she tousled mine. I looked up and Jo was standing in the doorway. For the first time ever I wished she would go away and shut herself in her room with her stupid irrational problem.

I didn't sleep well that night. It was muggy and I tossed my duvet aside in favour of a cool sheet. But as I turned my body this way and that, looking for comfort, the sheet became wrapped around my legs like a mummy and I was hotter than ever. I went down to the kitchen and there was a crumby plate and a banana skin on the draining board. The kitchen had that warm, burnt smell of fresh toast. After that I was able to drift off to sleep but woke up feeling cheated of the hours I needed. I knew I had been dreaming for my mind still felt busy as if it had been on a night shift. I grasped and grasped but any images had long since faded away.

I opened Jo's door.

'Good morning, how are you today?' I sang cheerily, like a Girl Guide leader on Prozac.

'Just one more day at home,' muttered Jo.

There were two paths to choose from and I took the one less travelled, as the poet recommends.

'OK, Jo.'

I shut the door on her and focused on chivvying Eliza along and getting myself ready for work. Life went on—a surprising thought, given that life, in many ways, had halted, stuck at some sort of junction.

The next few days were a blur, difficult and painful to recall. One day I would see biscuit crumbs in Jo's room and nearly leap with pure joy, but then I would spot more scattered across her window-sill for the birds and I would land back down with a thump. Sometimes she would eat a meal, usually on her own in the kitchen, and we would hear the obvious scrape of metal on china, but the more she seemed to eat, the more suspicious I became. She would go to the bathroom and all I would hear was the loud gush of water from the taps, the toilet flushing and, lastly, the swishing sound of Jo cleaning her teeth.

I desperately clung on to the slightest glimmer of hope, any sign, however small, that she might have started eating again, and without retching it all up afterwards and flushing those calories down the toilet. At this stage, she looked much the same so her body must have been retaining something from the food she frantically stuffed into her mouth, but then she stopped eating altogether. She had given up on school and now, it seemed, she had given up on herself.

Jo's appointment at the eating disorders clinic dangled like a lifeline, and when the date came through I arranged to take the day off work to get her there. All my hopes lay on this appointment. It was like gambling all your chips on one number of the roulette wheel. It was a painful, desperate hope for I knew failure here could mean losing everything. We would be left with no way out, or so I thought. It's hard now to remember a time when the hope of Lily Finnegan was an unknown entity.

I did the school run with Eliza, who seemed oblivious and

uninterested in what was happening to her sister, and then rushed back to wake Jo for the appointment. She tended to sleep in every morning, sometimes well into the afternoon, bereft of the energy food usually provides, I suppose. But when I returned, she had gone.

I knew I had to find her. We'd waited weeks for this appointment and presumably we would have to wait even longer for another one if we missed it. I thumped the empty bed in frustration and pressed my forehead against the cold of the window, hoping irrationally that she would just appear in the garden. I looked at my watch and saw that time was running out. My body tensed up, my teeth gritted together and my head pulsated. I kept looking at my watch and staring out of the window and, in between, pacing a path up and down the length of the lounge. I could only imagine she was with Scarlet, or had perhaps confided something to her.

Scarlet would be at school but I could leave a message on her mobile. Her recorded voice clicked in straight away.

'Hi, bummers, Scarlet here—if you're a fit guy, leave a message, runters back off.'

'Oh, hi, Scarlet—just checking to see if you've heard from Jo recently. I think she's forgotten her, er, medical appointment. Thanks.'

There was one other very obvious call to make.

Please don't let Alice answer, please don't let Alice answer, please…

'Hello.'

'Oh, hello, Alice. Why aren't you at work?'

'Lizzie. Are you phoning to check up on me?'

'No, I was just surprised you were there. Is Roger in?'

'He's at work, naturally.'

'Oh, of course.'

'Is there something I can help you with?'

'No, just checking to see if Jo had got the bus over there or something.'

'Has she gone missing?'

'No, no, of course not. Whatever made you think that?'

'The fact that you've phoned to see if she's here.' She wasn't a top lawyer for nothing.

'Well, yes, there is that. It's just that she had a medical appointment today and she's obviously forgotten about it.'

'Oh, dear. Is it to do with her weight loss?'

'Pardon?'

'Roger and I have noticed that she's lost a lot of weight.'

'Well, they do, don't they—teenagers.'

'Lizzie, I don't want to interfere. But I saw you at the doctor's that day with Jo. I presume she was there about her weight loss and I presume she'll have been referred to the eating disorders clinic and I wanted to say…'

I put it to you that you have been a bad mother who has let her own teenage daughter lose enough weight to make her sick, yes, sick. I also put it to you that I would have made a better mother to Jo, providing her with consistent parenting of the highest standard…

'Lizzie, are you still there?'

'Yes, sorry. What were you saying?'

'I was just reassuring you that you are doing the right thing. This is the normal route to take things and I'm sure she'll get the treatment she deserves.'

'Actually, Jo has a verruca. More than one, in fact. On both feet. And that's why she's lost weight. Oh, here she is, just in time to take her to the foot clinic. I'll leave you to get on. Bye.'

I thought about my final speech. On reflection, the bit about Jo losing weight because of her verrucas may have been a mistake. I looked at my watch again. Time had run out, my head was thumping and I had run out of ideas. Desperately I managed to hold myself together as I needed to be at my most persuasive, for it was time for the other telephone call.

'I'm sorry my daughter has missed her appointment today. We really would like another one. Well, she wasn't sure about it, you see, but now she's changed her mind. What? That's nearly three months away. I know, but I'm begging you, please. Please, I don't know what else to do. Please.'

I was told that if I was very anxious and felt that Jo's weight was dangerously low, the normal route would be to go back to my GP and ask him to put in an urgent re-referral. I slammed the phone down and sank to my knees.

The normal route. The same phrase Alice had used, but what did it actually mean? I could imagine Alice taking the normal route through life—school, Girl Guides, exams, university, sensible job, sensible shoes, safe sex, calorie-controlled diet, little black dress, sensible fitness regime, white bathroom, Ikea furniture, iPod, well-organised holidays, retirement plan, life insurance. All mapped out, all stamped and sealed with the approval of her friends, relatives, fellow lawyers and bank manager. Is that the route I had taken? School certainly, but then a series of strange jobs, including singing telegram and promoting a new restaurant while dressed as a chicken. Then sex with anyone, sex with Roger, sex with no one, no future plans, a lot of bungling, breakages and bluffing my way through. My life seemed to be based on a vague aim of just getting through each day without making too much of a prat of myself.

Yet, if I looked back far enough, I had been heading out on another route. Look at my early alternative holidays in huts up mountains, my alternative therapies as I tried to meditate my way into oblivion, the alternative Spanish literature and films from Japan I used to favour. Those knitted scarves, those home-made sandals, that African food I used to concoct. I was called Eliza then, sometimes Ellie, but never Lizzie. Ellie Smith, that was me. When did Lizzie come into existence?

It was Roger who came, a knight in a Marks and Spencer suit, to rescue me from strangedom. He dragged me back onto the normal route with his 'two children are enough, home improvement, put some money aside' philosophy. He deserved Alice. They deserved each other. But my time with him left me feeling confused, unsure of who I really was. I needed a different approach now, and so did Jo. We were shut in a box and until we decided to step outside it and really think deeply, we were going to suffocate one another.

I sat and waited for Jo to return, staring at the wall, staring at my life as it flashed up before me. Eventually the noise in my head was interrupted by the telephone ringing. It was my brother.

'Hi, Lizzie, it's George.'

'Jo.'

'Yes. Got the train here to the office. Walked from the station.'

'I'll come and get her.'

'No need, I'll run her home. Have a chat.'

'Thanks.'

When George arrived, he stepped over my threshold like an unwanted salesman.

'Sorry, George, I've got to get to work. You and Sue must come over some time.'

It isn't only teenagers who shut doors against the rest of the world.

Jo went straight to her room and I decided against a parental interrogation. If she didn't want to take the normal route, it was fine by me. But all other pathways seemed hidden from view.

Jo appeared cheerful the next morning. It was Saturday so there was no need to broach the subject of school. I risked suggesting that we spend some time together while Eliza was at her rehearsal. We decided to take a walk along the river to the film rental shop and maybe get out a DVD for the evening. I will never forget that walk. Jo had discarded her baggy clothes in favour of a flimsy dress.

'There might be mosquitoes by the river. Do you want to pop your trousers on?' I asked.

'No, I'm fine.'

We parked the car, got out and heads turned immediately. We walked towards the river in silence, not looking at anyone's face but aware, very aware. I wondered if this is what it would be like to be out with a disabled child, contorted in a wheelchair, shouting or screaming perhaps, so that equal amounts of sympathy and blame would be thrown at the mother.

Jo soon tired and we didn't make it as far as the rental shop. Back in the car, we sat looking ahead through the windscreen. I slid the keys into the ignition but didn't start the engine. There was so much I wanted to say but couldn't. In the end it was Jo who spoke first.

'I think I need help,' she said.

'Yes, yes, I think so.'

'Not the clinic. Not the doctor.'

'No, of course. I understand.'

'Something else, then.'

'Yes, another way. There'll be another way.'

The barrier had not been completely removed but a gap had appeared and I could see a chink of light through it.

Alice phoned back with a speech she had prepared earlier.

'It must have sounded as if I was interfering and I can assure you, Lizzie, this was by no means my intention. My only crime here is that I care about Jo, not as a mother—you're doing a perfectly good job at that—but as a friend, a friend to Roger and a friend to his family.'

'It's OK. It's all under control.' A weak defence.

'Believe me, the bond between a mother and daughter is strong and wonderful but very complex.'

'It's a bit difficult for you to comment, Alice. I mean…'

'I may not be a mother, I can't dispute that. But I am a daughter, and my mother and I are really close.'

'Oh, yeah? Which is why you imagined she wanted her bedroom done in pink.'

'And why you thought Jo wanted hers green.'

'She did want…didn't she?' I swallowed and took a deep breath as I inhaled a bitter truth.

'Lizzie, let's not argue, we're both on the same side here. But I will tell you that my mother loves me and I love her and the colour of her room doesn't matter that much to either of us. She might pretend otherwise, but my mother's always been there for me. She might have preferred me to have six children and work part time in the corner shop but I can live with that. And Jo knows you're there for her. Later, when she's older, the trivial things that seem to irritate her now won't matter. She knows you love her.'

'Well. Perhaps you should have been a psychologist.'

'It's closer to law than you think. They both require a great deal of analysis. Get help for Jo, Lizzie. Being a good mother doesn't always mean doing it all yourself.'

Why did Alice always have to know everything? She was trying to get one up on me, I thought. But underneath I knew she was not.

That night I prayed. I had never been religious and my spirituality was intermittent, coming at times of great joy or extreme sorrow. They say everyone prays when they are dying or giving birth, even the most hardened atheists. Extreme prayer, I call it, and the path of desperation usually ends with a cry for help from something or someone who can perform miracles. And I needed a miracle. I didn't get on my knees or recite the Lord's Prayer or anything like that. I just pleaded in my head, pleaded for a release from this nightmare, pleaded for a cure, and I bargained, bartered, quite prepared to give up everything—my job, my own dreams, my own health, anything—for Jo. Yet it didn't seem enough, and suddenly I felt compelled to write it down as if God were more able to read a letter than read my mind.

Please. Please make Jo better. Please let her eat again.
Please don't let her die. I will do anything to save her.

I stared at the piece of paper and my true feelings shouted back at me. Part of me wanted to add a postscript—*of course, it's probably not as bad as all that*—but there was a time for pretending and a time for facing the truth. A bit of dust on your jacket can be brushed off, but ingrained stains need a seriously hot cycle in the washing machine. There it was again, the washing-machine method of parenting. It doesn't come with any instructions, so just keep pressing the buttons until you get it right. And look for the switch at the side you didn't notice at first.

I wondered what to do with my piece of paper, my prayer. I couldn't get any more ridiculous so I took it outside, placed it on the barbecue and put a match to it. The paper curled and a flame leapt up like a hot tongue talking. It was as if I was burning all my old ideas, the conventionality of Alice and Roger, the rigidity of the medical profession, the last twenty years. Small slithers of ash flew up into the sky and I watched them spiral off. I felt like a child asking for Mary Poppins to come down on an umbrella and sort the family out. Little did I know that she was already on her way.

SIX

'I'LL refer you to the eating disorders clinic,' the doctor had said. 'There may be a waiting list.'

So I wasn't on my own. There were hundreds of us out there. What other diseases are there walking around the town? Hidden diseases—they must be everywhere. The world is infected with illnesses that have no rash, no high temperature, no high blood pressure. I'd never met anyone like me, or so I'd thought. But I must have. I must have seen someone in the high street, passed her by. Someone like me.

My mother didn't understand that I could end it all at any time. I chose not to eat. But I could if I wanted. I chose to look good. I chose to look thinner than Scarlet. I chose not to go to school. Not yet. But I could if I wanted. I really believed that then, that I could end it at any time. That I was in control. But control was controlling me. It took an angel to teach me that.

'Would you like a teensy-weensy bit of scrambled egg? Or a teensy-weensy bowl of soup?' my mother kept asking. Like I was baby bear or something.

Leave me in the kitchen where I can choose, I should have said. For every time I rejected her food, she looked at me as if I had stuck a fork into her.

I went to my room and lay on the bed. I felt safe there. My room. My bed. My thoughts. Staring at my ceiling. If I let my thoughts drift, I could play out my life as it should be. Winning all the school prizes with everyone clapping. Winning the Man Booker prize to a standing ovation. Receiving an award for bravery to cheers and whoops. An Oscar. The Nobel Peace Prize. An OBE. The cheering and applause ringing in my ears. My imagination could lift my spirits. Fantasy is better than reality.

I woke up in the night, hot and sweaty, and went down to the kitchen for a glass of water. The kitchen was quiet. Safe. At night it felt like my own kitchen. But if it was really my kitchen it would be tidier, in some sort of order. I had some water and then some toast. No butter or jam or anything. No extra calories. I put the plate on the draining board for Mum to admire. It wouldn't be good enough. I peeled a banana and laid the banana skin next to the plate. Like arranging a collage. Then I stuffed the banana down the plug hole. I mashed it down the tiny holes with my fingers and ran the tap while I did. It turned into glue, sticking around the outside of the plug. It took ages to force it down but in the end it was gone. Consumed by the plumbing system.

The next day I didn't want to go to school. I would go in the day after. I stayed in bed until Mum and Eliza had gone. Then I got up and weighed myself. I looked in the mirror. I didn't want to look like that. Grotesque. There were thick slabs of fat on my thighs. And my breasts were too big. I shouldn't have had that piece of toast. But dieting wasn't the answer. I knew that.

I opened my drawer and took out my magazine. *Celebrity Exercise Regimes* it said on the cover. I'd got it all wrong. One actress ran up and down the stairs twenty times a day. That wasn't enough for me, I would need more. I started straight

away. After a few frantic runs up and down, my calves began
to ache. I must have been so unfit. I carried on. Sometimes I
had to stop at the top of the stairs. Bend over and gasp for more
breath. I was hot, clammy, breathless, but I had to carry on. I
loved the rhythm of it. The predictability. I knew where I was
going: either up the stairs or back down again. I didn't have
to think.

I concentrated on breathing and keeping going. That was
enough to stop other thoughts. It was exhilarating. There was
a rush of blood to my head, and all around my body. I was
alive. I reached my target. Success. I would run up and down
more times the next day. Push myself further.

I collapsed onto the bed. Wow! I didn't need the eating disorders clinic, I thought. I wasn't like them. I had said the word
'anorexia' in my head but I hadn't written out the label and
attached it to myself. It was more like a warning or something.
I would write a list. A list to make me happy.

• *Run up and down stairs one hundred times a day.*
• *Add one more exercise regime to this list each day until
I have ten different activities.*

I would add eight more items to my list. After I'd run up
and down stairs some more.

Later, the doorbell rang. It was Scarlet.

'My God, Jo, you look terrible. Are you really ill?'

'Shouldn't you be at school?' I murmured, letting her in
reluctantly. I wasn't in a talking mood. I pulled my dressing-
gown around me and crossed my arms.

'I've got frees this afternoon. Jo, I didn't realise… What's
happened to you?'

'Nothing. I've been a bit poorly, that's all. I'll be back at school tomorrow. Do you want a coffee?'

She followed me into the kitchen. I busied myself with making the drinks. I fiddled with the taps and the cups and then started to put stuff into the dishwasher—all the stuff Mum had left piled up on the side. Scarlet perched on one of the stools. Then she started to cry.

'Is it your mum?' I asked.

'No, stupid, it's you.'

At first I didn't understand. Then I did. My mother had put her up to it. My mother was paranoid. She thought I was going to die. She thought Scarlet could save me.

'Do you want something to eat?' I asked. 'I've already eaten.' I pointed to the crumby plate with the smear of butter on the side that I'd left on the draining board.

'Oh, so you've eaten, then. I didn't think—'

'Don't listen to everything my mother says.' Then I laughed. It was an odd laugh. Different. Maybe because I hadn't heard myself laugh for a while.

'Everything went well when I saw my dad again at the weekend,' reported Scarlet, 'and Mum's more settled now. She's giving the house a spring clean and she's bought herself some new clothes. I think that's a sign she's moving on. What do you think?'

'Definitely.'

'I've kept my biology notes for you and I've got different people to copy the notes in your other subjects. So don't worry, it's all sorted.'

'I'll be back tomorrow so don't go to too much trouble, Scarlet.'

But I didn't go back to school and Scarlet came back again

with a pile of books. I may have been giving up on myself but Scarlet was still there, she kept on coming. She plonked the books down on the kitchen table and stared at me. I thought she was going to cry again. I looked through the books. Biology A Level syllabus, *Further Maths*, Book One, *The Catcher In The Rye*.

'It's a classic,' said Scarlet. 'Supposed to be one of the top fifty books to read before you die.' And then she looked down. As if she'd said something wrong. She carried on looking down as I glanced at the last book—*Eating Disorders: A Self-Help Guide*.

I stared at Scarlet. Eventually she looked up at me. She seemed nervous. Scared even.

'I haven't got an eating disorder.'

'We used to tell each other everything.'

'I mean I haven't got a proper eating disorder. Just a bit of one. And it's getting better.'

Scarlet hugged me. And when her hands hit the bones of my back, she carried on hugging me.

'I still love you,' she said.

Best friends are better than boyfriends, better than sisters. Better than…anyone. I wanted to tell her everything. Not just bits, hints, but the whole lot. But I couldn't. Was she still my best friend? I took a deep breath.

'I've got a problem but…well…it's kind of, you know…'

'Difficult to talk about,' said Scarlet. 'I know. I understand.'

Then she told me she was going to have another tattoo. A dolphin on her right ankle.

'Does it hurt?' I asked

'Yeah. But it'll be good practice for when I have my tongue pierced. Apparently that really does it. Your tongue swells up and everything. I can't wait.'

I laughed, because everyone's strange. One way or another.

'Will you come with me when I have it done?' Scarlet asked.

'Can't wait.' I grinned. Then I got a skewer out of the drawer and pretended I was going to do it right there, right then.

'I'm definitely coming back tomorrow,' I said. Maybe I believed it.

But then I decided not to go back. And never to go to the eating disorders clinic. I don't know why. I preferred to spend my time jogging instead. Along the towpath by the canal. I would go out without saying anything.

At first, I felt defiant, rebellious. I'd never been rebellious before. Not much anyway. I'd wanted to please, keep things steady. Especially after Dad had gone. Better to feel pious than guilty. Or something like that. Why should I feel guilty for missing school? It was my life. And it felt good, no one knowing where I was. Everyone wondering where I was. It felt good, for a while. But guilt seeps in slowly like water into a sponge. Soon I was soaked with the stuff. Should have, ought to—my mother's words had infiltrated my brain. Invaders. And it needed a rebellion to get rid of the invaders. But was I up to it? So as I kept up the steady pace of an easy run, I swung to and fro. From rebellious to guilty. From guilty to rebellious.

I focused my mind on thumping along the canal path. It seemed to stretch on for miles. And either side of the canal, wasteland. Miles and miles of wasteland. Overgrown grasses and small shrubs. Scattered rubbish. Patches of barren earth. Nothing much to look at except the path ahead.

Running on my own without permission. It was like I'd won a lifelong argument. Or had I? It didn't feel like it. I stopped running. There was a weir. I sat down and watched it. Watched the inevitable flow of the water. I wanted to go home and I didn't want to go home. There it was again: conflicting desires, conflicting thoughts. Unhappiness.

I don't remember going home. I don't remember what Mum said, but there wasn't much of a row. It hadn't been much of a rebellion.

One day Mum told me all about her plans for the future.

'I want to run my own sandwich business. Get my own place and do it better—really healthy food, no junk, no fat. Maybe have a sit-in service as well, more like a café really. At the moment, Trish and I do all the work and the owners get all the profit. It doesn't matter how hard we work, we still get the same wages. And the owner never listens to my ideas. I just think it would be so good to run my own business. Do you think I'm up to it, Jo?'

'Yeah. Course.'

She wanted reassurance. Maybe she wanted me to say how proud I was. Maybe she wanted me to ask questions. Maybe she wanted me to show more interest in her life. Maybe she wanted me to jump up and down, whoop with joy at having such a great mother. Like role reversal or something. I don't know. I didn't deliver. I didn't much care if she opened a café or not. I didn't much care about anything. Not then.

Uncle George and Auntie Sue called round. When Mum was at Trish's, dealing with the future.

'One of Victoria's friends had an eating disorder,' Auntie Sue said bluntly, 'and I think you have one, too. Are you anorexic, Jo? Bulimic?'

'No, I'm fine.'

'Victoria was a drug addict. She got out of it—and look at

her now. You don't ever think these things will happen to you. But they do. The worst thing we did was to try and sort it out ourselves. Victoria tried. We tried. In the end, she got better because we got help. Expert help.'

'I don't need help.'

'The first step is to admit you need help. It's all right, you don't have to do it now. Just think about it. As soon as you say, "I need help," everything else will follow on. That first step is the hardest, believe me. But you can only do it when you're ready.'

I ignored her. I didn't know what else to do. I'd already said it. I'd said it to Mum—'I need help.' But nothing had happened. Like those pointless wishes when you cut your birthday cake. There didn't seem much point saying it again to Auntie Sue. We chatted about restaurants, Victoria's wedding presents, something they'd seen at the cinema, holidays, Labradors. That was the surface talk. The verbal chat. The non-verbal stuff was different. Body language and facial expressions spoke of something else. Me. What I could do when I was ready. If I wanted to.

At that moment I hated Auntie Sue for knowing. And I loved her for being honest. Direct. Looking at me straight. I hated her for telling me what to do. I loved her for not telling me what to do. And I loved Uncle George for always being Uncle George. You knew where you were with him.

When Auntie Sue went to the bathroom, I told him.

'I'm getting help,' I said. 'For definite.'

'Good,' he said.

'Yeah,' I said.

I didn't eat. I looked better, I thought. Kind of. Some days I thought I looked thinner. Other days I thought I looked worse. It was food that was the problem. Not me. I was OK. But food was frightening. I was scared of it. Scared someone would force-feed me, stuff food into me until I exploded. Scared it would never come out again.

I ran away from food but I was intrigued by it. I would pick up a piece of fruit and turn it over and over in my hands. Like it was an ornament or a beautiful antique. Something to look at, admire. I would read books about food. Cookery books, recipe cards, stuff in magazines about nutrition, books on cake decorating. I wanted to know what Mum and Eliza were eating. I wanted to know what Scarlet had for school dinner. Face your demons. Like watching a horror movie for pleasure. Confront your fear.

I knew I was ill. I knew it was getting worse, spinning out of control. At the same time I thought everything was all right. I felt clever, inspired, healthy even. When you're muddled and confused, you don't even realise you're muddled and confused. But part of me must have known. Because I had told my mother.

Now I needed Mum to sort it all out for me, make it go away. Like she used to sort it out when I was bullied at school. Like she used to sort it out when I had a nightmare. I had handed the problem over to her. I was helpless.

There were three days when we didn't talk about it. Three days when I knew Mum was searching for answers, maybe not the obvious answers. She once told me she had had past life regression and found out she'd been a nurse in the Crimean War. Everyone who's been regressed has been a nurse in the Crimean War. Most of them were Florence Nightingale herself. Maybe I used to be a school dinner lady in a former life. Or someone at the circus—in one of those freak shows. It's weird, Mum doing stuff like that. Weird and cool, I think. Or maybe weird and dodgy.

Mum has meditated with Buddhists in the Himalayas. She can chant strange mantras in front of exotic candles, but not in front of Dad. I've seen photos of her in flowing kaftans with flowers in her hair, her fingers forming a peace sign. Sometimes I like looking at those photos. Sometimes I don't. That was what she was like. Then she had me and I changed her. She became just another mother at the school gate, blending into the background. It was better that way. But now I wanted her to dig deep for that old wisdom. People—hippies and all that—were happy then. Happy and kind of daring. For that time.

What about me? I wanted to do something daring. Not going to school, escaping to jog along the towpath without saying, running away to Uncle George's—that had all seemed daring. But they were everyone else's daring, too. If everyone rebels in the same way, it just becomes group behaviour. If everyone's different together, different turns into conventional.

Eventually Mum sat me down again for one of her chats. Makes her feel like a good mother.

'There are plenty of options for this sort of thing,' she said.

'This sort of thing.' She couldn't say the word yet but I felt better. More secure. Mum would know what to do. She knew a therapy for every problem. Somewhere among her piles of stuff from years ago she had books on every psychological disorder. They were dusty, the books. But that made them more magical. Was that what I was looking for? Magic?

People close to you can't help. They need help, too. It takes a stranger. A stranger to see your soul. A stranger like

Lily Finnegan—but not yet. In the meantime, I asked Mum to give me a list. Look at her old books, contact people, talk to whoever and then give me a list. I got it the next day. A list of choices. Close your eyes and stick a pin in one.

- *Wait for the eating disorders clinic appointment.*
- *Psychotherapy.*
- *Hypnotherapy.*
- *Past-life regression.*
- *Psychiatry.*
- *Behavioural Therapy.*
- *Eating disorders camp in Wiltshire (there may be a waiting list).*
- *Reiki.*
- *Reflexology.*

I panicked. 'There have to be ten,' I insisted.

'I'll look in my books,' Mum said.

'I thought you had, I thought that's where you got this list.'

'I've been on the Internet,' Mum explained.

That seemed wrong. It was too clinical, too modern. I needed an old potion or something. But there are angels on the Internet, there's magic on the Internet. I know that now. Since Lily Finnegan.

I looked at the nine options.

'I'll think about it,' I said.

'No!' Mum shouted. 'We've got to do something now.'

Then she went mad. Started crossing stuff off. Put a circle round 'psychiatry'. Underlined the eating disorders camp. As if it was up to her. As if… But part of me wanted her to decide.

'Whatever,' I shouted back. 'Do whatever you think.'

'But what do *you* think?'

'I think there have to be ten choices.'

Then it happened—she threw a glass at the wall. There was a loud crack, then a lot of little spiky, squeaky sounds. Bits of glass bouncing across the floor. It went on for ever and we stood there, not moving, not knowing what had happened. Then Mum put her hands over her mouth. Like in slow motion. She put her hands over her mouth and gasped. Like she couldn't believe what someone had done. Except it was her. Maybe she didn't know it was her. Can you go mad for a few seconds and then go back to normal again? Can you book in at the psychiatrist's reception and then be fine before you walk through the door? I looked at the pieces of glass. I looked at Mum. A few tears were dripping down her face, but it wasn't like she was crying. There was no sound. And still those hands, those hands over her mouth. If she went mad then she couldn't help me. So I cried, too. Then she put her hand on my shoulder and pulled it away.

'I love you,' she said, and went to get the dustpan and brush.

'I'll look at the list,' I mumbled, and took it upstairs.

It didn't fit. That word 'therapy'. Or 'psychiatry'. Especially not 'psychiatry'. That was for other people. Nutters. Screwed-up people. People one slice short of a pizza. You see them in the post office queue, talking to themselves, pulling odd faces, shouting out random words. What was that list even doing in my hand? My normal, sane hand. And never trust anything ending with -ology which isn't an exam. Or anything which sounds like Japanese food. As for eating disorders camp, well, it sounded like fat camp on its head and I needed another option. Option number ten. It came in the end, in the form of Lily, but not before I had to endure Eliza's big performance and Dad's big news.

I used to do dancing and singing when I was little. Especially dancing. I used to be good until my legs stretched out of control. I used to dance on the stage with a lot of annoying, giggling girls at the Saturday dancing school. We would practise and practise. Practice makes perfect, Miss Price, my dance teacher, used to say. I had a good sense of rhythm, she also used to say. I had a good sense of rhythm, Mum would say. And Dad. And Grandma. So it must have been true. Tell a fat girl she's got lovely hair and she won't know she's fat.

When I was eight, I got to dance in two dances in the annual show. And I was in the middle of the front row. Pink dancing shoes, a pink dress and matching hairband, knee-length white socks with a pink frilly bit sewn along the top. I walked onto the stage and saw Mum and Dad at the front, laughing. Laughing with pride, I thought. At the end everyone clapped. I loved it. It was as if the applause was a drug shot straight into the veins so the high was immediate, intense. I floated off that stage, cheeks rosy with excitement. I followed everyone into the room at the back and got changed in the middle of all the excited chatter. I sat down and leaned over my feet. One of my socks had rolled down to my ankle. It must have been like that all the time.

I wanted to be a ballerina or a dancer in a West End musical. I wanted more of that applause. I still get that feeling now when I imagine it. Then Eliza came along and started dancing at two and a half. She was cuter, more charismatic and didn't have to try so hard. She cast a tiny shadow over me which got bigger as she grew. Then one day I came top in the

Maths test and got a prize for my English story all in the same week. I didn't need to dance any more. I had found another way of making people happy.

Eliza's show was a musical especially written for youth theatre. Eliza was about the youngest performer. Still got the lead role, though. I'm trying to sound proud of my sister. I am, but there's something hiding behind the pride. Regret, maybe. I really don't know. The spotlight was on Eliza long before she walked onto the stage. I was kind of in the back row. But I'd had my day, in August, with my exam results. This was her day. In the week before the show, I felt OK, just OK. On the day, it was great. I did feel proud. That was my sister up there.

The theatre was part of the arts centre which used to be an old church but had bits built on the side which looked like Lego. There were rows and rows of seats but they'd all be filled with mums and dads. I wondered how many were divorced. Would I be able to tell? Dad came. I sat between him and Mum. As a barrier. Dad gave me a hug and some money for a new CD. He didn't say, 'Are you all right?' meaningfully, with a strange inflection, like some people did. Mum and Dad didn't look at each other before the performance. Their eyes were facing forward. We'd met Dad at the theatre. Mum and I were early and already in our seats. The best seats. After he hugged me (and gave out the guilt money), he said hello to Mum. Briefly. There was a pause. He looked at his watch. Still ten minutes to go.

'How are your restaurant plans coming along?' he asked Mum.

'Oh, early stages,' she replied. They talked across me, or through me, like I was the telephone wire.

'If you need any help—'

'Oh, no,' she said quickly. 'We've got loads of support—Nigel, Jim, Donovan…loads.'

A list. A list of men. Had Dad noticed? He had.

'So it's not a women-only enterprise, then,' he said with a laugh.

'No, but a woman will be in charge.'

'Of course. With some help from a few men.'

Verbal tennis. I think they were at deuce. I thought I'd serve something up.

'How's Alice, Dad?'

'Really well. She was asking after you. In fact, I wasn't going to say anything but Alice has got some really exciting news. Well, we both have. We want to tell you together. Can you come over next weekend?'

'That might be a bit difficult,' explained Mum, 'But we'll see what we can do. I'm sure we can come up with something.'

Mum was an expert on the vague and meaningless. Stalling. Avoiding. Evading.

The curtain went up and I felt excited. As if I were up there. I looked at my parents each side of me. I felt safe but vulnerable. I held Dad's hand. I squeezed Mum's hand. I wanted to put their hands together. But I didn't. Later, I tried to work out who was clapping for Eliza the hardest—Mum or Dad. After the show, we waited for Eliza. People came up and congratulated Mum. Like it was her.

'Eliza was wonderful, quite wonderful,' gushed one old lady.

'Thank you very much.' Mum beamed. Like it was her being complimented. Like she got the credit. Like she'd taught Eliza everything she knew. Perhaps she thought she had. Did she take the credit for my exam results? Can you take the credit but not take the blame?

When Eliza came out front, she was glowing. Her face stripped of make-up, her hair hanging down, her jeans on—she was my sister again. She came to me first. I hugged her.

'Well done, sis, you were great.' I meant it. But the words were forced. Her success emphasised my failure. The one thing I could do, I had given up on. Eliza got applause, I needed therapy. Life's a shit sometimes.

Dad came back for a coffee afterwards. He looked around the kitchen but he never seemed to notice that it was different now. That everything had changed and got in a muddle. I wanted him to bring round his lawnmower and his shears and all that stuff and sort out the outside. Now I know that the outside of anything doesn't much matter.

'I'm so proud of my girls,' he said.

Proud of Eliza for her performance, proud of me for sitting there, saying the right words.

'So what's your news, then?' asked Mum casually, as if she didn't care. As if she hadn't been guessing. As if she hadn't already guessed.

'Oh, well, I might as well tell you. I can't keep it to myself any longer. Alice and I are expecting a baby.'

'Well, well, well,' responded Mum meaninglessly.

'Great, I get a baby brother or sister. I can't wait,' enthused Eliza.

'Half-brother or sister,' corrected Mum.

'Jo?' Dad looked at me with concern. Had I allowed my face to race ahead of my thoughts? I hesitated. I wanted to ask questions, a million questions. But not in front of Mum. Maybe not even in front of Dad.

'Congratulations,' I mumbled.

I walked out to the car with Dad.

'Your car needs a good clean.' I laughed. And then I wrote my name in the dirt. I wanted to spray it on really. So he wouldn't forget me.

'The firstborn is special,' he said, smiling at me. But I didn't know if he meant me or the first of his new family. I waved him off as if saying goodbye to a lot more.

I ambled back down the driveway, my legs aching, my body exhausted. Mum was in the kitchen, singing. I stood in the doorway. She had a sharp knife in her hand. She was attacking a carrot.

'I'm making a stew for tomorrow,' she announced.

'Can I help?'

'Yes, please, Jo, that would be great. There's another knife in the drawer.'

So we peeled vegetables. Slowly and methodically. I scraped a thin layer of grainy, hard outer skin from the carrots. I bent my wrist round the misshapen, earthy potatoes. I chopped the green beans. Mum hummed instead of using words. There was so much to say and nothing that could be said. All that could be done was backtrack.

'Good show,' began Mum.

'Yeah, Eliza did well,' I continued.

We talked a bit. But not much. And we carried on peeling and chopping.

Then Mum went on a mission. A mission to cure me. A mission to put me in therapy. Like some American celebrity or something. But I could cure myself. I knew I could cure myself. Scarlet knew it—she'd given me a self-help book. Self— that meant me. I wanted help but I didn't want help. There it was again, wanting opposites. Being ripped down the middle.

I started to set myself targets, but they weren't proper targets—I know that now. They were ultimatums. If I eat an apple, I'll buy a new CD. If I don't eat anything for two days, I'll make myself sleep on the hard floor, without a duvet.

I kept hearing Mum on the phone, trying to talk quietly. Trying to sort it behind my back. I wanted to sort it together. To talk about it. But it hurt too much. She phoned the doctors. I think she phoned the eating disorders clinic again. I heard her begging down the phone. I could hear the whine in her voice. Like a kid wanting sweets in the supermarket. The *Yellow Pages* was left open at psychotherapy. I'd answer the phone to a soothing voice asking to speak to Mrs Trounce. Maybe she phoned the Samaritans, I don't know. I felt like I was a problem, an irritating problem that needed sorting out.

Then came the offers: 'Why don't we try this?'; 'This doctor sounded really nice'; 'I've heard this is very popular'— like it was a flavour of ice cream or something. I had a thousand ways of saying maybe, a million ways of saying no. Next came the dates. Set without consulting me, without asking. 'Saturday at two o'clock. Dad can have Eliza for the day.' 'Woodbury Psychotherapy Centre, eleven o'clock Tuesday. I've arranged the day off work.' 'I've nailed myself to the cross and sacrificed myself for you.' Then nothing. A whole weekend of nothing. Just Mum staring into her drink like it was a crystal ball. And looking like it was bad news.

Soon it was another Monday and Mum came home from work exhausted. Not physically exhausted like she'd run ten miles or something. Just exhausted with life. She got the sharp knife out again. Not more bloody stew, I thought. No. She cut a slice of lemon. She poured some gin into a glass.

She looked at it. Like she was casting a spell on it. Then she poured out a bit more. She opened the tonic. The fizz was like the splutter of a firework. Loud in the silence. Glug, glug, plonk. The lemon was in. The ice was in. Mum's medicine. Mum's drug. Mum's escape. She looked at me. She had something to say.

'I've been looking in the paper for premises for my café,' she said. That wasn't it.

'I've found another therapy option,' she said. That was it.

'There's an eating disorders society,' she began. 'There's a new local support group. Just started.'

'Great. Do we get a badge and a certificate?'

'You'd meet other girls like you.'

But I knew there were no other girls exactly like me, I was different. Surely I was different. They'd all be models or something. Maybe wannabe actresses. Models and actresses living on caffeine and nicotine.

'Or the therapies I already mentioned…'

'Do I have to?'

'This isn't going to go away, Jo.'

Another gulp of gin. She was trying to make it go away herself. Or at least fade into the background a bit.

'I can deal with it.'

'No, you can't, Jo. Just look at yourself. You've been saying you can deal with it for weeks now. I can't go on like this any more. I've started coming into your room at night to check you're still breathing, like when you were a baby. You don't realise what a fine line you're walking, Jo. In the end, I'll have to take you to the hospital to be tube fed. You're not far off that.'

The anger had gone from her voice. This time she was frightened. And fear spreads like fire.

'I want help, I just don't want therapy.'

Fear is illogical and leads to illogical words. But mothers rescue daughters in the end. And if mothers are too frightened to, then they rescue them by proxy.

'There's someone called Lily,' Mum said quietly. 'Lily Finnegan.'

And despite Mum's quiet, tired voice, the name resonated around the room. It bounced off the walls. It sung a lullaby to me. It calmed me as if the therapy started with a name.

'Who's Lily Finnegan?' I asked. The name melted on my tongue. It seemed familiar, as if I'd heard it a thousand times before. It didn't have the cold abruptness of Jo Trounce. It was warm and inviting. It begged me to meet her.

'I'm not really sure,' admitted Mum. 'Apparently it's best not to know too much then you won't have any set expectations about what will happen. She comes to your house and she does…well, whatever needs to be done. Sorry, that's all I can tell you at the moment. I'm finding out more tomorrow.'

I knew it was all psychobabble. For all we knew it could be some New Age know-it-all making money out of misfortune. I knew Mum was clutching at straws. And I knew she knew it, too. If this therapist, or whatever she was, had been called Sally Jones or Doris Block, I would have said no. But I said yes. I said yes because she was called Lily Finnegan.

SEVEN

I'M NOT sure now if I found Lily Finnegan or if she found me. It was the butcher who mentioned her to me, although I didn't tell Jo that, her being a vegetarian. If I had explained to her that the butcher was a vegetarian too, she would never have believed me. It would sound like a teacher who didn't know her five times table or a bishop who didn't believe in God. Mind you…

Sometimes when we want to look forward to a better future, we look back to the best of our past. Perhaps that's why I remembered my incense-burning, chanting, Buddhist days. I even hugged a tree once, but I never did get the moss stains out of my cheesecloth shirt so I gave that up pretty quickly. I wasn't really a Buddhist, of course, even though I had Buddhist statues in my flat at the time. In fact, I had other icons more to do with the Hindi religion and a cross over my bed. I was into diversity before anyone knew what diversity was.

'I am a Buddhist, Christian, Pagan, Jew, Muslim and Hindi,' I would announce, followed by a long speech as to why all religions were really philosophies and basically the same. I used to be called the church tart as I would switch from church to mosque to synagogue with the same ease as I later switched from Debenhams to Dorothy Perkins on a shopping spree.

When I look back, it's as though I'm thinking of a different person, someone else's life. What happened to the old me? I fell in love with Roger, I suppose, and then I had to adjust, as so many women do, to becoming what I thought he wanted. I wonder sometimes whether I really loved him, or whether it was the security I loved—having someone else to make the decisions and guide me back into a more conventional life, one my mother would have approved of. When we married, I could sense my mother's blessing, or so I thought, so I must have done the right thing. And I was happy—for a while.

What happened to the spiritual side of my life? Roger helped me intellectualise it, talked of proof and the human fear of death being the cause of all religious belief. I disagreed with him at first, but at the same time I wanted to fit in with him and his friends and family. I found myself getting married in a church, arranging a Christian funeral for my father, and having both girls christened. Conventional, safe, acceptable, and just spiritual enough without embarrassing anyone by actually talking about it.

Now I wanted prayer and meditation, reflection and guidance. The local fete at the vicarage was not going to help me so I found myself back at the Buddhist centre for a lunchtime meditation class, painfully aware of my sensible shoes and drip-dry cardigan. My memories may have been distorted: when I arrived at the Buddhist centre I was surprised to find a group of ordinary-looking people who were standing around chatting and drinking tea in a very ordinary way, and not a Tibetan monk in sight. I was introduced to somebody with an unpronounceable name who I remembered as Frank from the butcher's shop. Apparently he was now a Buddhist priest and a strict vegetarian.

'So you don't work at the butcher's any more then,' I commented.

'Oh, yes. Still handing out the pork chops and giblets,' he laughed.

Frank's laugh was huge, loud without being raucous and as infectious as measles so that I found myself laughing too without knowing why. He laughed with his whole body so that his shoulders bounced up and down like a puppet on strings. And the tone of it was ever so slightly filthy. For a Buddhist priest.

He was a tall man with broad shoulders but looked soft, like a big cuddly toy. I immediately relaxed and felt completely at ease about returning to a Buddhist centre after so many years. I had known Frank in my youth and I also recognised a lady who used to be Eliza's teacher at nursery school. It all felt familiar and comfortable, as if I was meant to be there.

Soon we were asked to make our way downstairs for our meditation session. At the bottom of the steps was a cool, airy room rather like a cellar. The walls were of painted white breeze blocks and there were some seats along the back of the room. At the front, incense and candles were burning on what looked like an altar. There was a statue of Buddha and a large Indian frieze at the back, as well as some smaller statues, and at one side of the room was a pile of cushions. A man with a beard showed me how to pile three cushions up and sit on them with my legs bent back and my knees on the floor. I remembered meditating in the lotus position all those years ago and had always struggled to empty my mind while I was focusing on cramp and a fear of breaking wind. This position was altogether more comfortable and gastrically safe.

'Position is everything,' the bearded man told me, and I bit my tongue to prevent myself making a witty quip back. I've always felt the need to make other people laugh when I'm nervous. But as soon as Frank the butcher started to talk, I was able to forget myself.

He told us to close our eyes and focus on breathing. I immediately sensed the warm air sliding into my nose and gently down into my lungs, which filled up and made my stomach rise, and then, after a momentary stillness, sink again so that I became aware of life itself inside me. And as the air breezed out of my nose again, my body became still, more solid, more defined.

Thoughts rushed into my mind, frantically at first, but I let them pass and soon my mind calmed and I was focused on the moment. Frank's voice was soothing, coaxing me into being right there, right then, with perfect awareness and total stillness as body and mind became one. I could have been there for three hours or three minutes, for time had lost its meaning and its grip on me. The only thing I was certain of was that I was meant to be there. I would find out why later.

'Is this your first time?' Frank asked me afterwards.

'For about twenty years, yes.'

'Ah, yes, I understand.'

Then he looked deep into my eyes as if he really did understand, understand everything that had happened, everything that I was feeling, and the warmth of his gaze melted something that was frozen inside me and drew out the emotions within. The next thing I knew I was crying, and along with the tears the words were flowing easily, effortlessly.

'There is always spiritual help for those who ask,' Frank was saying, 'but there is also human help. There's someone you may want to contact. I'll give you a name and a number and let you follow your intuition.'

'Thank you. I'm sorry.'

'You have nothing to be sorry about. If you'd kept that hidden deep inside you, then you would have had something to be sorry about. Come, share a drink with us.'

I could have done with a large gin and I suspect that I looked at the steaming mug of herbal tea with some disappointment. But it was soothing, like a child's medicine administered by a caring parent. I talked easily with the other meditators and there seemed to be plenty to say without the obvious 'And what do you do?' with its hidden subtext of 'How much is your house worth?' and 'Are you more successful than I am?' No questions, no judgements, no competition. I was taken back to my youth when having a polished floor and a clipped hedge were irrelevancies.

I strolled home easily, as if I were gliding through time. I knew that I had an important telephone number in my pocket, but somehow it didn't seem so important or urgent any more. I knew that Jo had rejected all the offers of treatment and help that had been offered to her and yet I knew she would agree to see Lily Finnegan. I don't know why, I just did. A step had been taken, we were on the escalator travelling up, we were in flow.

My easy thoughts were interrupted by a shrill cry from behind.

'Oi, you. Turn around.'

I swivelled round to see Alice's mother staggering up the street, waving a stick. The stick had been painted in black and white stripes like one of those sweets you hang on a Christmas tree. She was wearing a long purple skirt and what looked like a large version of a child's pink anorak complete with fur-lined hood. She had a battered white mother-of-the-bride style of hat perched on her wire brush of hair.

'Hello, it's Alice's mother, isn't it?'

'You can call me Dolly.'

'Hi, Dolly. Where are you off to?'

'My bleeding workaholic daughter instructed me to wait in some café, which is supposedly in this road, while she finishes off some very important work for some very important client. More important than her own mother, it would seem.'

'She probably meant Starbucks—it's just at the end of the street.'

'I don't want any American rubbish—let's go in the pub.'

The next thing I knew, Dolly and I were sitting in the King's Head with a pint of Guinness each and a bowl of peanuts between us.

'So, you were married to Roger, were you? Bit dull, isn't he?'

'Well…I suppose. It depends what you like in a man. Anyway, I imagine he and Alice… Anyway…'

'Oh, don't be polite on my account, my dear. Alice is as dull as he is. They deserve each other. But you're different.'

'You don't even know me.'

'I saw you in the DIY shop. You were talking to yourself. That's good enough for me.'

'Was I?'

'Oh, yes. Shows a sense of eccentricity. Or madness. Either will do. And I like the way you've dragged me into this pub. No, you're better off without Roger. When he retires, he'll do the garden and make a model of the *Cutty Sark* out of matchsticks. When you retire, you'll be like me.'

'I think I'd like that. You just say what you think.'

'You can when you're old, you can do what you like really. You can tuck your skirt in your knickers and waltz up the street swearing like a trooper. You can pinch the window-cleaner's bum, sit on your doorstep in your nightie and eat pickles out of the jar, and turn the telly right up loud to annoy the neighbours. I know, I've done most of them.'

'You can't do anything like that when you're middle-aged.'

'Don't worry, your day will come. Then you'll notice that people don't care what you do, they just laugh and secretly admire you.'

'Even Alice?'

'Oh, no, not Alice, she doesn't know how to laugh. That might involve creasing her porcelain face or, heaven forbid, letting her mascara run. If Alice should accidentally laugh one day, she'd think she was having an asthma attack—or an orgasm. She's a lawyer, her job is to catch people out, not live and let live. Come on, we need some more peanuts here, I seem to have spat most of them out onto the floor.'

We sipped our Guinness and popped peanuts into our mouths as if we'd been coming to the King's Head together for years. Every now and then Dolly made a personal comment about someone sitting nearby in a loud, clear voice. She also made unconnected random remarks about politicians, celebrities and members of her own family, especially her daughter, it seemed. Yet her words didn't seem to match the underlying warmth of her personality.

'All Americans think they own this planet,' she stated, as a party of New Yorkers walked past our table. 'I wonder whether they know how irritating they are. I mean, do they *really* want everyone to have a nice day?'

But the next thing I knew, the Americans had bought us each another pint of Guinness and were laughing along with this eccentric old Englishwoman who managed to persuade them she was a descendant of Shakespeare himself.

'These peanuts are off,' she shouted out to the barman. 'They're past their sell-by date. A bit like me.'

The barman roared with laughter, flirted with her and then gave us three more bags on the house. Every now and then I checked in my pocket to make sure Lily Finnegan's number was still there, but I felt comfortable and nearly happy in the pub with Dolly. I had needed this break from the anxiety that was my life with Jo and I knew it would give me the strength to carry on the fight for Jo's health which had taken over my life. I tried to ignore the clock on the wall and enjoy the brief diversion.

'Alice irons her sheets and her teatowels, and it wouldn't surprise me if she irons her knickers,' Dolly said. 'She needs to learn to let go, live a little.'

'A bit difficult with Roger, they're two of a kind,' I said. 'And they're both impossible on the phone. Everything's so…businesslike. I have to stop myself reading out my National Insurance number before we start, and if I make a joke it just seems to stun Alice into silence. I don't think she gets…'

But then I looked at Dolly. She had closed her eyes and folded her arms against me. Her silence was a solid, frozen silence and I found my sentence fading away as if I had forgotten my lines. Dolly said nothing for a while and then started to talk about a boyfriend Alice had had at school.

'He had hair you could fry bacon on, and by the smell of him, someone had,' she said, and then we were laughing again, together.

The rule had been laid down—only Dolly could criticise her daughter, and I realised that Alice had probably been right, that love between a mother and daughter is complex.

I wasn't sure if this strange conversation was particularly Buddhist but I was having a great time, and wasn't the pursuit of happiness on every Buddhist's agenda? I could only imagine what Alice would make of this.

Alice swept into the pub, beaming with gratitude as she found that I had been looking after her mother with such care. 'Oh, it's so lovely to see Mother out enjoying herself,' she said. 'You see, I'm far too dull to think of something like this. Roger must really miss having the fun factor in his life. And I guess you must be better in bed than I am.'

'What's going on here then?' came the very real, very uptight clipped tones of Alice.

'You told me to wait for you here and… What's your name?'

'Ellie.'

'Ellie's been keeping me company. So get off your high horse, take that broomstick out of your arse and come and have a drink with us.'

'Mother, I told you to wait in the café at the end of the street.'

'Sorry, it's partly my fault. I ran into Dolly and…'

'Dolly?'

'Yes, Dolly. Your mother.'

'Lizzie, my mother is called Ernestine, as she very well knows. I would hardly have a mother called Dolly.'

And as 'Dolly' roared with laughter, peanuts splattered out onto the table, followed by the bottom row of her false teeth.

I found myself sitting on the hall chair, holding Lily Finnegan's number in my hand as if it were a magic key. Perhaps it was. Doubt seeped into my mind slowly and I felt so very alone with it all. There was no one to answer my questions, smooth over my uncertainties. I hadn't seen Frank for years, why should I trust him? More importantly, why should I trust someone called Lily Finnegan when she was just a name on a piece of paper? I had no idea about her qualifications, her experience, her success rate. What would Dr Robinson think? Or Roger? Or Alice? And yet I found my mind turning more and more towards Dolly and I knew for certain that, however rudely, coarsely or abruptly she might put it, she would somehow approve. She might be flippant on the surface, of course—'Why not give it a go? You can't trust anyone who has to work for the NHS anyway,' I could hear her saying.

Trust, that was the key. I was expecting Jo and myself to trust someone we knew nothing about. It was like giving your house keys to a stranger and asking him to pop in and water your plants while you were away. The chances are you would lose everything and your plants would die. It was as if I were expected to trust humanity, human nature, serendipity itself. Trust that everything was happening as it was meant to, trust in the right outcome, in something greater than the world we live in. And I didn't know if I could do that. The longer I sat, the more I realised that there was one thing I could not do. I could not sit there doing nothing.

I rummaged through one of my piles of books for the *Yellow Pages*, flicked through it and pressed out a number.

'Frank, I need to talk about it all.'

I walked into the butcher's shop where Frank was wrapping up two lamb chops for an elderly lady who was trying to find her purse in the bottom of her shopping trolley.

'Here, let me,' I said, and reached down for it.

'It's all right, Flo, you can trust her, she won't walk off with your money.'

Then Frank patiently helped her count out the right change and handed her a small bunch of fresh rosemary.

'Here, chop this up and press it into the meat before you grill it. Your nephew will love it.'

'Perhaps I'll get some bacon for his breakfast—he's staying over, you know. I've put clean sheets on the bed and a folded towel on the end, like in a proper hotel.'

Frank sliced some bacon for her and once again helped her with her money. Then I opened the door and let her out. Frank called to a young lad to shout if it got busy, peeled off his apron and indicated that I should follow him out the back. While he scrubbed his hands, I leant against the wall and looked around the room. It was sparse, basic but served its purpose as somewhere to have a break and store a few miscellaneous objects. A couple of armchairs and an old wooden chair made up the furniture. Apart from that, there were two piles of books and magazines in the corner and two boxes next to one of the armchairs. I immediately felt at home. I thought about Frank and the old lady in the shop.

'You're very patient,' I said.

'That's what we offer,' he explained. 'Quality meat and quality service. Something more than the supermarkets.'

'Will you survive?' I asked.

'Yes, I think so. We have loyal customers and others who are coming back to us. I'm never going to make much money but that doesn't bother me.'

'But meat. You're a vegetarian.'

Frank looked at me seriously and said, 'I'm a vegetarian now but I've been a butcher since I stood here beside my father when I was sixteen. I don't have a problem with it. Other people might but I can't do anything about that. Everyone is on their own journey. Mine seems to be a journey of contradictions.'

'Perhaps everyone's is,' I said. 'Which brings me to my daughter.'

'First tea,' said Frank. 'Fennel and liquorice.'

'Sounds disgusting.'

'Trust me.'

I sat down in an old armchair in the corner while Frank put the kettle on. Unusually, I wasn't wearing my watch and I had no idea what the time was. It didn't seem to matter and I could have sat there for ever, curled up in the armchair, watching Frank make the tea. He seemed to be immersed in what he was doing, looking at the rack of mugs as if personally se-lecting the best one for me. He even handled the teabags gen-tly, as gently and lovingly as he had handled the old lady in his shop. Everything seemed to matter to Frank, yet nothing was desperate.

'I'm desperate,' I told Frank as I sipped my tea. It had a slightly bitter taste to it and yet it warmed my throat like honey.

'Go on,' he coaxed.

Then it all came out. Everything I had already told him

about Jo all over again. He didn't stop me and point this out, he just listened. Occasionally he asked me to confirm something, occasionally he said 'I understand' but the rest of the time he just listened.

'Have you phoned Lily Finnegan?' he asked eventually.

'That's just it, Frank. Can I call you Frank? Am I supposed to call you by your Buddhist name, only it sounds like I'm ordering a takeaway— No, I don't mean that.' I took a deep breath. I didn't need to make jokes with Frank, I didn't need to paint over my anxiety with flippancy. I knew I could just be myself.

'It's about Lily,' I continued. 'It's just that… Anyway, Lily, yes, I don't know her, I don't know if she's qualified. What if she makes it all worse? Then it would be my fault for rushing in and—'

'Whoa, slow down. Let's just think for a minute.' Frank leant over and patted my hand. 'Close your eyes, Ellie, your mind is too busy. Let's slow it all down.'

The next thing I knew he was telling me to focus on my breathing and to let it all go. I don't know how long we sat there like that but when I opened my eyes, the colours seemed brighter, the edges of everything sharper, the reason for being there clearer.

Frank handed me a pencil and a pad of paper.

'I have to go out front,' he said. 'Take your time and write down all the options. I'll be back.'

I looked at the paper in front of me. I wrote 'Lily Finnegan' at the top. I thought of everything I had tried to persuade Jo to do. I thought of my original list of nine choices. I put the pencil down. Lily Finnegan was the only option left.

* * *

At home later, I was back at the downstairs phone again, staring at Lily Finnegan's number. I knew I had to use it, but I was still hesitant. It seemed that Jo's future depended on me saying the right thing. Memories of sitting exams, my driving test, job interviews all flooded into my mind for I must have sensed that this was a pass/fail situation. And the stakes were high: Jo's life. I stared at the phone and it rang, as if I had willed it to. I picked it up quickly.

'Hello, is that Lily?' I asked, illogically.

'No, it's Alice.'

'Oh, I'm sorry, you'll have to get off the line. I'm about to make an important call.'

'Is everything all right, Lizzie? You sound anxious. Is it Jo?'

'Of course not, I was just needing to speak to a guy I met at my niece's wedding. He's pretty keen to speak to me actually.'

'And he's called Lily?'

'Yes, that's right, Lily. I know it sounds like a girl's name but he's Canadian. Anyway, if you're looking for Roger, he's not in, I'm afraid.'

'I know. He lives with me now.'

'Of course. I'm getting confused, waiting for this call from Gordon.'

'Gordon? Not Lily, then?'

'Gordon Lily, that's his name. Yes.'

'You seem to be getting rather confused about names, which brings me to Mother, or Dolly as you insist on calling her.'

'She told me to.' I was sounding like a twelve-year-old in the headmistress's study.

'I just wanted to warn you that mother is quite overweight

and she does have high blood pressure. She shouldn't get over-excited and she definitely should not be drinking.'

'Yes, Alice. Sorry, but I think—'

'I know you mean well, Lizzie, but I don't want Mother—'

'Enjoying herself?'

'Getting ill.'

'Don't you think Dolly—your mother—can decide what's best for her?'

'Of course not. She has a home help, she has me. She doesn't need to decide anything.'

I looked at Lily Finnegan's number growing damp in my hot hand. There were more important things in life than arguing with Alice.

'Well, Dolly's lucky she's got you. Sorry, not Dolly—Ermintrude.'

'Ernestine.'

'Anyway, I must make this call to Lily. I mean Gordon. Gordon Lily. Bye for now.'

I felt strangely nervous and thought I should practise what I wanted to say to Lily.

'Hi, my name's Lizzie Trounce—I got your number from the butcher…'

No, that didn't sound quite right.

'Hi, I got your number from the Buddhist centre. I understand you offer some sort of thing…help, whatever, to girls who have problems and stuff like that.'

I closed my eyes and took a deep breath. I had to be clear, confident, say exactly what I meant without fear, without holding back the raw facts.

'Hi, I'm Lizzie Trounce. I got your number from the Buddhist centre. I understand you offer therapy to people

who have eating disorders and my daughter would benefit from some help right now.'

That was it. I dialled the number carefully and held the receiver to my ear. It seemed to echo with my heavy breathing as I waited. The repetitive, monotonous ring tones were almost hypnotic until they were suddenly broken by a faint click, indicating the start of an answer phone message.

Hello, you have reached Lily Finnegan, as you were destined to. I've been expecting your call and I'm looking forward to hearing your message, which will tell me so much. I will get back to you.

I put the phone down quickly so that I could absorb the words, take in the gentle, almost breathy message and work out why I didn't immediately dismiss the speaker as cranky, despite the slight American accent, despite the less than clinical approach. I took a deep breath and dialled again. As I listened to the message once more, I rehearsed the words that I had prepared already. The long tone provided my cue.

'Hi, my name's Lizzie Trounce—I got your number from the butcher...but not in the butcher's shop or anything. Anyway, I understand you offer some sort of stuff—no, let me start again... Anyway, my daughter has a problem. Of sorts. Can you help? Thanks. Oh, hang on, I haven't left my number. It's, um, oh, yes, 729124. That's it. Thank you. Thank you so much.'

I tried to be positive and told myself that it would have been even worse if I hadn't prepared a message and at least I had left my number. I always thought there should be some sort of erase button available for all speaking situations so you could go back again after a blunder, wipe it out and say the right thing instead.

I stared at the phone and the desire to erase my anxious,

inarticulate message passed and a sense of relief washed over me, as if I had wrapped an unwanted present up in brown paper and posted it off somewhere far away.

'Yes, yes, yes,' I shouted, as if I had just won the lottery.

'Are you all right?'

'Ah, Jo, there you are. I just phoned Lily Finnegan and left a message. She'll phone soon, I imagine.'

Then Jo smiled and I realised that I hadn't seen her smile for some time. Did I really want to rub the smile off her face? Of course not, and yet I couldn't help myself, the need to know was so strong, and so I asked her one of my themed questions.

'So, did you eat your quiche, then?'

'Yeah.'

'You didn't…you know, afterwards?'

'No.'

'Good. That's good.'

What was the point? I didn't believe her. I went upstairs and into the bathroom. I sniffed around the toilet and the sink. Sometimes I would get a faint whiff of vomit or toothpaste which was a sign, a clue. On this occasion there was nothing to suggest the quiche had been chucked up again. It could have been hidden in Jo's room but I didn't dare look while she was in the house, and when she went out with a bag there was always a possibility that she took unwanted food with her to dump in a bin or hedgerow somewhere.

Once, I followed her into town. I kept to the other side of the road at a reasonable distance and had an alibi ready should she turn round and see me. She passed a rubbish bin without even slowing her pace or glancing at it. I felt an instant surge of relief but I couldn't stop following her. I needed to know for sure. I had no idea whether she knew I was there, but when she got into town she darted down a side street and into a gift shop. She must have walked right through (or else hidden herself somewhere in the shop) and I lost sight of her. I didn't just need an erase button for my conversations.

The more subtle and clever I became at trying to find out whether or not she was eating and keeping the food down, the more subtle and clever Jo became. I found some more food under a loose floorboard inside her cupboard and had to pretend I had found it by accident when I'd called in an electrician to see about putting in more power points.

After that, I didn't find any more hidden food in her room. Then, following a comment I had made about odours in the bathroom, I found some vomit in an alleyway near the house. Of course, it could have been some drunk reeling home on a Saturday night and so once again I was left with that dull ache you get in your stomach from not knowing.

We were playing games, pointless games, since all I really had to do was look at Jo to realise that she was eating nothing or very little. No wonder my inarticulate telephone message to Lily Finnegan had sounded so desperate. I didn't hear from Lily for three whole days. Every time the phone rang, I froze as if I were a film put on freeze frame, and then jumped up and almost ran to answer it. But it was never Lily.

I needed Lily Finnegan as much as Jo did, for I continued to spend my time watching, following, deducing. I just could not let go—it's impossible to let go of the baton if you don't have someone on your side to take it from you. But then came Lily and the race was on.

The next day, I returned from work to find two notes and the answering-machine flashing.

Mummy! I've gone to Rebecca's. Her mum says is it OK
if I stay the night??? Can you ring and say yes. Please,
please please!!! I must stay at Rebecca's—we're making up a dance. I will do my homework. I love you, Eliza.

MUM. GONE OUT. JO

I flicked the switch on the answering-machine and listened as I took off my coat and shoes.

You phoned, that's good. But I'm off phoning at the moment and have decided not to use it at all. So can your
daughter send an email to lily@lilyfinnegan.com? She
must email me and tell me the three most important
things about herself. That will be a good start.

There are some things in life you really need to slow
down—Sundays at home, walking along the beach at sunset,
making love, an intriguing dream, sipping champagne. You
feel like throwing a net over time and dragging it back so you
can relive the experience slowly, with complete immersion.
Then there are the things we long to speed up, wind on
quickly—cleaning or polishing absolutely anything, talking
to Alice, driving on the M25, having your legs waxed. The
process of getting Jo better needed speeding up. There was a
sense of urgency about it, yet I had waited for three days and
still did not have an appointment for her. I found myself tug-
ging at my hair in desperation. I couldn't settle, my mind was
shaken up, and that in turn seemed to shake up my body.
    I grabbed the phone and pressed out Lily's number. No
time for preparation, no room for fear or self-consciousness.

Sorry, this number is not available. Sorry, this number is not available.

'Shut up,' I shouted out as I slammed the phone down. Why did this bloody Lily Finnegan have to be so obscure? Couldn't she have a secretary, an appointment system, files and procedures, just like anyone else? But I knew that if she were just like anyone else, she would not have been acceptable to Jo. To us. There was nothing else for it, I would email her myself.

Hi, Lily,
Thanks for your telephone message. Jo's out at the moment. I wonder if we could make an appointment. I can take the time off work so any time of the day or evening would suit. It's getting rather urgent.
Regards,
Lizzie Trounce

By the time I had a made a cup of tea, a reply was waiting for me.

Dear Lizzie,
I look forward to receiving Jo's email.
With love, Lily

The butcher's was shut and I pounded on the door as if trying to wake the carcasses that were waiting to be sliced up. But I knew where to go next. I cut through the tranquillity of the Buddhist centre like a crack of lightning on a still day.

'Frank, I need to speak to you urgently.'

'Lizzie, welcome. Sit down a minute. Now, let's have some tea and we'll talk.'

'But…'

I had been going to say that there was no time to waste, yet somehow right there, right then, there was time. Time to reflect and consider. What difference would half an hour really make?

Frank handed me a mug of tea and waited for me to speak.

'I was just wondering about Lily Finnegan again. Where she's based. She only seems to be operating on the end of an email at the moment like some sort of psychological eBay.'

'Lily has her own way of doing things, I believe. I think you just have to go with her particular flow. And if it doesn't work, then we'll think again.'

We. Frank used the word 'we'. For the first time I felt as if I was not alone, that I had someone I could talk to, someone to help me carry the load. I smiled at that thought and looked up to see Frank smiling back at me. Then he turned to talk to a woman in a long black skirt who was eagerly pointing something out in a book. Frank had time for everyone, yet he managed to make each of us feel equally important. I realised that I couldn't bear it if he was perfect, like some sort of Buddha. Eventually he came over and, as if he could read my mind, said, 'Don't tell anyone, but I ate a lamb chop yesterday.'

He nodded over to the woman in the black skirt.

'I'm sure Marion could smell it on me. She was just showing me a piece of writing about the beauty and freedom of animals.'

'Will you be excommunicated?' I asked.

'I don't think the Pope has much interest in a vegetarian Buddhist butcher from Essex,' he laughed.

Then Frank turned his attention to someone else and I slipped out unnoticed.

I stood outside the Buddhist centre for a while just think-ing. I felt like I was sitting in the audience of a dull play just willing something, anything, to happen. The more I tried to move life and Jo and the world along, the more life seemed to put me on hold in an empty phone booth with nothing to listen to. I closed my eyes and willed Jo to be at home so I could ease her onto the next stage in the process—the first stage really. I prayed that Lily would offer an immediate ap-pointment, and somewhere in my thoughts I dreamt that something would happen to take my mind off these endless worries.

'Hello, Lizzie, isn't it? Victoria's wedding, remember?'

'Oh, yes, now, let me think—I met so many new people, Gordon, isn't it?'

Rule number one, remember his name but not so easily that he knows you've been thinking about him ever since you met.

'I didn't know you lived around here,' I said.

'I didn't but I'm house-hunting. I've just got a new job right over there.' He pointed to a firm of accountants.

'Well, I hope you and your wife will be very happy in this town.'

Rule number two, use subtle means to check that he's single. Or at least as subtle as you can manage in the circumstances.

'I'm on my own now. Divorced.'

'Oh, fantastic. I mean, fantastic that you're making a new start. I found that when I got divorced myself,' I said, remem-bering rule number three.

'Oh, did you move then?'

'Not exactly move, no. But I got a new washing machine.'

'Are you in a hurry?'

'Not at all, I've got loads of time. Well, not loads obviously.

Actually, I've urgently got to get back to my daughter and make sure she sends an important email. But later…'

'Sorry, I've kept you, haven't I? Men are not great at picking up hints, I'm afraid. I'll let you get on. Great to see you, Lizzie. Maybe we could have a drink when you've got more time.'

'Great. Maybe one Friday?'

'Mondays and Thursdays are good nights for me. Anyway, I'll ring.'

Then Gordon grinned at me, and without asking me for my number turned round and walked away, clutching his mac and briefcase. Gordon's last words rang in my ears as I wondered who he reminded me of.

When I got home, Jo was in the hall, putting on her trainers.

'I heard the message, I've emailed Lily and I'm off for a run,' she muttered.

'Has she emailed you back? Have you got an appointment?' My questions ran after her as she walked out of the front door and started limbering up on the path.

'We're going to use the power of the written word,' she shouted as she jogged off down the road.

Suddenly it was all moving too quickly but before I could throw more questions after Jo, a car drew up. It was Rebecca's mother, dropping Eliza off. Eliza greeted me with a scowl.

'You were meant to ring.'

'I forgot. I'm so sorry. You should have phoned me.'

'You were out and your mobile was switched off. You forgot about me.'

'I'm sorry. It's been a busy day. Look, I don't mind you staying over at Rebecca's, I'll run you over there…'

'It's too late.'

Good mothers let their daughters sleep round at their friends' houses. Good mothers organise wonderful sleep-overs for their daughters with midnight feasts of ginger beer and jelly, letting them sleep out under the stars, greeting them in the morning with milkshakes, toast and honey and hot steamy baths for everyone. Never mind the tiredness, ignore the mess, comfort the girls disturbed by the ghostly screeches of owls. A good mother lives in an Enid Blyton, timeless, Sunnybrook Farm world, all soft focus and dew.

I had failed Eliza, let her down and could see no way back into good mother land. I decided that another apology might just earn me a free ticket there.

'Sorry, Eliza, I'll make it up to you.'

'How?'

'A picnic?'

'I don't think so.'

'Maybe we could think about a trip to the theatre.'

'Better. But I'm going next week with the drama club, remember?'

'Some new clothes?'

'Spending money on me because you feel guilty is never a good idea.'

'Where did you get that from?'

'Daddy.'

'How would you like me to make it up to you, then?'

'That's up to you. Something different. Something unusual. You'll have to use your imagination, like you have with Jo.'

'Jo?'

'Yes, she told me. She's got to send emails to Lily Finnegan. Weird ones. Nothing to do with her stupid eating thing. She's obsessed with the computer so it'll work. Everything's going to be cool.'

'It's not that simple, Eliza, it's really not that simple. What else did Jo tell you?'

'Nothing. Just that.'

'She's supposed to go to an appointment. She's supposed to have therapy. Where is she? I wonder if she's got her mobile. I must sort this out.'

'Hey, what about my guilt present?'

I ran downstairs but Jo's mobile lay abandoned on the kitchen table. I would have to wait until she got home, then I would confront her, sort it out. I slid down into the armchair and put my head in my hands. I could smell an argument with Jo brewing slowly, just simmering gently in my mind, waiting for the heat to be turned up. I could sense Eliza's disappointment in my failure to come up with an exciting alternative to staying the night with Rebecca. I could see the piles of stuff in the corner still waiting to be sorted. I could still see Gordon walking away from me because of my insane preoccupation with Jo. And Alice. Alice was always there with a torch to light up all my bumbling, burbling inadequacies.

Wallpaper patterns repeat themselves over and over until someone decides to rip it all off and slap new paint on. Alarms carry on ringing and ringing and ringing until someone turns them off. The monotony of motorways, police dramas, acceptance speeches can make you want to scream. And I had failed to see what really needed changing. The world and I were ready to scream at Lizzie Trounce. Bring back Ellie Smith. But the place between two identities is a dark one, and it was about to get even darker. The phone rang. It was the phone call I had been dreading.

'Mrs Trounce?'

And I immediately knew it was Jo.

'It's St Michael's Hospital here. Don't worry, your daughter's stable. She collapsed while she was out running. Someone brought her in.'

And all I could think was that I had to get her out of there—it had to be the right thing to do. Or was I just pushing another button at random?

EIGHT

HE MUST have been a psychiatrist. The guy in the hospital who sat next to my bed. He sat next to my bed, stared at me and asked me loads of questions. In between the questions, he stared some more. Then he said his name was Steve.

'I'm Steve,' he said. 'Do you mind if I ask you some questions?'

I'm Steve. That's all. Like he was in disguise or something. An undercover psychiatrist. Just a nice guy asking questions without me having to face the truth. That I was mental. A nutter. He didn't wear a white coat, or thick glasses. His hair didn't stand up like an electrocuted hedgehog and he didn't stammer. But I knew he was a psychiatrist—he had odd socks on.

And then there were the questions.

'When you look in the mirror, do you sometimes feel that you are looking at someone else?…Who do you admire?… Which three words would best describe your father?'

He wasn't very good at his job. He didn't even know I was lying. I told him I had an eating disorder and that someone else had already asked those questions. I told him I was having treatment. I told him it was working. I told him I needed to go home and finish my therapy.

Did I want to go home? Yes and no. That was usually my answer to questions—yes and no. Pretty well covers it. I liked the clean white sheets, the way I was tucked between them. I felt safe, like I was in an envelope. Or a parcel. I liked one of the nurses. She laughed for no reason. She winked at me. She tucked me into my envelope. I didn't like the other nurse. The one with the trolley. She gave pills to everyone. Everyone except me. I didn't get pills, I got Steve. Steve, who couldn't admit he was a psychiatrist.

Two fat ladies came with the tea trolley.

'I'm nil by mouth,' I said.

'We wasn't told that,' said one of the fat ladies. Then she got a 'nil by mouth' sign and put it on my bed. I nearly laughed at that. I nearly cried too.

Then my mum came. A bit panicky but OK. She didn't tuck me in, she didn't wink at me but she was better than the nurse. I was more important to her. The nurse tucked everyone in.

'Perhaps this is for the best,' Mum said. 'You'll get some help here.'

She looked pleased. Pleased I was in hospital out of her way. Then she cried and said she didn't like the idea of me being in here. I cried a little bit. Hospitals are like that. People die in hospitals. It's like the end of everything. Perhaps she wasn't pleased, I thought, perhaps she was scared. Like me. For a moment I felt trapped. Like I'd been tied to the bed, kidnapped by the NHS. Mum was swaying. First she was on their side, then she was on mine. I needed her on my side and suddenly that was the most important thing.

'See that,' I said, pointing to the nil-by-mouth sign.

'That's ridiculous,' she said, and jumped up. Then she sat down again because she didn't know what to do. Just one more push should do it.

'I trust Lily Finnegan,' I said. 'She's an expert. They don't know what they're doing here. Nil by mouth—except for the pills.'

'Pills?' Mum started to look worried. One more push.

'This has scared me,' I said. 'Scared me into doing something. Doing something with Lily Finnegan. I've got to now. I don't want to end up here again.'

Funny thing was, I was telling the truth.

They brought Mum a cup of tea. The cup rattled on the saucer. She kept blinking. When she went to the toilet, I cried again. I cried for my mum. Then I saw her talking to the nurse. Then the doctor. Then the psychiatrist. She bent her head. She even cupped her hand over her mouth once. I expect she whispered. She talked to them one at a time, like someone spreading a rumour. I knew she was lying. I knew she was telling the same lies as I did. The next thing, I was in the car, going home. And Mum was giving it some.

'We're going to give it a go with Lily Finnegan,' she said. 'But if it doesn't work, we'll have to go back to the hospital. That's the deal.'

Why 'we'? Would she go into the hospital, too? On a drip? Being force-fed? Lying in the bed with me, tucked up by the nurse who winked?

Then Mum laughed. 'I had to sign for you, like you were a letter or a parcel,' she said.

Then she said, 'You'd better email Lily Finnegan when we get back.'

She didn't say, 'Or else I'll send you back to the hospital.'

But she thought it. She didn't say 'You were lying and you haven't emailed her yet.' But she thought it.

Mum didn't like being fobbed off with an email address. She wanted Lily Finnegan in person. Not some virtual Lily Finnegan in cyberspace. That's what she said. But I was OK about it.

I put Lily's address by my computer: lily@lilyfinnegan.com. I left it there to mature. I left it there while I thought. About what to write, mainly.

'Have you sent an email to Lily Finnegan yet?' Mum asked each day.

It was better than 'Have you eaten your toast?'

Then one day Mum didn't ask. But, anyway, the time felt right. I sat in front of the computer. I rested my fingers on the keyboard. I felt like I was about to give a piano recital. I was nervous. I thought about how much worse it would be if she was there in front of me. This is better, I thought. Easier anyway.

Lily Finnegan,
You know about me from my mother. Apparently I must write 3 things about myself. Here goes. Mum thinks I am starving to death. Mum thinks I will never be able to have children. Mum thinks I will never go back to school. I hope you can help.
Jo Trounce

I pressed send. I knew it was inadequate, not good enough. Perhaps I should write more. But I didn't know what to write. The words looked scary up on the screen. I had had those words in my mind before. Sometimes I had said some of those words. But to look at them, that was different. A photograph has more impact than the news read out on the radio. Seeing is believing. Your eyes don't lie, your mouth does that for you.

An hour later, I checked my inbox.

Dear Jo,
But what do you think?
With love,
Lily

With love? She'd never even met me. But she cared. From those ten words I knew she cared. Ten was my magic number. It always worked. This time my words flowed out of my fingers.

Dear Lily Finnegan,
I think I want to eat normally. So I can go to friends' houses. So I can eat in a restaurant. So it's not a problem any more. But I want to eat what I want to eat. I want to decide. And I don't want to eat too much. I'm scared of getting better suddenly. I want it to happen slowly. So I can get used to it. I want to eat but part of me doesn't want to eat. I want to go to school but part of me doesn't. Not eating sometimes makes me feel happy. But mostly I am very very sad. Sometimes I want to die. Sometimes I'm scared of getting older. I want my mum to be proud of me. Like she's proud of Eliza. Sometimes I think Dad is proud of me. But soon he'll have a new baby, a new family. I want to cry but I don't. No reason. That's what I think anyway.
From Jo Trounce

Tears welled up in my eyes. I blinked them back and swallowed my emotion. There was blood on the keyboard. I had splattered myself over the screen. I felt better. And I felt worse. The reply came almost immediately.

Dear Jo,
Well done, very well done. Now cry. Cry again tomorrow and email me after that. Do not contact me until you have cried twice. Wipe your tears with a white handkerchief and put the hanky in a shoe box. Trust me—you will have something to cry about.
With love, Lily

I had expected instructions but not that. I thought she'd write 'eat an apple' or something. Not 'cry twice'. And what made her think I'd have something to cry about? I couldn't just sit and turn on the waterworks like some actress thinking, My dog's dead, my dog's dead, over and over in her head, like they do.

I didn't have to do as Lily said. She would never know whether I'd cried or not. What was the point anyway? Why was I doing this? I thought. Boredom? Hope? Curiosity? Yet for some reason I opened the small drawer at the top of my oak chest and found a creased white handkerchief stuffed at the back. I switched to my outbox and found my message to Lily. I read it through. When I had finished, I put the moist hanky under my pillow.

The next day I was home alone. As usual. I slept. I read. I found I wanted to email Lily but I had to cry again first. And I had nothing to cry about. Actually, I had everything to cry about, but moments for crying pass. If you hold it back, it gets

into your system. It comes out in your sweat, piss, blood, shit.
That's what I thought. It was too late to cry about stuff that
had already happened. So I lay on my bed. Then watched TV.
The hours passed easily. Then Eliza came home. Then Mum.
A letter had arrived with good news. Nothing to cry about,
though Mum welled up a bit.

Dear Eliza,
You are the golden daughter. Looks like you're going to
be rich and famous, make your parents swell with pride.
Make your sister look like a waste of space.

Or words to that effect. I didn't actually get to read the letter.
'What does it mean?' asked Eliza, just needing confirma-
tion of her brilliance.
'They are just suggesting you audition for a stage school,
the Valentine Rose stage school. Apparently someone saw you
in your show and suggested to your drama teacher that you
apply. Your teacher seems very keen, I must say.'
'What about school?'
'You'll do ordinary lessons at Valentine Rose's as well as
dance, drama and singing. You'd still do your exams, keep all
your options open.'
But we all know they don't bother with exams at these
places. Or proper lessons. School for Eliza would be fun.
Doing what she loves doing. Still, good on her. I suppose.
'Well done, I'm proud of you, sis,' I said. And Mum
looked proud of me for saying the right thing. We had a
pride loop.
'I haven't got in yet.'
'You will,' I said confidently.

Later, I got out an old shoe box and went on the computer.
There was already a message for me.

Dear Jo,
I know you will have completed your assignment by
now. Well done. What I need to know now is what writ-
ing you do. Poems? Stories? Letters? What sort of writ-
ing would you do if you had a choice and plenty of time?
Keep going with this, you're doing great.
With love,
Lily

Dear Lily Finnegan,
I like writing lists. Lists of ten. That's about it really.
Jo Trounce

Dear Jo,
That's a great place to start. Put a heading: 'I want'—at
the top and write your list underneath. Take your time.
With love,
Lily

I got a paper and a pen. I lay on my bed. A good place to
think. I could look up at the stark, white ceiling. Nothing
there, nothing to get in the way. I could ask myself questions
and get the answers from my head. I wrote 'I want' and
thought about it. I knew what my mother wanted. I knew
what Eliza wanted. I knew what Scarlet wanted. And I knew
what they wanted from me. But 'I want' was simpler than
that. It didn't have to be complicated by other people.
Everybody knows what they want. Don't they? But I
couldn't be sure.

When we were younger, Scarlet and I would talk about what wishes we would make if a fairy came to grant us three of them. Scarlet said 'A golden dress' straight away, then 'A puppy' followed by 'A diamond necklace'.

'Why not wish for a tree that grows money?' I said. 'Then you could buy all those things and loads more.'

'There's nothing else I want,' she replied simply.

'Well, I would wish for all my wishes to come true for the rest of my life,' I said.

'That's cheating. You have to have three things that the fairy can magic up right there. Three things you can see.'

'Your mum wouldn't let you have a puppy anyway,' I pointed out.

'Then I would wish for her to let me. Instead of the golden dress.'

'But you can't see that wish. You said it had to be something you can see.'

Eventually we decided that all the best wishes were things you could see.

I looked at my 'I want' page. Now I wanted things you couldn't see. Things you couldn't get your hands on. Things to get your head around. Scarlet would be the same now. She would want her parents back together, an easy time at school, to fall in love, to be taller. Mum would want… But writing other people's 'I want' lists was a cinch. What about mine? I stared at the page. I thought about Lily being pleased. Whatever I wrote, she'd be pleased. There were no right answers. Definitely no wrong answers. Just honest answers. Answers that were right for me, and nobody else.

I want…
To be loved by everybody
To be successful

To be fit and healthy
To be thin
To make my parents proud
Alice to leave Dad and take the baby with her
Not to be clumsy
Not to have periods again
To earn lots of money
To give up school

I typed it, sent it and waited. No reply came for two days. In those two days, I kept looking at my list. I wasn't sure if I could be successful and earn lots of money if I gave up school. There were other contradictions. People didn't know what I wanted, so they might not do their bit.

Dear Jo,
Well done, this is a good list to start working from. By now, you may have spotted some contradictions. See if you can sort them out. Remember also that you cannot control other people, only how you react to them. Also make sure your list is specific so you may want to add a little detail. For example—to earn lots of money: How much? To be successful: At what? Also beware of negatives—they can be turned round into positive statements. Take your time to work on your list.
With love,
Lily

I thought she'd tell me to cross some of them off. Like being thin. But she didn't. I could keep what I wanted, it was my list. I started at the top and changed the first one. I want…to be lovable by being kind and confident. I was pleased with that. But would getting rid of Dad's baby be kind? Anyway, I couldn't control him, Lily said. I want…to have a successful and enjoyable job, earning in excess of the average wage. I liked that one, too. But, realistically, I couldn't give up school as well. So I added I want…to return to school and enjoy it. And I want…to be fit and healthy (so with periods, then).

I left the thin aim for a while as I wasn't sure what weight to put if I were to keep the fit and healthy aim. I wanted to be less than average, I knew that. Not to be clumsy was negative. I tried to rework it as a positive. Impossible. It was harder than I thought. I felt like crossing them out and putting 'Golden dress, diamond necklace and puppy'. Life was so much simpler back then. Why did it have to be so complicated? And who made it that way?

I left the complicated list and went for a walk. Walking is good for thinking, problem solving. The rhythm of your feet striding off stops you from agitating, you know, getting restless. And thoughts flow then, so useless thoughts can get washed away. And better ones stream in. Or something. I remembered Victoria's wedding day. Was that the last time I was happy? Or the first time I was unhappy? I had written a list some time then, I remembered that.

People looked at me as I walked along the canal path, but I couldn't read their faces. Sometimes people stare because I'm too fat, sometimes because I'm too thin. Sometimes because I've got a spot. When I got back, I stood in front of the mirror. I was too fat. I needed to keep the thin aim on my list. I rummaged in my drawer and found my old list.

To get all A grades at A level
To go to university

To get married
To have children
To be loved by everybody (Something hadn't changed,
then)
To be successful and earn a lot
To be really popular
To be fit and healthy
To be beautiful
To have more time

Had my aims changed that much? Or was it me who had complicated them? Complicated my ambition by not wanting to go to school. Complicated my desires by fear of the future. Complicated a wish to be beautiful by…by what?

My head was foggy and musty and clogged up. I decided to type up my old aims. I wrote a note at the bottom explaining that they used to be my aims. But now they were rusty.

Dear Jo,
What's stopping you from having these aims now? They are your aims. But you don't have to have them. You can amend them as you want. Cross out the ones you don't want any more and see how many are left.
With love,
Lily

Dear Lily,
I want all these aims. It's just that I can't have them. There are obstacles in the way. Or something.
Jo

Dear Jo,
Find someone you can trust outside of your family. Arrange an enjoyable trip out together or stay in and do something fun. Something you want to do. At some point during your get together, show your aims to your companion. Discuss together all the reasons why you can't have each aim—as many reasons as possible. Then write down SMART. This means specific, measurable, achievable, realistic targets. Together, check that your aims meet these criteria. This sounds like hard work so make sure you are somewhere relaxing and have fun too! Contact me in a week. Good luck. I know you're going to enjoy this assignment and that's important.
With love,
Lily

Somehow these had become my aims again. But they were old aims. Everything had changed. I looked at the list again. There was no mention of food. Wasn't this why I was writing to Lily? But then food had always been the barrier, not the aim. I realised I needed another aim: To be in control of my life. But, then, there would be eleven aims. I looked at the list. Which one would I sacrifice in order to have control? I needed to think about that one.

I did feel I was doing something about it all, I suppose. And when I shut my door and went on the computer, nobody came in. At first, Mum hovered outside the door. At first, Eliza wanted to come in and take her turn. The computer had been installed in my room. For course work and stuff. Famous, successful, popular girls didn't need to worry about course work. Eliza was allowed to use it. But not then. Not when I was working with Lily Finnegan. She was told to leave me alone when I was on the computer. For a few weeks, Mum said. Was there a time limit on getting better? Was I working against the clock?

'It's not fair,' Eliza protested. 'I don't have a computer in my room. You love Jo more than me.'

So Dad came round and installed one in her room. Eliza always got what she wanted. Maybe I should have whined more.

Scarlet came to see me again.

'You look better,' she said. 'Do you feel better?'

'Kind of.'

'I reckon you should take a year off and start again in year twelve next September. That way you won't have all that catching up to do.'

'That would be like going backwards.'

'Not really. You'd be having a break, that's all. For a year.' Was that my time limit? 'But you'd be ahead of me,' I said. 'You'd go to uni first.'

'Probably not. I'm taking a year out when I leave school. You'll be taking a year out now, that's all.'

'Why does everyone assume I'm going back?'

'Because you're clever.'

'Not that clever,' I said firmly. 'If I was that clever, I wouldn't be at home emailing some therapist every five minutes.'

'Is it helping?'

'I don't know yet.'

'Well, you look better,' said Scarlet. 'Do you feel better?'

Do all conversations go round in circles? Does life go round in circles? How do you get off the endless roundabout? You have to slow down and take a brave leap, I suppose.

'How's your mum?' I asked, leaping onto something else.

'Still very down. The doctor gave her a prescription for Prozac but she doesn't want to take it. I don't know what to do for the best, Jo. The thing is, she gets upset whenever I see my dad but I can't just stop seeing him. He'll get upset, for a start. Last week, I pretended I was staying with a friend so as not to upset her, but I felt awful. Mum's dragging me down with her.'

Scarlet started to cry. A few solitary tears and then it was over. She didn't say sorry. She just brushed them away and carried on.

'What do you think I should do, Jo?'

'Which friend did you say you were staying with?' I asked.

'Bethan from school.'

'I didn't know you were that friendly.'

'We weren't, but we're doing the same subjects this year. I felt awful asking her to cover for me. I've never minded lying before, to be honest. I mean…well, you know, the excuses I've given about homework, and all the times I've told Mum that I've never smoked or had so much as a sip of alcohol. I used to hint that I was out at the school youth club or something when I was trying to sneak into clubs under age. But this time I don't like it. Maybe I'm too old for lying, I don't know, but I'd rather tell her the truth. But…do you have this problem?'

'No, not really. My dad's having another baby. I don't think Mum likes that much.'

'God! What about you? I mean, bit of a shock, isn't it?'

'I don't mind. It's cool. Well, you know…'

'Yeah, I do. I'd hate it if my dad had another kid. I'd be well jealous. Probably get Herod on the phone straight away. I'd be screaming and shouting about it. But you're much more easy going. I admire you for that.'

Then Scarlet looked at me carefully, like she was deciding what to do with me.

'You need a night out,' she said. 'Dress up, go clubbing, have a laugh.'

'No, I'm not ready. Not yet.'

'OK, that's cool. What do you want to do, then? How about a bit of quality time with your best mate?'

I thought about Lily's instruction. I thought about inviting Scarlet on my day out. I had already planned to pack up a picnic for her and get the bus to Bramley Cross. There's a meadow near there with a stream at the bottom. We used to picnic there as kids. I was going to go there with Scarlet and talk about my lists, like Lily said. But I was frightened she wouldn't understand. And I was even more frightened that she would.

'Did you used to go on picnics when you were a kid?' I asked.

'Yeah, awful things. Wasps everywhere, flat lemonade and squashed egg sandwiches. My parents' idea of a lovely family day out. I don't think so. I think they read too much Enid Blyton when they were younger.'

'I just like having coffee in Tramps,' I said. 'And having a laugh. Like usual.'

'Yeah,' Scarlet sighed. 'We've had some good times there. We'll meet Saturday, then, as usual. OK?'

I liked some things being the same, it helped me cope with the changes. Scarlet and I had a sort of history. Like a married couple. Weird or what?

'Where would you go for a really special day out?' I asked.

'I'd go to London in a stretch limo and eat at the Ritz and then have a box in some posh theatre and then go on to an exclusive club, once I'd escaped from the paparazzi, of course.'

'And I suppose you'd be wearing a golden dress.'
'Of course.'

And so Scarlet had told me what to do for my day out. She always knew what to do. Use your imagination. So I didn't mention the day out or the list or Lily's instructions. For I'd already decided to take Grocer with me. Grocer had been my friend when I was very young. We'd drifted apart but I always knew he'd be there when I needed him. And I needed him then. For my trip. For my list. We decided to walk along the disused railway line. It was a bit overgrown because no one really went there. We cycled to the old station, dumped our bikes and walked. The wide track, where the trains had once run, cut through a wooded area in a clean straight line that seemed to stretch on for ever. It had become full of potholes and bumps so you couldn't really cycle along it. But walking was fine and I wanted to be moving. It helped me think. It helped Grocer talk, I remembered that. I read the list out.

'You can achieve these easily,' Grocer said straight away. 'In fact, if you think about it, you've already achieved some of them. And you're on target for the rest. If you go back to school this year or next, you'll get As, or good grades anyway.'

'I want As.'

'What's wrong with Bs so long as you can get on the course you want?'

'I want to get the best grades I can.'

'Then change it to "the best grades I can" on your "I want" list. Now, what about this one—to be successful and earn a lot?'

'I want to be a writer or a journalist,' I said. Where did that come from?

Grocer was smiling. He had a way of putting words into my head. Everything felt right. As it should be.

'Now, what about this popular thing?' said Grocer. 'I suppose that means having some friends, which you've got.'

'I don't have many friends,' I admitted.

'Where is there a quantity specified in your aim?'

And so we worked through the list. Grocer was logical. Positive. Enthusiastic. I saw the problem, he saw the solution. When we got to beauty, he put an idea into my head about inner beauty. I wanted outer beauty.

My head was buzzing. I needed to stop. Let it sit in my mind for a bit. I remembered a stream which ran through the woods next to the old railway path. We crunched our way down into the wooded area, weaving between the trees. Like a slalom course or something. We found the stream. Water made me relax. So long as we were on our own. Nobody watching.

'Let's go and stand in the water. What do you think? There's something about water flowing round your feet.' I don't know if I said that or Grocer. It came to the same thing.

We peeled off our shoes and socks. We rolled up our trousers. And we stood in the water. Still. Like statues in a fountain or something.

'Imagine all our problems flowing out of our feet and being washed downstream.'

Why not? I closed my eyes. With my eyes shut the water seemed louder. More powerful. Magical. When I opened them, Grocer had gone. I walked back towards the railway track.

I heard a rustle in the trees. I saw something move.

'I need confidence,' I said, hoping Grocer would come

back. 'I can look confident on the outside but it's not the real thing. My confidence is dead low. Ground-level stuff. Maybe that's what I've got to sort out. But if I looked good...'

Grocer had gone and Growler had arrived. Grocer and Growler, I had almost forgotten Growler.

'You're not actually sorting out the food problem, are you?' Growler said.

'Aren't I?' I said, or was that Grocer?

Then the movement in the trees turned into Scarlet.

'Hello,' she said. 'I heard you talking to yourself.'

Embarrassment is the worst emotion. I'd rather be angry—you can walk away from that. Or sad. You can hide from that one. Envy you can cover up with a smile and a load of the right words said in the right way. But embarrassment is right there on your face. It makes itself known. Shouts out. Can't be covered up. I looked down at my feet so Scarlet couldn't see my red face. But I was too late.

'There's nothing wrong with talking to yourself, I do it all the time.'

Scarlet shrugged her shoulders. She didn't care. She didn't know it was even worse, that I'd been talking to my pretend friend from when I was little. She didn't know I had to ask an imaginary friend to help with my list because I'd been too embarrassed to ask her. I felt sick. I wanted to lie face down in the stream and stop breathing. I wanted to run off but my feet were stuck. And my mouth. I just stood there. I wanted to cry but I didn't know how.

'Do you remember the stream? It's down there somewhere. Let's go and paddle in it.'

And we ran through the trees again. Perhaps I could have asked Scarlet to help with my list. I thought about asking her anyway. I thought about my list. I realised I had sorted it out myself. With a bit of help from my imagination.

'Do you remember when we were little?' I said. 'You wanted a golden dress, a puppy and a diamond necklace.'

Scarlet laughed.

'I reckon that's still what I want,' she said. 'I might say I want to pass my exams or get with Dominic Bradshaw, but underneath I really want a golden dress, a puppy and a diamond necklace.'

Scarlet pulled out a bag of plums from her jacket pocket. She took one out and then threw the bag down onto the damp grass. She ate it leaning forward, bending over the plum so the juice could drip down onto the ground. She wiped her mouth with her sleeve. She hadn't changed much.

I took a plum. I ate it, too. I didn't think about it.

'How's stuff at home?' I asked.

Did I want to know? I was there with my list stuffed into my pocket. My problems stuffed right inside me. My earlier embarrassment still stuck to my skin like old sweat. I wasn't sure if I cared about anyone else. Did I even care about me? Then Scarlet was talking and I was listening.

'You're lucky, having a sister. There's just me for my parents to fight over. Sometimes they don't tell me enough and sometimes they tell me too much. At least I've got you to talk to, you've been through it all so you understand. God, Jo, I don't know what I'd do if I didn't have you to talk to. I'd go mad I reckon and then I'd...'

'Start talking to yourself?'

Scarlet laughed. I laughed. I was laughing at myself. I'd never done that before. I took another plum. So did Scarlet.

Some things never change. Scarlet never changed. She was always there, the same, reliable. Just there. One day I would talk to her properly. About everything. The way she talked to me. She talked to me and I talked to a virtual friend. She confided in me and I confided in a virtual therapist. So long as you have an imagination, an imaginary friend will never let you down. So long as you have email, a therapist on the net couldn't let you down. But she could. And she did.

NINE

I WANTED to run away, like a scared child running away from home. I wanted to escape far, far away to somewhere unknown, where I would be anonymous, where no one would realise I was a mother with responsibilities. I wanted to run away and come back when it was all over and I cried because I couldn't do that. I was trapped in a life gone wrong.

I drank on my own that night, the day after Jo had come out of the hospital. It had been a brave decision, taking her home and putting my faith in an unknown, unseen therapist called Lily Finnegan. Yet I felt cowardly, afraid, as if I wasn't quite facing up to something. I wanted to run away from my responsibilities and yet I did not want anyone else taking on the responsibility for my daughter. This is a very analytical way of saying I felt like a failed mother and I needed a drink.

I had already slipped into the habit of pouring myself a large gin and tonic or a glass of red wine whenever I felt tension creeping in, that tension which grew out of my preoccupied mind. A little bit of alcohol takes away the intensity of fear, numbs the pain that thoughts of an unknown future can cause. But that night I drained the wine bottle and topped up my escape with a couple of gins. Mother's ruin, they used to call it. Well, yes.

In the morning, my head had wanted to stay on the pillow but my sandpaper throat was calling out for liquid, like a shrivelled leaf gasping for rain. So I dragged myself to the bathroom and leant on the sink, then pulled my head up to face myself in the mirror. I was a strange shade of green. I splashed water on my face, then cupped some in my hand and slurped it down. Carelessly, I threw myself into the first items of clothing I laid my hands on, croaked a goodbye to Jo and poured Eliza into the bus.

I usually walked into work, saving on fares or car parking and giving me twenty minutes' gym-free exercise. But that day I took the car and even that made me feel heavy with effort. I don't remember the journey to work—my mind was switched to automatic, too busy focusing on regret and self-recrimination. Somehow I got into town, parked, and ground my way towards the sandwich bar, my head still throbbing. I tried to smile as I walked into the shop but my face felt as if it might crack like dry mud in the heat. At least, I thought, I would be able to get through the routine of the day without anyone realising how I was really feeling.

'You look awful,' declared Trish as I tried to force another smile. 'Get yourself a strong coffee or something.'

'I'm fine, never felt better,' I wheezed. 'Sorry I'm a bit late, by the way.'

I opted for a large glass of water and then worked hard buttering bread and pouring out hot coffees. It was the pre-business rush and our customers were too preoccupied with the urgency of making more money to notice my grey skin and shaky hands. A hangover, period pains and the stress of bringing up a teenage daughter were a lethal combination, and as the morning progressed I wondered if I might just lie down and die.

'Hello, you look terrible. Can I have a cup of tea? I haven't got any money but that won't matter, will it?'

'Hello, Dolly. Come out the back and I'll have one with you.'

We went into the small, cramped room behind the shop and I quickly moved my coat off the chair and hung it up. The rush was over and I was beginning to feel better. I sat down with Dolly and we sipped our drinks and chatted like old friends. Dolly appeared to be wearing an entire Manchester United football kit and had a whistle round her neck.

'I'm supposed to be meeting Alice. She wants to take me to the chiropodist, but I'm not having some filthy man running his hands up my leg. That's why I'm dressed as a lesbian. Anyway, there's nothing wrong with my feet. Alice won't be happy until I've got every disease in her medical dictionary.'

Trish called me from the front of the shop.

'Won't be a sec,' I told Dolly.

'If that's Alice, don't tell her I'm here,' Dolly shouted out loudly.

There stood Alice in her immaculate suit, hair, nails and lifestyle. I wiped my buttery fingers down the front of my stripey shirt which, in the haze of early morning, I had felt sure went well with my checked trousers. I pushed my greasy hair behind my ear and tried to smile. My muscles still weren't co-operating.

'Are you all right, Lizzie?'

'Absolutely great. Never felt better. Shouldn't you be at work?'

'I am supposed to be liaising with Mother about her chiropody appointment. I felt sure that I saw her coming into this…establishment.'

Trish grinned and tried to focus on the coffee-machine.

'No, I haven't seen her.'

'I'll wait, then.'

'We're pretty busy, actually, Alice.'

Alice glanced around the empty shop.

'Getting ready for the rush,' I added. But Alice was quite prepared to wait for as long as it took me to come up with the goods—Dolly. I was sure Alice suspected I was harbouring her criminal mother and was quite willing to sit in surveillance until Dolly was forced out of hiding.

'Can I get you a coffee or something?' I asked, reluctantly.

'A coffee and a croissant please, Lizzie.'

'Takeout? Only there isn't a lot of room to sit in here. It's lovely over in the square opposite.'

We all looked out of the window.

'The rain is definitely easing off now,' I added.

'I'm fine in here,' said Alice, perching herself on one of the stools. 'So, this is the sandwich bar. I can't say I've been in here before. We have Starbucks conveniently located round the corner from the office, so I can just send my secretary out for a cappuccino when I need one. The drinks machine in the office is just dire, as you can well imagine. Roger says you might be starting up your own sandwich business.'

'More a restaurant really. Probably a chain of restaurants. Exclusive. Very upmarket.'

'That's marvellous. If you need any help on the legal side…'

'Here we are, one coffee and a croissant.'

'How much do I owe you?'

'No, that's all right. It's on the house.'

'No, Lizzie, I insist. Business is business. Besides, I'm sure the owner wouldn't like the idea of you giving the goods away.'

'All right, that'll be £3.25, then.'

Alice handed me her credit card. Trish was really concentrating on cleaning the machine by now.

Out the back, Dolly started coughing and wheezing, sounding like a lawn mower running over a cat. Trish was ahead of me and started coughing and spluttering herself. I joined in and threw in a few sneezes for good measure.

'I'm sure that's Mother at the back of the shop,' said Alice.

The evidence before me suggests that not only did you know the whereabouts of the missing person, but that you knowingly held her against her will and tried to cover up the evidence using distraction techniques. I put it to you that you have deliberately hidden an elderly woman in a sandwich bar...

Alice glared at me and pushed her way through to the back room.

'Come on, Mother, we've got an appointment, haven't we?' Alice was saying, as if her teeth were glued together.

Mother and daughter emerged from the back room, Dolly whinging like a teenage daughter while her daughter was reprimanding her like a stern mother. As they reached the shop entrance, Alice turned and looked at me suspiciously.

'It's all right, Lizzie, I don't blame you,' she said, though I felt sure that she did.

A couple of hours later Alice returned. I ducked down behind the counter and held my breath.

'I'm sorry, she's out in the van,' Trish told her.

'Oh, well, when she returns from her delivery, perhaps you would be so kind as to give her this.'

Alice handed something over the counter to Trish. A summons, perhaps? I couldn't see what it was from my hiding place but I tried to stretch my neck up a little to have a look. I'm not exactly sure how it happened, but somewhere in the process, I knocked over a cup.

'Shit,' I muttered. This was followed by a silence where everyone, including me, decided what to say.

'Oh, hello, Alice, I was just down in the cellar,' I said cheerily, pulling myself up from the floor.

'I thought you were out in the van?'

'I was, but the quickest route from the car park is through the cellar.'

Trish had said something else at the same time, I wasn't sure what. I may have felt flustered and inadequate, as I always did during these ordeals with Alice, but at least my hangover had completely disappeared. Perhaps Alice had some use after all.

'Can we talk?' Alice asked.

Trish shuffled her feet, desperately thinking of a way to help me out, but there was no escape.

'Can you manage for a minute?' I said to Trish, and asked her to bring us some coffee.

'Just water for me,' Alice said firmly. 'I've reached my quota of caffeine for the day.'

Alice must have heard about Jo's trip to the hospital, I told myself. I realised that I was not up to discussing Jo with anyone, let alone Alice. I was still feeling raw and vulnerable and very, very frightened. I wouldn't be able to hold it together and if I broke down, Alice would probably be as comforting as a nightie made from Brillo pads. But Alice, it seemed, had other matters on her mind.

'It's about Mother,' she began.

'Oh, that's great,' I said, rather too enthusiastically.

'No, it's not great, Lizzie, I'm very concerned about her.'

'Why? What have I done?' I asked. 'If it's about hiding her out the back, I really didn't mean—'

'No, it's not that. Well, it's linked, I suppose. You see, Mother really likes you. I think you're the sort of daughter she would have selected, given the choice.'

I wasn't entirely sure what to say. 'I'm sorry,' I spluttered out, eventually. 'I'm sure she loves you underneath.'

'Of course she loves me, but all she's ever wanted is grandchildren and I've kept her waiting far too long. Naturally, she's delighted that I'm pregnant but bemused as to why I intend to return to work quickly and employ a nanny. It's going to take her a while to sort this out in her mind.'

'Easy,' I said. 'Dolly could look after the baby and that way—'

'No, that won't be possible. And for once Mother agrees.'

'You two need to get together and have a really good, honest talk,' I said.

'Hard for any mother and daughter, I imagine, but that's not what this is all about.'

Then Alice pulled out a notebook which she consulted before continuing.

'I have laid out a plan of action which will help Mother cope with her various appointments. And point three involves you.'

It felt as if I was sitting in front of my boss or a bank manager and my hangover was beginning to kick back in again.

'Oh, lighten up, Alice,' I said a little angrily, then muttered an apology.

Alice looked stunned for a moment and then said, 'Don't think I don't want to. Do you really imagine I like the sound of my own bloody, uptight, lawyer's voice? It's just that… Oh, fuck it.'

Alice looked even more stunned, and perhaps even a little pleased with herself. From behind the counter, Trish gave an audible cheer.

'Look, I don't mind helping you out with your mother. Just tell me what you want me to do.'

'It's just appointments. She's awkward with me, keeps implying that she's interfering with my career. Well, perhaps she is. Anyway, if you could just be, well, a sort of back-up, I suppose. You work shorter hours than me and Mother seems to trust you.'

'OK. I'm sure she can't have that many appointments.'

'Mother is not at all well, you have to understand that.'

I didn't believe Alice for a minute. Dolly was the toughest, most robust lady I had ever met. I always imagined that if someone ran her over, she would just get up again, dust herself down and shout out some suitable abuse. But how wrong I was.

After Alice left, I remembered the package she had handed to Trish earlier. It was a brown paper bag with a book inside.

'I suppose this is some sort of business book,' I said.

Trish glanced at the title and handed it to me. *The Anorexic Child* was written across the cover with a line drawing of a mother and child standing apart from each other.

'Alice thinks Jo's anorexic,' I said to Trish.

'Maybe she's right. It happens.'

I didn't want Trish to know. I didn't want Alice to know. I didn't want anyone to know. I thought they would all blame me.

'It's not your fault,' said Trish simply.

It was the best thing she could have said. And the worst. I found myself crying all over the salami and cucumber. Why did I care what Trish or Alice or anyone thought? Dolly seemed to me to be the happiest person on earth and she clearly didn't give a bunion what anybody thought of her. In fact, she seemed to thrive on showing her worst side at every opportunity. But I liked her worst side, I liked all sides of her. She was gutsy and funny and she didn't care. Perhaps that's the definition of happiness—being who you want to be. I just needed to know exactly who I was first.

Weekends were the worst. Weekends were when the whole world seemed to be judging us, jumping to conclusions, pointing fingers, throwing blame into the air. Occasionally on a Sunday Jo would come into town with me or even help out at the supermarket. She would sometimes slouch out in a big, baggy jumper, her hair in a dragged-through-the-hedge style, her hands thrust into pockets of wide-legged, ripped jeans. At other times she would spend hours getting herself ready for such outings, and when she came downstairs in a flimsy dress and ill-applied bright blue eyeshadow and pink lipstick, I would hastily look at my watch or check that I had put my purse into my handbag.

Once she came into town with me in a pair of shorts and a T-shirt which clearly belonged to her much younger sister. She'd obviously found it easy to fit them on her diminishing frame but the resulting effect was like one of those pipe-cleaner men I used to make as a child. She may as well have written 'I am anorexic' across her tiny white top.

It took us some time to park so I told Jo we would have to hurry as I needed to get back to do some chores. I simply didn't have the time to stop and talk to a couple of old friends I saw, or even pause to throw them a cheery wave or a grin. I suppose Jo too must have noticed the judgers and starers, the whisperers and mutterers, but she seemed oblivious to it all. In fact, I had a suspicion that she thought she looked good in Eliza's shorts and part of me longed to tell her that she was a freak, an oddity, a very sick girl.

Was I ashamed of my daughter at that time? Not really, I just wanted us to be left alone to deal with things in our own way. I didn't want anecdotes from well-meaning acquaintances, unprofessional advice, more judgements. I felt angry more than anything, and I directed that anger randomly in all sorts of directions as if I had picked up a rifle and was firing it anywhere and everywhere. And some of the shots were bound to hit the wrong target.

Underneath the anger, I was in a state of permanent desperation, like someone in a desert crawling across the sand in the faint hope of an oasis. Like a tramp so hungry he turns to the rubbish bins outside a restaurant, delving amongst the flies and the dirt for someone's discarded food. I was hungry, hungry for knowledge because knowledge was power—or so it seemed.

With despair running though my blood, I would long for opportunities to surf the net, needing more and more information, as if this was armour against the desperation. I went straight to the worst-case scenarios, poignant personal stories that slapped me into realisation.

'How I held my dying daughter in my arms'... 'Julie: her story, her illness, her death.'

I would read pseudo-psychological articles, based more on opinion than research:

'Rejecting food is rejecting your mother'... 'Strict parents risk eating disordered daughters'... 'Parents who are too lenient with adolescents can cause disturbance such as eating disorders...'

Perhaps I just needed to prove to myself that there were no easy answers, that involving Lily was the best thing any mother could do. Yet I would not be made redundant, I had to remain in charge, in control. I needed to take on the role of supervisor, keeping an eye on Jo's therapy, checking Jo's progress. I would oversee the recovery programme, I decided, like a manager or a mother superior.

So I emailed Lily myself to air my concerns, in the hope she would keep me in the picture.

Dear Lily,
Just to let you know that Jo seems a lot happier since she's been in contact with you. The trouble is she's still on the fizzy cola diet! They just don't seem to do cola with added minerals and vitamins—a definite gap in the market! I'm sure she'll be fine in the end but she's understandably anxious. She's not going to school at the moment so I'm keen to help. Anything I can do? Do please let me know.
With kind regards,
Lizzie Trounce

Dear Lizzie,
Between your words, I can sense how worried you are

and I understand how you must be feeling. Unfortunately I am unable to communicate with other members of the family while I am working with Jo. My relationship with Jo is based on complete trust. She is doing very well so I suggest you ask Jo herself what the best way to help is. And accept her suggestions, whatever they are.
With love,
Lily
cc Jo

I immediately wrote an angry reply, pointing out that I was paying for the therapy and that once she started the face-to-face contacts with Jo, it would be me arranging the appointments. And apart from anything else I was her mother and I had the right…

I stopped. *Did* I have the right to know everything that was happening in Jo's life? I deleted the message before sending it, deciding it would be better to respond when I had calmed myself down. I heard Jo come back from her walk and so I left the computer and headed for the drinks cabinet. Then I remembered my awful morning in the sandwich bar when I was dressed like a contestant on Trinny and Susannah and made an idiot of myself in front of Alice, of all people. No doubt she would have repeated it all back to Roger.

You had a lucky escape from your first wife, darling. She looked like she was auditioning for a part in *Annie* and she had old people, including Mother, hidden round the back. Not only that but she was hiding in a fantasy cellar which apparently has a secret passage from a non-existent car park. I think she's really lost the plot now, no wonder her daughter…

I put the gin bottle back in the cupboard and decided to meditate instead. Frank would have been proud of me. At the start of my meditation, my mind was all over the place. Thoughts of Jo's first day at school years ago kept flashing up, joined by memories of her school trips away. Eventually, I was able to let those thoughts pass and I settled into a deeper part of my mind, all sense of time melting away. I was aware of the distant sound of Eliza humming and the tap-tap from Jo who was upstairs on the computer. My mind was washed over with calming blues and greens as I felt myself sinking into a heavy, relaxed state. As soon as I opened my eyes twenty minutes later, I knew what I had to do.

Jo got in before me.

'I see you've been nosing around, emailing Lily Finnegan,' she accused.

'I want to know how to help, that's all.'

'Butt out of my business, that would be a good start.'

If I had learnt anything, it was to walk away when Jo was in one of her defensive moods. I used to battle it out until she backed down, until I had won, but I had never felt better for it.

'OK, then,' I replied calmly, and went to get tea ready for Eliza and me.

I opened the fridge to find a few eggs, a bowl of limp lettuce, half a tomato and some old bacon. We had run out of milk, butter and anything else that would provide my family with a well-balanced, nutritious meal. I knew there were some packet soups in the cupboard and some microwave meals in the freezer but that seemed like cheating. I had only been pretending to be a good mother, like those experts in magazines who call themselves Doctor until someone finds them out. I looked over at the pile of pans and plates in the sink and realised I had nothing clean to cook with or serve a meal on anyway.

Jo came into the kitchen but did not apologise for herself, just reopened the conversation.

'Actually, my point about butting out was serious, although…well, I could have picked different words. The thing is, I need space to get better in, if you know what I mean.'

'I can't help, then,' I said sulkily. Something made me think about Alice and Dolly.

'You can and you do,' reassured Jo. 'I know you're there for me. You found Lily, didn't you?'

'So the best thing I can do is nothing.'

'Yeah. And believe in me. Oh, and don't leave food lying around hoping I'll eat it. Don't ask me if I've eaten anything either. It's all pressure—just let me do it.'

'It's hard for me to do nothing, it doesn't feel normal.'

'None of this is normal,' Jo pointed out.

'That's true. It's as if life is on hold.'

'You should get on with stuff. That would really help me. If I saw you just getting on with stuff.'

'I'll try.'

I looked at the sink and I looked at Jo. I had two daughters in the house who treated me like a servant, and a cook, a counsellor, a teacher, a cleaner, a taxi service. I had taken on a thousand roles and left the most important one out—a manager.

'Jo, can you and Eliza wash up the pans and put the things in the dishwasher while I go and shop for some food?' I asked.

I waited. Jo stared at me. There was a moment when I knew it could go either way.

'OK,' she said eventually.

That had been too easy so I ran out of the house before anything went wrong.

Soon I was back in the kitchen, tossing a salad while the fresh fish sizzled under the grill and the potatoes baked in the oven. The girls had cleaned up the kitchen and Eliza was reluctantly laying the table. Jo made her excuses as usual.

'I think I'll go and ring Scarlet, she's going through a tough time. Her parents have split.'

'You didn't tell me, Jo.'

'It's just happened.'

'Is Scarlet all right?'

'She cries a lot.'

'Oh, dear, that's not good. Still, I'm sure you can make her laugh.'

Suddenly I felt an urge to hug Jo. We were talking properly, I was cooking properly, and there was a glimmer of our old, easy relationship. I took her in my arms and was immediately aware of the hard jutting spine on my hand, like a rigid, knotted stick attached to her back. Her pointed shoulders angled out like handlebars. Cuddling Jo had lost its softness. Looking at Jo and especially touching her was a constant reminder of the way her body had been mistreated and abused. I felt nurturing and rejecting at the same time, I felt pity and anger—and nausea. Jo's bones formed a barrier between us.

She went off to make her call and I stared at the door she had closed behind her. Suddenly I was aware of the smell of burning and rushed to the grill to rescue the trout. I scraped off the black bits from the outside of the fish and tried to disguise the whole meal with mayonnaise. Still, the salad and the baked potatoes were fine. I tried to focus on them but the smell of burning lingered for the rest of the evening. And I still couldn't concentrate on anything.

Jo had told me to get on with my life, so on my next day off I decided to call in at the estate agent's to enquire about shops to let. After five minutes with the spotty commercial properties specialist, who looked like he was a member of the under-fourteens football team, I felt confused and out of my depth. The rents sounded astronomical to me if I wanted a decent location, and whichever property I took on would involve a fair amount of refurbishment to make it suitable for my purpose. I realised I wasn't even clear about what that purpose was. I wanted something different from the sandwich bar but nothing too ambitious.

'So what's your decision, Mrs Trounce?'

'Sorry?'

'Shall I arrange for you to look round some of these premises?'

'I don't know. Can I take the details and go through them all first?'

'Of course. Have a browse and then give me a ring. Here's my card.'

I looked at the rectangle in my hand with its flying blue-bird in one corner and 'Digger Smith' across the centre in some sort of gothic typeface. How can a fourteen-year-old called Digger have his own business card?

I stood outside the estate agent's and stared at the wedge

of paper in my hands. If I had still been with Roger, he would have looked through them all with me, or maybe without me, and with his eye for business he would have put them into priority order and then sorted out all the financial details. Meanwhile, I didn't even know what all the financial details were that I had to sort out. There were times, practical times, when I actually missed Roger—when the boiler packed up that weekend, when my car broke down, when we had mice nesting in the attic. And now, when I found myself being carried away by unfamiliar currents, sinking with no one to throw me a lifeline. I cursed myself for needing anyone, especially a man, especially an ex-husband, but at the same time it seemed unfair that brilliant, competent Alice had Roger to herself when she didn't even need him. Not in the practical, common-sense way. Perhaps all she really needed was a father for her child and I wondered why she hadn't got round that one. Didn't successful, independent career-women visit a sperm bank, whatever that was? Barclays without the overdraft, I suppose…

'Hello, you seem lost in thought. Something important?'

'I was just thinking about sperm banks.'

Gordon laughed. I cringed and imagined that erase button again. But somehow we ended up going for a coffee.

I showed him the details of the shops to rent and as I talked, I surprised myself with more knowledge than I'd credited myself with.

'This one is quite a bit cheaper than the high street,' I explained, 'but I reckon George Street is an up-and-coming area. There are a couple of interesting shops opened opposite and it's on a route through to a commercial area so I think there'll be a lot of passing trade.'

'Are you going for a bank loan for the up-front expenditure?' Gordon asked.

'Yes, I'm going to do a business plan. I've never done one before but it can't be that difficult.'

I could feel my confidence filling up inside me like good wine being poured slowly into a waiting glass. This was what I had really needed, someone to talk things through with.

'I'll tell you what,' said Gordon, 'why don't I run up a business plan based on what you've told me and you can have a look and see if it's any help?'

'Great. Thanks. If you don't mind.'

I leant out of the tower window, my golden hair shining in the early evening sun. I looked out over the fields and meadows of the kingdom and saw a knight on a white steed dressed in the shiniest of armour. He seemed to be coming my way and…

'Sorry, Gordon, what was that?'

'I was saying that another option would be if I were to invest some money in your enterprise. I know you'll need to think about it, but it would be a good plan for both of us. I believe it would be a good investment for me and that way you'll know my help will be on a purely business basis.'

Gordon carried on talking and I felt myself glazing over. I remember reading somewhere that we should all do what we're good at and pass the rest on to the experts in their field. I was good at customer service, ideas, dreams. Meeting Gordon meant I could pass the rest on to him as he seemed so keen. It was as if my guardian angel had sent him along to solve all my problems. I felt enthusiastic and inspired, my status would go up several notches as I turned from employee to employer. I would prove to Roger, Alice and the rest of the world that I could be a success. I would be living my dream.

I looked at Gordon who was busy making notes on the back of one of the estate agent's sheets. I felt happy and excited but also had a sense of unease.

Gordon looked up from his jottings.

'Are you all right?' he asked.

'I think I'm just scared,' I said.

He patted my hand. 'That's normal. I'll tell you what, why don't you sleep on all this and in the meantime let me take you out for dinner tonight?'

Suddenly the business faded into insignificance. Gordon was asking me out on a date and I felt flustered and nervous, like a thirteen-year-old about to have her first snog. I looked terrible, the house was a tip so I wouldn't be able to ask him in for coffee, Jo was round at Scarlet's and it was late notice to get a babysitter, and Eliza had her audition the next day and I wanted to ease her into an early night. The problems stacked up in front of me like a landslide rolling down the hillside and blocking the path.

'I can't make it tonight,' I said. 'How about Friday?'

'Saturday would be better for me.'

'Great. Saturday it is.'

Then I watched Gordon thoughtfully as he tapped our date into his electronic organiser.

I took an excited Eliza to her audition at the Valentine Rose Performing Arts College (or Val's stage school, as it was known). Roger phoned and told her to 'break a leg' and Alice had sent her a good-luck card with instructions on being a good thespian, which the girls found hilarious. I simply looked forward to spending time with my younger daughter— I was all too aware that recently my energy had been totally focused on Jo.

I was surprised to find that Valentine Rose was an actual person, in fact an actress turned drama teacher who owned and ran the school. Valentine was larger than life in every sense of the word, and boomed out a greeting to us as if she were in a Shakespearian production and we were at the back of the stalls. She had a deep, penetrating voice which had that 'trained' quality to it, enunciating every syllable and sound of each word. Off guard, I thought I detected a slight hint of a Yorkshire accent and wondered if Valentine Rose was her real name. She was probably known to her family as Val Braithwaite or something altogether more earthy. She wore a long, flowing kaftan which looked familiar, and I wondered if it was one of my relics from the seventies which had found its way into her wardrobe via the charity shop. She jangled with beads and baubles and I smelt a musty mixture of herbs and smoke.

As we looked round the school, Valentine greeted any passing student by name, adding a personal comment relating to a recent audition or performance in class. I liked her obvious pride in her school and I realised this was what I wanted for my café, a personal touch and regular customers so that it would be more like a club. But perhaps I was expecting the impossible. We were introduced to some of the staff—an effeminate dance teacher called Jasper and two drama teachers who spoke to us as if reciting their lines. The place was, in short, very theatrical, and its staff and pupils very dramatic. There was no mistaking it for an ordinary school, though it was not exactly Fame Academy either.

Eliza went off eagerly to her audition while I waited with other parents in an empty classroom. I thought about my imminent date with Gordon and realised I would have to explain myself to the girls. Jo was never far from my thoughts and I immediately recalled her tantrum and 'illness' when I had first met Gordon at Victoria's wedding. I knew I had to proceed with caution and wondered about the casual, drop-it-into-the-conversation approach:

'Oh, didn't I tell you? I'm just off for a quick snack with some guy I met, can't even remember his name, friend of Uncle George's. Don't really feel like it actually but I don't want to let Uncle George down. Oh, this old thing? Well, I thought I'd better not go smelling of salami.'

That didn't sound quite right. I would never let either of the girls go out with someone if they didn't even know his name. No, far better to sit them down and explain it all properly so there would be no mystery, no secrets. I tried another tack in my head:

'I'm having dinner with a very reliable and sensible man called Gordon. He's not taking the place of your father but I hope he will be a friend to all of us. Yes, I have dressed up tonight as I want to impress Gordon for he's a charming man and he may be helping me with my business idea so it will be worth making…'

No, that sounded like I was expecting wedding bells and was asking the girls to be bridesmaids. I imagined myself pleading with Jo not to sulk as I handed her my posy of flowers.

'Are you all right?'

I realised that all the other parents were staring at me and the man next to me had moved to a different seat.

'Sorry, I'm auditioning myself next week. Royal Shakespeare Company. Have to practise my lines. Lady Macbeth.'

'I don't remember Lady Macbeth telling off her teenage daughter for sulking at a wedding,' one father muttered.

'Modern interpretation,' I said. 'I wonder how they're all getting on in there?'

I wish I hadn't asked as this opened up the opportunity for some of the more competitive parents to ask other questions in order to eye up the opposition.

'Has your daughter done her LAMDA exams?'

'Has your son been in any major productions?'

'Does your daughter have professional singing lessons?'

I suspected there was only one place available and that our offspring were competing for it while we sat there quite helpless and unable to control the outcome. I think one couple, particularly the proud, pushy father, would have been more than happy to have settled it between ourselves, perhaps with an arm-wrestling competition. Eventually, the conversation ground to a halt and we took it in turns to stare at the door as if on sentry duty. I flicked through a couple of magazines but didn't really concentrate. Every now and then I glanced at my watch and tapped it, for the hands seemed to have stopped moving.

Eliza was the first to come and get me, looking flushed and happy.

'Did it go all right?' I asked.

'Yeah, great,' she replied.

'Good luck with the audition,' one man shouted after us.

'The audition's over,' I shouted back before I realised what he meant. I just managed to shout, 'Out damn spot,' before we were out of earshot.

For the next few weeks, the slap of letters landing on the hall floor was immediately followed by the sound of Eliza thumping down the stairs to check the post. The letter eventually arrived and Eliza stood there holding it in her hand as though it were a priceless antique. She opened it slowly and we stared at her as she stared at the letter. Suddenly she screamed, threw the letter in the air, hugged me and then hugged Jo. She rushed off, no doubt to make phone call after phone call to her friends. I picked up the letter and read what I already knew was there.

'She's got in,' I said to Jo unnecessarily. 'I'm so proud of both my girls.'

Jo looked doubtful. I nearly made reference to her past academic record but that seemed irrelevant somehow.

'I'm proud of your bravery and determination,' I said quietly. 'You're having to deal with a lot at the moment and yet somehow you manage to be a good and supportive friend to Scarlet and nice to Eliza and encourage me with my café plans. I'm so proud of you.'

And as I said it, I realised it was true. And I could think of so much more I could praise Jo about. I had forgotten what a wonderfully funny, generous and articulate young woman she was growing into. She was more than a set of exam results, more than an eating disorder.

Eliza rushed back in, literally jumping for joy.

'I must phone Uncle George, have you got his number?'

I scrutinised Jo's face, her posture, her general demeanour

for signs of envy or even bitterness and resentment. Certainly the words she chose to say to Eliza were the right ones.

'Well done, sis,' she said.

'Why don't we all get a DVD out tonight and relax, as a family?' I suggested, turning into the perfect mother without really trying. And then, when I went to my well-stocked fridge to get out some fresh food, I noticed that Jo had eaten the left-over salad and a yoghurt. Jo was eating, Eliza's dream was coming true and so was mine.

Eliza Trounce shone last night in this innovative production of *Macbeth*. As Lady Macbeth's daughter, she stole the show in the wedding scene. The first-night party was held in the exclusive West End restaurant Ellie's, which is owned by the star's mother and her partner, Gordon. Eliza's sister Joanna, who writes our medical column, was seen accompanied by Prince Harry...

This should have been the end of our story. A happy family, their problems behind them and a sunset ahead. But as I turned the page, expecting to see the credits, I realised there was another chapter of anguish to come. That's the trouble with life: there never is a perfect rainbow, just the dream of one.

TEN

I LIKED the lists. I got really good at writing lists. Lily sent emails telling me how good they were. She didn't need to, I already knew. The point about lists is that they order your mind, your thoughts. But not your life. My thoughts had become tangled and knotted. I'd made the wrong connections. Sometimes my lists had been negative, contradictory, circular. But they got better. The first list I made had been practical and unemotional. By the end of the list phase, I could even make lists around a feeling. I began to link emotions to events, feelings to actions. My early lists focused on other people. Gradually they became lists about me.

Then Lily told me the lists were finished. I could move on to the next phase. I didn't want to. I liked my lists. I knew I could do them. I had doubts about being able to write anything longer, more creative. Or fluid.

Dear Jo,
This week I want you to write me a story. Take your time. It can be as long or as short as you want. I want you to write about a girl. She can be any age you like. She can be anybody you like. The title of the story is 'Girl in a

Box'. Ask for help if you need it. Always ask for help when you need it.
With love, Lily

Dear Lily,
I don't know where to start. Can you help?
From Jo

Dear Jo,
Well done for asking for help. It is always good to ask for help when you need it. Think about <u>all</u> sources of help. Think about the meaning of inspiration and then you will have the help you need. Once you under-stand this, you will lift up your pen and the words will flow like wine.
With love,
Lily

Strangely, I never wondered whether Lily Finnegan was one slice short of a sandwich.

GIRL IN A BOX

She is in a box. She is waiting for someone to come and let her out. She knows the inside of the box very well now. A strip of daylight slithers through the gap between the lid and the side of the box. So now she can see as well as feel the smoothness of the pine. She can feel and see her body, which is bent and curled to best fit into the re-stricted space. The wood is warm and dry, silky and per-fectly even. The light dances over the wood grain as she

senses her own breathing, her own very slight move-
ments. Yes, she knows the inside of the box very well and
she knows her position in it. But she does not know how
it will look when she steps out of the box. She has been
told there is a label on the outside but from her position
she can not read it.

She hears footsteps and then the faint muttering of
someone reading the label—'Girl in a Box'. The footsteps
echo into the distance and more arrive, more mutterings,
more words being read aloud. There must be more than
one label on the outside of the box. Person after person,
reader after reader comes to the box and reads a label. She
listens to the words, every one of them different.

'Intelligent', 'reliable', 'screwed up', 'self-destructive',
'jealous', 'friendly', 'frightened', 'articulate', 'controlling',
'out of control'. The labels are sometimes accurate, sometimes inaccurate and sometimes contradictory.

Eventually a stranger lifts the lid and she steps out and
looks back at herself. She realises that the labels have
been written by the visitors to the box. They are not de-
scriptions, they are opinions. And opinions are as different as the people who give them. She learns that she can
take the labels off as she chooses and write some of her
own.

She looks around and sees other boxes, some with people inside and some with people outside looking back at
themselves. They are all at different stages in the process.

It is always a stranger who can let a girl out of the
box, for a stranger does not waste time writing out a new
box label.

I emailed the attachment to Lily.

Dear Jo,
I loved this story. Now write another story called 'Taking the Steering-Wheel in a New Car'.
With love,
Lily

    I wrote the next story and was pleased with it. It made me feel good so I set about writing more. First I asked for inspiration. Then I let my thoughts flow. At first I edited my thoughts before they were written down, then I didn't. Gradually I wrote better and better stories. But then she set me another challenge.

Dear Jo,
Feelings are often expressed best in a poem. Pick a feeling and write a poem about it. You have already shown me that you write well and use words in an imaginative, innovative way so I know you will be able to tackle this task.
With love,
Lily

    I had never written a poem before. But Lily believed I could do it and my stories had been good. Only Lily would read it, and that made me feel safe.

Fear

Fear is invisible
Until we tie it on tight
To an object of our choice—
Spiders, rainstorms, snakes, blood
Or, in my case—food.
Then we ban the object from our lives

Instead of snatching out the fear
And drowning it with love
Love of ourselves.

As a poem, I didn't rate it much. As something else, I did. Writing wasn't about getting good marks, it was about truth. I added a postscript to my email:

PS. I am ready to write about food. Maybe even talk about it. I want to meet you now.
With love,
Jo

Dear Jo,
You are doing very well. Now write down everything. Keep a journal and also you must write about a journey. Do not get in touch with me until I contact you.
With love,
Lily

Dear Lily,
When will that be?
With love,
Jo

But I didn't get a reply. I didn't like that. Until then, all the tasks given to me were to take a few days, a week, or maybe two weeks. I always received a reply straight away, as if Lily were waiting for me. There for only me. Suddenly I didn't know how long it would be—days? Weeks? I didn't know. I wanted to know. Knowing was believing. Knowing was control. Knowing was power. Suddenly I knew what I had to do. I grabbed my pen and paper and wrote as I thought.

I sent my thoughts on 'knowing' to Lily. They bounced right back. I was angry. I wrote about anger. That bounced back too. I printed it out and put it in the top drawer of my desk. Writing about anger got rid of it, like it had leaked out of me and into the page.

The next day, I heard my mum on the phone to Gordon. She was talking about where they were going to meet. Suddenly I was alone. Mum was running after Gordon, Dad was with Alice and soon a baby, Eliza was off to stage school. I was going nowhere. Lily was gone. I had no one. They were all on their own journeys and I was being left behind. Home alone. Mum and Eliza had forgotten about my eating disorder. Dad didn't even seem to know. Scarlet was busy drying her mother's tears. She liked tears and I had none. The school had written to Mum and said I should take the rest of the academic year off. They weren't bothered. My eating disorder was powerless. I had to do something, my journey had stopped. I was standing at a fork in the road. I had to move forward if I didn't want to be left standing. But I chose the wrong path.

Before I went, I needed to see everyone. I phoned Scarlet and arranged to meet her at the coffee-bar. A sudden downpour meant I had to run the last hundred metres. I pulled my jacket over my head as I tried to sprint. Puddles had formed almost instantly and my shoes let in the water. Perhaps they dragged me down. After that short jog, I was gasping for breath. Exhausted. My limbs ached. I had to lean against the wall and I thought I was going to faint.

'Are you all right?' A young waiter put his hand on my shoulder. He pulled it away quickly.

'Yeah. Not used to running,' I panted. I made my way to a table and pulled off my wet jacket.

Scarlet arrived soon afterwards. She dripped her way towards the table. We ordered coffee. The waiter looked over from time to time. Curious. Questions were written on his face in clear ink.

'Scarlet, you know I have anorexia.' I said the words before I swallowed them, as I was tempted to do.

'Yeah, you told me, well not in so many words. I mean, you hint at things, don't you?'

'Do I?'

'I expect we all do. Are you…getting better?' Scarlet asked nervously.

'I was, but my therapist has let me down.'

'Bastard. What's she done?'

'She won't reply to my emails. I feel stuck. I have to do something.'

'Has she given you some advice and that?'

'Write. She wants me to write about it. So that I'll be able to talk.'

'Well, you're talking now.'

'Yes, but I'm not really talking.'

'I keep a diary,' Scarlet said. 'It's a lockable diary, you know, private. I keep it so I can write down everything without worrying about anyone seeing it. I look back on my diary and I think, Shit, was I really that hung up on that munted guy? Or else I think, Did I really get that upset over something so pathetic? Then when I'm like in the middle of some crisis, like with my parents, I know I'll look back one day and think, So what?'

'Yes, but in therapy you need your therapist to read the stuff. And Lily Finnegan's done a runner.'

'Do you want me to read your stuff?' offered Scarlet.

'No, you've got enough to worry about.'

'Sometimes it helps to think about other people's problems for a change.'

'Yeah.'

We sipped our coffee for a while, distracted by a family who had come in out of the rain.

'I told you to bring your coat but, oh, no, you always know best, don't you!' snapped the mother at a sullen young girl. The mother's lips were pressed tightly together. Like a purse. Lines creased from her lips towards her sucked-in cheeks. She pushed the girl roughly into the seat. She studied the menu. The father and son sat down, too. Glances were made but no one really looked at anyone else. None of them spoke.

'Is there such thing as a happy family?' Scarlet pondered.

I thought about my family. I looked at the miserable family nearby.

'Perhaps my mum's right,' I said. 'Perhaps you do have to laugh.'

'You have to laugh, you have to cry,' Scarlet added.

I looked back at the family. They were ordering drinks now as if nothing had happened.

'How's your mum?' I asked Scarlet.

'Still crying.'

'Oh, dear.'

'Don't worry, she'll soon be all cried out. I'm going to my dad's this weekend. She says she doesn't like it but she understands. That's good enough. They're never going to get on like your parents do, that's for sure.'

'Oh, yeah. Still, if you pretend something for long enough, it becomes real. Keep on faking it till you're making it, or some such shit. I think I'll pretend to be a successful film star.' I laughed.

Then we thought of all the things we could pretend till they happened. And we laughed. We really laughed. I felt better. Scarlet laughed till she cried, then talked about her mum again. This really was my best thing—sitting in the coffee-shop with Scarlet. I thought about that. And I nearly cried, too.

'You can talk to me about anything,' Scarlet said. 'That's what friends are for.'

'I know. Eliza has loads of mates but they don't talk or anything. Just dance about being immature.'

'If my mum had a best friend, she'd have found it easier,' Scarlet said.

And I thought about my mum. And I thought about how I hadn't really truly talked to anyone yet. Not properly. Not out loud. But I was starting to. It was just like reading the emails out loud really. I knew I would start with Scarlet. I just had to make myself do it. She was looking at me, like she was waiting for something.

'I will get over my anorexia,' I told Scarlet. 'I have a sense of the future.'

'That's good. If you realise it's just a passing phase, like boy bands or green eyeshadow, you move on. I don't completely understand it all, Jo, but I do know it's not your fault. Stuff like that kind of happens.'

'I don't completely understand it either,' I confessed, 'But I'm getting there.'

'Loads of girls at school throw up and stuff.'

'Do they?'

'Yeah, and other stuff, too. Caroline Webb cuts herself, Monica Sadler is obsessed with fire—she's always lighting matches and getting weird about it.'

'How do you know this stuff? Do they talk to you?'

'Shit, no. Sometimes my mum knows their mum, sometimes it's a rumour that kind of fits. But they're all secrets, and secrets are very dangerous.'

'You're very wise,' I said.

'You wouldn't like to tell the new physics teacher that, would you?'

The next weekend I went with Eliza to stay with Dad. Alice was at her mother's again but she'd left a congratulations card for Eliza. Dad wanted to take us out for a meal to celebrate.

I took a deep breath. 'I have difficulty eating,' I began. 'My stomach's been playing up again.'

'She's anorexic,' said Eliza. 'Even if she eats it, she'll have to throw up afterwards.'

I punched Eliza on the arm, pretty hard. Eliza practised her drama skills.

'I know,' said Dad. 'Are you having some sort of therapy yet?'

'Only by email,' Eliza piped up.

'I'll be seeing her face to face soon,' I explained. 'And it's already made a difference.'

Dad looked me up and down. His thoughts were very loud.

'I know, let's go to the roller-skating rink, then Eliza and I can have something to eat and you can if you feel like it or else you can just carry on skating. Problem solved.'

As it happened, I had a sandwich. Mum would have been proud of me. But I tried not to think of her. Dad skated for a bit, then he got bored. He went to the bar. They were show-ing football on a wide screen. Perhaps he'd have a son next time, I thought. Then I tried not to think about that either.

The next night, Dad went out. He never changed his plans. Eliza and I watched television. We watched a documentary about missing persons. There were men and women who had gone out for work one morning as usual, but they never came back. No one knew where they were. No one knew if they were alive. Sometimes a missing person came back. Some-times a missing person was found—but not often.

One man was found in London. He had left a good job. He walked the city streets at night, he went round and round on the Circle Line by day. He said his life before had been like going round and round on the Circle Line. One woman went and lived with another man. She had another child with him. She never got round to telling her first family, slipped her mind or some-thing. There was a seventeen-year-old boy who hated school. Great things were expected of him. Nobody expected him to go and live at Heathrow airport. But he did. For three years. He said he only meant to go for a week to show them. To show them what? He didn't say. I liked him. I liked all of them. It's easy to get stuck—in an airport, on the Circle Line, in a family.

Eliza laughed at some of the people on the programme. She said they were stupid.

'You need to have a better understanding of people than that,' I said, 'if you're going to be an actress.'

'I can act stupid,' said Eliza, and did a silly impersonation of the man on the Circle Line. I laughed. Eliza doesn't think that deeply. That's why she's so happy.

Mum came to collect us the next day. She tried to stay in the car and beep the horn.

'Why doesn't she come in?' Dad muttered. 'Has she completely lost the use of her legs?'

In the end, Mum came through the door.

'Coo-ee!' she called. She had a new floral dress on. She smiled like a Stepford wife.

'Sorry, Roger, I was just trying to speed things up. I'm meeting Gordon this evening.'

'Oh, yes, I meant to ask—how is the restaurant plan going? You must be very busy.'

'Yes, that's why I'm having a night out away from it all.'

'Sounds like a good idea. Well, they're all packed and ready to go.'

Mum had got her message across but would never know if it had been received or not. I heard the frustration in her laugh.

When we got home, I phoned Uncle George.

'How's it all going?' he asked.

'Not great.'

'Takes time.'

'I'm not patient.'

'Me neither. Too slow?'

'At the moment.'

'Anything I can do?'

'Send me an email.'

'Sure. You send one back.'

'OK, then.'

'Mum and Eliza OK?'

'Yeah. Susan?'

'Yes.'

'Victoria?'

'Great. I think.'

'Not sure?'

'Always worry.'
'Like Mum.'
'Yeah, runs in the family.'
'Anxious parent syndrome.'
'Difficult daughter syndrome.'
We laughed.
'I'll email, then, Jo.'
'Thanks.'
'Bye.'
'Bye.'

Dear Jo,
I have only ever sent business emails. I keep wanting to ask you for a quote or to clarify a contract. Be patient, Jo, you'll get there. We all have difficult times. When I was your age, I ran away from home. I'd been dumped by a girl—Gloria Pratt. Trouble is, you can run away from the causes of your feelings but not the feelings themselves. I ran away and still felt bad. I think Victoria was running away as well, escaping. Stick with it—you'll be fine. Come and stay if you want, have a change of scene—or am I encouraging you to run away after all? Funny, this is the longest email I've ever sent. My finger aches. Susan sends her love. With love, Uncle George

Dear Uncle George,
I hope Gloria Pratt is having a shitty life.
Sometimes people don't run away from something, but towards something else. I think I'm in limbo. I feel like I'm in a rowing boat—I've left the shore but the new shore is nowhere in sight. I need to get there quickly

before I drown. I'll go back to school next year, I know
that. It's the bit between now and then I'm scared about.
Love to Susan, and Victoria when you see her.
Love Jo
PS Thank you for being my Lily Finnegan!

Dear Frank,
I wanted to thank you for introducing me to Lily Finnegan.
Where did you find her? Do you know her? I don't even
know where she's based—is she local? She's taking a bit
of a break from me at the moment, and that's cool. But
if you know anything, please please please tell me.
Love Jo

Dear Jo,
Do you know, I can't even remember who told me about
Lily—I think it was my Buddhist friend I met on retreat.
She is now on a longer retreat in the Himalayas, I believe.
I have heard remarkable things about Lily Finnegan so
I am glad she is helping you. Let me know if there's any-
thing else I can do, Jo. And if you want to come and see
me at any time, we can have a longer chat.
With love
Frank

   I went to the Buddhist centre when I was out jogging.
There was a big man there. Looked like my old teddy bear.
   'Jo,' he said, 'I'm Frank. Come and meditate with us.'
   'Just tell me where she is, then. I've got to know where she
is. I haven't got time to meditate. You don't understand, I've
got to find her.'

'I don't know, Jo. I'm so sorry.'

'Then why did you ask me to come? What was the point?'

'I wanted to help, that's all. Help you feel better. Your email sounded like you were having a difficult time.'

'Well, I am, I am. But why would you care?'

'Why wouldn't I? Look, we're going to meditate now. Join us if you want and then we'll talk some more.'

'About Lily?'

'And about you.'

'I don't know how to meditate,' I said. 'Is it just sitting there, thinking?'

'It's sitting there, not thinking really.'

That sounded easy but it wasn't. I kept thinking, I couldn't stop it. Afterwards, Frank said that was OK. He said there was no such thing as doing it wrong.

'Like life,' he said. 'There's no such thing as doing it wrong. You learn, that's all.'

'Lily Finnegan, I've got to find her. I can't cope without her.' And then I cried. I felt stupid but I didn't tell Frank. He probably would have said, 'There's no such thing as feeling stupid.'

I wondered if there was any such thing as Lily Finnegan. But I didn't really want to ask.

'Is there any such thing as Lily Finnegan?' I asked.

'Of course. Just because something's not standing in front of you doesn't mean it doesn't exist. She's probably thinking of you right now.'

That made me feel a lot better.

'You have a lot of people who love you, Jo.' He meant my mum. I might have known he'd be on her side. But I stayed a bit longer. I wanted to.

Frank spoke slowly and carefully, like every word mattered.

And he wanted to know all about me. Not about exams or eating. And he didn't ask all the usual boring adult questions like 'Do you have a boyfriend?' He asked about music and books and life and me. But he didn't know where Lily was. So he said.

Was I eating at that time? I really can't remember. It wouldn't have been much anyway. I was still underweight—I can see that from looking back at photos taken around that time. I didn't feel underweight. If I thought about food I got scared, then I didn't eat it. But I became so preoccupied with finding out about Lily that I forgot sometimes. I just ate something without thinking. Then there would be days and days without eating. I had stopped feeling hungry. And if I did eat something, I felt strange—kind of full and bloated. Kind of poisoned or something.

I had begun to understand. It was the lists and the stories. They weren't about food. They were about control, expectations, finding myself, loads of stuff—but not food. Food was just a symptom, a by-product. It was me I had to look at, not what was left on the plate. I feel sure I would have been all right then if only…if only other people had played their part. But everyone around me was busy. Or just not there.

I wondered if they'd notice if I went. I wondered if they'd care. It would be a test. I remember when I was about three or four, in the sitting room with Mum and Dad. I had been showing them my drawings. Then the neighbours came round, an old, grim-looking couple. Mr and Mrs Slater. They talked to Mum and Dad about a fence. I drew a fence and tried to show them.

'Not now, Jo,' Mum said. So I went away and hid. I hid under the bed. The dust made me cough. Then I lay still. I heard the front door slam. I heard Mum and Dad arguing. The kettle. The rattle of teacups. Soon they would wonder where I was, I thought. Soon they would worry. Then they would find me. Then everything would be all right. After a long time, I heard my name being called. Mum found me.

'What an earth are you doing under there? Come down and have your tea.' That was it. No hugs and kisses. No big reunion. No tears of relief.

I didn't run away to be found. I didn't run away to escape. I ran away to find Lily Finnegan. I knew I had to do something. I knew I had to do it on my own. I would go to all the local therapy centres, I would go to the three Finnegans in the telephone directory, I would shout her name out in the street. I knew if I found her, everything would be all right.

I could have phoned people up, I could have surfed the net. But I wanted to physically find her. To pound the streets. To walk and walk and walk until I got what I wanted. I wanted it to be a journey, to notch up the miles, to feel it in my muscles. I wanted to find Lily, but I wanted to find her in my own way. This would be my journey, my quest.

I wanted to just walk out of the door with nothing in my pocket. Like the runaways on the documentary. That seemed incredible to me. The ultimate freedom. But practicality won through. Still, I kept preparation to a minimum. I didn't want it to be like a holiday or getting ready for school. It had to be different, new. I stuffed money, a few clothes, a toothbrush, a comb, paper and pens and a sleeping bag in a rucksack. I took my phone. I took my passport—I don't know why. Three minutes' preparation. Then I walked into town.

Time stretched out before me. I had no deadlines, no ap-

pointments, no schedule. I understood the freedom of the runaways. But I wasn't like them, I would go back. When I'd
found Lily. When I'd sorted everything out. I wasn't escaping, I was confronting. I wasn't running away, I was running
towards.

It was a twenty-minute walk into town along the main
roads but I took the longer route, the back way. So I wouldn't
be seen. I knew I would have to avoid the west end of town
where Mum's café was and the Buddhist centre, but the other
side of town would be OK. How often do you see people you
know in town, anyway? But I saw someone I knew straight
away. It was a friend of my mother's. I should smile and say
hello. I should say, 'Thank you for asking, I'm feeling much
better now.' I should be the perfect daughter. As if my mother
was standing behind me. But she wasn't. I had a choice. I
could cross the road. I could look the other way. Or I could
smile and say hello. It was up to me.

'Hello.' I smiled and carried on walking.

I could decide what to say. I could decide where to go. I
decided to go to the library.

I had always loved books. Not just reading them, I loved
being surrounded by them. I loved the look of them, the feel
of them—and the idea of them. Books were an escape, a safe
place to go, a therapy, a source. Books mapped out my history. I could pinpoint an exact time in my childhood by what
I had been reading. *Anne of Green Gables*; *The Lion, the
Witch and the Wardrobe*; *Harry Potter*; *Little Women*—I could
tell you where I was as I finished each one. I was always called
'bookish'. I never knew if that was praise or criticism. Praise
from the adults, dissing by my peers, I reckon.

I walked into the library and felt at home. Books are the

most interesting wallpaper, the best furniture. Furnish a room with books and you will be rich, someone said. I never talked about my passion for books, it wasn't cool. Some people understood about books, some people didn't. At school I talked about CDs. I talked about TV. And boys. Not books. Not often anyway. I ran my fingers along a row of books. The spines felt familiar and important. Sideways words caught my eye. Columns of colours marched in front of me like soldiers. Every now and then I pulled one out and read the back cover. I put it back on the shelf. Lovingly, with care. I took my time, I had plenty of that. I just walked around, looking, feeling, sensing. Libraries always have the same smell. Any town, any country—the same mixture of new and old, paper and wood.

Eventually I logged on to a computer and flashed up the library catalogue. Lily Finnegan had not written any psychology books. I went to the information desk. A lady in a brown cardigan handed me the town guide and the *Yellow Pages*. I made a list of therapy centres. I read the paper. I took down a book of Van Gogh paintings. I turned the pages. I read a short story from a compilation. I read the notices on the wall. I wondered if I could sleep there, hide behind the chairs when they locked up. It would be easy, I thought.

I went out into the street. I noticed more stuff, loads more stuff. I had time to notice. The dust and dirt outside the library had all blown into one corner by the old telephone box. The bench was cracked at one end. The wood was split open. Like an old cedar. A lady sat at the other end, staring into space. A shopping basket on her knee. Empty. Her glasses crooked like they had slipped off one ear. A handful of dry leaves lay under the bench with an old tin can. But there were no trees in sight. I walked around the sharp corner of a concrete building. I heard snatches of conversation from shoppers. Meaningless, trivial, strange, out of context.

'It'll do for a Friday, but not a Saturday.'

'She would say that, wouldn't she? Obviously. I mean she would.'

'I'll kill him and then he'll be sorry.'

I came to the Church Lane Therapy and Healing Centre. The window was a patchwork of notices. So many therapies. So many disorders. What would they think if I went in and asked about Lily Finnegan? I thought. Then I thought again. Did it matter? They must have seen everything, they were therapeutic people. I walked in. There was a smell of cinnamon and orange. The lady behind the desk smiled at me kindly. She waited for me to speak.

'I'm trying to trace a therapist called Lily Finnegan,' I said.

'I don't think we have anyone of that name. I'll just ask.' She disappeared through an open door. She came back with a man. He smiled kindly.

'What sort of therapy are you looking for?' he almost whispered.

'I'm looking for a therapist. I've been emailing her. She's called Lily Finnegan.'

'I don't know her, I'm afraid. Is there someone else you'd like to see?'

'No, it's all right. Thank you.'

'That's all right. I'm only sorry we can't help. Do come in at any time and have a browse.' His arm swept across to indicate the back wall where three shelves of books and a large rack of leaflets lay.

I smiled. I didn't feel awkward. That had been easy. I walked to two other therapy centres and one woman's semi, which was listed as a therapy centre. They were all kind. No one had heard of Lily Finnegan.

I had one more place to call at. It was a private house again.

'Come in, come in,' welcomed the lady who answered the door. She was dressed in a long black robe with a sort of lace shawl. Kind of Victorian or something.

She took me into the lounge where two men and three women were sitting on the floor. In the lotus position.

'I'm sorry, I think I've made a mistake. I just came to make an enquiry,' I said.

'Are you not here for our yoga group, then?' piped up one of the ladies. She had a strange squeaky voice, like a puppet.

'No.' I felt awkward. But the lady who had answered the door put her arm round me. She gave me a squeeze.

'Don't worry, we haven't started. Enquire away.'

'I'm looking for a therapist called Lily Finnegan. I wondered if you knew her.'

I was expecting slow head nods, another wasted call. But the lady with the squeaky voice said, 'I've heard that name somewhere.'

I raised my eyebrows in hope.

'I know,' she continued. 'It's from an Irish folk tale. That's all I know. I can't remember the reference, but she did help people in the story, I think.'

My face must have looked despondent. The lady who had answered the door hugged me again.

'Do you know about synchronicity?' she asked.

'Like Carl Jung?' I said.

'Yes, that's it. It's all about meaningful coincidences. You were meant to come here, I sense it.'

I left them to their yoga. It was getting late. The talk of folk tales made me think about the library again. I would sleep there. It was a risk. I had never taken any risks in my life. It was about time. I had nothing to lose.

I hid behind the chairs as planned. But then I heard the cleaners arrive. I crept into a small office and I got inside a cupboard. They didn't clean the office anyway. There were no security cameras upstairs in the main part of the library, only downstairs in Reception. Locked inside the library— what freedom. The strangest thing was, I didn't think about home. I didn't worry. I was too busy trying to get by in this strange new life. If I had thought about home, I would have known how anxious they'd be. Then I would have felt guilty, in the wrong. But I knew that finding Lily Finnegan was the right thing to do. And I knew that I would find her. In the end.

ELEVEN

'LET go a little,' Frank told me during one of my increasingly frequent heart-to-hearts. 'You've lit the touch paper, now you need to stand back at a safe distance. Let go of Jo and Lily, just a little.'

But I couldn't let go unless I knew for certain that Jo was getting better, and tracking down Lily was to become something of an obsession for both of us. Maybe Jo *was* getting better—I couldn't decide. I was fairly certain she had stopped losing weight and I clung to this positive thought as if hanging on in a tube train taking a bend at full speed. If I let go of it, I would collapse in a heap on the ground.

'Aren't you supposed to be meeting Gordon one evening?' Frank said. 'That will take your mind off things, which makes the letting go and the letting be a lot easier. You have to do something for yourself every now and then, we all do.'

I tossed this advice around in my mind for days until eventually it just seemed easier to go on my date with Gordon than to keep thinking about it.

'If you don't take care of yourself,' Trish had said, 'you won't be fit to take care of anyone else.'

She had a point. Frank had a point. And so, with some hesitancy, my relationship with Gordon began.

Before I got ready for my big night out, my mind leapt ahead to the end of the evening when Gordon might want to come in for coffee. I looked at the piles of junk in each room, the clutter of my life which just wouldn't go away. In the end I decided just to tackle the lounge so I could bundle him in there quickly, keeping the hall light off. I moved all the piles up to my bedroom, plumped up the cushions on the settee and dusted the mantelpiece. It had been fairly easy, but when I went back up to my bedroom to get changed, I realised all I had done was shift the problem somewhere else. Eliza came in as I stared at the new chaos.

'You should take some of this stuff to the charity shop,' she said.

'If only I had the time.'

'It's right next to your café,' Eliza said. 'Just take one bag in each day. Jo and I could help you on Saturday.'

'If only it were that simple,' I said, knowing it all needed sorting out first and some of the stuff would have to be stored in the loft. The task just seemed too enormous. Then I remembered something Frank had said about each journey starting with one step.

At least my frantic attempt at clearing up had taken my mind off my date with Gordon, which I approached nervously as if I were a teenager going out with a boy for the first time. I spent ages meticulously applying my make-up and my new mascara and took even longer over my hair. Eliza had already organised some of the piles at one side of the room so that there was a little more space in the bedroom for me to stand and consider myself in the full-length mirror. I changed my outfit several times until I was confident I looked like the sort of person Gordon would like to be seen out with. I chose the red dress and the pointy shoes, only momentarily wondering whether Gordon might prefer the grey.

Eliza joined in with my excitement, thoughtfully considering my small selection of lipsticks and picking out a pair of hooped earrings which she told me would look 'very theatrical'. Jo had gone out to Scarlet's house but had promised to be back before seven when Gordon had arranged to pick me up. With ten minutes to go, I sensed that Jo was about to let me down, perhaps even setting out tō ruin my evening. In the same way she is trying to ruin my life, I found myself thinking, but quickly screwed up that thought and binned it to the back of my mind. At that time I was often ashamed of my own thoughts, which could churn guilt round in my head like dirty washing on fast spin.

I considered not phoning Scarlet at all but knew I had to and, as I tapped out the number, I realised any pleasure I might have that evening, any enjoyment, any spontaneity was almost completely dependent on this phone call. On Jo. She seemed to have total control over my emotions, my life, my destiny. I knew a good mother would put her daughter's needs first, but I nevertheless felt myself silently praying—or was that wishing? I could never tell the difference—that my daughter would walk through the door even as I dialled Scarlet's number.

'Jo's not here right now.'

I almost punched the air with relief. She must have left already.

'Jo's on her way,' I explained to Eliza. 'Will you be all right for five minutes? Perhaps I'd better wait until she gets here.'

But Eliza insisted on going next door to wait with our

neighbour, whose kitchen resembled a small cake shop and who doted on Eliza, cooing over her in the same tone she used with her five overweight cats.

Gordon arrived exactly on time and took me to a new Greek restaurant I had been dying to try ever since I heard Roger going on about it. Perhaps part of me hoped he would be there.

Lizzie, you look stunning. No, Alice is throwing up at the moment and has completely gone off sex so there seemed little point in her coming. Is this your new boy-friend? Well, I can't pretend I'm not jealous…

I scanned the restaurant but the only face I recognised was that of Mrs Marshall from Eliza's school. I waved heartily just in case she was the sort to spread rumours. The restaurant was on two floors and we were taken downstairs where the lights were dim and candles flickered on the tables despite it still being daylight outside. We were early and only two other tables were occupied, yet there was a cosy atmosphere and, as the tables were crammed closely together, I was glad of the lack of other diners. Greek music played in the background and pictures of ancient Greek monuments adorned the whitewashed walls.

We ordered our food quickly and started to talk. At first it seemed less like a date and more like a policy meeting or business networking because Gordon seemed intent on discussing the details of my café plans. Then he picked up on my unease as I shuffled in my seat, my mind distracted by thoughts of Jo, and he changed the subject.

'How are your daughters?' Gordon asked.

'Fine, just fine. Did I tell you about Eliza getting a place at Valentine Rose's?'

I then found myself doing most of the talking for whenever I asked Gordon about his life, he gave short, noncommittal answers. He was an excellent listener, I decided, and he made me feel important. As the evening rolled on, my anxiety about Jo eased into a dull, manageable ache, always there but no longer piercing into me like the unbearable screech of a dentist's drill. Pleasure had successfully anaesthetised the pain and the rest of the evening passed quickly and pleasantly.

When Gordon dropped me off at home, he kissed me on both cheeks but his eyes spoke of more to come.

'Coffee?' I asked, thinking about the hours I had spent preparing the lounge.

'I would come in but I've got a breakfast meeting in the morning,' he almost whispered. 'Still, once I've settled into my new job, you'll never get rid of me.'

I almost forgot to laugh but it didn't matter for we both knew this was the beginning of something. I made a firm decision not to ponder on what Jo would think. Not then. Not until I had savoured the moment and its aftertaste.

I waved Gordon off and swivelled round to see the house in total darkness. Not a single light was on, not even Jo's. I glanced at my watch. It was only a quarter past ten. A hundred questions poured into my mind, like buffalo stampeding, but there was really only one question—and one answer. For a moment, I didn't move.

It was the moment I had rehearsed over and over in my mind so many times. When Jo was younger, I would lose sight of her for a split second—on the beach, in the supermarket, at the playground. And in that split second I would rehearse my lines as a stunned parent making her heartfelt, emotional appeal on the television: 'If anyone has seen anything, however trivial…'

So many thoughts in that split second, but I had always tried to keep the thought of death out of my mind. This time I failed. I saw death as soon as I saw my neighbour running out of the house to reassure me that Eliza was tucked up in the spare bedroom. I saw death as I marched into the house, leaving my neighbour on the path, muttering details about hot chocolate and bedtime stories.

I searched the house, frantically flicking on light switches as I rushed around like a rat in a maze. I didn't even know what I was looking for—perhaps a note, perhaps a clue, perhaps even Jo herself. And all the time, that cruel cocktail of guilt and blame bubbled up inside me like an evil witch's brew. I blamed myself for going out with Gordon, I immersed myself in guilt for going out with Gordon. And I was sinking into deep, deep shame for even thinking about going out with Gordon when my daughter needed me to be there for her. I believed that I alone could have prevented her disappearance, and perhaps even her disorder. And that responsibility lay on me like a heavy coat on a hot day.

Suddenly the practical side of my mind overrode despair and I found myself robotically acting out a logical sequence of actions. First I phoned Jo's mobile.

'Hi, Jo. Not sure what's happened but I need to know you're safe. Can you call back—whatever time of the day or night. Please call. I love you. Whatever you've done. Not that you've… Just call, darling. Please.'

Then I phoned my neighbour.

'No, nothing's wrong. Just a misunderstanding with Jo. Teenagers, eh? You didn't by any chance see…? No, I thought not. Well thanks for having Eliza. No, no point in disturbing her now.'

I took a deep breath. I had to keep control. I couldn't afford to lose it now. I knew I had to do the big phone round next, make a list of all the friends and acquaintances she may have called and get my finger pressing those telephone digits. My anxiety pushed aside any feelings I had of being judged a bad parent, bad enough to lose a daughter. I just wanted her back and the bargaining with God started straight away—I would have done anything, given anything, just to know she was safe.

'George, Jo's gone missing again. Has she turned up there? No, you stay there in case she turns up. Yes. I'll let you know as soon as I hear anything.'

'Scarlet, sorry your mum had to wake you up. Have you any idea where she might be?'

'Hi, I know you haven't seen Jo for a while, I got your number from her address book. Well, if you hear anything…'

Please don't let it be Alice, please don't let it be Alice.

'Alice, can I speak to Roger please? It's personal… Hi, Roger, I'm sure it's nothing but Jo's gone walkabout again. Yes, I'm just going to call the police. No, you stay there just in case. I'll call you. Don't tell Alice. Because it's none of her bloody business, that's why.'

'Hi, Frank, I hope you don't mind, I didn't know who else to call.'

'Aren't you going to send out a patrol car or something? You don't seem to understand, my daughter is missing—anything could have happened. What do you mean—as soon as we have an officer available? I'm not reporting a leaky tap here, my daughter is missing. Missing!'

I knew that the police officer had heard it all before, night after night, week after week. Most missing teenagers reappear within twenty-four hours, he told me, and he had no reason to suspect that this story was going to be any different, anything other than routine. Perhaps that should have comforted me in some way but it didn't.

I stared at the drinks cupboard but the doorbell rang before I tossed my coin. It was Frank, and as soon as I saw him I burst into uncontrollable tears. He guided me into the sitting room like I was a blind woman and eased me down into the armchair. He perched on the edge of the chair, put his arm around me and drew out the rest of my tears with gentle, encouraging remarks.

'Let it all out', 'It's all right, Ellie', and even 'There, there'. Frank had resorted to the name he first knew me by, a life-time ago.

I cried for the absence of Jo, I cried out of fear and despera-tion and I cried over all that had gone before. This time I really cried, not just a few tears but endless, desperate sobbing. I had maintained such control over the previous few months and I sensed that all that was being swept away by an overwhelm-ing flood of emotion like I had never experienced before. I tried to speak but the sobbing strangled my words and Frank soothed me into believing that I had time, that talking could come later.

'Have you looked in Jo's room?' Frank asked softly.

'Maybe not properly,' I said.

So we made our way upstairs and reluctantly looked through her papers, her drawers, under her bed, in her cupboard. Frank switched on the computer but I had no password to access her email. I felt like an intruder into her soul, a thief of her mind as I read her stories, her lists, her diary even, looking for clues which might hint at her whereabouts but finding instead clues about her life, a life that existed beyond my guidance now. Jo had been busy growing up, and that process of maturation un-folded in the notebooks and journals I held in my hand.

I stood for a few moments staring at my daughter's diary,

reluctant to open it for fear of finding blame. Did she blame me, her mother, for all that had happened? Was I about to read the evidence here in her room where love, I thought, justified my intrusion? But I found no blame, only guilt. Guilt and blame are woven so tightly together that the two can never be untangled, so if Jo was feeling the guilt, who was activating the blame? I already knew, of course, but the words on the page screamed out a loud message.

I feel I'm letting Mum down... I don't want Mum to be upset about this... I'm going to prove to Mum that I can beat this... All this mixed in with angry comments like *What do they know anyway?* and *No one even tries to understand.*

Just when I thought the river had run its course, I cried again. I had cried for myself and now I cried for Jo and what she had been through.

'There's something that might be important here,' Frank said suddenly, holding a scrap of paper in his hand.

I snatched it off him for I was the mother, I was the one who should have found the clue: *I must find Lily. I will email the Buddhist centre and get her details. Then I will go to her.*

'Did she?' I snapped. 'Did she get Lily's details from you?'

'No, I didn't have any. Only the email address. I'd forgotten about it, about how she wanted to find Lily.'

'But she contacted you about it? Why the hell didn't you mention it before?'

I sank back down onto Jo's bed.

'I'm sorry, I'm uptight,' I apologised simply. 'Perhaps Jo's all right, just out there looking for Lily. Perhaps she's already found her. I'll send Lily an email. Perhaps Lily's already sent me one. And I'll phone her.'

A chink of optimism spurred me into frenzied activity,

first on the phone, where I was able to leave a gabbled message, then on the computer.

Dear Lily,
Jo has gone missing. We think she is looking for you. Please let me know as soon as you see her. Tel No. 729124. With kind regards
Lizzie Trounce

I looked at my message. It was positive. I felt so sure Jo would turn up that I was almost able to drown out my nagging doubts with optimism. But my optimism shone like a torch with an old battery, fading with every minute.

'You should try and get some sleep,' Frank suggested, but we both knew that was impossible as we tried to imagine Jo's thinking, tried to work out where she would have gone to find Lily. We were like detectives on a cheap TV programme.

We drew up a shortlist of therapy centres. We wrote down the details of the three Finnegan families in the telephone directory and tried ringing them but only got one muffled, irate response, and we surfed the net until dawn. The activity calmed me, gave me the focus I needed, and I even managed a cup of tea and a small piece of toast. I wanted to get out and check some of our leads as soon as possible but Frank sensibly suggested that the police would have the resources to do this more quickly. We phoned the station for the fifth time and this time we were told that they were on their way.

I sat numbly on the couch, staring at the wall in front of me, my mind exhausted with its all-night rehearsing of worst-case scenarios. Eventually the doorbell trilled through the house and I shuffled wearily into the hall, my expectations low.

I opened the door to a uniformed man and woman, more like a boy and girl really. I invited them in and they sat side by side on the couch, like a young couple meeting her parents for the first time. The policewoman introduced herself as Linda and her partner as Darren. It was clear that Linda was going to be doing most of the talking and, as if to confirm this, Darren reached into his pocket and pulled out a notepad and pen.

Darren had the last remnants of acne on his chin and his jet-black hair was cut short with a piece at the front that stood up like a tuft of grass. Linda removed her hat to reveal blonde hair pulled back into a neat bun, and then sat up very straight on the edge of my couch with her knees together as if she had been taught how to sit in an old-fashioned deportment class, but the slightly nasal Essex accent dispelled any such thoughts from my mind.

I gave them Jo's details and the photograph I had ready. They went through the motions and so did I.

'Has she ever run off before?'

'No, not really.'

'Have you checked with friends and family members?'

'Friends? Oh, yes, everyone.'

'Where did she like to hang out in the evenings?'

'She generally stayed at home.'

'Where was she when you last saw her?'

'At home.'

'Has she been upset about anything recently?'

'Well, she's a teenager, you know how it is.'

'But have there been any specific incidents, any family rows?'

'I explained all that. I gave you a list of therapy centres. And that name—Lily Finnegan. That's who to start with. I already told you.'

'If you could just explain one more time, Mrs Trounce.'

So I did. And this time I even said the words—'eating disorder'. This time I told it straight, barely flinching. I didn't bother to dampen it down with the language of good mother gone bad—'It's just a phase', 'You know how young girls are', 'She knew she had my full support'. But did she really know? If Jo had known that, really known that, then why did she feel the need to run away and look for Lily Finnegan?

'You've done really well, Mrs Trounce,' said the post-adolescent policewoman.

I had. I felt I had stripped myself naked and let them and Frank see me as I really am. The policewoman nodded the sympathetic nod of someone who has seen it all before and as they left, her colleague shut his notebook firmly. I wondered how long it would be before he opened it again, for the interview had been routine, repetitive and with no trace of the urgency it deserved.

Frank started making plans, practical plans and then carrying them out—getting Eliza ready for school, printing off more photos of Jo. While the printer groaned out its images, Eliza pulled on her school clothes and Frank made her a sandwich. I just stood there, like a maypole with dancers around me. Soon the door crashed shut, the echo of lace-ups on paving disappeared and still I stood. Numb.

Frank pressed a cup of tea into my hand and I drained it like a machine. Then the doorbell rang and Frank answered it. I was aware of Alice's brittle voice in the hallway and I felt even worse. Frank showed Alice and Dolly in.

'Shouldn't you be at work?' I asked automatically.

'We're here to help,' said Dolly. 'We would have been here earlier but apparently the world would have ended if lawyer-of-the-year here hadn't sent some vital emails and delivered some dull-looking document.'

'You've taken the day off work, Alice?' I must have sounded surprised.

'Of course. When I heard about Jo, I phoned the office straight away. I never even got ready for work, that's why I'm dressed like this.'

I looked at Alice in her pencil skirt and cream blouse and was hard pressed to see any difference from her usual work attire.

'She hasn't got her jacket on,' Dolly pointed out helpfully.

'I think Ellie and I should go out and try and find Jo while you two stay here in case she comes back,' Frank suggested.

Then the telephone rang again.

'Oh, hello, Gordon. Yes it was a lovely evening but I really can't talk right now. I have no idea when I'll be free again. I'm sorry, it's just that something's come up.'

Alice looked from the phone to Frank then back at the phone again. She looked at me in my creased red dress and smudged mascara and raised an eyebrow.

All the evidence put before me suggests that you are a brazen hussy.

'I'll have a very quick shower,' I said, and left Frank to write down mobile phone numbers for Alice and Dolly.

The cool shower rejuvenated me immediately and I washed quickly and efficiently. I pulled on an old long green skirt and loose collarless shirt, and decided my old granny boots would be ideal for pounding the streets. Something made me go into Jo's room and I saw on the bed a green cardigan she hardly ever wore. I sniffed it, held it to my cheek and put that on, too. I didn't stop to reapply make-up, just quickly brushed my teeth and tugged a comb through my wild hair. I glanced at the gypsy figure in the mirror, so different to the one who had gone out with Gordon the night before, and hurried downstairs to Frank.

Dolly was sitting in front of the television, eating a bag of crisps, and Alice was trying to collect magazines together and arrange them on the coffee-table. I had no choice but to leave them to it.

As Frank and I were about to get into his car, we saw Scarlet sprinting up the road. Her cheeks lived up to her name as she leant against the car door, gasping for breath.

'Jo's texted me, she's fine right now, and the dinner lady saw her coming out of the library this morning.'

I silently thanked God, and Buddha and Mohammed for good measure, as well as any passing angels and even fate itself. For I knew that at nine o'clock that morning Jo had been alive and was almost certainly still alive, and the sun was parting the early clouds, and people were spinning their way into their daily routines. It was the night-time that was frightening, darkness where the danger lurked, and safety for your children came with the dawn.

'Thanks, Scarlet, I could hug you.' And I did.

'I'd better get back to school.'

I phoned the police with the latest information while Frank drove. As we made our way along the high street, I scrutinised every face on the pavement, momentarily seeing Jo in any young girl who had her head bent down in an adolescent stoop. She was everywhere and nowhere.

'Slow down, I can't see. That might have been her going into Dorothy Perkins. Can you slow down a bit more?'

By now we were crawling along the main street looking like a funeral cortège in a Nissan Micra. Cars behind us were honking their horns and pedestrians were staring through the car windows to see who these dodgy kerb crawlers were.

'We're from the council,' I shouted out to one group of on-lookers, which seemed to satisfy them.

'Just tell them the truth,' Frank said, placing the pile of photos on my lap. And soon we had most of the town on the look out for Jo.

Eventually we parked and strode purposefully into the library.

'You must have seen her, she was spotted coming out of the library this morning. You must have a record of who logged on to the computers. And surely you've got closed-circuit TV cameras? Don't kids nick books from the library any more? I know we did.'

In contrast, Frank spoke slowly and thoughtfully and was able to glean that Jo had taken out two items of fiction early that morning, both books of Irish folk tales. My spirits lifted and any doubts I had about the accuracy of the morning's sighting melted away. I could smell optimism in the air.

We decided to tackle the therapy centres on foot, which we did like despondent salesmen unable to get a hit. Nobody had heard of Lily but we did discover that we were following in the footsteps of Jo as time and again we heard that someone else had made the same enquiry earlier.

Then we called round to an address listed in the telephone directory as L. Finnegan, although the number hadn't matched Lily's.

'Do I look like a bleeding Lily?' seethed a huge dark-haired man with a tattoo across his cheek who turned out to be called Len.

'You're the second lot who have accused me of being a Lily. Now sling your hook. Just because my mate Jim has moved in doesn't mean I want to be known as Lily.' His voice faded as he sensed we did not require this information.

'Now clear off,' he added, as he pushed his hair behind one ear and slammed the door shut.

'You've got to laugh,' I said to Frank as we hurried back up the path. And we did—laugh, that is. It wasn't really all that funny but laughter is more than a response to something comical. It's a release, an outpouring of so many emotions including, ironically, sadness. I realised then that what I always said was true—you really do have to laugh. To survive.

Frank and I had a gut-aching, back-bending, raucous laugh as we left Len's house. I leant against him as my giggling nearly knocked me off balance and Frank tipped his head back and let out an uninhibited roar into the hazy, traffic-fumed air. Drunk with humour, we wove our way along the pavement, propping each other up, tripping over our own feet and pausing every now and then to catch our breath. Happiness can creep up on you in the most unlikely circumstances.

With everything to hope for, we made our way back home where I was greeted by an immaculate-looking kitchen.

'I wanted to do something to help,' said Alice. 'I don't usually do housework—we have a cleaner—but I thought I could put my organisational skills to good use.'

I looked more closely and saw that nothing was actually any cleaner but the plants had been placed in height order along the window-sill and everything had been tidied away somewhere or other.

'I told her not to stick her nose in,' said Dolly, 'but don't worry, I made sure she didn't go upstairs and snoop through your personal stuff.'

'Mother, you know I would never do anything like that,' said Alice, sounding as though she would have been prepared to take an oath on the bible.

'You read Roger's diary. And you check his suits for credit-card slips. Still, he had an affair with you so I expect he'll do it again.'

Alice had the decency to look embarrassed but she put up a solid legal argument.

'You know perfectly well that Roger and I were just acquaintances to begin with. I have proof of staying in separate rooms when we had to attend the same business conference,' she said, and hastily changed the subject.

'There are three messages, which I've written down on this notepad. They're all from someone called Gordon. I took the liberty of explaining the situation and Gordon volunteered to help, although he had to consult his diary. By the third telephone call he realised that he had an urgent pre-scheduled appointment but he asked if you might contact him at your earliest convenience.'

'I'm sure he didn't say "at your earliest convenience",' said Dolly.

'Actually, that's exactly what he said. In fact, he sounded like a solid, reliable gentleman.'

Frank saw Alice and Dolly off while I rushed upstairs to check the emails. I thought there might be something from Scarlet or Lily, or even someone we had met that day. But it was even better and I let out a gasp of relief as soon as I saw Jo's name on the list. My fingers fumbled clumsily over the keyboard as I frantically tried to open the message. In my

hurry I opened an old message and had to sit back, take a deep
breath and start again, trying to maintain control.

I'm fine. Lily has made me realise a lot of stuff. First, you
were probably worried. So sorry. Second, I knew the answer lay with Lily. It did. I'm going to be fine now I've
found Lily. I just need a couple more days. Lily is looking after me so I'm OK. Don't worry about me, worry
about yourself. I love you.
Jo

   Salt water stung my already sore eyes. Jo had found Lily
and these were the first positive words I had heard from her
in a long time. I called Frank up to show him the message.
   'I can't thank you enough for today, Frank.'
   'That's OK, Ellie, I'm just so pleased that Jo's safe. I'm
going now, but I'll ring you later. I think you've learnt a lot
about life and about yourself today.'
   Then he looked back at the message on the screen.
   '"Worry about yourself",' Frank quoted. 'That's an interesting line.'
   'Not really. She's just trying to reassure me.'
   'I think she's suggesting you both need to make changes,'
Frank observed. 'Maybe the idea came from Lily herself.'
   I smiled. The idea that Lily Finnegan had an interest in my
welfare made me feel warm and comfortable. Suddenly I felt
eight years old again on that rainy night when my grandmother had tucked me up in bed with a steaming mug of hot
chocolate. That last night of real childhood before my mother
died. Somehow, everything was connected.

TWELVE

The Legend of Lily Finnegan

IT WAS told in years gone by that the wisest of the wisest women of Ireland lived at the top of Purple Mountain in an old, old cottage enveloped by Irish mountain mist which could only be seen by those bringing questions they could not answer by themselves.

From the very top of Purple Mountain, so called because of the acres and acres of heather, the wisest of the wisest, Lily Finnegan, could see everywhere and everyone below her. She could even see the thoughts of the folk beneath, which floated out of their minds up and up and up to the very top of Purple Mountain. And when these thoughts and hopes and dreams floated up, Lily would collect them and store them in little glass bottles which she kept on shelves in the hay barn beside her old, old cottage.

Every now and then, she would take down some of the glass bottles and look at some of the thoughts and hopes and dreams of the folk in the valleys below and she would stir in a spoonful of truth before sending them back down the mountainside to seek out the very places they came from. For that is how your dreams come true.

Now this tale concerns young Shona O'Shea, who had thoughts and hopes and dreams in abundance, so many that Lily Finnegan had the largest glass bottle of all for Shona O'Shea, but despite the abundance of Shona's hopes and dreams, none of them ever came true.

So it was that Shona O'Shea and her young sister walked through the village to the mountain pass and set off on a journey to the top of Purple Mountain, seeking Lily Finnegan. They planned to ask her what poison had fallen into their hopes and dreams, although Shona's sister kept very quiet, for had not some of her dreams already come true? And had she not already discovered that everything comes to those who wait?

I liked writing in the library. I could concentrate, kind of. But my mind wandered off in the middle of my story, like it does. Sometimes I don't even know what I'm thinking about, but sometimes I do. Like then. Right then I was thinking about journeys—the journey in the Irish folk tale and the journey Lily, the real Lily, had talked about. Before she dumped me.

Most of my questions began with why. Not who or what or when or where. Always why. I remembered that Lily Finnegan had told me to go on a journey or write about a journey, but I couldn't be sure which. She was fading away. Everything was fading away. And why would I need to write about a journey anyway? What had that got to do with anything? And why, why, why had she deserted me? Then I realised my questions were linked.

When you go on a journey, you leave stuff behind. You leave people behind, possessions behind, and sometimes your old life. I was only in the library, only two miles from home, but I had left everything behind. And everyone. Including part of me. The part that was there in my house, with my family. The part of me that was with my friends. The part of me that was on show to the world. On your own, you're different. On my own, I'm different. Maybe I'm more real on my own. Honest. No one to pretend to. No one to impress. No one to wind up. No one to compare myself to.

So I'd left my mother and sister and Scarlet and Dad and Lily behind. And I was in the library. The house of answers. It was all making sense. Or something. Then I emailed my mum.

I loved the library. I always have. Any library in any town feels familiar, like I've been there before. Like déjà vu. I love thinking of how many words make up a library. I love thinking of all that wisdom, all that creative stuff.

Most of all I love the order, the predictability, the organisation. Rows and rows of books in sections. Sections labelled History, Psychology, Travel and all that. Each section in alphabetical order of author, or in subsections of countries or medical conditions or historical periods. Or whatever. Each book with a number and a second number. Like 101.23 or 97.4. Like a maths test, where there are questions and answers. One answer to every question. You know where you are in a library. The books have in them what it says on the cover. Usually. And they are catalogued. Catalogued on the computer, and in filing cabinets at the back of the library. And the library has its own language. Like another planet or something. Where the magazine racks are, it says Periodicals. Like there should be tampons. Where you borrow the books, it says Checking Out. Like you're sussing the guys.

Best of all, there is no food or drink allowed in the library.

No one to say, 'Oh, go on,' no one to judge when you don't take a biscuit. You can't have food in a library. Food is messy and disordered and unpredictable. It doesn't come in sections, it all meshes together so you don't know what's what. So, no food or drink. Just words to eat, facts to digest, ideas to consume.

I remember when I was little, I had a plate in three sections. A fish finger would be in one section, some peas in another, and a little potato in the third. All neat and tidy and ordered. That's how it would be in a library if they served food there.

They had books about food. Cookery books, books about food from different countries, books on growing food, the history of food—everything. They had books about anorexia, bulimia, teenage problems. The questions were in these books. The answers were in these books. But I didn't want to read them. Not then. Not yet. I wanted to write.

The lady at the desk gave me some more paper and a pen, and a warm smile. She smiled because she worked here, with books. She had walls of books all around her. She was safe. And she smiled because I was in the library every day. Looking at books. Writing. Doing stuff she approved of. I looked at her thin hips, her flat chest. She wouldn't approve of eating in the library.

'Are you still writing?' she asked. She was still smiling.

'Yeah.'

'Something interesting?'

'Yeah. The legend of Lily Finnegan.'

'What's that, then? A story?'

'Yes. It's written in the style of an Irish legend.'

'That's really interesting. What made you write that?'

I thought about how I had always liked writing. And how I got into writing lists. Lily had moved me on somehow and there

I was making up an Irish folk tale. Weird. Writing was like puking up over the page or taking a load of laxatives. An emptying out. Getting stuff out of you but in disguise. Or something like that. I explained to the librarian about the legend.

'Someone told me about Lily Finnegan.'

'Lily Finnegan? You mean…?'

'Yes, an Irish woman from some sort of legend. Maybe you've heard of her, only I couldn't find any reference to it in your library. So I thought I would make it up myself. I don't know why really.'

'There was a Lily Finnegan who worked here, although, come to think of it, that might have been Lily Finlay.'

I thought about that. It didn't seem right. Lily Finnegan wasn't the sort of name you forgot.

Then the librarian said, 'I'm sure if there had been a legend, we'd have known about it here.'

'That's what I thought.'

'Can I read it?'

Like showing someone your puke, your shit, I thought.

'I suppose so.'

The librarian read it and she still smiled. I didn't mind her reading it. I'd sent stuff to Lily and she must have read it. But for some reason I was nervous. Like the librarian was an examiner or something. But I didn't mind.

'It's good,' she said. 'It's the right style, too, for an Irish legend. How's it going to end?'

'I don't know yet. Well, I'm not sure.'

'It engages the reader, makes you want to know what's going to happen.'

'Yes. Yes, it does.'

Then suddenly I didn't know what to say to the librarian.

That happens sometimes. I can talk to someone and then suddenly I feel embarrassed, worried I might say the wrong thing. But I wanted to find Lily so I took a deep breath. I made myself say it.

'Can you find out, do you think, if her name was Lily Finnegan—the woman who used to work here? You see, I'm trying to find someone with that name. It's someone I know about. From the Internet.'

The librarian said, 'Sure, no problem. I'll ask Megan—she's worked here for years.' So it was all right. Asking her was all right. If you don't ask, you don't get. I know that now but I still don't always ask.

Shona O'Shea and her sister walked along the narrow mossy path which lay in the shadow of Purple Mountain. They turned onto the mountain track which had become overgrown with misuse. At first, they had to fight their way through the undergrowth, but soon the path became easier to follow and cut across the heather like a sandbank in the ocean. The mountain track zig-zagged through the purple but was nevertheless steep and they climbed it slowly and arduously.

When they reached the first of the small lakes, they stopped again. Shona stared into the glassy surface of the deep blue water.

'Where is the top of this mountain?' she sighed.

She looked into the lake and saw the mountaintop shimmering in front of her. So Shona knew they were on the right track and could reassure her sister who needed no reassurance.

When they reached the second of the small lakes, they

stopped and stood beside it. Shona stared into the glassy surface of the deep blue water.

'Will we ever get there?' she sighed.

She looked into the lake and once more saw the mountaintop shimmering in front of her. And her face, staring right back at her from the top of the mountain. So Shona knew they were on the right track and that they would get there. She reassured her sister who needed no reassurance.

The librarian came back and said it was true—Lily Finnegan used to work there, but she left. She must have left to train as a therapist, I thought. But I didn't say it.

'I remember seeing pictures of her retirement party,' said the librarian.

Retirement? That was all wrong. Lily Finnegan was too young. Young but experienced, youthful but wise, cool but with some authority. She wore deep purples and mauves, the flowing clothes of the eccentric and psychic. I knew what she was like. Her picture had hung in my mind for weeks.

'I don't think it's the same Lily Finnegan,' I said firmly, 'not the one who's been emailing me.'

'Oh, it isn't,' the librarian said. 'Megan thinks she died about six years ago.' I was at a crossroads or a T-junction or something. No, a roundabout. A roundabout with roads spiking out in different directions. One signpost told me that this was another Lily, another signpost told me that Megan was misinformed, another told me that I was living in some sort of ghost story. Or was it a case of stolen identity? Or perhaps it didn't really matter one way or the other.

'It really doesn't matter one way or the other,' I said. Then I burst into tears.

I cried because someone who had loved books had died. I cried because someone called Lily Finnegan had died. I cried from confusion and doubt and hope and despair. And I cried from not knowing. I was in the house of answers and I knew nothing.

The librarian eased me out of the chair and steered me towards her office at the back, then she made me a cup of coffee. She didn't ask questions. She didn't expect anything. So I talked.

'I've been sleeping in your library. My mum knows I'm safe—she thinks I'm with Lily Finnegan. Well, I am in a way. She's always kind of there in the background. I'm talking about her, writing about her, thinking about her. You see, she used to email me. About not eating properly. No, not about that at all. About life. About what I want. I had to email her back and it helped. It really helped, putting it into words without having to say it. Then she told me to go on a journey and write about it. And when she abandoned me, I tried to find her. I'm still trying to find her, but I'm stuck. Writing it down isn't really enough, is it? And I'm ready to talk now, I'm really ready to talk.'

'I think you probably are.'

'Sorry, am I going on?'

'Don't apologise. Never apologise for who you are. Be yourself and you've got nothing to be sorry about.'

I started to cry again. I don't know why. I used to cry when people were horrible to me at school. But I was crying because someone was being nice to me. Weird.

'I've been watching you,' the librarian said. 'I've seen you writing away there and looking at all the books. Not just looking at them, being absorbed in them. The way you hold them,

I can tell you know how precious they are, how important. Sorry, I must sound a bit daft.'

'Don't apologise for who you are,' I said, and we laughed.

We laughed like I used to with Scarlet at school—you know—when we were laughing in assembly or something. Crying and laughing are like the same thing when you think about it—letting out how you feel really loudly, really obviously, so everyone can see.

'Don't knock writing therapy,' she said. 'All these writers of all these books—why do you think they wrote them? Not to make money, not to be famous. It's their therapy, that's all. Writers bleed their lives all over the pages, believe me.'

And I did.

'You should go home,' she said, 'Sort things out.'

'When I've finished my coffee,' I said, 'And when I've finished my journey.'

When they reached the third lake, Shona stared into the glassy surface of the deep blue water and sighed.

'Who will we see when we reach the top?' she asked.

She looked into the lake and saw the mountaintop shimmering in front of her. And her face smiling back at her, right there on top of the mountain. She stared and stared but she could only see herself.

'There's no one at the top of Purple Mountain, look in the lake,' she told her sister who had no need to look.

I showed it to the librarian.

'It's too simple,' I said.

'Life is simple,' said the librarian. 'Simple but not easy.'

* * *

I went and bought chips and then I went home. Was that when I discovered I could eat on my own? I spent ages in the shop, sprinkling on the salt and splashing on the vinegar. Then I walked to the canal and sat down on a bench. I spread the salt around with my finger. Then I shook the bag of chips so they were just right. I thought they might make me fat. But I planned to walk home briskly along the canal path. Jog even. Eating always comes with guilt but the shame had gone. I enjoyed eating the chips—the sting of the vinegar on my throat, the soft warm potato bursting out of the crisp outer layer. It was the texture I liked more than the taste. And the comfort of something hot going inside. Like putting on a duffel coat in the snow. Ignore the guilt, that's the best thing. On your own you eat without judgement. You eat to please yourself. You throw away the bits you don't want. Everyone should eat on their own.

The librarian had liked me. She hadn't told me off for sleeping in her library. She accepted me. When someone accepts you and likes you, you can like yourself. Maybe I had read too many of those self-help books in the library. My head was full of 'Accept yourself', 'Love yourself', 'Be yourself', 'Live your own life'. So I went home to live my own life. I would accept myself and be myself and eat when I wanted to. Simple. But not easy.

'Jo, thank God you're all right. It's so lovely to see you, darling.' The creases on my mother's forehead disappeared. 'There's some soup on the stove.'

I went to my room and began typing out my story for when Lily came back. Mum came to my room with questions on her lips. But she wanted the answers without having to ask the questions. She sat on the bed and made a statement instead.

'You saw Lily.'

'She works in the library.'

'The library?'

'Yes.'

'I expect she was a great help.'

'Yes.'

She knew I was lying but she let me lie. I thought about Mum. She wanted to help. She just didn't know how.

'Everything's going to be all right now,' I told her. 'I'm taking small steps on a long journey.'

More from one of those books.

'I just wanted to tell you,' she said awkwardly, 'that I'm not going to see Gordon any more. And I might put the café on hold for a bit.'

Real martyrs kill themselves for a cause. They don't just slash their wrists and let you watch.

Had I ever been totally honest with Mum? I remember when I was five and she said I was tall and elegant and that I'd make a good dancer. Right, like dancers are all tall. Crap. Dancers are petite and fragile. And anorexic. Something in common, then. Anyway, I told her I liked dancing. I don't know why. It seemed the right thing to say. That's how I ended up at dancing classes. Until Eliza got better than me.

I got loads of positives for saying what she wanted to hear—'I like school', 'I like the cardigans you buy me', 'I want to be a doctor', 'I've eaten in town'. It was easy to make Mum happy—just lie. Soon I'd forgotten what I really did like. Like those actors in the soaps on telly. After a few years they turn into their characters.

I had been honest with Lily. Honesty by email is pretty easy. I was honest with the librarian. I think I'd been honest with Scarlet. Perhaps you can only be honest with people who are honest back.

'I want you to go ahead with your café,' I said honestly.

'Jo, it's not important. At the moment, I need to give you more time. I—'

'No, don't. You just make me feel so fucking guilty when you do this.'

She didn't flinch at the swearing. But she bristled at the criticism.

'I want to be honest with you, Jo.' It was catching. 'I want to do what's right for you but I always seem to get it so wrong. Of course I want to go ahead with the café but not if it means you won't eat.'

'Do what you want,' I snapped.

What was the connection between opening a café and me not eating? What was the connection between food and getting my life back from my mother? What was the connection between the librarian and Lily Finnegan?

I carried on typing up my story. I changed some words as I did it. Thought of better ones, better ways of saying the same thing. It was like pottery or something. No, sculpture—it was like sculpture. I was crafting my story into the shape I wanted. And I was immersed in my craft. Totally. I didn't hear Eliza playing music in her room. Not really. I knew Mum was making sandwiches in the kitchen, but I wasn't conscious of it. There was no past and no future. There was no envy or guilt or disappointment. There was no eating disorder. There was only writing. Not writing like your fingers bouncing off the keyboard, not writing like doing an essay for your teacher or jotting down a letter or note for someone else. It was deep writing, deep as your soul. Writing with total control of your mind and body. Writing by being there. In that moment. For yourself and nobody else.

This was being alive. If you were drowning, then nothing else would matter except getting to the surface. If you knew you couldn't drown, you'd see the fish, the coral, the beauty of it all.

Then I found myself leaning closer to the screen. Like I was myopic or something. I hadn't realised it was getting dark. I switched on the lamp and illuminated my thoughts. I looked at my clock, checked it against my watch. Nine o'clock, somehow it was nine o'clock. No wonder I was hungry.

The next day Scarlet came round. She gave me a huge hug.

'I was so worried about you,' she said. 'Perhaps you only know how much you love someone when they disappear. Come here, give me another hug. We've got some catching up to do.'

It was like I'd been gone a year or something. I realised that I'd missed Scarlet, too. Everything was easy with Scarlet. No pressure. Only a tiny bit of pretence.

'Did you find Lily?' she asked.

'Only a dead one,' I replied.

'How's the eating going?'

The only person who ever asked.

'I'm eating again but only on my own.'

'That's cool.'

Simple, and every now and then easy as well.

'What are you going to do now?'

'Try and send my story to Lily, I suppose.'

'Is it bouncing back?'

'I haven't tried yet—I want to be sure. Before I try I have to be sure it will go through. I couldn't stand it if it didn't get through.'

Scarlet looked at me carefully and said, 'Feel the fear and do it anyway.' She goes to the library, too.

'Do you want any books or stuff from school?' Scarlet asked. 'Or are you just going to wait until next September?'

'I'm changing my subjects,' I told her. 'I'm going to do history, English and philosophy.'

'When did you decide that?'

'Just now.'

'I thought you wanted to be a doctor?'

'No, a writer.'

'That's cool, really cool.'

'Let's put some pizza in the microwave.'

We did. And I found I could eat with Scarlet.

Then life was pretty good. No school, no pressure. No one talking about soup on the stove, no one minding what I did. I was free. Sometimes I went out. For the whole day. I even stayed another night in the library. I went to the canal. I walked around town. I sat in the cinema. I watched runners sweating round the track at the stadium. Whatever I wanted. I never told Mum where I was. She didn't ask. She struggled not to ask. Looked like someone was gripping her round the throat sometimes. She was all contorted, like a murder victim. But she didn't ask. I was in control.

Mum carried on looking at premises for her café. Because I said she could. She didn't see Gordon. I hadn't given permission for that. I might do later, I thought. It was up to me.

Eliza didn't bother much with school. She was waiting to

go to Valentine Rose's or whatever it was called. That's all she thought about. She went on and on about it. She didn't care what I thought. She didn't care where I was. She was obsessed with herself.

'Ninety-seven per cent of performers are unemployed,' I told her.

'Then I shall be one of the two per cent.'

'Three per cent,' I corrected her. I may have sneered.

'I want you to be in the front row at my opening night on Broadway,' she told me.

'Why?'

'Because you're my sister.'

I never knew whether to love Eliza or hate her. I usually did both. I sometimes cooked pizza for Eliza. Once I brought her some chips back from town. I don't know if it was because I loved her or because I wanted her to be fat.

The only thing I couldn't do was make Lily Finnegan reply to my emails. So I didn't send any. I thought there might be a way to make her reply.

If this bounces back I shall kill myself.

If this bounces back I shall find you and...

If this bounces back I shall stop eating again.

I didn't know if she was sending stuff back or if there was something wrong with her email. If it was her email, it would be mended by now, I thought, so now I'll know.

In the end, I sent it and I put, *Please read my story about a journey.* That's all. No provisos.

If the next band to come on the radio is American, she'll read it.

If my 10p lands heads up, she'll read it.

If I throw my pen and it lands on the window-sill, she'll read it.

It didn't bounce back. But she didn't reply either. But, then, I hadn't asked for a reply. You get what you ask for. At least my pen had landed on the window-sill. Then it occurred to me: because of Lily's connection with Frank, I had made assumptions. I just assumed she lived in our area. Perhaps she didn't. Perhaps she didn't even live in our country. Perhaps she flew over when the time was right. There was something American about her. Or even Irish. An American of Irish descent.

Something had happened to me when I ran away. Something good. Something had happened to Mum, too. There were changes. There was a shift forward. I was like a car in a traffic jam. Stop, start, stop, start. But I hadn't found out much about Lily Finnegan on my journey. That journey lay ahead. I hadn't really asked her anything about herself. I had asked to meet her but I hadn't asked her where she lived or anything. If she was local. Or young. Or old. Or short. Or tall. Nothing. And all I had to do was ask. I was like Mum—wanting answers without the questions. My story hadn't bounced back. She was reading it. She would reply, I knew. Then I could ask her what I needed to know.

I had to meet her soon, I thought. I would tell her about running away to find her. Once she knew how desperate I was, she would come. I understood now, about the writing coming first. And the talking to other people—Scarlet, Frank, the librarian. And very nearly Mum. Now I knew the next step was to talk to Lily. Face to face. She would understand that, surely she would understand that. I had to be patient. Small steps. I had to get on with the rest of my life while I waited to meet Lily in the flesh. So I decided to start my novel. I got a pen and some paper and wrote some character sketches.

Josephine

Beautiful and confident. Heads turn when she walks into the room. She loves her job in the book shop. She is great with children and they flock there to hear her read stories. She has always been intuitive and now she learns that she is psychic. She has suppressed her psychic powers but now wants to use them for the good of mankind. She has long, dark hair, large brown eyes. She is very slim. Like a model.

I felt excited. I felt driven. My life had meaning. I had control over everything. Nothing could go wrong now, I thought. When Lily Finnegan replied, I could tell her I was better. I didn't want anything to change. Then Dad phoned.

'Great news, you have a little sister. We've called her Lily.'

I nearly said 'Congratulations' like I should have. Like I would have.

'You can't call her Lily,' I said instead.

'Well, we have, after Alice's grandmother. You must come and see her.'

'Who? Alice's grandmother?'

'Don't be daft, Jo. Please come and see your sister. And me—I want to see you, Jo.'

'Not if she's called Lily—it's the wrong name.'

There was a silence. I thought he'd put the phone down for a minute.

'I'll always love you, Jo, you'll always be special. Nothing's changed.'

'Then prove it and change the baby's name.'

'Oh, grow up, Jo.'

But I didn't want to grow up. And I would do anything to stop myself from doing so.

THIRTEEN

ALTHOUGH I knew deep inside that there had been some progress with Jo, I still couldn't settle my mind because it was all moving far too slowly for me. I desperately wanted the old Jo back right now, as if nothing had happened. I wanted her to wake up one morning, tell me she was better and tuck into a big bowl of cornflakes. I wanted to be sitting in some space in the future, looking back and laughing about Jo's 'little hiccup' that she went through as part of growing up, like flu or chickenpox or tonsillitis—occasions when I had nursed Jo back to health, when it had seemed endless but where a bright sunny day arrived when it was all over and very soon forgotten. And I wanted to see Lily Finnegan in the flesh, touch her hand and feel the trust that could not be properly formed with such a vague, unknown person who was just a name on a computer, a recorded voice on a telephone.

I knew, of course, that Jo had not met Lily when she had escaped into town. But I had let it go. That phrase 'let go' seemed to be shouting at me from every corner, everywhere I went. It was like one of those summer songs that you hear every time you switch on the radio or the TV or go into a café or a shop, and which follows you on holiday wherever you are in the world. Everyone I spoke to seemed to be telling me to let go—Dolly, Alice and, especially, Frank. I would open a newspaper and see those two words staring back at me; I would walk down the high street and hear them as part of a stranger's conversation. It was as if the universe was shouting 'let go' to me until eventually I heard, and knew what it meant. I understood. In order to get close to Jo again, I had to cut the rope and let go. Yet still I tried to cling on to that rope. Maybe, I thought, I didn't need to know who Lily Finnegan was, but I sensed that if I knew more, the letting go would be easier.

Frank knew how much I yearned for more information, information to reassure me that I had taken the right path, so he rang me one day because he had heard something—not much, but something.

'Lily Finnegan's name came up today,' he said.

'How? When? Where is she?'

'Whoa, hold on. I don't know that much. One of my Buddhist friends has just come back from India. She was telling me that it had been a difficult decision to go because her sister had been struggling since suddenly becoming a widow three years previously. It seems the grief process was taking a long time and her sister was slipping into deep depression—'

'So her sister saw Lily Finnegan,' I interrupted. 'Can I speak to her? Can she tell me where she is?'

'Like Jo, she's been doing most of the communication by email but they did meet once. I think it was in a café.'

'Lily lives around here, then?'

'Yes, she does. I don't know any more than that, I'm afraid, but leave it with me and I'll see what I can find out.'

'Thank you, Frank, you're an angel.'

'In the meantime, get on with your life. Do something for *you* every day.'

But information was on my mind, and I realised that not only did I need to know more about Lily, I needed to know more about eating disorders. The Internet had given me a range of highly personal, intimate, heart-wrenching stories but all they had taught me was that eating disorders came in more shapes and sizes than a woman's shoe. The book Alice had given me—*The Anorexic Child*—had been well intentioned but was, in fact, a series of articles from psychiatric journals which were about as easy to follow as a tax form translated into Latin.

I decided to look for a layman's book on the subject, written for parents, but when I got to the book shop, I felt that stigma about eating disorders creeping into my mind. The more I learnt about anorexia, the more I realised how ignorant the general public was, how ignorant I had been. It was complex, with layers of causes all interwoven and firing off each other. I was just beginning to understand that I was not to blame but I was aware that others would not have that understanding. I stared at the book I wanted and looked around the shop nervously. For a moment I wondered whether to choose two other unrelated books and sandwich my chosen one between them. Then I thought about Dolly and I realised how ridiculously self-conscious I was being, so in the end I walked up to the cashier, quite openly holding up *Helping Your Teenager With An Eating Disorder* for all to see. Why should I care what ridiculous judgements people made?

'I'm studying to be a psychotherapist,' I explained to the cashier. 'This is one of our set texts.'

I then ran so quickly for the door that I fell over my feet and my bags went skimming across the floor. A member of staff helped me to my feet and collected my things, glancing at the book's title as she dropped it back into the bag.

'It's for a friend,' I explained.

'I thought it was for your studies,' said a familiar voice, and I looked up to see it was the cashier who had come to my rescue.

As I left the shop, at least I managed to laugh at myself. But I knew I still had a lot to let go of.

I read the book during quiet periods at work. At first I hid it behind the covers of Delia Smith's cookery course then, gradually, I let go of the shame that came from blaming myself and read it openly, even discussing it a little with Trish. I soaked up every word, but the book seemed to list all the things I had already done wrong in alphabetical order, and the self-blame started to surface again. I half expected a large hand to slide out of the book and point an accusing finger at me. There was one interesting chapter that considered the parents of the eating disordered teenager, suggesting that even their history might have some relevance. I immediately thought about my own mother and began to see patterns in the chaos.

When Jo's problems had set in, it had been the first time I had really wanted my mother since I was a child. She would have loved and supported me through all the anxiety and bewilderment. She would have known what to do, and I desperately wished she could have been there with us. But all I had was a memory. Losing her when I was eight years old meant that by the time I was an adult, not having a mother was a way of life, like being tall or not suiting yellow. I thought of her at life-changing events—my wedding, the births of my children and so on—but only with a passing regret. Jo's eating disorder probably counted as a life-changing event, but this time the regret was delivered in lorryloads. I wished she was with me and all I could do was look back, remember and imagine.

My mother used to read me childhood poems every night at bedtime—Walter de la Mare, Robert Louis Stevenson, A. A. Milne. She was always there for me, cooking my favourite meal of sausage and mash, taking me to the park on my red bicycle, teaching me how to read *Peter and Jane*.

I remember having an argument at school with my best friend, who vowed she would never speak to me again. I rushed home, tears like rain, sobbing so hard that I couldn't get the words out. Mummy sat me down and gave me a clean white handkerchief, a raspberry milkshake and time to talk about the disaster. Her words soothed, reassured and explained gently how the world of friendship worked. That was the essence of good motherhood—making everything better—and she never let me down.

How could I live up to such sainthood? It was like trying to model my parenting skills on that perfectly meek and gentle Mother Mary whose immaculate parenting was destined to produce a perfect offspring. Whenever I let Jo down, I sensed a bitter taste of failure. I tried to explain all this to Frank.

'Jo's eating disorder is not your fault,' Frank reassured me.

'But I haven't exactly handled it very well. In fact, I've done everything wrong,' I said, waving my new book in the air. 'I've been trying to coax her into eating, I've been nervous around food, I've insisted on knowing everything she's eaten that day—you name it, I've done it wrong.'

Frank smiled sympathetically then slowly leaned over the table and gently eased the book out of my hand. He walked across to the bin and threw it in.

'You are the expert on your child,' he said, 'and she's getting gradually better. So what's the point of slapping yourself in the face over it?'

'But what if it comes back again?'

'Then you'll deal with it. Why should you have known exactly how to handle it? You're not a trained clinical psychologist. But you've learnt a lot and will be able to cope better and better. And don't forget, this is the first real hiccup you've had with Jo. You've been a great mum.'

I tried digesting this for a moment, then asked, 'Did you find out any more about Lily?'

'Only that they used to meet in the Gallery Café. Apparently Lily knew the owner and they used to give her a quiet corner if she needed to meet clients informally.'

'Brilliant,' I said.

'I think it was a while ago, Ellie,' said Frank, and looked at me doubtfully.

I went straight to the Gallery Café on my way home, half expecting to see Lily herself dishing out advice along with the cappuccinos and cakes. I rather resented paying for a coffee when it was a perk in my job all day, but I felt I had to buy something in order to interrogate the staff. Most of the boys and girls behind the counter appeared too young to have an employment history there, but an older lady said she remembered a regular customer who was a therapist.

'Gary and Noreen, who used to own this place, knew her. I think Noreen might have been her sister or something. She used to sit over there. She was quite old, I think, but I remember her eyes, her lovely face. There was something about her—you couldn't take your eyes off her. She was like a magnet.'

I knew that was her.

'Does she still come in?' I asked.

'Not since Gary and Noreen left. They went up to Birmingham.'

Easy, I thought, all I needed was a surname and a telephone directory.

'What was their surname?' I asked, rummaging in my bag for a pencil.

'Smith.'

'Oh.'

I put the pencil away again. 'Do you know what happened to Lily, the therapist?'

'No idea.'

Someone behind me who was waiting to place an order coughed meaningfully and I had to accept that this was a dead end. I slumped down at one of the tables and sipped my coffee, staring out at the rain. Before I left I gave my telephone number to the girl behind the counter.

'Look, if you remember anything else, can you give me a ring?' I asked. 'It's really important.'

'Are you a private detective?' she asked.

'Something like that.'

The girl shrugged and put the piece of paper with my number between the jars on the shelf behind her. The whole experience had left me feeling dejected and frustrated. I remembered Frank's advice, to let go and do something for myself. I realised that what I really wanted was to see Gordon again. I hadn't spoken to him since the morning after the night of Jo's disappearance when I had been so cold, almost rude on the phone. I couldn't face speaking to him on the telephone and wondered about forgetting him altogether. But I knew I deserved another chance and decided a quick, humble apology was in order and email was the safest route.

* * *

The next day, I sat down and tried to compose a suitable message, one that I hoped would result in Gordon wanting to see me again.

Hi, Gordon!
   Just a quick apology if I was a bit offhand on the phone the other day. Teenage daughter problems as usual! We really must meet up some time. I'll give you a ring soonish.

I read it through for signs of honesty. It was flippant and vague and sounded as if I had as much intention of meeting him again as I had of going for a girls' weekend away with Alice.

Dear Gordon,
   I am so sorry I was rude on the phone. Jo had gone missing and I was frantic, as you can imagine. When would you like to meet? How about Thursday? My treat to make up for being so offhand. I'm really looking forward to seeing you again.

I didn't know whether that was honest or not, but for some reason I didn't want to send it. Perhaps I felt I didn't deserve to have such an attentive male friend. Perhaps I was scared of taking the relationship a step further. Perhaps I was still worried about upsetting Jo. I pressed delete. Then immediately realised that I had pressed send. Maybe it was my destiny to be with Gordon after all. Jo would have to get used to the idea of me having a new partner some time. I couldn't protect her from everything in life, though I could have prevented Roger, Alice and the new baby suddenly turning up five minutes later. I would have if I'd known. For Jo's sake.

I answered the door in my pyjamas.

'Oh, Roger, come in. I wasn't…' But then I wondered if Jo had arranged all this.

'I know you weren't expecting us but…'

'Us?'

'Alice and Lily are in the car.'

'Lily? Do you mean…?'

'The baby's called Lily—didn't the girls tell you?'

'Oh, yes, I think they did. I've been so busy what with the caf—restaurant and Gordon and everything.'

'Can we come in, then?'

'We usually arrange visits, Roger.'

'Yes, but Jo seemed upset and confused about the baby. I thought this was the best way. She's got to accept it sooner or later.'

'We were just going out…'

Roger looked me up and down as I stood there in my nightwear.

'Can we come in?'

Then Eliza sprinted down the stairs and put her seal on the negotiation.

'Oh, the baby, the baby. I can't wait to see my new sister.'

'Half-sister,' I corrected.

Part of me wanted to see Alice as a new mother. She would have had to shed all those designer suits in favour of a baggy shirt—complete with patch of sick on the shoulder—to cover up that postnatal flab. And I admit it would have given me great pleasure to see bags under her eyes at last, but why should I match that with my large, unflattering pyjamas? So

I told Eliza to let them in and call Jo down while I went to get changed.

Suddenly it seemed really important that I looked good, and that I looked busy, maybe tell them that I had more premises to view. I opened my wardrobe and scraped the hangers across the rail, trying to pick an outfit which was flattering, sophisticated, young. It was a chilly morning and a jumper would have been most suitable but I spotted a flimsy, slightly bohemian white blouse that I hadn't worn for ages. I knew I looked good in that and it would go so well with the new green skirt I had bought from the market a few days earlier. The skirt had not been my usual style but Eliza had raved about it, telling me I looked very 'floaty', like a fairy. Damn, the green skirt was in the wash. I delved into the washing basket as if trying to secure a prize in the lucky dip. I held the skirt against my nose and then to the light. There were no obvious marks but it did need ironing.

I heard the low drone of awkward conversation from downstairs, interspersed with excited squeals from Eliza. I could slide into the kitchen unnoticed and run a warm iron over my chosen skirt. I threw on my grubby dressing-gown and made it safely into the kitchen, aware that I hadn't even brushed my hair. I plugged in the iron and spread the skirt over the ironing board. I had an itch in an awkward place at the base of my spine so I reached my hand up the bottom of my dressing gown and was giving it a thorough scratch.

Then Alice came in.

Her stomach was as flat as a teatray, her clothes and make-up immaculate, and I wondered whether she had simply ordered her baby over the Internet together with a team of people to look after the child while Alice got her beauty sleep.

Alice smiled warmly at me. For some reason she always took a rather unnecessary interest in my life and was, in her own rather formal way, quite friendly. But I found that the easiest way for me to operate was to keep a distance from both her and Roger, as is usual in such situations. I just wished Alice would play her part more enthusiastically—years of clever legal practice, I suppose.

'Hi, Lizzie.' She smiled, striding elegantly into the kitchen and perching on the edge of the stool, not a leaking breast or eyebag in sight. She tucked one ankle behind the other, her back held upright in broomhandle straightness.

I smiled with my mouth then refocused on my ironing.

'Congratulations,' I muttered eventually.

'I'm sure this isn't your idea of a perfect weekend—us lot turning up like this.'

I pressed too hard with my iron.

'I really don't mind.'

'It's not exactly my idea of fun either. I can imagine a life with just Roger and baby Lily,' she continued, 'and I suspect you're happy just being left alone with the girls.'

'I allow Roger proper organised access,' I explained. I could defend myself as well as any lawyer.

'Yes, I know, you're very good.' Alice thought for a moment. 'I suppose I'm just acknowledging that life is not made up of perfect families and we have to make the best of things, not fight against it.'

I wasn't sure I was ready for all this honesty. I was only just beginning to be honest with myself, in private, and this was all a bit too much. Pretence is so much more comfortable.

'Well, I'm glad we've got that straight,' I said, and put my hand on the hot iron.

'Run it under the cold tap,' said Alice.

'It's fine.' I winced. 'Now I really must go and get changed.'

'I'll come and help you.'

Oh, that would be lovely, then we can be girls together doing each other's make-up, giggling over Roger, trying each other's clothes on and generally being all pally and huggy and girly and excited. Maybe we could…

But I just pulled a face. Probably one of horror, which I tried to disguise by sneezing in a rather odd way.

'I don't want to intrude,' Alice explained, 'I just think Roger needs some time with the girls, and while Lily is asleep they can all talk without having to pussyfoot around me.'

Why did Alice have to be so bloody nice?

'I'm sure Jo and Eliza are pleased to see all of you. Eliza's very excited about the baby.'

Sometimes I sensed that there was a nice person hidden inside of me just bursting to get out. After all, Alice was OK and none of this was her fault. I just hoped she never had a baby boy—she had everything else I hadn't got.

'Are you off to see Frank? Or maybe Gordon?'

'No, Geoff actually.'

Alice looked impressed. Or maybe shocked, I wasn't too sure. Then I saw complications ahead if she should let slip to Jo about my three boyfriends.

'Actually, Geoff is the owner of some premises I'm considering for my new…restaurant.'

Then Alice sat on the bed and watched me as I scrunch dried my hair. With all the problems with Jo, I had cancelled two hair appointments and had let it grow to my shoulders. I pulled on my green skirt and put some beads round my neck.

'You look fabulous.'

I stared into Alice's eyes for signs of sarcasm but detected none. I was confused.

'Hardly, but you do. You've just had a baby and you look like you've just stepped out of the pages of *Vogue*.'

'But you, Lizzie, you're so…so individual. I dress like a lawyer, speak like a lawyer and behave like a bloody lawyer. As Mother keeps informing me, I'm dull, dull, dull.'

'What did you say?' I asked, wondering if my inner voice had just been speaking a bit too loudly. But as if to confirm it really had been the enviable Alice speaking, she burst into tears.

'That'll be your hormones,' I said knowingly, and handed her a tissue.

'No, I've always been envious of you.'

Some people just refuse to read the scripts they've been given.

Alice quickly pulled herself together and tried to move the conversation on as if nothing had happened. But I needed to pull her back, make sense out of what had sounded like pure nonsense but which I hoped might have some truth in it.

'Why an earth would you be envious of me?' I asked.

'I don't really know,' Alice said unhelpfully, but then she saw my confusion and carried on. 'I used to think it was because you had daughters and I didn't, but that situation has changed now. On reflection, I think it's your haphazardness I envy.'

And I was none the wiser.

Then Alice looked at me thoughtfully and said, 'Roger couldn't understand why Jo was so upset about Lily's name.'

'Maybe it's because she has a sort of friend called Lily. Had. Someone who helped her when she was a bit confused about things.'

'Lily Finnegan?'

'Yes. How do you…?'

'She's the writing therapist, isn't she? She's meant to be very good.'

Alice was taking small, careful steps into our lives and I felt, well, very British about it. You read about American couples asking ex-husbands and wives to their weddings and gushing out treacly announcements like, 'He'll always be my best friend.' They even bequeath personal possessions to ex-spouses in their wills and somewhere along the way wife number one and wife number two become best friends. Well, it wasn't going to happen here. The Americans have already given us Starbucks and Jerry Springer—isn't that enough?

Yet I wanted more from Alice, more information, even if it meant opening the door a little wider. I still kept the hospital number by the bedside, I still dropped occasional hints to Jo about the merits of the eating disorders clinic and I still found myself praying, with eyes squeezed desperately tight, that I was doing the right thing. I needed reassurance about Lily and now it seemed that Alice, of all people, held the key.

Yet Alice was invading my space. I didn't want her in my bedroom, watching me as I threw myself into my old clothes, and I didn't want to watch her downstairs as she threw herself into my family.

'It's probably easiest if you all leave when I do,' I announced suddenly.

'Whenever I try to build bridges, you knock them down again. I'm really not too sure what it is you're so frightened of.'

What was I frightened of? That the girls would like Alice more than me because she had her hair done in a posh salon and wore clothes from somewhere so exclusive and sophisticated that I'd never even heard of it? That Alice was judging me, my clothes from the market and my untidy house, which resembled a stage setting from *Oliver?* Was I frightened that she was laughing at my café plans while she herself was probably buying up the whole town and planning to take over a small country? Was it envy or insecurity or something else? Where did it all start, this wanting my family all to myself with no outside interference? And why had I started questioning my life, questioning my values and questioning myself?

Maybe only Lily Finnegan knew the answers.

'How do you know Lily Finnegan?' I asked Alice, eventually.

'I had an eating disorder myself.'

This was one of those occasions when a little pebble of information that had been dropped into my mind felt like an enormous boulder. Pictures rushed into my head like a slide show on fast forward. I saw Alice and Jo, and maybe even Lily Finnegan herself, chatting amiably over the common bond of eating disorders while I stood on the sidelines, still not able to understand.

Oh, Jo, let me help you confront that side salad for I have been there too and I know exactly how you are feeling. I can tell you what to do, show you the way, be your substitute mother if you like. We can faint over a plate of chips together, bond by throwing up that pizza we wished we'd never had.

That one simple sentence from Alice set up a theory of a conspiracy against me. And it stopped me from pretending any more. Mind you, I was experienced at the next best thing—damage limitation.

'Yes, well, of course Jo went through a sticky patch like that herself, as teenagers do. Still, at least she's over it now.'

'It's not your fault,' Alice said simply. Another boulder.

'Actually,' I said, trying to look and sound casual, 'I need to get in touch with Lily but I seem to have lost her details. I know where she lives but I can't for the life of me remember... Anyway, I've lost her number too and, would you believe it, her email address. Still, I guess that's what comes from being haphazard.'

'Doesn't Jo have her details?'

'Jo's a lot better now, I didn't want to drag it all up again. I just wanted to get in touch with Lily about someone else. Yes, that's it. I need to give her details to a friend. Only I don't have them. Oh, and I need to know her precise qualifications.'

'Have you forgotten those, too?'

I smiled and tried to look haphazard.

'The truth of the matter is,' Alice said, 'I haven't seen Lily since she lived in Moulsham Street and, of course, she's moved since then, after the fire. I must confess I thought she had moved over to the States but her name came up the other day.'

'When? What did you hear?'

'I do believe her name came up in court. A woman was using her depression as an explanation for her crime.'

'Diminished responsibility?'

'Something like that. Anyway, I'm not at liberty to disclose the details of the case.'

'But you could find out some more about Lily. Not that it's important. Just if you've got time.'

'Lizzie, I can tell it *is* important and I'll make it my business to ask the right questions in the right quarters.'

I experienced a sudden surge of gratitude and, strangely, I wanted to hug Alice, but somewhere in my bedroom a mobile phone began to ring. As it was a standard ring tone set on a moderate volume setting, rather than my loud clinky version of 'Children of the Revolution', I guessed correctly that it was Alice's.

'Good morning, Alice Anderson speaking. Oh, dear. Yes, I see. Where can I find her now? I see. Yes, of course, I'll be there straight away.'

Alice beeped her phone off and turned towards me.

'Mother's had a fall outside the King's Head. She's not seriously hurt apparently but they've taken her to Casualty as a precaution.'

Alice seemed to be thinking about something else.

'Oh, dear, Lily will need feeding in a minute. Let me think what the best course of action would be.'

Right on cue, the baby began to cry and Roger immediately started shouting for Alice.

Surely Alice was about to lose her cool exterior. I looked at her for signs of rising panic but she remained completely controlled. I couldn't bear it any longer, she'd made herself too nice to dislike. And she knew Lily Finnegan.

'I'll go to Casualty if you like,' I said. 'I am supposed to be the back-up.'

'But what about Gordon, or Frank—er, no, Geoff. I don't know, but isn't someone waiting for you?'

'They'll keep,' I said casually. I could do cool, too.

As I drove towards the hospital, some of Alice's words suddenly came back to me like the words of some half-remembered song. Was I mistaken or had she told me that she envied me? And why was that so important to me?

It was ridiculous. How could anyone envy me? And yet I smiled to myself as if perhaps they could. Then I realised that I had probably been caught out by clever lawyer banter and that Alice must have a hidden agenda. And why did she tell me that she had had an eating disorder? It surely couldn't be true... As I turned into the hospital car park, I realised that I had been interrogating myself again. Alice may be a top lawyer, but I could be both the accused and the prosecuting counsel. And the judge, come to think of it.

I heard Dolly as soon as I walked into Casualty. She was leading a choir of student doctors and nurses in an off-key rendition of 'Jailhouse Rock'.

'Ah, Ellie, come and meet these lovely, lovely, lovely doctors.'

'Dolly, you're drunk.'

'I should bloody well hope I am. Otherwise I'm suing the King's Head.'

A serious-looking doctor took me to one side.

'Are you related to Mrs Anderson?'

'Yes, of course,' I lied.

'She clearly fell over due to excess alcohol consumption. Luckily there are no broken bones or serious injuries, just a few bruises.'

'Fine, I'll take her home, then.'

'I wonder if I might give you some information about alcohol dependency. We do run a—'

'She's not an alcoholic, she was just celebrating becoming a grandmother.'

'She was on her own.'

'There's no rule that we can only enjoy ourselves in a group. I think you're confusing celebrating with line dancing.'

'If I can be blunt, I suspect that years of alcohol consumption may have resulted in some neurological disorder, on top of her other problems. She hasn't been making a lot of sense.'

'Of course she hasn't, she's hammered. Anyway, she's an eccentric, so even when she's sober she doesn't always make sense by any ordinary definition. That's why I like her.'

'That's very interesting. I'd like your mother to come in for some more tests. I'd like to see if she behaves normally.'

'Well, she doesn't, I'm glad to say. What is normal anyway? I've been normal for the last twenty years and I'm ashamed and embarrassed by it. What about you?'

'I don't think this is very helpful. I'll leave you to take your mother home and we'll send out a further appointment. If you could just ensure that she attends.'

By now Dolly had worked her way through the entire back catalogue of Elvis and had moved on to songs from *The Sound of Music*.

'Come on, I'll get you home, Dolly.'

'What did the doctor say?'

'He said you weren't normal.'

'Oh, that's lovely. What a kind man.'

Dolly's flat was like a cross between a junk shop and a temple hit by a tornado. There were piles of books everywhere and boxes of miscellaneous, mostly unidentifiable objects. And amongst this car boot sale of knick-knacks were candles and incense sticks.

'I thought you had a home help.'

'She's on her holidays.'

'Don't they send a replacement?'

'They did, but I sacked her. She kept tidying up.'

'Isn't that what they're meant to do?'

'The usual one doesn't. She just drinks coffee.'

It was easy to make myself at home in Dolly's flat. It was a home from home, I suppose, and I soon found myself making a pot of tea and a pile of toast and jam.

'I had a bit of a chat with Alice today.'

'Did you see my granddaughter?'

'Yes, she's lovely. Anyway, Alice told me she'd had an eating disorder when she was younger. And that Lily Finnegan helped her.'

'I don't know about that. She didn't stick with Lily for long. She went to some private psychiatrist. She doesn't trust anyone who's not wearing a suit and tie.'

'Did you ever meet Lily?'

'I can't remember now. Yes, I think I did but I don't really remember. I heard she died but I can't be sure. Pity, she could have helped your Jo out.'

'She is.'

'Well done, that was a good move.'

And for the first time I felt I had done the right thing. Perhaps I was a good mother after all.

And the Mother of the Year award goes to…

'You're daydreaming again,' said Dolly.

'Alice said something else. She said she was envious of me.'

'I expect she is. Think about it. You allow yourself to have faults, some of the time anyway. Never mind, right now what

I need to complete my sobering up is a trip to Aqua Land. I need a soak in the jacuzzi and a sauna. Are you coming? You can use some of my swimming gear—go into the bedroom and delve around in the third box on the right, it's all in there.'

Until I met Dolly, I think the word 'spontaneity' had been crossed out of my internal dictionary.

In an oversized spotted swimming costume, I lay back in the spa pool while Dolly splashed her arms and legs about like an octopus having a fit. Everyone else was on the opposite side of the pool, staring at Dolly's armbands and pink bath hat.

'Hello, Jo said you were here.'

'Oh, Gordon, hi.'

'So you're Gordon,' said Dolly. 'Come on in, I'm going into the steam room.'

There was a small commotion while Dolly called over to two young male attendants to help her walk to the sauna.

'Who's that?' Gordon asked.

'My ex-husband's future mother-in-law. She's teaching me how not to be self-conscious in public. I'm doing quite well.'

Then Gordon and I lay back together in the bubbles, both with plenty of flesh on display, both looking slightly flushed. This, I decided, was a great opportunity to get to know each other more intimately.

'This is a great opportunity to talk business,' said Gordon.

I closed my eyes and pretended I was somewhere else.

FOURTEEN

MY MOTHER is turning into an honest woman. She's been admitting her faults and everything. Of course, she always adds, 'Nobody's perfect', or 'Everyone has faults'. In case we think she's the only one. She also means most people have more faults than she does. But she doesn't say it. Not in so many words.

I like people with faults. Eliza's crap at maths. And she talks too much. Scarlet's a crybaby and she talks too much. Dad doesn't say enough. I like Mum better now she's got faults. I remember when I was little, choosing a doll with one blue eye and one brown. Must have been a mistake in the factory, the shop lady had said. I loved that doll. I loved her even more when one eye wouldn't stay open, like she was winking or something. Mum said it was wear and tear. Well, we all have wear and tear.

Can babies have faults? Perhaps they haven't had enough wear and tear to have developed faults. That's why they seem so frigging perfect. Unless they're born odd or something. I wanted Dad's baby to have faults but she didn't. She will once she's had some wear and tear. Eliza drooled over the baby. But later when I asked her whether she liked me or the baby best, she said, 'You, silly,' and hugged me. Immature question really.

I hated Dad turning up like that. How can you run away if someone chases after you? But he didn't look at the baby much. It mostly slept anyway. Mum didn't look at the baby at all. She ran away. I hadn't thought of Mum not liking the baby before. Good to know you don't have to grow up totally.

Dad was being so great I pretended to like the baby. And Alice. I didn't mention the baby's name. Neither did Dad. Or Alice. They called it 'the baby'. When you pretend to like someone, you end up liking them anyway.

Alice told me she used to have an eating disorder. Perhaps it'll be hereditary. Then I had a bad thought: I wished she'd died from it. So I was nice to her to make up for the bad thought. She got better, though. I looked at her. I wondered if she was completely better. Underneath.

'Would you like a cake?' I asked her.

'No, thanks, Jo.'

Not enough evidence really. She was slim but not bony. Pretty, I suppose. I wondered if it was the baby Mum was running away from. Then Alice left us alone with Dad.

After they'd all gone, I went on the computer. An email from Scarlet and an email from Lily. I decided to look at Lily's message last. Like eating the veg first and saving the chips till afterwards.

Hi!
Just got back from Dad's. He gave me £10! I can get used to this separated parents thing! He tried to cook me an omelette but it tasted like a leather jacket! When

I got back, Mum cried. Then I told her about the omelette and she cheered up. Then I told her about the £10
and she gave me £20. So—do you want to come shopping with me Friday after school???
PS Jimmy Bradshaw is going out with Noelle!

Hi Scarlet,
Not Noelle with the acne????
Yeah, shopping would be cool. See you in the coffee-
bar at 4.
Dad and the baby came round! It wasn't as bad as I
thought. Didn't get any money out of it though!!!
See you,
Jo

I hesitated before opening Lily's message. I knew she would
have read my story, the Irish folk tale. I thought of the question she had told me to ask—'What's the worst thing that can
happen?' I had dissed that a bit. But, hey, that was one useful
question. Better than 'Why are you trying to fuck my life up?'
    'What's the worst thing that can happen?'
    'The baby dies' or 'The baby grows up to be perfect'?
Sometimes the worst is the best and the best is the worst.
    I looked at the message waiting to be opened. What's the
worst thing that can happen? Lily says she hates my story. I
said it out loud: 'Lily says she hates my story.' It sounded all
wrong. Unlikely. So I opened the message.

Hi, Jo,
Great story. How's it going to end?
With love, Lily

Dear Lily,
Back to lists:
1. Are you going to tell me where you've been?
2. Did you know you caused me to run away?
3. Did you realise that the story is already finished?
4. I need to meet you now. I also need to know where you are.
With love, Jo

Dear Jo,
You can never go back.
We are only responsible for ourselves.
Only you know if anything is finished.
You will meet me one day.
Love Lily

Dear Lily,
How? When?

There were no more messages after that, but I decided I would email the next day and arrange to meet. On my terms. I set the time, I set the place. Then I read through my story again. Was it finished? Aren't all endings a little ambiguous? When is anything finished? It's been hard to find a true beginning and an exact end to my own story, this one. From a wedding to a party. But weren't those occasions just picked at random? We don't even know if it's fully finished when we're dead. It's easier to find a beginning. That Lily Finnegan existed, that was how my story began. My Irish legend, I mean. The story of me really began at birth, my birth. This is just a chapter.

Change can be a beginning. Or an end. Or just a change.

What happened when I decided to have a surprise party for my mum's birthday? Was that a beginning? Or just a different place from which to look at my life? And where did I get the idea? From Lily, of course. She planted so many seeds in my life, but subtly, without me realising. Like the school gardener creeping in at night.

This was the first time I'd decided to do something for Mum. And not just to make me feel like a good girl. I suppose this was being grown-up and it wasn't as bad as I thought. Lily had made me write a list—the good things about being grown-up. I couldn't think of many. Not at first. Then I noticed that sometimes it tasted quite good. It was like when I said, for years, that I didn't like Marmite. Then one day I took a bite of Eliza's Marmite on toast by mistake. It was lovely. Had I changed or had I always liked Marmite but never known it?

I was turning into a nun or something. Or Cliff Richard. I decided to phone round first and get myself a list. A guest list. Dad was well chuffed I'd phoned.

'Of course I'll come. The baby's too young to leave so Alice won't be able to make it. To be honest, I could do with a break from the baby.'

Double whammy. Cool.

Uncle George, Auntie Sue, Victoria and Stuart, neighbours, Trish from the café. Everyone wanted to come. It's easier to ask for support for someone else. Easier than asking for yourself. If someone said no, it would not be me being rejected.

I found Gordon's phone number in Mum's book. He was polite. And vague.

'In principle, of course I'd like to come, but my new job is very demanding and at the moment I'm tied up with so many evening meetings. Does your mum know you're phoning?'

'Sort of.'

'Ah, I would need to know she's expecting me.'

'That would spoil the surprise.'

'I'll think about it.'

Bastard.

I ate a packet of crisps while I was on the phone. And an apple. It was good thinking about other people. Then I got bored because no one else was in. So I weighed myself. Was I better? Is it normal to take notice of every crumb that goes in your mouth? Everyone worries about what they look like. Don't they?

Why do I look in the mirror and think OK, then look again and see someone the size of a bouncy castle? Sometimes I'm OK, sometimes I'm not. Sometimes I can eat, sometimes I can't. Sometimes I'm scared, sometimes I don't give a toss. I was better, but I felt like one of those volcanoes—dormant. That's it, dormant. It was under control but not dead and buried.

It was good to leave the house. Like lifting the lid of your coffin and climbing out. It was liberty, escape, life. It was good to see people. Chosen people. People who hadn't said the wrong thing at the wrong time. Alice had said the wrong thing—'Let's bond together over our awful, debilitating anorexia.' Or something like that. I bet she belongs to some group, talking about it endlessly. I bet she surfs the net, researches it all and then talks to some bulimic from Wolverhampton—'Isn't it sad?' ' No one understands.' 'We are victims of society.' She said other stuff, too. She tried too hard. Like when you try to score a goal in netball to save your team from losing. You always lose then. When you're twelve-nil up, the ball slides in like a wet fish.

So I went to see people. I went to see Frank because I couldn't find his phone number. He wasn't at the Buddhist centre. Then I remembered he was a butcher. He was pleased to see me.

'Hi, Jo, come out the back. Tom, can you manage for a bit?'

'Do you ever eat your meat, Frank? I mean, you are a Buddhist.'

'I did have a lamb chop the other day.'

'You're not a very good Buddhist, are you?'

He laughed. 'An elderly customer of mine invited me round for dinner when her nephew let her down. She didn't know I was a veggie and had gone to a lot of trouble. Sometimes you have to do things for the greater good.'

'Cool. I'm having a party for my mum—for the greater good. Will you come?'

'Of course. Anything for you and your mum. And I'll bring some of my veggie sausages and pies.'

'Not lamb chops, then.'

I'd been so busy arranging Mum's party that I'd almost forgotten about emailing Lily. I'd been thinking about getting her address and visiting her if she lived near town. But it seemed more important to see Frank and then Scarlet. Funny how priorities change. Like your mind shuffles things about when you're sleeping. I really wanted to make sure Scarlet was OK. Shit time with her family. That's when you need a friend. I thought about Frank's lamb chop, his greater good. I liked that. So I texted Scarlet and we met in the café. I told her about the baby.

'Was it all right? Seeing it with your dad and that?'

'It felt funny.'

'Of course it did. Still, it could have been worse, I suppose. Alice could already have six daughters or something. At least you haven't got all that.'

Dinner plate half-full or what?

'What about your dad?' I asked.

'OK. I'm getting used to it all. Talking to you is cool. Like the poet says, they fuck you up, your mum and dad. Still, they were probably fucked up by their mums and dads.'

'Yeah, that's true. My mum's mum went and died on her.'

'That's probably why she loves you too much.'

'How's school?' I asked.

'All right, but I wish you were there. What are you going to do till September?'

'Organise a party for my mum to start with.'

'Great. I'll come.'

'Neat.'

We got more coffee. And an almond croissant—to share. Some other people from school came in and stared at me. I put a huge piece of almond croissant in my mouth. And stared back.

'What are people saying about me?' I asked.

'Nothing. They're too busy talking about themselves.'

'How's your mum?' I asked.

'On Valium or something,' said Scarlet. Then she cried. What was it with this café?

'She'll be all right,' I said.

'Oh, it's not that,' said Scarlet.

'What is it, then?'

'I don't know. Sometimes I cry for no reason, everyone does.'

Sometimes I hold it back for no reason.

Scarlet thought for a moment and then said, 'Maybe it *is* my mum. I've been so worried about her. Or maybe it's just pressure at school—there's more homework in the sixth form. Or maybe it's just life. Still, you have to let it out, else you get eczema or asthma.'

'I thought you were born with that stuff.'

'Your mind is your body, your body is your mind.'

Then we went shopping. I didn't try anything on. I didn't have any money. I saw a great skirt. But I was worried it might not fit. Scarlet bought a huge purple skirt and a black corset. Cool. I thought about the red top I'd bought at Dad's that time. I might wear it, I thought. One day. Maybe for the party. Another surprise for Mum.

We got bored with clothes and went into the second-hand book shop. I picked up an old book. The pages were worn and thinning from being turned over and over. It was a little bit yellow. The print was old-fashioned. I thought about the hundreds of people who must have read it. Then I found an old copy of *Anne of Green Gables*. I read the first page. I nearly forgot Scarlet was there. I looked up and she was leaning against the wall. Looking at me.

'Sorry,' I said. 'You don't like books that much.'

'It was my idea to come here.'

'Why?'

'Because I knew you'd like it, stupid.'

Then we went to get our make-up done in Debenhams. Because I knew Scarlet would like it. We linked arms on the way there. Like we were in a dance or something. And we laughed at nothing.

The next day I went to see the librarian. I was like a prisoner just out of jail. I was catching up with everything. She asked about my writing. I showed her. While she read it, I looked at her face. To see if it matched the face she showed me afterwards.

When they reached the fourth lake, Shona stared into the glassy surface of the deep blue water and sighed.

'Who will we see when we reach the top?' she asked again.

She looked into the lake and saw the mountaintop shimmering in front of her. And her face smiling back at her, right there on top of the mountain.

'If you keep asking the same questions, you will keep getting the same answers,' said her sister.

So they went on up to the fifth lake and Shona looked into the water again.

'Show me what Lily Finnegan looks like so I will recognise her when I see her.'

She looked into the lake and she saw hope.

The librarian smiled while she read it. And she smiled when she looked up at me.

'I can't wait to find out what happens when they reach the top,' she said.

'But they don't need to reach the top,' I explained. 'It was the journey that was important.'

Then I told the librarian about the book. The one I was planning to write. I would be a famous writer. More famous than Eliza, I hoped.

Then the librarian offered me a job. I told her I was only free until I went back to school. She said that was ideal. It was only to cover while someone was on long-term sick leave.

'What's wrong with her?' I asked.

'Cancer,' she said, 'but there's hope.'

There's always hope.

'It's only putting books back on shelves, that sort of thing.'

'Perfect.'

* * *

I told my mum. And my sister. My mum was pleased. Eliza didn't care. I phoned Dad to tell him. Alice answered so I put the phone straight down again.

With the money I earned I would buy a skirt to go with my red top.

Then Eliza told Mum about the party. I hated her for that. It was meant to be a surprise.

'I'm not sure about having a party,' said Mum. 'I don't know who to ask.'

'I've already asked people. Everyone wants to come— Dad, Uncle George, Victoria and Stuart…'

'What do you mean, you've already asked?'

'I thought you'd be pleased.'

Then Mum went ape-shit. She squawked like a parrot. She bellowed like a hippo. She roared like a whole bloody jungle. She was a one-woman zoo. Stampeding right at me. I had to shout back, to be heard.

'One rule for you, one rule for me,' I began. 'It was OK for you to do stuff without asking—like decorating my room a colour I didn't want and making me do science so I can have a career I don't want, and telling me what to wear and how to have my hair and…and telling me what to eat and when to eat and how to eat.'

Then it all came out. Specifics. All the times I'd been told what to do. All the times I hadn't been consulted. All the times I'd been manipulated. Like I'd been saving it all up. Or something.

Then Mum stopped shouting. She stopped everything. She just stopped. Like her batteries had run out.

Suddenly she slumped down into a chair. She stared at the wall and she started talking. Like she was talking to the wallpaper or something.

'I had to tell you what to do when you were little. That's how you learn. By rules and boundaries. You had to be told to say please and thank you, like any child. You had to be told how to hold your knife and fork properly. And I bought clothes I could afford, that washed easily. But you had some choices, you always had some choices.'

'But I'm grown-up now. You have to let me do things for myself. Make all my own choices.'

'I know. It's just difficult to change, that's all. Anyway, this was about you making a choice for me, without consulting me. This is about the party.'

'Well, now you know how it feels!' I snapped, and went up to my room. Mum always left me alone when I did that. Not this time. She burst in—without asking.

'Don't storm off like that. No wonder we never resolve anything, you always like to leave it hanging in the air. I was trying to explain. I was also trying to apologise. I know I've made mistakes. I know I caused your eating disorder.'

Then she sat on my bed and cried.

'Do you want me to phone everyone back?' I asked.

'That would be even worse,' she said.

'Well, it seems to me like there are two choices, we either cancel or have the party.'

'Or…' began Mum. But there wasn't really another choice.

We sat in silence. Words had been thrown in the air. They had to settle down.

'I will let you grow up, I promise,' said Mum.

'But I'm not even sure I want to grow up.'

'Growing up doesn't mean you're on your own. I'll always be your mum till I…'

Some words are best not thrown into the air.

Apparently there's a tribe in Africa where there is no word for guilt. I don't believe that—surely they would just go round nicking everything. Unless there's so much morality they don't need guilt.

'Nothing's your fault,' I said to Mum.

I felt a bit churned up so I phoned Scarlet.

'Hi,' I said. 'Just had a row with Mum. I'm feeling a bit shit. Make me laugh.'

'I'll ring you back, Jo, I'm a bit tied up—I've got a friend round.'

'What friend? Anyway, I only wanted to talk for a minute. I need to—'

'Yeah, well, it's always about what you need, isn't it?' Scarlet snapped sharply.

'Forget it. I'll phone someone else. Anyway, I only phoned you because Charlotte was out.'

I threw the phone down. I went to bed and pulled the covers over my head. To make myself disappear. To make it all go away. I was too angry to cry. Scarlet didn't deserve my tears. I'd show her I didn't care. I tried to read but I couldn't concentrate. Then Mum knocked on my door.

'Is everything all right?' she asked through the crack. 'Only if it's about the party…'

'She's had an argument with Scarlet,' Eliza shouted as she danced past. 'Best to leave her alone.'

I didn't think Mum was able to do that. But she did. Eliza said something helpful the next day, too.

'You should ask Dolly to the party. Mum likes her.'

I decided to go and see her—I knew where she lived. I was a bit nervous, I'd only met her once. And she was Alice's mother.

She lived near the town in the ground floor flat of a large terraced house with a red and blue door and big sunflowers growing in the tiny garden at the front. There were gnomes lined up by the tree, like they were waiting for the bus or something. I rang the doorbell and heard the first eight notes of 'We Wish You a Merry Christmas' chiming out. Everything made me smile.

'Ah, Jo,' Dolly said as if she were expecting me. 'Come on in.'

She was wearing pyjama trousers, a frilly white blouse and pearls. Perhaps she'd been in the middle of getting dressed. I didn't like to ask.

'Sit down,' she told me, and I moved a bunch of bananas and a top hat so that I could. 'Now, I'm going to make you one of my famous smoothies,' she announced, and disappeared into the kitchen.

I looked around. It was like someone had been looking for something, turned everything upside down and then left it like that. I could hear Dolly chopping fruit. Then singing loudly. And way out of tune. While the blender was whirring she sang even louder. And more out of tune. She brought in a jug of green slush. It looked like a pond.

'Kiwi fruit,' she explained, 'and banana, peach and grape juice. Delicious.'

She poured out two glasses. She slurped hers like a six-year-old and got a green moustache. I laughed. She didn't care. I thought about Alice. It didn't fit.

'Alice is different from you,' I said.

'Her way of rebelling. She knows I hate normal. I'm proud of her, though, but don't tell her.'

'Why not?'

Dolly thought for a moment, and then she said, 'I don't know,' and shrugged her shoulders. Then laughed at herself.

'I'll put some music on,' she said. 'Do you like jazz?'

'I don't know.' I shrugged my shoulders. Then laughed at myself.

The music made me tap my feet up and down on the floor. It made me feel happy. It made me think of old-fashioned parties and dancing and drinks with fruit floating on the top. It was summer music. I thought of lawns with daisies. I thought of big hats and bare shoulders. Dolly made trumpet noises and swayed about. It was Dolly's music. It was very Dolly.

'I'll play you Elvis later,' she said. Like she didn't want me to go.

Next thing I knew we were playing Scrabble. I'd forgotten all about Scarlet and Mum and Lily.

'P-L-I-P,' she spelt out as she put the letters down. 'Plip.'

'There's no such word,' I challenged.

'Yes, there is—the sound of ice in a drink.'

She didn't care about rules. I wished I could be like that.

'No, I can't make a word,' I said.

Dolly winked at me. It was a challenge.

'S-I-L-S-Y. Silsy,' I said. 'How you feel when someone's horrible to you.'

'Brilliant. You get sixty points for that.'

'How do you work that out?'

'The artesian scoring system. So much better.'

The artesian scoring system allowed Dolly to declare herself the winner. She was mad. I'd forgotten about Mum's party. Then I remembered.

'I'd love to come. How exciting.'

And then I felt excited too. I didn't want to go home. I thought about Scarlet.

'Penny for your thoughts,' Dolly said.

'Had an argument with my best friend,' I mumbled.

'You poor thing, you must feel awful. There's nothing worse than having an argument hanging over you. Unless you're my age, then it's wonderful. Still, you'll feel better when you've spoken to her.'

Then she handed me the phone.

'I'm not phoning Scarlet. It was her fault. She should phone me.'

Then I cried. This was getting to be a habit. Dolly put her arm around me. My head rested on her shoulder. The frill of her blouse tickled my nose and made me sneeze.

'Bless your heart and soul,' she said, and I felt safe.

Then Dolly told me that the best thing for me to do was say sorry. Even though I'd done nothing wrong. She went into the kitchen and sang. I tapped out the number.

'Hi, Scarlet.'

'Hi, Jo, thanks a million for phoning.'

'I'm sorry.'

'I'm sorry too.'

'Text me, yeah?'

'Yeah. I'll ring you and I'll tell you what's happened, Jo. It's complicated. It's not you.'

'Love you.'

'Love you too.'

That was it. Simple. No problem. It hadn't been my fault. I felt good again. Suddenly everything seemed easy.

Dolly came back in with a big box and a bag of mints. 'Let's play Twister,' she said. She didn't ask about Scarlet,

she was too busy enjoying herself. I'd never had a gran. I always thought they had to smell of lavender. And have bad
hips. And tell you to sit up straight. And tut at your clothes
and hair, like Scarlet's gran. I looked at Dolly in her pearls
and pyjamas. She was supposed to put her left foot on a red
circle and her right hand on a yellow one. But she got her
walking stick and used that instead of her hand. Then I remembered she was old.

'Your go,' she shouted.

Then we had to stop. Dolly needed to sit in an armchair,
get her breath back.

'That's the trouble with having a brain that's sixteen and
a body that's seventy-two,' she said. 'It makes me want to
scream. But I haven't got the energy to go down to the old
railway tunnel.'

'Railway tunnel?'

'You know, at Newman's Corner. It's where I go and have
a good scream. Anyway, I've had enough now.'

And I knew it was time to go.

Dear Lily,
I would like to meet you outside the library at five
o'clock on Thursday. Looking forward to seeing you.
With love,
Jo

Dear Jo,
I can't make it then. Still, I'm sure we'll meet soon.
With lots and lots of love,
Lily

I didn't mind, I was starting my job the next day. And Lily was right, surely we would meet soon.

On my first day at the library, I was so nervous. I felt so young. I felt like people were looking at me. Waiting for me to make a mistake. It wasn't like school. It was new. I didn't know where anything was—not even the paper clips. I didn't know anyone's name. Did I feel like that the first time I went to school? I couldn't remember. When something is familiar, you don't remember it as unfamiliar. When you know someone, you don't remember not knowing someone.

The staff were old. Or middle-aged. So they were kind to me. One of them called me duck. It was OK being the youngest and being looked after. I'd taken a packed lunch in with me. The librarian said they all did. There was a coffee-bar nearby but it got crowded, and it cost. I had put a few things in the lunch box. Three of us sat round a table out the back. Someone put the kettle on as I opened my lunch box. Mum had added a sandwich. I stared at it. I felt hot. Everyone was looking at me. I felt dizzy and a bit faint.

'Are you all right, duck?'

I closed the box.

'Here, have a glass of water. You're not used to being on your feet all day.'

I sipped my water and felt better. Comforted. Nobody said, 'Finish your lunch', or 'Waste not, want not', or 'Think of the starving children in Africa'. But it was easier to eat than not eat. I ate an apple and a banana. I felt great. Like I'd passed an exam.

In the afternoon, I put books back on the shelves. They were all on a trolley. I felt important, pushing my trolley round the library. I wanted to see someone I knew but they were all at school. I had a lot of time to think. I thought about my panic. Was it all coming back again?

The mountain had been easy to climb to begin with. Once they had decided to climb it, it was just a matter of walking in the right direction. Now, after the fifth lake, it had become very steep and uneven. A mist had fallen on the mountainside like soft muslin and Shona and her sister could hardly see where they were going. Shona could not see the top of the mountain and could barely see the path. For a while, it felt like they were going downhill again, and they stumbled over loose rocks and narrow crevices in the land. 'Remember Lily Finnegan and hope,' Shona told herself.

There was a boy who came into the library. Spiky black hair. Cool clothes. Tall. A bit gangly maybe.

'Have you g-got Ted Hughes?' he asked. He looked at the carpet. Maybe he'd dropped something.

I took him to the poetry section.

'There's this one,' I said, pulling a Ted Hughes selection off the shelf. 'It's sort of a greatest hits.'

He grinned. It was lopsided.

'I was looking for *Birthday Letters*,' he said.

I couldn't find it. I showed him how to look it up on the computer. Both copies were out. I showed him how to reserve one.

'Thanks,' he said. 'Do you work here every day?' He rubbed his left eye and shuffled his feet.

'Yes,' I said. I wanted to say something else. I couldn't think of anything.

'I really like Ted Hughes,' I said eventually. 'And Sylvia Plath.'

'Have you read *The Bell Jar*?' he asked.

'No, just some of her poetry.'

'You can borrow my copy if you want. I'll bring it in. If you want, that is, though you do work in a library. Still, it's up to you. I can pop in tomorrow, whatever you think.' He spoke very quickly. He must have been in a hurry so I said, 'Thanks. See you.' And went back to my trolley.

I phoned Scarlet up as soon as I got home from work.

'There was a boy in the library today. Really cool. We're looking at some poetry together tomorrow.'

'Cool. Look, Jo, I've got something to tell you. Can you come round?'

'Going to Scarlet's,' I shouted.

'What time will you…?' I didn't hear the rest.

I ran nearly all the way to Scarlet's. She only lived four streets away in a house nearly the same as ours. Blue door, though. And a lawn mown into stripes. Inside, it was so tidy, like a show house or something. It smelt of polish and that stuff you put on windows. Scarlet had told me that when her mum gets stressed she cleans and polishes. When she gets really stressed, she scrubs.

Scarlet had been crying again. She's like a tap or something.

'Is it your parents?' I asked. I wanted to tell her about the boy in the library.

'Sort of,' she sniffed. 'We're moving. To Birmingham.'

'You can't be! What about school? What about me?'

'I'll be going to a new school and everything.'

'Why?'

'Mum wants a fresh start. I've got two aunts who live up there—her sisters. I won't know anyone.'

'You'll know your aunts, I suppose. Have you got any cousins?'

'Yeah, they're awful.'

'Can't you persuade your mum to stay?'

'She's set on it. The house is on the market. And the thing is, she's dead happy now she's decided we're moving.'

'You could live with your dad,' I suggested.

'I don't think Mum would like that. Anyway, he's not that near. For school and that.'

I thought about the unfairness of our lives.

'We're kind of in between, aren't we?' I said. 'I mean, we're nearly grown-up, we're well up for deciding our own stuff and yet all the big decisions are made for us. Unfair or what?'

'Perhaps it won't be that bad in Birmingham.'

'I don't want you to go, you're my best friend,' I blurted out. I felt like crying myself.

When I said that, Scarlet cried all over again and that set me off too. I hate injustice.

I walked home slowly. I tried to imagine going back to school without Scarlet. It seemed impossible. I had thought Scarlet would always be there. Phoning wouldn't be enough. Or emailing or texting. I had to see her—do stuff together. I felt like someone was dying. My stomach was churned up, I felt sick. Maybe the world didn't like me. Maybe God hated me or something. Why did bad stuff always happen to me? Then I realised it had really happened to Scarlet. Even so. When things went wrong I felt fat. And ugly. And hopeless. Like it was all out of control. I knew I wouldn't be able to eat for the rest of the day.

When I got home, my eyes were red. My skin was blotchy. Mum and Eliza saw me so I told them about Scarlet.

'I wonder if Scarlet's mum would let her live with us during term time,' Mum said.

'That's not fair,' squawked Eliza. 'I'll have to have a friend to stay too.'

Mum ignored her.

'I don't think Scarlet's mum would let her but thanks for offering, Mum, you're cool.'

I thought about the story of Jekyll and Hyde. Then I thought about life without Scarlet. Eliza had loads of friends. So many I got them muddled up. So many she probably did too. I had one friend and she was moving away. Mum and Eliza had felt sorry for Scarlet. But what about me? I wondered if this was what divorce felt like. I cried again and this time I didn't know what I was crying about. Maybe it was contagious.

The boy came into the library the next day but I was on my break. He left the book in an envelope for me. With a note—'from Anthony'. I said his name in my head. I didn't want a boyfriend but it was a lovely feeling knowing I could have one. When I was ready.

When I got paid, I spent my money on a black taffeta skirt to go with my red top. It was cool. I didn't show Mum or Eliza. I decided to surprise them the next morning. I got dressed and came down for a cup of tea, without milk. Eliza asked if she could try it on. She was envious. Then I showed Mum.

'That's not the sort of thing you usually wear,' she said doubtfully.

'That's the whole point.'

'Well, it'll be great for a party or something. Not really suitable for the library, though. Perhaps you should get changed.'

Mothers can cut you down to size. Mothers can decide where you live. Mothers can decide what you wear. Mothers can offer to have your best friend to stay. Mothers can make you feel clever and pretty and loved. Or not. I wondered when all of that ended. I had thought of something good about growing up. Mothers can change but what makes them change? The look on my face maybe.

'What am I talking about?' she piped up suddenly. 'Of course you can wear it to the library if you want to. You'll be the most beautiful librarian there. That'll get a few noses out of a few books.' And then she kissed me like a kid.

So I went to the library in my new outfit. Anthony didn't come in. That wasn't why I'd worn it. Still…

Then Mum tried even harder. This time she changed her mind about the party and said she was looking forward to it. She said it had been a great idea.

Dear Lily,
I think I'm better. I have more good days than bad days. My mum says everyone has good and bad days so maybe it's normal. Mum and I had a row about a party but it's all right now. Most things get right in the end. The party's on 31st August from 7:30 p.m.
You're invited! Can we meet before then? It would feel funny to meet for the first time at the party. I can come to yours if you want. What's your address?
Love Jo.

Dear Jo,
Of course I'll come. I'm looking forward to it. See you there!
Love Lily

I stared at the email. There was something odd about it. I suddenly thought that I might already know Lily Finnegan. And she might know me.

Dear Lily,
Who are you?
Love Jo

But I got no answer. I felt curious, angry, intrigued, let down, fish-slapped, disappointed, nervous. Most of all, I felt that life was changing too fast. My world was spinning too quickly. I was unbalanced and I wanted it to stop. I wanted the world to stop so I could think, work things out, make some decisions. My friend was leaving, I liked the boy in the library, I was scared about the boy in the library. My mum was lovely, then awful, then lovely again. September was coming round too quickly, the days were disappearing, just disappearing.

Even Lily had let me down once. When she had disappeared I ran away, but I felt she was showing me something. Now I felt like running away all over again, because if I already knew her then she never really existed. I decided to take a walk down to the old railway tunnel at Newman's Corner.

FIFTEEN

PLEASE don't let it be Roger, please don't let it be Roger.

'Oh, hello, Roger, just calling to see how everyone is.'

'Is there a change in the arrangements?'

'No, no. Why should there be?'

'Is Jo all right?'

'Fine. And how about you and the…er…baby?'

'Lizzie, do you want something?'

'No. Mind you, if Alice is there, while I'm on the phone…'

'I'll just get her. She's only got a few minutes. She's due to feed Lily at two-forty.'

I heard strained whispering in the background, then the sound of the phone being picked up again.

'Alice, I wondered if you'd come up with anything more about Lily.'

'Only that I'm finding it hard to keep her to a schedule.'

'I meant Lily Finnegan.'

'Ah, yes. I did ask my colleague. The woman I mentioned, the defendant claiming clinical depression as an influence on her crime, is in contempt of court, it seems. Perjury, technically, and her defence has been ripped apart by Nigel Haversham. Marvellous young lawyer.'

'And Lily Finnegan?'

'Well, that's just it, the woman lied. Hadn't been treated by Lily for years, it seems. Tried to change the date on her documentation. However, I will ask Nigel—he must have had contact with Lily to form part of his prosecution. Next time I see him, I'll have a word.'

'When will that be?'

'Thursday the fifth at two-fifteen.'

'That's ages away. Won't you run into him before that?'

'We all run to a very tight schedule, Lizzie. In some ways I wish… Anyway, I have to go, it's two-forty.'

I decided to take a walk down Moulsham Street on the outskirts of town, thinking that perhaps I could find where Lily used to live. There was very little logic to this as it wasn't likely she'd have chalked a forwarding address on the front wall. But I might see someone to ask, I thought, or pick up some sort of clue.

Unexpectedly, I felt quite emotional when I arrived at the top of Moulsham Street, as if I were visiting a shrine or some sacred place after a long pilgrimage. Perhaps in some ways I was. I sauntered slowly past a row of old Victorian terraces, wondering if I would sense some sort of divine vibe coming from one of the buildings. As I approached number forty-three, I did feel something. I imagined someone looking at me, watching over me in some way. I looked up and there was a small child staring out of the window. He stuck his tongue out at me and ran off. One of the houses was empty with a battered 'For Sale' sign outside, leaning to one side as if disheartened by the empty building behind, which was clearly in need of some repair.

I sat on the wall in front of it and put my head in my hands. It had been a futile journey and I wondered what on earth I was doing there. Half-heartedly, I decided to stroll along the rest of the street and then power-walk my way back to the car. The houses continued in much the same pattern, except for a corner shop right at the end. Knowing that corner shops are often a good source of information, my spirits lifted a little as I went in to clutch at this particular straw. I grabbed a newspaper I didn't really want and went up to the counter.

'Hi, lovely day,' I said.

'Yes, and a good thing too. I hope it lasts, my niece is getting married next weekend. It's going to be a big do, she's marrying Thomas Badger of Badger, Henman and Smith. Thomas is the son, of course, but he'll go into the firm. The best man is the son of that actor off the telly—you know, the one lives up at Moulsham Lodge.'

Brilliant, I thought, this was the sort of shopkeeper you normally dreaded but the sort I most needed right then.

'You don't happen to know if Lily Finnegan lives around here?'

'Used to live at number forty-eight. Gone now, of course.'

'You don't happen to know where?'

'Well, it's complicated isn't it?' she said. 'And I'm not one to gossip.'

I waited but nothing came.

'So you don't know, then?'

'Not really, no,' she muttered, clearly disappointed in herself.

I walked straight back up the street and found that number forty-eight was the empty house where I had sat pondering on the wall. I walked round the back, half expecting to see Lily sitting there, waiting for me, but all I saw was a garden of nettles and parched grasses. I peered in at the window and saw that the kitchen had been burnt out at some point. The house was waiting for someone to put some heart and soul back into it again, to give it life. I felt sad seeing such neglect and had a strong urge to get back to my home and family. I would come back and talk to the neighbours, I decided, but seeing a house unlived in, frozen in time, there seemed to be no great urgency, as if life could stand still whenever we chose it to.

As I walked back to the car, I wondered what had made me come searching for Lily's history. What exactly had I been expecting to find? And it occurred to me that all these weeks I had not really been searching for Lily at all, I had been searching for myself. And I realised that I had been looking in completely the wrong place. I looked back up the road behind me where Lily had once lived. I knew from experience that when you stop looking for something, it generally turns up.

I got into the car and drove away slowly, feeling dizzy with emotion. What I needed, I decided, was to go home, forget about Lily and get on with my life, supporting both my daughters in the best way I could. When I got back, the girls were out and I walked around the house as if looking at it for the first time. The lounge was still tidy from when I had cleared it for Gordon's visit, the kitchen was better since Alice had tidied it the day Jo had gone missing, and some of the stuff had been shifted out of the bedroom. I could see light shining through the debris, a way out of the chaos, and felt a sudden surge of energy. I started to tidy up, made a list of jobs that needed doing around the house, flung open the kitchen cupboards and the fridge—and stopped to think. I felt calm, controlled, as if life had slowed down just a little. But I knew I could always feel calmer and I knew how.

* * *

'You look wonderful, Ellie,' Frank told me after the meditation session.

'Thanks. Not exactly designer. I got these at the market and the skirt came from a charity shop.'

I indicated the long, off-white, crumpled-look skirt which topped my old granny boots.

'I didn't mean the clothes, I meant you—you look so healthy and relaxed, at ease with yourself.'

'Maybe I'm in love.'

'Are you?'

'I don't know. I don't think so. Gordon's lovely but…I don't know. I never seem to know what I want.'

Congratulations, Mrs Trounce—you have won first prize. Now, would you like the car, the holiday, £5,000 in cash or £5,000 worth of groceries?

Oh, I don't know. I've got a car but it needs changing, and a holiday would be nice, but then again… The money maybe, but then how much is the holiday worth? Oh, I have no idea…

I'll have to hurry you, Mrs Trounce.

Oh—I'll have the groceries. Oh, damn. Damn, damn damn. Why did I choose the dullest, most practical…?

'Sorry Frank, what was that?'

'I was just asking what Gordon was like, that's all.'

'He's kind and very well organised, very sensible and reliable. He's helping me look into running my own café—he's very knowledgeable about that sort of thing. Yes, a good antidote to my scattiness, I think. Keeps me on the straight and narrow, doesn't get carried away with fantasies or any romantic notions. Yes, you know where you are with Gordon. Like Sainsbury's.'

'You should bring him here, get him meditating.'

'No, he'd never do anything like this.'

'I meant to ask you, are you still teaching yoga?' Frank asked.

'No, I still practise it occasionally but I haven't taught it since Jo was born. Why?'

'We want to start some yoga classes here at the Buddhist centre. Nobody would need to be a Buddhist to join but it would fit in with our general philosophy.'

'I'm a bit rusty, Frank.'

'There's this course in India. We might be able to fund someone to go.'

'India?'

'Gordon could go with you, if you like.'

'But Jo, and Eliza…'

'What are fathers for?'

'Then there's my job…'

'I wanted to talk to you about that too. We're thinking of starting a vegetarian café here. We need someone to run it. Some of the profits would go to the centre and we wouldn't be able to pay much, but if it was combined with yoga teaching…well, think about it anyway.'

'I've looked at the figures and the Buddhist café is a no-go, I'm afraid,' Gordon advised me as we sat over coffee at the back of the sandwich bar.

'I think that's very sound advice,' agreed Alice, shutting her file. Did she have a file on me? I decided not to ask.

'Do you have a file on me, Alice?'

'Just a few notes. I thought we could talk about Gordon and

I both being partners in your business. I'm keen to get involved in something else now I've cut down my hours with the firm.'

It has just been announced that Alice Anderson and Gordon Grant have just put in a bid to take over the entire sandwich business in the South East of England. Shares are rocketing sky high at the news of the apparent takeover…

'I'd better help Trish, it's getting busy again.'
I showed Alice and Gordon out, almost wishing I hadn't asked their advice. But they both had business minds and the logic that I lacked. And I knew they were right. If I was going to make money, I had to make the business my own.

I decided to email Lily and ask her some direct questions about her qualifications. I would be businesslike, efficient and expectant of a direct answer. I sat up straight in my chair like Alice. I coughed in a thoughtful way like Gordon. The computer keyboard was in front of me but it looked confusing, like the flight deck on a Boeing 747. My mind was refusing to connect with my fingers; instead it was revisiting all the emails I had already sent Lily Finnegan—demanding, needy, desperate. I had simply wanted to know what was happening to Jo, I had wanted to get my hands on it and I had thought that that was being a good mother. Now I was insisting on information about Lily herself, questioning her credentials. Then suddenly all that floated out of my mind. The keyboard came properly into focus and I began to write an altogether different sort of note from the one I had planned. This one would leave me naked, exposed, unable to hide behind my roles as mother, organiser and would-be businesswoman. Yet I knew that this was what I needed to communicate more than anything.

Dear Lily,
This may sound stupid but I don't know who I am any more. There is more to me than being a mother, more to me than wanting to run my own business, more to me than what I do day in, day out. The better Jo gets, the more confused I get. And the worst thing is, I'm not entirely sure what I'm confused about. I just sense I need help. I'm sorry but I don't know who else to tell this to.
Love Lizzie

Dear Lizzie,
Why are you sorry?
Love Lily

Dear Lily,
I'm sorry because this is not like me. I am usually strong and in control. I am not really like this and that is one of the reasons I feel confused.
Love Lizzie

Dear Lizzie,
Never be sorry for being honest. Never be sorry for being vulnerable. Now write a list of who you are.
Love Lily

Dear Lily,
A mother, a future businesswoman (of sorts), a middle-aged woman, an ex-wife. Someone who wants the best for her children, someone who wants to be someone,

someone who wants to prove herself to the world, someone who mucks up and gets a lot of stuff wrong. But this list seems inadequate somehow—as if I've lost part of myself along the way.
Love Lizzie

Dear Lizzie,
Take away the roles from the list, strip away how you spend your time and think about the authentic you. You will need to ask the people you love how they see you.
Love Lily

Dear Lily,
I can't do that. This is private. Nobody knows I'm communicating with you.
Love Lizzie

Dear Lizzie,
What are you frightened of? Take your time before you answer that question.
Love Lily

What *was* I frightened of? I was frightened of being found out. I had never contacted a therapist or anyone like it in my life. I had never so much as read the alternative health section in the Sunday papers or answered any quizzes about myself in women's magazines. I didn't do self-analysis, let alone involve anyone else in the process. I was frightened of being found out. Yet it was wider than that: being found out also meant that I might be showing people a part of myself I preferred to keep private. I wanted to choose what I showed to the outside world. For someone who didn't do self-analysis,

I was suddenly diving straight into myself. In fact, I realised, the process had started with Jo's problems. I had never wanted to look closely at myself and my life until Jo had been made to look closely at hers. Daughter showed mother the way.

When you bring your children up, it forces you to look at your own childhood. It can help you understand, help you to cope, and it can help you accept. I had never looked back on my own childhood so much, never seen so much of myself in Jo as when she became a teenager. Never had I wanted to understand so much until Jo was tackling her eating disorder.

I was used to telling amusing anecdotes about my child-hood—the time when my friend and I got caught eating tomatoes in the greenhouse and denied it, even though we were covered in red juice and pulp; and the time when my knickers fell down in the school gym, or the time when my mother...

Suddenly I knew what I was truly frightened of, and when I told Lily she coaxed me into writing about it. For the first time in my life I wrote pages and pages about my mother. The mother who had read to me at night but had withdrawn this privilege whenever I was deemed to be naughty, leaving me abandoned and cold with no nightlight and no words of reassurance that I would see her in the morning. My mother, who could prepare the perfect meal and serve it with love yet could, on one of her tired and tearful days, burn the sausages and leave the potatoes lumpy. I remember one occasion when I had commented on this innocently enough.

'This isn't very nice, Mummy,' I had said, with the innate honesty of a six-year-old.

And without saying anything she scraped my meal into the bin and left me crying while she marched out of the kitchen with tears of her own.

Later I had retold this story, with embellishments and filtering out the emotion, to amuse my own children. One day, maybe Jo and Eliza will laugh with their children about what had happened at their mealtimes.

The real, honest memories reminded me that my mother could calm me or snap at me as the mood took her. Her voice came in shades of black and white, pleasure and pain.

My darling angel... You should be ashamed of yourself... I'm so proud of you, you're such a clever girl... Don't be so stupid... Get out from under my feet, can't you see you're in the way?... I don't think that's the sort of friend you want, she's really not your type... Well done, you must take after me.

Sainthood is easily given to anyone who dies young. We want to remember the good times which, over the years, we mould into perfection. Speaking ill of the dead feels like a sin, so we let the bad memories melt away and are left with pure goodness—a saint, an angel. I loved my mother and she loved me. And as I wrote the truth, I realised that love and perfection are not even distant relatives.

I wrote about the good and the bad, the anger and the love, the pain and the regret. Then, when I had bled my mother dry, I found hidden wounds from my father and gouged them out too—the puss and the poison, the scars and the scabs. I could do this for a stranger, a stranger who was not a stranger, for there was both a closeness and a distance.

Then Lily Finnegan sent me a final message:

Let yourself be known.

And I understood. And understanding my past meant that I could make decisions about my future.

SIXTEEN

I STARTED visiting Dolly and phoning her. She was old but well cool. I took her bits of shopping. Like I was a Girl Guide or something. But I wasn't doing it for her. Not totally. I was doing it for me. I wanted to be like her. Strong. Eccentric. Not giving a shit. Sometimes I wanted to be like Scarlet. Cool. Popular. Tattooed. Pierced. I sort of wanted to be like my sister. And I wanted to be like that music presenter on the TV.

'Just be yourself,' Dolly said. 'Why be anyone else? Far too much effort, just be yourself.'

'There's bits I'd change,' I said. 'I'm not perfect.'

'I should bloody well hope you aren't.'

'You are,' I said, and hugged her. 'You're just right.'

'No, I'm not. But I have great faults.'

'So you wouldn't change anything, then?'

'I'd like to be immortal,' she said. And looked sad.

I found my mother crying at the computer.

'I've been writing to Lily,' she said. Like that explained everything. In a way it did.

'First you took over my life, now you're taking over my therapist,' I snapped. Then I regretted it. Regret is usually followed by diverting the blame. Not this time.

'I'm sorry,' I said. That was all. That was enough. There's a lot in that word 'sorry'. It's simple to say and hard to say. It comes with a feeling which can be hard to feel. It's kind of humbling. It's simple but never easy as the librarian would say.

'It's OK,' Mum said. 'I should have asked you first.'

'I'm sure we share Lily with hundreds of people.' It never felt like that, though.

Then I remembered something I'd been thinking about. Something strange.

'I think we might already know Lily,' I said to her.

'What makes you think that?'

'You don't think we know her, then? You don't think Lily Finnegan is a pseudonym or something?'

'I didn't recognise her voice on the answering-machine.'

I decided I would listen to the answering-machine later, just to be sure.

Then Mum said something strange. 'I've heard things. That she went to America and came back. But not to Moulsham Street.'

'Moulsham Street?'

'Apparently she used to live there.'

Mum thought for a moment and added, 'I walked along Moulsham Street. Her old house was empty, quite empty.'

'She's definitely coming to the party,' I said. I hadn't wanted Mum to know. Like Lily was mine or something. But she had told me about Moulsham Street. It was like at school when you work in pairs. Two heads are better than one. Or something.

'What are you writing about?' I asked. I didn't want them to write about me. Behind my back.

'My mother, my childhood,' she said. Then she started fiddling around in the sink.

I felt sorry for Mum. I made her a cup of tea. I knew how she felt. When you start writing, it's like stripping yourself down to the skeleton. Your emotions pour out in your blood, your deepest feelings are ripped out with your guts.

I had moved on. I was writing a book, an Irish folk tale and a diary. Less blood but just as effective. Before the days of writing for Lily, I wrote from the brain—clever words, articulate, educated, meticulously planned. Now I wrote from deep inside, filtering my ideas through my brain. (Sounds a bit up myself, but it's true.) Lily had made me write, made me write more than lists, more than course work. Now I wrote because I wanted to. Because I needed to.

Writing a diary is like clearing your handbag out: chucking out used tickets, discarded leaflets, stuff that accumulates in there day after day. Sometimes I said the wrong thing, sometimes I did the wrong thing, sometimes Eliza or Mum said or did the wrong thing. It all went in my diary, because it happened. It happened, that's all. And at the end of the day, you close the diary. Each day brings a fresh page. Writing was no longer therapy, it was a way of life.

'Keep a journal,' I advised Mum. Like I was her therapist or something.

Lily was still there. I would be meeting her. Yet for the moment life carried on without her. And with her. And still I wondered.

SEVENTEEN

IT WAS Jo who told me to keep a journal—as if she were my therapist or something. It helped me to see everything clearly once I saw my mind written out on a piece of paper. As I converted my thoughts into the written word and then poured them out into my diary, they seemed to organise themselves into some kind of coherent logic. The only thing I couldn't work out in my mind was whether we already knew Lily Finnegan, as Jo suspected. It seemed totally unlikely, ludicrous even, yet the idea gnawed away at the logical part of my mind until I suddenly found myself accusing all and sundry of being Lily Finnegan in disguise.

'Frank, are you, in fact, Lily?'

'I beg your pardon?'

'Are you Lily Finnegan in disguise? She seems to know more about us than we've ever told her.'

'I'm told that's what she's like—she has a strong intuition. I think you'll find Lily Finnegan is Lily Finnegan. Have you thought any more about India, by the way?'

'Yes, I've been trying to. Gordon told me to write all the pros on one piece of paper and all the cons on the other, then give each a percentage weight. Then, apparently, I'll be able

to work out which would be the most favourable decision
based on these figures.'

'And?'

'And I didn't understand a word he was saying. I can't
seem to make decisions these days—I used to go with my gut
feeling, intuition, I suppose.'

'And how can you tune into your intuition now, do you think?'

'I usually just kind of imagine myself in different situations.'

'Visualisation.'

'Just letting my mind run away with me, really.'

I am serving coffees in my very own café, Lizzie's
Coffee House. The place is brimming over with busy
shoppers and office workers, mobiles buzzing, bags of
shopping stuffed under tables topped with steaming
mugs of cappuccino or pots of Earl Grey. Out the back,
Gordon is scrutinising the accounts, Alice is fine-tooth-
combing the employment contracts. Money flies into
my hands and out again and life has speeded up like the
final spurt in a competitive race. When I finally sit down
and take a short break, I try and work out whether I am
fulfilling my dream and what exactly that dream had
been in the first place.

Now I am somewhere quieter. I am stirring tomato
and basil soup, breathing in its rich aroma, which mixes
perfectly with that of the freshly baked granary rolls. I
lovingly arrange the oat cakes onto an earthenware platter and glide easily over to a table of women, who look
up at me and quietly pass their empty plates across with
soft words of appreciation. The café is busy and tran-
quil, humming with easy conversation and gentle laugh-

ter. Contentment is poured out with the soup and teas, acceptance and gratitude are the currencies I deal in. When I ease myself into a comfortable chair to take my break, I try and work out whether I am fulfilling my dream, and I realise that it was never really a dream but an intuitive desire which I had sent up into the air…

'Do dreams just happen or do we make them happen?' I asked Frank.

'I always love your questions,' said Frank, who never seemed to answer them. Perhaps that was why I had thought he was Lily Finnegan.

The next person I accused was a completely unlikely candidate and I knew I was really clutching at straws.

'Are you Lily Finnegan? Only you said you knew her and we all know ourselves when you think about it and it might have been your way of not lying in a clever lawyer sort of way and—'

'Can I stop you there just one minute? I think I've lost you. Are you, in fact, asking me if I am Lily Finnegan?'

'In a word, yes, I am.'

'Three words, actually. I don't completely understand what it is you are accusing me of, but I can assure you that I am Alice Anderson and have all the right documents to prove it. I told Jo exactly the same thing yesterday.'

'Sorry, I don't know what came over me. I think I've lost the plot.'

'No, not at all. You're bound to want to know more about Jo's therapist. It's only natural to want information about her—you haven't lost the plot at all. Now, tell me, Lizzie, how are your business plans developing?'

'I've handed in my notice at the sandwich bar.'

'Good.'

'But I'm not starting up my own business, I'm going back to being a yoga teacher and I shall be running a small café at the Buddhist centre for a nominal wage.'

'I was wrong. You really have lost the plot. I fear you may have made an inadvisable decision from a business perspective.'

And that was when I knew for certain that I had made exactly the right decision.

'You're not Lily, are you?' I said to Dolly in the King's Head.

She laughed. I nearly managed to laugh at myself.

'Jo asked me that—what a pair! You're both barking mad.'

I knew that was one of the highest compliments Dolly could pay. Translated, it meant that she liked mother and daughter very well indeed. Then I told Dolly about my plans at the Buddhist centre.

'That's wonderful,' she said. 'You'll be serving nutritious wholemeal vegetarian food in the mode of loving kindness.'

'Yes, I suppose I will.'

'Which means you'll give me my tea and scones for free.'

'Why not? And you might be interested in my yoga classes for older people.'

'No, I wouldn't. I don't want to do yoga with a load of whinging old codgers. No, you can put me in a group with young men, young men in skimpy gym gear. Talking of which, let's challenge those two to a game of darts.'

And we did. I felt younger and more frivolous with Dolly than I did with most people half her age. She must have read my thoughts.

'Live your life to the full,' she said, staring into my eyes as if trying to make me understand. 'I mean that. You never know what's round the corner, so live your life one day at a time, to the full.'

I had run out of people to accuse of being Lily Finnegan. It was ridiculous, I knew, for all I had to do was email Lily herself and ask if we already knew her. A simple question that required a yes or no answer, but I knew that Lily generally answered my questions with another question. And, anyway, Jo had invited her to the party. All I had to do was wait and meet the surprise guest. The guest of honour.

EIGHTEEN

SOMETIMES you remember stuff for no reason. Like I remember meeting Scarlet in the coffee-bar that time when we had the blueberry muffins. I don't know why, nothing much happened. I just remember it really clearly. It was two days before the death, seven days before the funeral and ten days before Mum's birthday party.

We went to the usual coffee-bar after I'd finished work. We ordered two mochas and Scarlet asked for a blueberry muffin. I looked at the muffins. My hand automatically went to my stomach. My mind automatically switched to calorie-counter mode. Was I normal? I listened to two girls behind us.

'I'd love a chocolate cake but I'd better not.'

'Oh, go on, let's be naughty.'

Then a lady at a table with her husband.

'That was gorgeous but I shouldn't have eaten it.'

I ordered a muffin too. They automatically came with a serving of guilt. I was normal. I just didn't like normal all that much.

When I looked in the mirror, I saw different people. I told Scarlet. To see if she recommended psychiatry or something.

'Oh, I'm like that,' she said happily. 'Sometimes I look fat and ugly and sometimes I'm OK. Sometimes I even look good.'

'Don't be stupid. How can you look fat?'

Scarlet laughed. 'I have no idea. Perhaps our brains are not properly connected to our eyes.'

I drank my coffee and ate my muffin and waited for the guilt. It didn't come. Perhaps I'd gone beyond normal.

'Now for my great news,' Scarlet announced. She had been desperate to tell me something. 'I'm going out with Gareth Brooks.'

'Gareth Brooks?'

'The very one. We're going to the cinema tonight.'

I wanted to go to the cinema. I wanted to go to a film with Scarlet. She was moving to Birmingham, surely it was more important to go with me.

'Is it all right if Gareth comes to your mum's party with me?'

At least she asked. Didn't just turn up like they were glued together or something. I wanted to say no. I wanted to tell her that she and I were going to serve the drinks. Just the two of us.

'Yeah, that's great,' I said instead. 'Anthony's probably coming.'

'Anthony from the library? Cool. Hey, why don't you two come to the film tonight?'

'Anthony can't make it tonight.'

The hole I had dug for myself was deep enough so I went home.

Sometimes I made bargains with myself. If I ask Anthony to the party and he says yes, I'll let Mum go out with Gordon. Or Frank. Whoever. Mum asked me if Gordon was coming. And Frank. Casually, while she was peeling the carrots. But it wasn't casual really, there was a desperation in the way she scraped at the vegetables. Like she had to know. Like everything depended on my answer.

Scarlet was looking forward to the party. I don't know why—I mean, it was my mum's birthday party. She hardly mentioned the move to Birmingham. But she gave me a train timetable so I could visit her. I'd have to cross London on the tube and catch another train. Scarlet had already done it loads of times to visit her aunts. It felt scary. Something you usually did with other people. Lily had once written that you should do something scary every day. Then we decided once a week was probably enough.

My scary bit of action was to ask Anthony to the party. How scary was that? On a scale of one to ten, about a nine. Well, you have to leave room at the top for shark attacks and being stuck in a burning building. And going back to school after an eating disorder.

Anthony came into the library a lot. We usually talked about Ted Hughes and Sylvia Plath. We had started talking about Auden and once he even mentioned Chaucer. But only in passing. I wasn't sure about asking him to the party. It was going to be difficult to switch the conversation from poetry to that. He might not even come into the library, I thought. But he did.

'Hi.'

'Hi.'

'I've brought some books back.'

'Do you need help checking them back in?'

'No, I'm fine.'

I walked to the computer with him, the one that allowed you to check your own books in and out.

'I always offer to help people,' I explained, 'because the machines are forever going wrong.'

I paused. I saw an opening. Like a burglar spotting a loose window with the silver just inside.

'I've been helping my mum a bit recently…'

There was the link. I felt like one of those presenters on morning television—'Thank you, Mrs Brown, for showing us your talking budgie. And talking of birds, let's go over to page three modal, Cherise…' Inane.

'I've been helping my mum a bit recently, she's starting a new job and it's her birthday so I'm throwing a party, only I've got some mates coming too, so it won't just be olds. Should be a laugh.'

'Oh, right.'

'You can come if you want. Check it out.'

'I don't want to bring this one back yet, I just want to renew it. How do I do that?'

It was like when you wipe something off the computer by mistake and have to start again. I showed Anthony how to renew his book and decided to have another go. By now it had equalled shark-infested water on the scariness scale.

What's the worst that can happen? I asked myself over and over again. As if being rejected wasn't so bad really.

'My party, well, not really my party, but Scarlet's coming and—'

'I'd love to come.'

'Cool.'

'Should I buy your mum a present or something?'

'No, of course not. I'll see you there, then.'

'Just one thing.'

'Yeah?'

'I don't know where you live.'

I walked home slowly along the canal path. I wanted to hug myself, I wanted to skip along the path singing. I wanted to enjoy the best day of my life on my own, sit in my happiness like a fly in a jam factory. I felt like I'd just passed one hundred exams, been selected for a top job, made a million out of my best-seller. And it was all for me. I didn't rush home to tell Mum and Eliza or rush home to tell Scarlet. Some things are too good to share straight away. Like chocolate.

When I got home, I caught Eliza standing in front of the mirror sideways. She had lifted her jumper and was staring at her stomach. Mum came upstairs to tell me something. We both stood for a second in Eliza's doorway, staring at her. Judgements only take one second.

'Do I look bloated?' Eliza asked suddenly.

'Of course not,' said Mum. 'Now, you're not going to be silly, are you?'

'I'm not that stupid.' Eliza laughed and bounced on her bed.

So that was how they saw me—silly and stupid. I went to my room. I remembered what Lily had told me. About not being able to control other people. Or what they said. Or what they thought. I could only control me.

Did I think I was silly and stupid? I didn't know. I needed to work it out. I went to my room and got out my pen and a pad of paper.

NINETEEN

I LOOKED out of the window and saw a familiar silver BMW parked at the top of the drive.

Please don't let it be Alice, please don't let it be Alice.

The doorbell rang.

Please don't let it be Alice.

'Oh, hello, Alice, shouldn't you be at work? Are you all right?'

'Let's go in. You'd better put the kettle on.'

'What's happened?'

'I've just come from the hospital. It's not good news, I'm afraid.'

'Jo? I don't believe it, I thought she was getting better but I did wonder if the library would be too much for her what with being on her feet all day and she was talking about going back to school but perhaps it's still a bit soon, oh, I don't know, oh, what am I going on about, I need to go to the hospital right now, there's no time to waste and, oh, how come you were there, she didn't phone you, did she, only I've been here all the time, oh, never mind, I'd better just—'

'Lizzie! Lizzie—it's not Jo.'

'Oh, thank God. I knew it wasn't Jo actually, she's fine now. So what…?'

'It's Mother. She passed away about an hour ago.'

'Passed away where? You mean…'

'Yes, she died.'

I sank back onto the kitchen chair and a thousand questions rushed into my head, then straight out again. Then nothing. The tap dripped, the traffic buzzed outside, the radiator clunked. Noise and silence mixed together, thoughts and emptiness took turns to occupy the space inside my head.

'I'll put the kettle on,' said Alice gently, and patted my arm with sympathy.

'But I'd only just got to know her. We had plans. She was going to come to India with me, we were about to start philosophy classes. She was *eccentric*. She was outrageous and hilarious and I thought she'd go on like that for ever. She showed me how to enjoy myself. She can't leave me now, we'd only just begun.'

'She was very fond of you, I know.'

I cried then. I cried because Dolly was gone, I cried because part of me was relieved it wasn't Jo and I cried because I had begun to pretend that Dolly was my missing mother. Alice pressed a mug of sugary tea into my hand and it was only then that I remembered who I was and who Dolly was.

'I'm sorry, Alice, she was your mother, you must feel…'

'I don't feel anything really, just numb. I wasn't expecting this. At first I thought she'd been overdoing things.'

'I never meant to…'

'No, it turns out she knew she was dying. Anyway, there are practicalities to address now, the funeral to arrange, her possessions to sort, the will to consider and the health authority to sue. Are you going to be all right, Lizzie? Can I call anyone?'

'No, I'm fine. She was your mother. If there's anything…'

But Alice was in control, she jotted down some notes on a piece of paper and slid it into a file. Families and friends, connections and distances, duty and pleasure. Are the relationships we have to work at any more worthwhile than those that are easy and effortless?

Then Alice picked up her briefcase, lined up the mugs on the draining board and looked at me. She was about to say goodbye as she would at the end of any meeting. But I couldn't let her go like that, with all that barbed wire around her, with her mind controlling her emotions with such effortful efficiency. So I hugged her. And as I held her, so she let go. She cried like a toddler, pounding her fists against my shoulder in a mixture of anger and despair.

'She never gave me a chance,' she sobbed. 'Never gave me a chance to say I loved her.'

Then Alice pulled away and fell heavily onto the kitchen chair.

'She was so…so exasperating,' she said. 'If only she'd told me. I knew she was ill. But…it was too quick. If only she'd *told* me.'

'That wasn't her style,' I said. 'She was like someone who spoke her mind, but she didn't really. She loved you and was proud of you but…'

'I know. Personally I shall have an enforced policy of telling my daughter that I love her and reciprocation will be fully encouraged.'

I laughed out loud. I couldn't help it.

'What? What did I say?'

'It was the way you said it.' I smiled.

'You sound just like Mother.'

And with that we both cried. Cried because both our worlds would be very different without Dolly, and cried because perhaps we finally understood each other. Eventually, Alice noticed that it was nine forty-two, as if that had some significance, and she left looking slightly lost and bewildered.

I phoned in sick and sat for a while in the kitchen, for how long I don't know. It could have been ten minutes, it could have been an hour. As all my thoughts melted away, Dolly's voice came through from a recent memory: 'Live your life to the full.' So at lunchtime I went to the King's Head, ordered a pint of Guinness and some peanuts and drank a toast to my old friend Dolly.

I told Jo as soon as she got in from the library and the colour immediately drained from her face. I had to fetch her a glass of water and sit her down. It was surprising how quickly and how completely Dolly had seeped into our hearts and become a part of our day-to-day living and breathing. Jo was shocked from the sudden loss and I worried in case this set her back onto the path of self-destruction.

'Are you all right?' I asked gently.

'Of course I'm fucking not,' she snapped, and ran upstairs.

After a while I followed her up, sat on the side of her bed and clasped her hand.

'Sorry, Mum, I wasn't expecting it, that's all. Tell me what happened.'

I told her all I knew and we sat quietly together in shared grief. Words were not needed. I sent up a silent prayer to Dolly and for just a flicker of a moment there seemed to be some joy in our sadness.

'I love you,' I said.
'I love you too.'

The next couple of days were a blur of tears and laughter, bewilderment and gradual acceptance. A life had ended and yet life went on. So much had been lost and yet, as I stood beside Jo, I felt that something had been gained.

'Lizzie, it's Roger.'

'I thought the girls were coming to you next week.'

'They are but I wondered if you could come over this evening.'

'Whatever for?'

'It seems Alice's mother has requested that you organise the funeral. She's left some quite specific instructions— they're entirely unsuitable, of course.'

'I bet they are.'

'Anyway, we need to talk to you, make sure the funeral doesn't turn into some sort of fiasco. For Alice's sake.'

'I can be there at about eight-thirty.'

'Seven-thirty would suit us better.'

'We'll call it eight, then.'

'Fine.'

'Fine.'

During the week, I kept myself busy at work and at home. The house was clean and tidy now and the fruit bowl overflowing. But there was something that wasn't quite right. I realised it was the endless walls of magnolia, the curtains chosen by Roger, the symmetrical shelves with books placed out of reach. There was nothing of me in the house, so I set about painting some colour into my life. I bought a couple of free-standing bookcases and an old corner cupboard which had no practical use but which had character and a history you could only guess at. I even bought two packets of sunflower seeds. By the time the day of the funeral came round, the house had started to become a home.

The girls and I arrived at the church dressed in yellows and reds and purples, as Dolly had instructed.

'There seems to be some sort of wedding on,' said Alice. 'We can't go in yet.'

I looked her up and down.

'I don't own any bright colours, do I?' she explained. 'Still, I haven't worn black.'

'No,' I said, admiring her dark grey suit.

'In fact, I've added just a touch of flamboyance for Mother's sake.' Alice sheepishly pulled a red spotted hand-kerchief out of her pocket and quickly stuffed it back in again. We all stood around awkwardly, waiting for the coffin to arrive. Repetitions of 'She was a wonderful character', 'It's a sad loss', and 'She'll be greatly missed' bounced around the colourful crowd of mourners like a company of actors practising their lines.

A short, balding man in a suit and tie approached Alice.

'I'm the photographer. I wonder if I could take a group photo.'

'We're not the wedding party, they're still inside the church. I think there's been some sort of hold-up.'

'No, no, I'm the photographer for the funeral.'

There were some parts of Dolly's arrangements I had omitted to share with Alice because I'd thought she might start to cry again. Instead, she opted for a little light shouting.

'I'll leave the mourners' shot, then,' the short photographer squeaked, taking a few steps backwards. 'Do you want me to carry on with the shots of the coffin arriving?'

'Oh, do what you want.'

'Look,' someone called out, 'here comes the stretch limo.'

The coffin had arrived just as the wedding party was emerging from the church. If I wasn't mistaken, some of the wedding party must have started their celebrations before the ceremony. Even the bride was finding it hard to walk in a straight line. No wonder their service had overrun, I thought. They probably had difficulty slurring their vows out.

When they saw the white stretch limo, complete with balloons attached to the front, they understandably thought this was the vehicle that was to take the bride and groom to their reception. They all seemed to surge towards it, throwing confetti, most of which landed on the coffin as it was being taken out of its unusual hearse by four bearers dressed in striped jackets and boaters.

A red-faced vicar ran out of the church porch and tried to duck and dive his way through the wedding and funeral guests towards the coffin-bearers.

'Round the back, round the back,' he shouted, as if directing some unwanted tradesmen.

He wiped his brow with a large handkerchief and tried to separate the two groups so that the funeral could begin with some dignity. This was difficult when the mother of the groom's wide-brimmed wedding hat had been tossed onto the coffin and a number of half-cut wedding guests were doing the conga behind it.

'I knew this would be a fiasco. Typical Mother,' Alice muttered.

'Dolly hardly arranged for this to happen,' I pointed out.

'Don't you believe it.'

We somehow managed to get inside the church, everyone sitting in their right places and Dolly at the front, the wedding hat having been discreetly removed. A more subdued, reflective atmosphere settled on the packed church. The vicar was talking earnestly to Alice but I couldn't catch what they were saying. He eventually shrugged his shoulders as if to say, Well, it can't be any worse than the wedding. Alice glared at me as if I were to blame for something. The man at the organ seemed reluctant to begin and the congregation was getting restless. After a brief chat with the vicar, the organ player eventually struck up the opening chords of 'Blue Suede Shoes' and eventually everyone joined in with the singing.

The 'hymns' may have been unusual, even irreverent and, to some people, inappropriate, but the readings were not. Dolly had selected some beautiful poetry, as well as words of wisdom from those she admired including Ghandi, Desmond Tutu, Mother Teresa and John Cleese. It was a strange mix of the ridiculous and the sentimental, the reflective and the downright silly. Like Dolly herself. Jo and I exchanged warm glances. Whatever anyone thought, every single person left the church with a smiling face. Quite an achievement for a funeral.

'I only met her a few times,' Jo said, 'but that was very Dolly.'

'You're absolutely right,' I said, agreeing with Jo in a way that was becoming increasingly common. Or was it? Maybe it just didn't matter any more whether we agreed or not, so long as we understood.

'Are we still having your party?' Eliza asked.

'Of course,' Jo and I said in unison, then I added, 'It will be sad not having Dolly there to liven things up, but she would have wanted us to go ahead with it.'

'How do you know?'

'I just do. I sometimes think I knew Dolly better than any-one I've ever known, even after a relatively short time. Frank thinks we knew each other in a former life.'

'Did you know her better than us, then?' Eliza asked.

'Probably,' Jo said, 'because we're still growing up and changing all the time. Dolly wasn't likely to change much at her age. Older people don't.'

'What about Mum?' said Eliza. 'She's changed.'

'Have I?'

Then both girls laughed as if they knew something I didn't. I linked arms with my daughters, one on each side, as we made our way to the King's Head for the wake. Jo dabbed a few tears away and I squeezed her hand. It was a short walk to the pub and yet it felt like the end of a very long journey.

We arrived to the sound of Elvis blaring out of the jukebox, as arranged. All the regulars had turned up and were busy tell-ing Alice what a great mum she'd had. She looked both be-mused and proud.

'Are you going to say a few words?' I asked Alice.

'Now, that would have been a good idea but I can't, I didn't think to prepare a speech.'

'It doesn't have to be a speech, just propose a toast or something.'

'I haven't prepared that either.'

'Just do something off the cuff.'

'To be frank, I prefer to have these things set out, a few notes jotted down on a small card so that I can deliver it with—'

'Real feeling?'

'I'll get Roger to say something. He does spontaneous a little better than I do.'

'That's new.'

Roger tapped a spoon against his glass and coughed.

'Excuse me, ladies and gentlemen, can I have your attention please? Thank you. I'd like to propose a toast to Ernestine but…'

'Who's Ernestine?' whispered Eliza.

'It's what most sensible people call Dolly,' I said.

'I'll call her Dolly, then.'

'I'd like to propose a toast, but before I do I would like to sincerely thank the Reverend Green for agreeing to take this most unusual service.'

Roger paused for laughter. There wasn't any.

'This most unusual service, and I have to explain that it was Dolly's wishes, not ours, but perhaps anyway I should thank Lizzie for organising the event.'

'Who's Lizzie?' shouted out one of the pub regulars.

'It's what sensible people call me,' I shouted back.

'Hey, it's Ellie!' And everyone from the King's Head cheered a drunken cheer.

'Ellie?' said Jo.

'Yes, it's what I used to be known as.'

'It's a lovely name. Better than Lizzie.'

'Yes, it is.'

I had already made a fool of myself by shouting out so I may as well continue in the same vein, I thought. Dolly's vein.

'Let the dancing begin,' I shouted, and grabbed Frank for a jive.

'Where's Gordon?' Frank asked.

'He had an important meeting. Couldn't be changed. He didn't have any windows available next week or something.'

'Does he sell double glazing, then?' Frank winked and looked rather pleased with himself.

My feet were aching a bit so I was glad when a slow dance came up. I cried a little into Frank's shoulder and he squeezed me tighter. During the evening we all cried from time to time, easily and naturally—Jo, Alice, Frank and several others. And yet it was in many ways a joyful celebration. A celebration of life.

'This is the best funeral I've ever been to,' Eliza said.

'You've never been to any others,' Jo pointed out. 'Still, you might be right, this is better than some weddings.'

Later, Jo and I talked for hours about the strange world we live in. We wondered what aliens from another planet would make of us. How we spend so much time and money on the remaining bit of hair on our heads, how we are all born with different bodies yet aspire to have the same dimensions and, strangest of all, how we eat when we're not even hungry. We didn't just talk: we really talked.

TWENTY

IT'S PHILOSOPHY really. Talking to Mum and Scarlet and people like Frank. It's philosophy—the meaning of life, the bigger picture. You hear people in the library talking about the soaps or their neighbour's new car or the sale in Dorothy Perkins. But I've always liked talking about important stuff. It's thinking out loud really, and getting to hear other thoughts from other heads.

TWENTY-ONE

I DON'T remember consciously making a decision to become a vegetarian. Frank certainly didn't try and convert me, I think it began because of having a fridge full of fresh organic vegetables, unusual cheeses and healthy pasta and pulses. Then it just evolved out of what I enjoyed cooking for the family.

As my birthday party drew nearer, I started to worry about it, anxiously asking myself a million questions. Would there be enough food? Would anyone actually turn up? Would I just spend my party wishing Dolly was there? What on earth was I going to say to Gordon? Or Roger? Or anyone? How would I feel meeting Lily Finnegan at last? I began to wish that Eliza hadn't let the cat out of the bag, that it had remained the surprise party Jo had intended. You don't worry about what you don't know about so sometimes it's best not to know. I could tell that Jo was worrying about something too, maybe connected with the party but most likely to do with that boy from the library Eliza told me about. Eliza was making a habit of telling me things I didn't need to know. I didn't confront Jo. It was part of growing up and no one can do your growing up for you. I couldn't expect my daughters to tell me everything.

TWENTY-TWO

MUM was so uptight about the party. I said, 'What's the worst that can happen?' Like I was Lily Finnegan or something. I told her there were more important things to worry about. Like world peace. I didn't tell Mum I was worrying too, or what I was worrying about. You don't have to tell your parents everything.

Then their journey took an unexpected turning. Shona and her sister sensed that they were no longer climbing but were going downhill. They turned round and tried to go back the way they had just come but soon realised that in the heavy mist and darkening skies, they had lost all sense of direction.

'Help!' called Shona.

'There's no point calling,' sighed her sister. 'There's no one to hear you.'

'There's Lily Finnegan,' Shona said. 'She might hear us.'

Then they heard a faint cry in the distance. The noises got closer and closer, and soon Shona and her sister could distinguish different voices. It was the villagers who had climbed up Purple Mountain to help them.

'Thank you so much for coming. Are you coming to help us up the mountain or down the mountain?'

'That's up to you,' said the Miller.

'It depends if you still need Lily Finnegan,' added the Blacksmith.

'Everyone needs Lily Finnegan,' said Shona.

On the morning of Mum's party, Eliza and I prepared the buffet. Mum shifted furniture about.

'This will look better once I've got rid of the carpet and polished up the floorboards,' she said. 'In the meantime, let's move the big armchair so it covers the stain on the carpet.'

She had bought the food—piles of Italian bread and granary rolls and fresh salad stuff. A few dips. That sort of thing. Our neighbour had made a cake. It was pink and had a frill round it.

'We could make it all up into sandwiches and rolls,' Mum said. She was obsessed. I wondered if there was a name for her obsession. Sandwicha nervosa. We ignored her and put the bread into baskets and arranged the rest on plates. Mum said it looked good. We took the wine out of the boxes and lined the bottles up—white, red, white, red, white, red. All in order.

'Is your boyfriend coming?' Eliza asked.

'Shut up, squirt.'

Eliza laughed. She didn't care about anything. Like Dolly. I muddled the wine bottles up—white, white, red, white, red, red, red, white. I looked at them. At first it made me feel uncomfortable, seeing them out of order. Then I got used to it. Then I liked them being random like that.

Scarlet came early.

'My boyfriend's coming later. I thought I'd come early and give you a hand.'

'I'll miss you when you go,' I said. Like I was soppy or something.

'I'll miss you too, but we'll always keep in touch. We should go to the same uni. That would be cool. I'll invite you to my wedding.'

'And my son's christening.'

'And my daughter's graduation.'

'And my granddaughter's nativity play.'

Suddenly the future was funny. Something to laugh about. It took the fear away.

'We will keep in touch, won't we?' I said.

'Of course we will, we've got to.'

Then we hugged and cried and all that stuff. I didn't hold back. So between us we cried bucketloads. Like a torrential downpour.

'Do you really have to move?'

'Yeah. Life changes. All the time. Can't control it really, just have to go with it. I'll speak to you every day, though.'

'You'd better.'

'Anyway, let's not think about it any more, I haven't gone yet. Let's have a laugh. Let's enjoy the party.'

We went up to get changed. Scarlet loved my red top. We did each other's hair and make-up. We stood back and looked at ourselves in the mirror.

'You look great,' Scarlet said.

I smiled. I thought maybe I did.

Then everyone arrived at once. They time it, the middle-aged. They get an invitation that says half past seven. They don't want to be the first. They don't want to seem desperate. They don't want people to know the only time they go out is to their kids' parents' evening. But they can't come at eight-thirty. That would be too late. So they all come at eight. In a crowd. All the same. All squeaking the same stuff—'How lovely to see you', 'These can't be your daughters, *surely*', 'My my, they're so grown up'. 'Wonderful', 'Lovely', 'Marvellous', 'Lovely', 'Gorgeous', 'Lovely'. Flossed teeth, sculpted hair, suits, jackets, beige, black, brown, careful, sensible shoes, predictable, expected. All made in the same factory. No rejects. Not that you could notice.

Gordon and Mum talked awkwardly. Frank was different from everyone else. He looked kind of different. And Mum. She flowed. She looked cool. I was proud, kind of. I'd done my bit. Been a good girl. So when Anthony came, he and Scarlet and her boyfriend Gareth and me went upstairs. Put decent music on. Mucked about. Had a laugh. Like we used to.

Eliza and her stupid friends tried to come in. Then they went to listen to her *Chicago* CD. Her friends preferred our music but they always did what Eliza said. Control, or what?

I went downstairs to see if anyone new had arrived. They were all standing around with glasses attached to their hands, plates balanced on their other hands, talking crap. Smiling because that's what you do. Not because there was anything to smile about. 'My mother's finally died,' one of them said. Everyone smiled. 'My dog's got to be put down,' another said. They carried on smiling.

There were plenty of neighbours, the other workers from the sandwich bar, a couple of people from the library, Dad, Uncle George's lot. The usual culprits. No one new. I spoke to the nice librarian who had let me sleep there.

'How's the story coming on?' she asked.

'Nearly finished,' I said. 'Then I'm starting my novel.'

'Good for you. I'm proud of you,' she said. Like I was her daughter or something.

Then I spotted a lady I didn't know. I couldn't remember inviting her. She looked bored. Could it be?

'Do you want a drink?' I asked.

'Thank you, I'll have some orange juice. You must be Jo.'

'Yes. Are you…?'

'I live at number fourteen, thank you for the invitation.'

'That's OK.'

It wasn't her.

I went upstairs again. I went down a couple more times. Same standing about. Same talk. Same people.

'Is Lily Finnegan here?' asked Scarlet.

'I don't know,' I said.

I thought about everyone downstairs.

'No,' I said eventually. 'It doesn't look like she made it.'

'That's a pity,' said Scarlet.

Where was Lily? Had she let me down yet again? Disappeared when I needed her? But did I need her? My friends were laughing, my friends were having a good time, I was having a good time. I'd been so sure that I already knew her, that she already knew me. Yet everyone who knew about my problem was downstairs with a drink and a nibble and not inclined to come up and find me. There was, of course, one person missing.

'Who's Lily Finnegan?' asked Anthony.

'Someone who made me see myself differently. Someone who gets feelings out of a ballpoint pen, or a keyboard.'

'Not so much a person as a concept, then.'

I smiled. I liked Anthony. When you start to like yourself, you tend to like most people. I realised that Lily was probably downstairs. Somewhere. But it didn't matter. I wanted to spend time with Scarlet. And Anthony. My friends. People who would always be there. Whatever I did.

TWENTY-THREE

IT DAWNED on me that day of my birthday party that for the first time in my life I was happy. I had had a good enough life, with moments of happiness scattered over the years like buttercups at the side of a canal full of rubbish. Yet negativity had always flowed somewhere beneath the surface. Now happiness was just there, existing, being. Now my life was just a few bits of occasional litter in a meadowful of flowers, positivity growing up from the earth beneath me. I always thought I would be happy once Jo was happy. Was she happy? Sometimes. But my happiness was not dependent on it, not linked by some sort of invisible cord. I was just happy being, and doing—doing was important.

I used to imagine the opposite, that happiness was lying on a sun lounger, a piña colada by my side, with someone vaguely Italian massaging my shoulders. Not a care in the world, nothing to do and nothing to think about. How could I have confused happiness with boredom? Why did I imagine satisfaction came from doing nothing? I also used to believe that happiness was brought to you by someone on a plate and handed to you. I thought for a while that person was Gordon.

Why? I don't know what I was thinking of! Gordon was a
lovely man, but he was the bringer of order, organisation,
pension plans and British Home Stores socks. Not happiness,
not my happiness.

He was at the party, of course, thanks to Jo. But I needed
to explain to him, he deserved that. If only he hadn't got in
first.

I had rehearsed the gentle let-down in my mind, so that by
the time Gordon arrived at the party, I would have my lines
word perfect.

'Hi, Gordon, thanks for coming. I've been meaning to
catch up with you actually.'

'Yes, it's been a while, hasn't it?'

'I know, but I've just been so busy working with
Frank to get ready for the vegetarian café opening, and
then of course there's my trip to India to arrange. Well,
the thing is, it's simply not fair on you. I just don't have
the time for a relationship in all honesty. The last thing
I want is to upset you. I hope you understand.'

'But we're so right for each other. You're the most
intriguing, beautiful, wonderful woman I've ever met.'

'I know, but I'm just not looking for a relationship at
the moment.'

'But I was falling head over heels in love with you.
I find you physically irresistible. I have to tell you that
I am totally heartbroken, but I just have to accept it, I
suppose. I do understand. I just feel so utterly privileged
to have met you. Now, if you'll excuse me, I just need
a few moments on my own.'

The only downside of my imaginings is that I rather depend on the other players sticking to the script, a script that they've never ever read. There's a fault in the procedure somewhere.

I was relieved to see Gordon arrive. This was going to be so much easier with the backdrop of a party—I could let him down gently and then circulate as if nothing had happened.

'Hi, Gordon, thanks for coming. I've been meaning to catch up with you actually.'

Let him down gently, let him down gently.

'Yes, it's been a while, hasn't it?'

'I know, but I've just been…'

'The thing is, Lizzie, I'm just not ready for a relationship.'

'No, hang on, I haven't finished saying my bit yet.'

'The last thing I want is to upset you. I hope you understand.'

'But that's my line. This isn't right, this isn't right at all.'

'I didn't realise you were going to be this upset. I thought…'

'Of course I'm upset. I'm the one supposed to be letting you down gently.'

Unfortunately, I was beginning to speak rather loudly at this point. The chatter around us suddenly stopped and everyone looked on just as I delivered my final adolescent-style whinge.

'It's not fair. I'm supposed to be dumping you.'

There was a momentary silence and then Gordon began to laugh. Everyone else joined in and Frank slapped me on the back.

'There's never a dull moment with you, Ellie,' he said. 'It's all so wonderfully haphazard.' Then he laughed again. I joined in, I thought I may as well.

'I'm sorry, Gordon,' I said later. 'Sometimes I can be more immature than my children.'

'It's OK, Lizzie. Look, I was going to say that I hope we can still be good friends. It sounds rather clichéd but I mean it. We both know we're not suited as a couple but we get on, we complement each other.'

Damn, that was better than the speech I'd written for him. And I knew that if I could be friends with Gordon, which I certainly could, then I could be friends with Roger. After all, I had long suspected that they were twins separated at birth.

'Ellie, I've put Queen on, liven things up a bit.'

'Well done, Frank. Good choice.'

'By the way, you look lovely this evening.'

'Thanks.'

'I hope we'll get to know each other really well while we work together on the yoga and café projects.'

'I'm not sure I want to be a Buddhist, Frank.'

'You don't have to be. Buddhists are the most embracing of all religions. The Dalai Lama himself pointed out that no one would go to a restaurant that served only one meal. It's the choice and variety that makes it a good restaurant, something for everyone. And that's what makes it a good world.'

'But is it a good world?'

'Yes, potentially. And it's a better world for having you in it, Ellie.'

I wasn't sure if Frank was flirting with me or not. Then I realised that it didn't matter really. I was looking forward to spending more time with him, and then—who knows? One thing I was sure of was that Dolly would have approved. A vegetarian butcher who was a Buddhist priest and a Queen fan. All he needed to do was paint his ceiling purple and he would have been perfect in her eyes.

'What colour are your ceilings?' I asked Frank.

'The usual white.'

'Oh.'

'I've just painted my bathroom ceiling purple,' Gordon chipped in. Life could be very strange at times.

As I circulated, I felt proud of Jo for organising the party. She had invited all the right people and I felt important, the centre of attention. Just like I was at the birthday parties I had as a child. It felt good to be that child again, just for one evening. Of course I looked out for Lily, I even asked some of the neighbours questions or made strange statements which made them look at me in that quizzical, how-much-has-she-had way.

'Am I right in thinking you are sometimes known as Lily?'

'You don't look like I expected you to.'

'You are her, aren't you? You must be.'

Then it dawned on me that it didn't really matter if she was there or not, so long as she was somewhere. Same with Jo really. I heard her laughing upstairs with friends and I smiled to myself. She was in her moment and I was in mine. I no longer needed Lily, for I was done with analysing my life. I was too busy living it, just like I used to.

The mind can be sharply focused or it can wander off on its own like a stray cat searching for food, so one minute I was scanning the room for signs of Lily, the next moment I was too busy dancing with Frank to give it another thought. Strange, it had all seemed so important the day before. But Lily had always been food for thought so the next day curiosity tempted me straight onto my emails. My intuition paid off, the only new message highlighted with the familiar blue strip was from Lily.

Dear Lizzie and Jo,

Thank you for a lovely party. I know now that you do not need Lily Finnegan any more. There is one last task to complete, though. I want you to write your story, the story of you both and what you have been through. I want you both to write your own stories independently, from your own individual points of view. This will be your challenge. This will be your closure. And then you can share your experience with anyone or no one. You have a choice. You always have choices, remember that.

With love,

Lily

I called Jo to read the message. She stood at my shoulder for a long time, reading it carefully. Then she said, 'Scroll down, there's more.'

I hadn't noticed, but she was right—there was a photograph underneath. A photo of a lady of around sixty or so. She had a warm, inviting face, its roundness topped by a mop of grey, curly hair. She looked so ordinary and yet so extraordinary. Underneath was a caption: LILY FINNEGAN—1940-2000. She had died six years previously.

'I don't understand,' I almost whispered. 'Is it a voice from beyond the grave? Or is someone playing a sick joke on us?'

'She died six years ago,' said Jo. 'Like the Lily Finnegan who used to work in the library, the one I was told about. Look. Look at the books. The photo was actually taken in our library.'

I leant back in the chair and held my head in my hands, weighed down by the sheer quantity of questions which had been delivered into my mind. Then I sat up and moved my face nearer the screen, squinting at the picture, searching for clues. I narrowed my eyes until the picture blurred and I thought I sensed a mauve aura around Lily's face—for it was Lily, I knew it was Lily Finnegan, not just someone called Lily Finnegan by way of a duplicate christening, but the Lily Finnegan who had helped my daughter, held both our hands and collected our tears. This was the woman who had rescued her and yet at the same time I knew it was not possible.

I clung onto the impossibility for a while, needing to believe that this was an angel, that Lily Finnegan surpassed reality, convention and earthly dimensions. Eventually logic took over with the authority of a teacher in a classroom of unruly children. I had to accept that someone had taken over the business, taken on the brand name of Lily Finnegan, just as someone might take over the sandwich shop, keeping its name with all the goodwill and associated quality that goes with it. Lily Finnegan's quality was continuing under new management. She wanted us to know this but to accept her anonymity. But could I accept that I would probably never know who she was? I smiled at the picture on the screen as if she could see me and would smile back. The present owner of the name of Lily Finnegan was doing her proud, whoever she was.

So that brings my story to an end, although it is not an end. Everything passes but nothing ends. Even Lily Finnegan's story goes on and on, in spite of the fact that she had already died. Maybe Dolly's story goes on, for the mark she left on me lives still. Everything else also continues: this is not a story where Jo recovers totally, where I find myself completely, and where we all live happily ever after in a permanent cottage in the everlasting woods. We are all still on journeys. There is still life to live, choices to be made, uncertainties to face. The success of my new ventures is uncertain—indeed, all our futures are uncertain—and my new relationships are uncertain so I can't write a conclusion. There are always loose ends, always emotions to unravel, always outcomes to await. The only thing that is certain is uncertainty.

I didn't ever find Lily Finnegan in the flesh, yet I found her in my life. For Lily was more than a person, she was a belief. A belief in humanity, hope and life carrying on.

TWENTY-FOUR

Now here they were, near the top of the mountain, with all the villagers to help them, and they still could not see the old, old cottage in the mist.

'I want to know why my dreams do not come true and why my hopes are not fulfilled,' said Shona.

'Then it seems you should be able to answer that question for yourself,' said the Potter.

'But I've tried,' said Shona.

'Maybe your hopes and dreams are not clear enough.'

'Maybe you are hoping for the wrong things.'

'Maybe you're not thinking of the consequences.'

'Maybe you are trying too hard to control and master your life.'

All the villagers gave a different answer and each answer added something new to the answer before.

Slowly the mist cleared and Shona, her sister and all the villagers could clearly see the path to take them back down to their village at the foot of Purple Mountain. Shona had not met Lily Finnegan and yet sensed that she had. For after that, she noticed that some, just some, of her dreams did come true and the rest might come true in time. Hope went up the mountain and hope came down again.

I read the Irish folk tale through. It was interesting, but not brilliant. It was a warm-up really. Like stretching before a football game. Or blowing a bit of warm air down a trumpet before playing. I was ready to do something bigger. I would do as Lily Finnegan suggested, I would write about my eating disorder. Maybe I would have more to say than I thought. Mum thought an angel had touched our lives. She was right. Kind of.

I had one more day before I went back to school. Different subjects. Different hopes and dreams. My own. This time, my own.

When I got to work I saw her, the person I had been wanting to see—the kind librarian who had read my story and had told me about Lily Finnegan who had worked here and then died. The librarian who had allowed me to cry. Who had listened. Who had been a stranger and a friend. All that seemed to be a long time ago.

'I can't believe the summer is nearly over,' she said.

When Shona got to the foot of Purple Mountain and returned home, she sat by the log fire and thought about her journey. She had discovered such a lot and knew that there was someone she needed to thank. Someone who had now stirred the spoonfuls of truth into her hopes and dreams. She opened the door and stepped out into the night. There stood the wisest of the wisest women of Ireland, down from the mist of Purple Mountain.

'Thank you so so much, Lily Finnegan,' said Shona. 'Thank you so, so much.'

Anthony didn't come in that day. Maybe I would see him there again. Or somewhere. Maybe I wouldn't. Nancy had made a cake for me and at our teabreak they all gave me a card and a present. I knew it was a book and I tore the paper off to see which one. *One Hundred Traditional Irish Stories* retold by Sean Leary. I held it to my nose. Like it was a flower or something. I felt part of something. Part of the library. Part of the world of books and writing. I was kind of proud of myself. Maybe other people were proud of me too. But being proud of myself was major.

After our break I finished putting the books onto the shelf. Then I put on my jacket and grabbed my bag.

I turned round and looked at the librarian. I smiled and she smiled back. Like we both knew something special.

'Thank you so so much,' I said.

Read all about it…

MORE ABOUT THIS BOOK

2 Questions for your reading group

3 Inspiration

5 Sources of help and information

MORE ABOUT THE AUTHOR

6 Author biography

7 Q&A on writing

10 A writer's life

11 Top ten books

12 A day in the life

WE RECOMMEND

13 Clare Shaw's future projects

14 If you enjoyed *The Mother and Daughter Diaries*, we know you'll love…

2

Read all about it…

QUESTIONS FOR YOUR READING GROUP

1. How did Lizzie change during the story? And Jo?

2. All the characters in the story have plenty of faults and yet we like them. Why?

3. What is Lizzie's relationship with food? To what extent do all women have an uneasy attitude to food?

4. How do you think Lizzie's childhood experiences affected her attitude to her own daughters?

5. Do you have to write about your problems for writing to be therapeutic?

6. Do you blame Lizzie for Jo's problems? What might have been the contributing causes?

7. How would a night out with Frank differ from a night out with Gordon?

8. What effect did Dolly have on the other characters?

9. What do you think Jo, Eliza and Scarlett will be doing when they are twenty-five years old?

10. Was Lizzie justified in being irritated by Alice?

11. How had the communication between Lizzie and Jo changed by the end of the book?

12. Do you think it mattered who Lily Finnegan was?

INSPIRATION

I started to write this book when both my teenage daughters were becoming independent while still needing plenty of parental support. I found it difficult to let my eldest daughter, in particular, grow up and make her own mistakes. Like all mums, I wanted to protect her from the big, bad outside world and make life as easy as possible for her. So I began a book about letting go and letting your daughters grow up.

At the same time, I became increasingly aware that many of my daughters' friends were developing eating disorders and when I became involved with one family in particular, I realised how emotionally devastating this problem is. I had had pre-conceived ideas about eating disorders occurring because young girls aspired to be like models and pop stars. I soon learnt that it is more complex than this and is as much to do with control. Sometimes, it can be linked to a fear of growing up. This fitted in well with the original theme of the book so I spoke with other families who were kind enough to share their experiences of having an anorexic teenager with me.

At about this time, a psychotherapist friend of mine told me about the benefits of journalling – 'When things go wrong, spew it out onto the page,' she told me. So I did. And it worked. I have since discovered that while this is no sub-stitute for counselling or therapy, many psycho-therapists recommend writing about problems. Personally, I find any sort of writing therapeutic – poems, stories, novels – there is something very uplifting about the creative process. And it was wonderful to give one of my characters this insight – Jo gains as much from writing her stories as she does from writing about her

"...I began a book about letting go and letting your daughters grow up..."

Read all about it...

"...I was fed up with seeing caricatures of teenagers..."

Finally, I was fed up with seeing caricatures of teenagers on my television screen. All teenagers are different but most of the ones I know are funny, articulate, caring and inspirational, even if they are a little confused! As for Dolly, I think she is simply the eccentric old lady I hope I become when I am older.

Read all about it...

SOURCES OF HELP AND INFORMATION

Websites

• The eating disorders association/beating eating disorders: www.b-eat.co.uk

• Something Fishy: www.somethingfishy.org

• Research and Information: www.eatingresearch.com

• ANRAD (Anorexia Nervosa and related eating disorders) www.anred.com

Books

• *Overcoming Anorexia Nervosa* by Christopher Freeman (Constable and Robinson)

• *Alice in the Looking Glass* by Jo and Alice Kingsley (Piatkus)

• *Talking about Anorexia* by Maroushka Monro (Sheldon Press)

• *Susie Orbach on Eating* by Susie Orbach (Penguin)

The Mother and Daughter Diaries is a fictional novel and does not set out to advocate any particular cure or source of help for anorexia. Eating disorders are best helped in association with a professional. The websites and books listed may be useful. Please note that these are my personal recommendations.

Inclusion on this list does not indicate recommendation by the publisher, or any representation as to the content of these sources. Nor does it indicate that any of these entities have endorsed *The Mother and Daughter Diaries* or use of their listings here.

6

AUTHOR BIOGRAPHY

Clare Shaw got her first taste for writing when she was asked to read out her story *The Snail and the Caterpillar* to the rest of her class of nine year olds. The story made the pupils laugh and the teacher cry, so Clare learnt at an early age that writing was an emotional business. Her effort at maths also made the teacher cry and Clare then knew for certain that writing rather than accountancy would be her destiny.

Leaving school, she trained and worked as a speech and language therapist before discovering that she still preferred writing to talking. So she became a freelance writer contributing to parents magazines and writing five books offering advice to parents, including *Prepare Your Child for School* and *Help Your Child Be Confident*. Clare then produced two daughters so that she could put her own advice into practice. This proved impossible so she returned to speech therapy and started to talk to people again. But the call of the word processor was loud and Clare wrote two plays – *Hothouse,* performed in 2006, and *The Glenn Miller Neurosis Programme,* performed in 2007. *The Mother and Daughter Diaries* is her first novel.

Behind every woman writer is a man bringing her cups of tea, and John boils her kettle at their home in Essex with help from their two daughters, Emma and Jessica.

Further information can be found on the websites www.clareshaw.com and www.mirabooks.co.uk/clareshaw

6

Read all about it…

Q&A ON WRITING

1. What do you love most about being a writer?

I love the fact that a book starts with just one idea in my head which then spreads like ripples so that soon I have characters who make my one small idea grow into a story. When I look at the finished book, it's amazing to think that it all started with just one single thought. I love starting a book – the excitement of getting those first words down – and I love ending it. The bit in the middle can involve a lot a blood, sweat and tears but it's worth it.

2. Where do you go for inspiration?

People are my main inspiration and it's not unusual for me to strike up a conversation on a train or a bus. Everyone is a potential character, everyone has a story to tell and everyone has something unique or quirky about them. If I get stuck when I'm in the middle of writing, I go into the countryside, preferably near flowing water. I live on the Essex-Suffolk borders and there are some great river and coastal walks in the area. Sometimes inspiration comes when you are least expecting it and so I try and keep a notepad with me at all times.

"...Everyone is a potential character..."

3. What one piece of advice would you give a writer wanting to start a career?

The difference between successful people and failures is that successful people never give up. Also, become self-critical: throw anything away which is not good enough, even if you have spent hours on it, and be prepared to write, re-write and write again until you are completely satisfied. Find a good agent whose opinion you trust. I owe a lot to my agent, Judith Murdoch, whose experience and insight has proved to be invaluable.

4. Which book do you wish you had written?

The Remains of the Day by Kazuo Ishiguro. The two main characters clearly love each other and cannot say. It is agonising to read, you can feel all their suppressed emotion almost bursting through. It is what the characters do not say which is important.

5. When did you start writing?

As soon as I could hold a 2B pencil. I remember reading my story out to the class when I was about eight years old and getting a gold star for it. I remember getting my Brownie writers' badge and I remember writing a scene for the school nativity play. Later I turned to writing non-fiction, including articles for magazines and four books for parents. Eventually I joined an evening writing class at Essex University and I was instantly addicted to writing fiction. I write plays – two have been performed – and now books – *The Mother and Daughter Diaries* is the first.

"... I was instantly addicted to writing fiction..."

6. Where do your characters come from and do they ever surprise you as you write?

I am not entirely sure where they come from, they seem to come out of the air and infiltrate my brain. I do character sketches to start with but as I write, they evolve and in this way they can take you by surprise. On a bad day, I have even been known to argue with them! Frank the butcher came from a butcher's shop in Colchester where I live. I used to look through the window as I walked past and see this jolly-looking man serving meat. One day, I found myself thinking how odd it would be if he were a vegetarian. He emerged out of that one thought.

Read all about it....

7. Do you have a favourite character that you've created and what is it you like about that character?

I love Dolly as she really does not mind what other people think of her, which leaves her completely free to enjoy her life. She is one of those British eccentrics we all love. Whenever I had a Dolly scene to write, I couldn't get onto the computer fast enough as I knew she'd make me laugh and feel all warm inside.

10

Read all about it...

A WRITER'S LIFE

Pen or Computer?
Both. But words flow out of your brain and into your pen-holding arm in a different way and can be more creative.

PC or Laptop?
Mostly laptop because I've just got a new one.

Music or Silence?
Mostly silence but Mozart, Beethoven and Vivaldi have all helped me out on occasion.

Morning or Night?
Any time the mood takes me and it's always best to follow your mood.

Coffee or Tea?
Tea, brought to me by John, my personal tea maker who knows how I like it.

Your Guilty Reading Pleasure
Psychologies magazine – I've always been more interested in the mind than in make-up.

The First Book You Loved
The Narnia books by CS Lewis. And *Anne of Green Gables* by LM Montgomery – I always wished I'd been adopted by Matthew and Marilla.

The Last Book You Read
The Lovers' Room by Steven Carroll – another MIRA® book and a cracking read.

Read all about it...

TOP TEN BOOKS

The Remains of the Day – Kazuo Ishiguro

Birdsong – Sebastian Faulks

Unless – Carol Shields

Cat's Eye – Margaret Atwood

Behind the Scenes at the Museum – Kate Atkinson

The Hours – Michael Cunningham

Rebecca – Daphne du Maurier

Tess of the D'Urbervilles – Thomas Hardy

Ethan Frome – Edith Wharton

Saturday – Ian McEwan

Read all about it...

"...My family is the most important part of my life..."

A DAY IN THE LIFE

I'm an early riser and usually find my mind has been active while I've been asleep, so I sometimes have a thought or two to jot down before I do anything else – writing is addictive and I'm completely hooked.

After breakfast, I meditate for twenty minutes, which empties my mind of the mundane and gets the creative cells firing. I spend most of the morning writing and stop to check my e-mails at lunch time – there's usually something to deal with, whether it's about the website I'm setting up or a reply to an enquiry I've made connected to some research I'm doing for the book I'm writing.

After lunch, anything could happen – sometimes more writing, sometimes research, which might mean visiting a location or just meeting someone who does a particular job one of my characters might have. If I require thinking time, I take a long walk and generally talk to myself. Sometimes I am reassured to run into someone else talking to him- or herself and wonder whether he or she might be a writer. Or mad. Or both.

My family is the most important part of my life and I like to spend the evenings with my husband John and two daughters, Emma and Jessica, whenever possible. Writing is a solitary occupation so I try and have some people contact to keep me relatively sane. I go to a philosophy class each week and attend a playwrights group whenever I can.

When I go to bed at night, I send up a huge thank you to the cosmos that I am living the life I love. Unless I'm stuck on part of my book, in which case I start planning another career. But then I wake up in the morning with an idea and I'm hooked again...

CLARE SHAW'S FUTURE PROJECTS

I am currently working on my next book, tentatively called *Cloudbusting Day*. It has themes of clouds, loss, obsession and a bit of archaeology. Like *The Mother and Daughter Diaries*, it reflects my view that life is a mixture of the funny and the serious, the happy and the sad.

I am also working on a new play called *The Other Roof*, which is about suicide but is strangely optimistic (life's odd mix again).

Read all about it...

14

Read all about it...

If you enjoyed *The Mother and Daughter Diaries*, we know you'll love...

Wednesdays at Four by Debbie Macomber

Every week a group of women meet, each has her own share of worries and troubles. Cancer survivor Lydia is anxious about her ageing mother. Alix's wedding plans have been hijacked by her meddling friends. Self-contained Colette's husband has only been dead a year but she's pregnant with another man's child. As friendships deepen these women start to confide in each other, but will listening and sharing be enough?

Everything Must Go by Elizabeth Flock

To those on the outside, the Powells are a happy family, but then a devastating accident destroys their fragile façade. When seven-year-old Henry is blamed for the tragedy, he tries desperately to make his parents happy again, but as he grows up, he questions if the guilt his parents have burdened him with has left him unable to escape his anguished family or their painful past...

The Butterfly House by Marcia Preston

Roberta and Cynthia are destined to be best friends forever. Unable to cope with her alcoholic mother, Roberta finds Cynthia's house the perfect carefree refuge. Cynthia's mother keeps beautiful butterflies and she's everything Roberta wishes her own mother could be. Years later, a stranger knocks on Roberta's door, forcing her to begin a journey back to childhood. But is she ready to know the truth about what happened on that tragic night ten years ago?